THE KNITPICKER

A Crabapple Yarns Mystery

Jaime Marsman

ALSO BY
JAIME MARSMAN...

A Crabapple Yarns Mystery Series:

Book One: The Knitting Fairy
Book Two: The Brief Haunting of Raspberry Hill

THE KNITPICKER

A Crabapple Yarns Mystery

Jaime Marsman

PRAISE FOR "THE KNITTING FAIRY"

What do you get when you combine a novice to the world of fiber working in a yarn shop with the owner, a mysterious, fairy-tale inspired character? You get Jaime Marsman's magical, whimsical story of "The Knitting Fairy" which is sure to be enjoyed by knitters everywhere. **Penny Sitler, Executive Director of The Knitting Guild Association (TKGA), tkga.com**

"Whenever an author combines stories and stitches, I smile. Jaime Marsman has done just that in her new book, 'The Knitting Fairy'. With a nod to Agatha Christie as well as fairy tales about Brownies who appear when no-one is looking to complete domestic tasks for those in need, Marsman has crafted a tale that combines mystery, fun, and knitting. Filled with phrases like, "she kitchnered Old Mrs. Harrison's toes together," "Oh, honey, let's go home and cable," and "as Louise reached into her small knitting bag, I had a distinct feeling of foreboding," knitters will find themselves laughing through each chapter, wondering who the knitting fairy could be!" **Donna Druchunas, author of six knitting books including Arctic Lace, sheeptoshawl.com**

"Amidst the characters, humour, and mystery is the fun of witnessing a non-knitter's assumptions and observations turn to affection and obsession. It made me wish to be a new knitter again!" **Sally Melville, sallymelvilleknits.com, sallymelvilleknits.blogspot.com**

"A page turning mystery with yarn shops and knitting - what else could you ask for!" **Carol Feller, Author of Contemporary Irish Knits**

A heartwarming and witty novel, guaranteed to make you smile. Molly Stevenson's new found love of yarn brings her comfort and friendship but leaves her with many unanswered questions. Appealing to the non-knitter as much as the knitaholic, this wonderful and enthralling mystery detailing the weird and wonderful goings on in Crabapple Yarns knitting store, will have you totally hooked." **UK Hand Knitting Association, ukhandknitting.com**

"It is obvious that Ms. Marsman is writing about what she knows: books, libraries and yarns. I really enjoyed following Molly's adventures in learning to knit and solving mysteries. The Knitting Fairy always keeps you guessing!" **Alissa Barton, Owner, Knitting Fairy Yarn Studio, knittingfairy.com**

"What I loved best about The Knitting Fairy is how perfectly Jaime captured that as knitters we actually fall in love with knitting. She reminded me of the butterflies, excitement, and joy of falling in love with my first skein of luxury yarn, falling in love with perfectly tensioned stitches and the euphoria of completing my first project. Not only did The Knitting Fairy remind me of why I fell in love with knitting in the first place, it made me pause (as a deadline-driven professional) to think that I still need to stop and smell the roses from time to time." **Kristin Omdahl, Author of 6 knitting books, styledbykristin.com**

The Knitpicker

Thank you, God.

KNITTING

The Merriam-Webster definition:**

- To form by interlacing yarn or thread in a series of connected loops with needles
- To tie together

The definition that should be in the dictionary:

- The mystifying and magical process whereby linear fiber is twisted and reshaped by needles of varying sizes not only knitting fabric together, but hearts and minds as well resulting in lifetime friendships, a sense of self-satisfaction and personal identity.

**knit. 2012. In *Merriam-Webster.com*. Retrieved June 22, 2012, from http://www.merriam- webster.com/dictionary/knit

CHAPTER 1

A person who can keep a secret is the scariest kind of person there is. They… I'm sorry… what did you say? Yes, you're right. Axe murderers are scary, too. Thank you. That is an excellent point. But, cheer up, you can generally see THEM coming. You'll <u>probably</u> have a chance to duck…or, maybe, even run if you tend to be one of the observant kind. A true secret keeper, however, now that's something you never see coming. You won't even realize that you were supposed to duck. And you'll NEVER get the chance to run.

The problem with secrets is that you just don't know that they are there. You can't see them. You probably wouldn't want to. I doubt many secrets are pretty. But, what is also true is that sometimes you can't see a secret keeper either. Oh. You can see them. (Please. Stop being so literal.) You probably see them every day, but you never <u>see</u> them. Do you know what I mean? You never see the awfulness locked inside.

Because it does have to be awful, doesn't it? What else could it be but awful to hold something horrible inside of you? Something that pounds at your heart, fluttering with angry wings, demanding… relentlessly – to be set free. How do you silence the voice screaming in your head, "Let me out. Let me out."?

"Let me out."
Day after day.

"Please, let me out."
Week after week.

"Out."
"Out."
"Out."
Year after year.

Because, you know, that is the goal of every secret. It is what they want. They don't want to be invisible. They don't want to be unheard. They want out. They want to be free. They want to be told. Only then can they rest in peace.

The true secret keepers of this world know how to keep them quiet. They know how to stuff them down and back in. They know how to <u>not tell</u>*. So, the secrets get smart. They smile to themselves and pretend to disappear. They sit quietly, with their hands folded primly in their laps, and, gradually, little by little, they gather dust and fade into the background. If you listen quietly, you can almost hear them chuckling. "Let them think that we are sleeping," they seem to say. But, deep down... you know. They are not sleeping. They are waiting. Because nothing can wait like an untold secret. And it's possible that the secrets themselves know the most terrible secret... that just because you are invisible doesn't mean that you're not there. It doesn't mean that someone can't, by sheer coincidence, stumble upon you. It doesn't mean that you don't exist. Secrets do exist. We know they do, even if we don't know where they are. And, with each year that passes, they grow just a little bit bigger. Just a little bit deadlier. And, still, they wait.*

"Ooohhh. I like that last line," a voice behind me cooed. "It's so mysterious." There was a snort, "And really cheesy. You'll never win with that."

I spun in my chair, "Natalie," I scolded, putting a hand over my heart for emphasis - you always need to be extra literal with Natalie. "You scared me. What were you thinking sneaking up on me like that?"

She grinned unrepentantly, flipping her blond hair over her shoulder. "I was thinking... 'Hey – I wonder what my competition is up to?'"

I rolled my eyes, "I am not your competition," I said patiently, like I haven't said this already, possibly many times already. "We're friends. Who are both..."

"Trying to beat each other in a story-writing competition." Natalie made her eyes big and wide, the idea obviously gaining steam. "Yeah. That could work... Two friends, driven apart by murderous jealousy..."

I snorted, "Now that's cheesy," I said. "I think you'd better think of another opener." I looked at my computer screen smugly. My opening was quite brilliant. I knew it. And Natalie knew it too. I hit save again (one couldn't be too careful) and closed the lid. As I am so incredibly old and experienced, I recognized the signs of a Natalie that was up to something. She was clutching a notebook rather tightly to herself. Could it be? It was only fair. I would have to be tricky. And quick. She was surprisingly strong for someone her size. What could I do? The pitter patter of tiny little feet entering the room gave me exactly what I needed. "What does Abraham Lincoln have in his mouth?" I asked, pretending to jump a bit with shock and looking over her right shoulder. (I hope you remember that Abraham Lincoln was the very strange, very opinionated, little dog that lives at Raspberry Hill…. otherwise that last question probably made absolutely no sense, did it?)

"Oh no," she gasped spinning on her right foot to confront her wayward four-legged owner… err… I mean… dog. "What is it this time?"

You know what? I'm sure I'll feel bad about it later, but in the meantime, I grabbed her notebook as she spun to see the alleged bad dog performing his latest feat of terror. She shrieked in indignation even as I nimbly hopped backward to escape her reach. "I can't believe you…" she was laughing and horrified at the same time. I fought her off bravely, swatting her with her own notebook until she fell backward over the end of the sofa. Triumphantly, I opened her notebook as she shrieked out dire warnings of doom if I even dared to…

"It was a dark and stormy night…" I read out loud before she regained her sense of balance. I raised my eyebrows. "Seriously?" I demanded, hooting with laughter. "That's your opening line?"

She huffed and flipped the hair back from her face, rising coolly from the sofa. "You only think that's my story," she said with remarkable composure, but the red creeping up her neck was giving her away.

Ok. Now I really was starting to feel a little bad and I handed her back her notepad. "I'm sure it's going to be great," I said, pausing thoughtfully, "after you get rid of that first line."

"Never underestimate the value of a classic," she said primly. "You'll see."

I guess we would.

CHAPTER 2

I t was a mystery story contest. Natalie thought she was going to win, hands down, because she lived in a haunted house. "I KNOW scary," she had said, trying her best to keep her face serious. "I've lived a mystery. I'm a natural for this story-writing thing."

What Natalie didn't know was that I had also lived a mystery AND I used to work in a library. That definitely gave ME an edge. I've read every story Amelda Tartan has ever written. Haven't you? Except, of course, her newest book, which was the reason for her visit to Springgate. She was going on a long, long book tour, and no one was more surprised than us when we heard that "Bookworms", the wee little bookstore in Springgate was going to be one of her first stops. Apparently, she had spent several summers here as a child with an elderly aunt and had fond memories. I, personally, didn't care what her reasons were. I just wanted to meet her. In my younger years, when I had more time for reading, I literally GOBBLED her books up. You know how it is. Some books are good. And some books are amazing. There are some books that you look forward to reading, and then there are the books that you stalk the poor bookstore worker for waiting for them to put the first one out on the shelf. Well. It's not like I've ever done that. It's just an example, of course.

I can still remember the feeling, after my first Amelda Tartan book, I'm sure you know what I mean... that amazing feeling after you finish a great book... like your head is fuzzy and disconnected and floating.... Like you're only half living in the real world and the other half of you is still living in the book. Like you've suddenly re-discovered a new and exciting zest for life, but have no idea how to make things different. You're walking through the rest of your day and it just mists around you like a cloud... like a dream that you can't wake up from.

The characters that you spent so much time with peeking out from behind corners. You're so enthralled with the world that the author spun out of words for you -- and devastated at the same time that it's over and it isn't real. I love that feeling. I also love that you're not looking at me like I'm crazy. It's so nice to meet a kindred spirit.

When I discovered that Amelda was a prolific author, I had chomped through the "Tartan" section of our local library with the calculated precision and determination of an army drill team. Even the librarian had been impressed. And woe to the unfortunate individual who held up my reading plan with an overdue book. Ahem. Hypothetically speaking, of course.

My first Amelda book was "The Home Wrecker," much to the horror of my mother, who was most emphatic that a young girl should not be reading such things. What she didn't realize was that it was not an immoral book by any means. It was about a husband who marries his 4th wife and she begins to suspect... well... in hindsight, I doubt my mother would have approved of that plot either.

Her latest series was based on a family of people who didn't always tell each other the truth. It was so delicious. In the last book, the daughter, Kate, found out that her dad was not just a plumber, but an undercover agent of a foreign government. Did you hear that? FOREIGN government. As in... not the American government. Let me tell you – DRAMA. And mystery at its finest. If, I admit a little bit implausible. After all, don't you think she should have wondered why a plumber would be gone overnight or for days at a time? Or why her sink always had a leak? I know. But it made for some great late-night reading. And really miserable mornings. In the newest book, we were going to find out what secrets Kate was hiding. I. Could. Not. Wait.

So, in honor of Ms. Tartan's arrival, the town was putting on a story contest, and the winner, chosen by a secret (of course) committee, would have the honor of reading a portion of her story at the "Welcome Amelda" party. Doesn't that sound exciting? So now Natalie and I were embroiled in a battle of the pens to see who could create the most entertaining mystery story. As you can see, it was going to be a battle to the death. Literally. Well... fictionally literally. Probably.

The only requirements were that it had to be less than 50,000 words and had to use at least one character from Ms. Tartan's works.

I wasn't sure what Natalie was writing about, but I had a sneaking suspicion that her main character was going to be "Scout". Do you know who Scout was? You guessed it. The family dog. She has a soft spot a mile wide for her own little fur ball. Which was a bummer. It was a good angle. People love stories about dogs, don't they? Yeah. Me? I wasn't sure yet what my angle was going to be. Obviously, it was someone with a really big secret (otherwise my incredibly brilliant opener was a total waste of time). But, here's the problem…if someone was a good secret keeper, you'd never know they had a secret to keep, would you? So, there has to be some sort of "occurrence" that either brings this horrible secret out into the light or a diary is uncovered where the (rather stupid) character writes out her thoughts… or something. And then… there's the fact that pretty much everyone in Ms. Tartan's books has secrets. And she pretty much revealed them all in previous works. So what else was there left to reveal? Maybe Kate's dad really WAS a plumber?

Sigh.

Is this what all writers go through? I bet it is. They write a really good opening (if I do say so myself) and then spend the rest of the story wondering what happens next…trying to live up to the promise of their opening lines? I don't know. Truth be told, I was out of ideas. Please don't tell Natalie.

Since Crabapple Yarns was still temporarily housed at Raspberry Hill, my world had gotten much, much smaller – even though, ironically, I was living in the biggest house I had ever lived in. Not that my life used to be big, you know. But it used to be a little bigger than this. Not that I'm complaining. I love living here, the creaky floors and cavernous rooms are strangely homey. I was even developing a certain fondness for Abraham Lincoln, despite the fact that he had doggy breath and growled anytime I got closer than 2.25 feet. Yes. In case you're wondering… I measured it. But I fiercely missed the sweet independence of my little apartment over the store.

It's just that I was starting to feel a little… crowded. I know. Crowded in a big house sounds strange, but it's true. At first, it was fun living with Jack and Natalie and Natalie's mom, Celia. It was nice to be part of a family again. And then, when Natalie's grandmother, Rose, and Rose's imposter-friend, Abigail (gracious – and you think books have drama?) appeared, it was even merrier. You know…as in… the more the merrier? I even got brave and moved back to my original room instead of sharing one with Natalie. After all, once you've seen a detached head in your bathroom closet, there's not a whole lot to be scared of anymore, is there? But still… something was missing and I was feeling restless.

Or maybe I was feeling lonely.

Have you ever noticed that you can feel lonelier when you are with people than you are when you're by yourself? Why is that? Natalie and Jack were in love and getting married at Christmas. You can imagine how nauseating THAT was. Celia and Rose and Abigail were inseparable. Even Abraham Lincoln preferred the company of others. And, if you can't even make friends with a dog, what are your chances in real life? Huh? Huh? Yeah. See. You don't know either. Do you ever wonder if people really like you… or if they just pretend because you do nice things for them or they're being polite? Yeah. Me, too. The problem is that you'll never, ever, really, really know, will you? It's just not possible. You can ask them, of course, but what are the odds that someone will say, "You know, you're right. I really don't like you. Glad we got that straightened out. Good chat. Thanks for asking. And while you're here, will you show me how to fix this dropped stitch?"

I wandered into the store area where Carolyn was busy re-arranging the baby yarn display. Yesterday, right before we were about to close, a large shipment of self-striping, softer than a cloud and – can you believe it – machine washable wool blend was delivered. If you're not a knitter, you probably won't understand the beauty of that glorious combination, but if you are… you would want to get yourself some of this yarn! Obviously, Carolyn couldn't wait to get her hands on it. I smiled to myself. Truth be told, I wanted to get my hands on it again, too. And even though it was not my time to work, I went to help.

Carolyn grinned happily at me as I approached, "Good morning, Molly," she said. "I couldn't wait another minute to see how this would look on the shelf. I'm thinking of making a sample with this yarn. Which pattern do you like?" She nodded towards the table with three patterns on it. I picked them up. The choices were comprised of a little hooded baby sweater, a little blanket that gathered up into a bunny head with long, droopy ears, and a cardigan with a sweet little collar.

"Well…." I said slowly… "you could do the cardigan and I could do the blanket."

She laughed. "It's calling you too, isn't it?"

Loudly. (What? If you've never heard yarn talking, then I suggest you put this book down immediately and head to your local yarn store. You'll see what I mean right away.)

An hour later we were snuggled down onto the couch and love seat and she was doing a gauge for her little sweater. A gauge is what you do when you want to be sure you are knitting with the right needles so that everything will turn out the exact right size. Gauges were rather boring. I was opting to skip the gauge. After all, how could a baby blanket not fit? Carolyn did not approve of my little gauge vacation, and I could see her frowning at my knitting when she didn't think I was looking. I rolled my eyes and finished the cast on. It's important to live up to your own standards, you know, not someone else's. Even in the little things. Isn't it amazing how many life lessons you can get from knitting? Another life lesson that I'm sure I would have to learn someday would be the value of gauge. But, that's not going to be today.

"So, how's the mystery story going, dear?" she asked.

I sighed. "It started off really good. But now I'm stuck."

Her smile was kind, "I hear that it is a common affliction amongst writers," she said, "but it often passes. Just keep writing."

Just keep writing? How can you "just keep writing" when you have nothing to write? I paused to reflect. Carolyn was pretty old and had seen a lot (I'm sure) in her lifetime. She might just be of some assistance in my quest for secrets. I pretended to study my knitting pattern, "How can you tell if someone is keeping a secret?" I asked Carolyn, looking up to catch her reaction.

Her little mouth dropped open. "What are you talking about?" she asked, looking around the store area quickly. "Has something happened?" Was it just me or did she look a little scared? Then again, with everything that had happened in this house, it was probably appropriate to be a little scared when someone asked a question like that.

"No. No. It's nothing like that," I hastened to assure her. "That's what I'm stuck on. I started off with a big long section on how secrets like to hide, and you don't know that they're there, but they're there just waiting for their chance to come to the surface. But I can't figure out what the secret should be. And, if you're going to talk about secrets, there should really be a big, juicy one, right? I suppose I could give up and go in another direction. But I really like my opener."

She stared at me for a long time. "Secrets are meant to stay secrets," she said, clearing her throat delicately. "I think that's the whole point."

"I know," I said patiently, "that's the problem. And the point. If I want to write about secrets, then someone needs to have one. But which character has another secret? And how do I know it's even there? And what is it?"

Carolyn paused thoughtfully, "Everyone has secrets, Molly," she said slowly. "If you're looking for a really big secret maybe you should look for the person who is trying to start over."

Something in her tone gave me a shiver in the warm store. "Trying to start over?" I squeaked. "What do you mean?"

"Well," Carolyn said, "it's been my experience that when someone is carrying a really big secret - they try to get away from it. To bury it and start over. So that's what you could look for. Start there and then start digging."

It sounded like good advice. But now I had another question.

"And do they?" I asked curiously. Her head tilted questioningly, "Get away from it by starting over?"

She smiled, almost sadly, her long fingers plucking at her yarn absentmindedly, "You can never really start over, my dear."

Her mood was beginning to affect me, and I lowered my voice to almost a whisper, "Why not?"

"Because the ghosts always follow you."

CHAPTER 3

T he ghosts always follow you. But it was her words that followed me. They snuck up behind me when I was helping with the lunch dishes and tapped me on the shoulder. I shrugged them away, but they clung to my shoulders like a small child riding piggy-back. I couldn't knit. When I tried to read the instructions in the pattern, the letters picked themselves up and rearranged themselves into the same five words over and over again. And then they just sat there laughing at me. It was really annoying. Perhaps I would change my mind and write a story about a little old lady who put an idea in someone's head and she went crazy. You know what they say… "Write what you know".

To calm myself down, I decided that, after dinner, I would walk down to Ryan's bakery and see if he had any great ideas about how to think up some horrible secrets for my story. Or if he had any ideas on how to get the ghosts to leave me alone. Or if he had anything tasty left-over that he would like me to eat for him. Distraction, I believe, must be the key.

So what do you think? Do you think that everyone has secrets? Do you? Are they deep and terrible? I know. You can't tell me. Or maybe you can. Maybe you're not meant to be a secret keeper. I don't know. It's confusing, isn't it? The big question is… would you feel better if you told your secret? Or would you regret it forever because it was a secret and needed to stay that way? At this point, I'd welcome any input. Seriously.

I guess that's the biggest dilemma, isn't it? Is the real point of a secret to stay hidden or to come out? Are secrets that never come to light unfulfilled? Or fulfilled? Are the secret keepers of the world the good guys… or the bad guys?

What did you say? That depends on the secret? Thanks. That's not exactly helpful.

Ryan was not at the bakery. The nerve of him. So Mr. Morrie was my next victim… I mean… the person, I was going to visit. Unfortunately, he was busy "doing his books"… whatever that means. I'm not really a business person. I hate adding up numbers with the expectation that they are going to come out the same – or match the bank statement – or whatever numbers are supposed to do. If you're adding them up just to see if they match the bank statement, isn't that kind of a waste of time? I mean, the bank has already told you what the number is supposed to be, so why argue with them? I'm sure they have really big calculators that know how to add just fine. What victory is there in achieving the same mathematical result as they have? Mr. Morrie, however, saw nothing helpful in the advice that I tried to give him and kept saying, "Shush." So I left. I'm sure he was sad to see me go. I bet when he was old and gray, he would regret "doing his books" when he could have been talking to me. What? Oh yeah, he was already old and gray.

As I stepped outside of Mr. Morrie's door, I couldn't resist going to look at the "old" Crabapple Yarns. The store that was now still condemned. Poor Carolyn. She was deep in the process of getting her store "un-condemned", but this was apparently a lengthy process involving lawyers and red tape. Red tape is no fun.

I walked up to the door so that I could peer in through the window and was slightly appalled to see dirty footprints on the sidewalk. I compared them to my shoes. Wow. They were huge. And, judging by the tracks, more than one person had tromped their way…

"Hey, you!" a voice yelled. I jumped so hard that I was sure that Mr. Morrie was going to come out and see what the big noise was that was me falling back to earth.

I landed on my rear. Hard. And found myself looking up into the slightly alarmed face of Ryan.

"I'm so sorry, Molly," he said contritely, even though I could tell that he was trying not to laugh. "I didn't mean to scare you. Honest."

I accepted his hand up with as much dignity as I could muster. It wasn't much, I can tell you that. "If I've broken my tailbone," I said, wincing a little as I straightened fully, "I'll never forgive you, because I'm certainly not going to be able to go to the doctor with a broken rear end, so it will never heal properly and for the rest of my life I'll be forced to…"

The rest of my very amusing diatribe was cut off when Ryan all but picked me up and pulled me around the side of the building, holding me back with one hand while he peeked his shaggy redhead around the corner comically.

"You make a rotten spy," I said grumpily, still trying to brush off the dirt on the aforementioned rear end. "What's the matter? Hiding from your customers? Did you run out of coffee cake again? I told you to make a few extras on Fridays. People really need coffee cake on…"

He pulled his head back, "Shhhhh," he said urgently, "I think he's coming."

Curiosity overcame the grumpiness. It was a quick battle, but a strong one. When one falls down, one expects a little sympathy, doesn't one? But, then again, if one is stubborn and holds a grudge, one isn't going to get to know everything. I know. It's a bummer. And a dilemma.

I tried to push around Ryan to see what he was looking at, but his long arms kept me firmly at bay. "I can't believe this," I hissed. "Let me see or else I'm going to…"

He grinned down at me, "You'll what?" His arm loosened and he stepped away from me just a bit. The challenge in his words was definitely meant to deter me, but I knew the same tricks that he did. And I wasn't falling for it. At least not today. I had just enough time to pop my head around the corner to see the tail end of a tall man in a suit get back into his very suburban-looking sedan and drive away.

"Who was that?" I demanded.

"Who?" Ryan asked innocently. He stepped back around the corner, swinging his arms nonchalantly.

"That man that just drove away." I gave him my best *DO NOT mess me with stare*. Why? I have no idea. I don't think it has ever worked with anyone in my entire life. Ever.

Ryan sighed, "I don't know who he was," he confessed, his eyes avoiding mine neatly. "I just didn't like the look of him."

A sudden thought occurred to me, "Ryan," I gasped, "you're not gambling, are you?"

"Gambling?" he sputtered. "He-… err… heavens no. Why would you ask me that?" His look indicated a serious doubt about my current state of mind.

I shrugged uncomfortably, thinking of Pete, Rachel's brother who had ended up with a broken leg after meeting with the people who wanted their gambling money back. Wait. Don't jump to conclusions. THEY didn't break his leg… he actually broke it running away from them… but you know… still… not people you want to mess with. "You're ducking a guy in a suit." I tugged at my hair anxiously, "Just like Pete…"

His face softened with concern, and he pulled me into a one-armed hug, "Of course not," he said in a gentle voice. "I really don't know who that was. I just didn't want to talk to him. So, I ducked." This time, his eyes met mine, but there was a distant look in his eyes that said he was telling the truth… but not telling the whole truth. My face must have conveyed what I was feeling, as it usually did, because he pulled me forward and kissed the top of my head affectionately. It was a move that usually melted me. But not today. Today, I had the unpleasant feeling that Ryan had secrets, too.

"So do you think that everyone has secrets, Natalie?" I asked, munching on toast for breakfast. I feel so bad for everyone who doesn't live with their own personal baker. Isn't it sad that most people are forced to exist with bread and jelly that comes from a grocery store? Jack, however, enriched our lives with homemade bread, oh, pardon me, homemade 7-grain bread, while Ryan kept us well-supplied with his own version of jelly. I was really going to miss living here.

You know, when I wasn't living here anymore. I'm not sure when that would be, but when it was, I would. Do you know what I mean?

She paused in her efforts of feeding Abraham Lincoln the crusts of her own toast. "Yes," she said, "I think so. There's always something to hide, isn't there? If it isn't a personal secret, it's something you've done or something your family has done or…" she glanced down to give Abraham Lincoln a significant look, "or something your dear little dog has done."

I shuddered theatrically. "I'm not sure if the world is ready to hear Abraham Lincoln's secrets."

She smirked. "Me, either." He looked up at both of us with a small head tilt that had Natalie rubbing his ugly little ears affectionately. "It's amazing how cute he can be when he wants to," she murmured. I tried to nod in agreement, but lying is wrong.

Also, I didn't want to be distracted by Abraham Lincoln's antics this morning. I wasn't done discussing secrets. "So what would you consider the worst secret ever?"

She quirked her eyebrow at me, and an arrow of guilt pierced my heart. "I'm sorry," I murmured. "I'm being insensitive. You've already lived through the worst secret ever."

She shrugged her shoulders, "It wasn't my worst secret," she said.

I gaped at her, "Are you telling me that you have a secret that is worse than your grandmother…"

She laughed and held up her hand, "Stop. Stop. What I meant was that even though that was a horrible secret, it actually turned out to be the best thing that ever happened to me."

I could see her point. Because of the mistakes her grandmother and mother had made, she was engaged to a handsome, sweet guy, was reconciled with her mother, and now had a complete and beautiful little family. So, I guess it is true that God can turn all things into good. But, where did that leave me in my quest for secrets?

"You know," Natalie said thoughtfully, "we found the answers to my questions at the library. Maybe you could too."

Hmmmm…the library… now why didn't I think of that? I'm so ashamed.

"Good morning, Mrs. Goldmyer," I said as sweetly as I could. Huh. It's amazing how much heartburn one can get from toast and jam. What? I'm sure it must have been what I ate – it would be totally rude to attribute my current state of indigestion on the face that was currently staring back at me.

I repeated my greeting. She lifted one hand to check the state of her bun, and once assured that not a hair was out of place, she smiled frostily at me before turning away towards her office.

"Well. That went well," the voice to my left said. I squeaked a little scream and spun to face… Natalie. "You didn't think I was going to let you go into enemy territory all by yourself, did you?" she asked, grinning unrepentantly.

"Well. You could have given me some warning instead of sneaking up on me like that," I said, patting my heart for emphasis (I seem to do that a lot around her).

She shook her head, "It just wouldn't be as fun, MollyDear." I have no idea why she thinks it's so funny to call me that.

We entered the library slowly, my heart smiling as we did so. I hope that, no matter how long I live, my heart always smiles when it sees books. I think that's healthy.

"Where should we start?" I wondered out loud. My feet were already inching their way towards my favorite authors. Even though I owned most of the books that I absolutely loved, it was still fun to see them in the library.

Natalie had, obviously, already thought things through a bit better than me. She pulled me by the arm towards the little room with the computer that sat like a piece of Tupperware in a china cabinet. "With the computer, of course," she said. "Where else?"

"Well," I said, "you know, there's always the card catalog, or we could start in the crime section and…"

She shrugged her shoulder at me, her grip firm on my sleeve, "Total waste of time," she said dismissively. "Takes way too long."

She sat down and quickly logged herself in. I really have a lot of respect for people who can do that, don't you? She stretched her arms in front of her, bending her fingers back and cracking her knuckles before she looked at me. "Now," she said, "what should we search for?"

Huh. That was a good question. Strangely, now that I was here, I wasn't so sure. How do you explain something that is a feeling in a way that a cold, logical computer would understand? Natalie saw my dilemma. Or, at least, she saw my hesitation and decided to take charge. She's really good at that. I tried not to let it happen too often. No sense in her getting an inflated sense of importance, right?

"What you need," she said with false sympathy, "is something that inspires you to get over this terrible writer's block. The best way to get ideas is to read, read, read. But, I think it's probably just as important to read the type of book that you're trying to write. So…."

"I never said that I had writer's block," I objected, fidgeting in my seat. "Besides… I think I'll just go and poke through the mystery section…"

"Don't be silly," she waved her hand at me. "Let's do this the right way. How about…" and here she began typing, "Secrets and murders…" she paused to wait for the computer to catch up to her brain. "Whoa. Ok. That's way too many results."

She was still muttering and pressing buttons when I decided to leave her to it and retreat quietly back into the library. Computers are all well and good, but really, they are no match for actually talking to the books… I mean… looking at the books. Don't be silly. I don't know anyone who talks to books, do you?

I headed straight for my favorite section. Now the only question was… which of my friends would be the most helpful to me right now? On one hand, I could really use someone coolly logical. Sherlock would have no problem deducing the biggest, juiciest secret ever. It was just what I needed – a brilliant plot with perfect logic. Maybe I should read up on his cases in the hopes that some of his investigative skills would rub off on me. Or maybe Hercule Poirot. Maybe just standing next to these books was good for me, as I could feel my powers of logic already rising to the surface to point out the flaw in my plan. There was some serious doubt on my part (and I'm sure yours), that I had the necessary… umm…. shall we say… little grey cells… (ha ha ha… pardon the little mystery humor) necessary to write like that. Or even think like that. What did you say? Oh. You were just clearing your throat, right? Good.

Maybe instead what I needed was some nice… ah ha… Victoria Holt. Now that girl knew how to write secrets, let me tell you. Why, I remember in one of her books, the daughter finds out that… oh, sorry, no spoilers here. You might want to read it yourself.

I was just in the process of pulling one or two books from the shelf when Natalie came striding down the aisle brandishing a sheet of paper triumphantly.

"I've got it!" she exclaimed. "We just needed to be more specific." A sinister smile began to bloom. It was a little creepy. "So, I looked up secrets and axe murderers."

I choked. "Axe murderers? That seems a bit melodramatic, don't you think?"

"I love melodrama," she said. "It's just what we need. Besides, don't you reference axe murderers in your introduction?"

"We?" I teased. "Does someone else need a wee bit of help with their teensy-weensy writer's block?"

She rolled her eyes and held up her paper again, "A mere slip of the tongue, my friend…" she paused for dramatic effect. "I found a book that sounds deliciously promising."

"What's it called?" I found myself asking… just like she wanted me to.

"The Axe Murderer of Springiegate."

"The Axe Murderer of Springgate?" I asked in astonishment.

"No," she corrected me patiently, "Springiegate." She held up the paper for me to see. "Look, there's an extra 'ie' in there – Springiegate."

We stared at each other. "Weird."

Natalie had obligingly written down the proper Dewey Decimal system number, and we went in search of "The Axe Murderer of Springiegate." But it wasn't on the shelf.

It wasn't on any of the surrounding shelves either – you know, how sometimes people pick up a book and then decide they don't want it anymore and just leave it on the wrong shelf... or the floor.... I know you would never do that, but some people do. It's super annoying. Especially when you were a librarian and had to put all the books back from whence they came.

Mrs. Goldmyer came along as we were shifting books around. "Ladies," she said, "if you would kindly refrain from taking apart the whole library, I would appreciate it."

"We were just looking for a book," I protested weakly. "We weren't moving anything around. And, if we did, we put them right back..." My guilty conscience had me wondering if Mrs. Goldmyer had ventured past Victoria Holt lately.

"Actually," Natalie interrupted, rolling her eyes, "maybe you can help us find the book we're looking for." A royal tilt of the head was her only answer. "The Axe Murderer of Springiegate."

Mrs. Goldmyer stared at her for 30 long seconds, not once blinking. It was a little awkward. I started to get worried and cleared my throat. She blinked, "I'm sorry," she said, politely. "I was waiting to hear the actual title. You cannot possibly wish to read such an absurd-sounding book."

"But it's listed in the card catalog," Natalie protested.

"Then," she said with an aggrieved sigh, "I suggest you use the brain you were given and find it on the shelf where it belongs. And," she continued, raising her voice over the protests of ours, "if it is not on the shelf, I suggest you do what most people do when they can't find a book in the library."

"Oh?" Natalie asked sarcastically. "And what might that be?"

"Assume it's checked-out." Her beady little eyes glowed with malicious self-righteous triumph (or at least that's how it looked to me), and she spun on her heel and left us standing there.

Well, I have to admit, despite being a former librarian... that particular scenario had actually not occurred to me. Once again, I'm so ashamed.

It wasn't until much later that I found myself wondering an important question....who else could possibly want to read "The Axe Murderer of Springiegate"?

CHAPTER 4

"It will be here on Friday."

I looked up from my knitting, "Excuse me?" I asked as politely as I could, which wasn't too politely. I tend to get a little cranky when someone interrupts me in the middle of a pattern. Are you like that too? There's nothing worse than, right in the middle of a tricky little YO, SK2P, having to stop and lose your train of thought. Then, when you're ready to go back to your knitting, you have no idea where you are and you have to count it all back out across the row. Well, I'm sure that there are worse things. At the moment, though, I couldn't think of anything else.

She waved her arms theatrically, "The Axe Murderer of Springiegate, dummy."

"Oh." It was all I could say … I was mentally chanting the place I was temporarily holding in my head of my stitch pattern.

"It certainly wasn't an easy book to find," Natalie continued. "I couldn't find it on any of my normal book buying sites, and the only one I could find was on a used book site and it cost an arm and a leg… plus shipping. It was literally the only copy out there."

I sighed and let my mental pattern-chanting go. "Then why would you buy it?"

She patted my arm comfortingly, "For you, MollyDear," she said. "You know I would do anything to help you get over this terrible writer's block."

I eyed her suspiciously. Yeah. Right. I don't think it was MY writer's block that she was worried about.

"Oh, and Ryan called," she said. "He can't have dinner with you tonight. He's busy making a special-order birthday cake for a customer."

"Well, that stinks," I said, heart sinking. "I wanted to talk to him tonight."

Her face was sympathetic. "Well, I know we're a poor substitute, but Jack and I would love to have dinner with you tonight. We were just going to discuss some wedding plans anyways."

I shuddered internally, the last time Natalie and Jack "discussed" some wedding plans, there was shouting and yelling and… I'm pretty sure Natalie threw a vase. She claimed that it had "fallen" out of the china cabinet. Amazingly, it must have also magically opened the glass door before throwing itself out to its death. Poor thing. And that was only to discuss if they should hang tulle or lace from the banisters. No. I don't know who won that argument. I'm not embarrassed to admit that I went into hiding.

"Thanks," I said, smiling as brightly as I could, "but I have some shopping to do in town, so I'll just go ahead and do that. You guys have a great time." I couldn't help an evil little chuckle, "And maybe you should 'discuss' your plans far, far away from the china cabinet this time."

She swatted me half-heartedly, face heating slightly, "It fell out of the cabinet," she insisted.

"Who knew someone could have such strong feelings about lace versus tulle," I couldn't help but tease back.

I left Raspberry Hill with her still muttering about "MollyDear" and "know-it-alls". Thankfully, she didn't harbor grudges and let me use Mr. Darcy without too much groveling. It was only about a mile into town, but it was a mile of haunted forest. I'm not kidding. Well, maybe I'm kidding. But I'm not. In the daytime, it didn't bother me, but at night… things lurked. I was sure of it.

I didn't really have shopping to do, but I would at least stop and buy a caramel apple at the candy store so that I wasn't a liar. And then, I was going to do some breaking and entering. I parked downtown, leaving Mr. Darcy securely locked and snug in a parallel parking place. Aren't you impressed? I said "parallel parking". True, there wasn't anyone else in the spot behind or in front of me, but hey – it's still considered parallel parking, right? Right.

I was just finishing up the delicious caramel coating on the outside of my apple as I approached Roberts Alley. I decided to stop by and say "Hi" to Ryan for a minute (and throw away the apple – why do they bother sticking that in the middle of all that caramel when no one ever eats it?) before finishing the rest of my errands. That's weird. It looked like all of the lights were off. Strange. But, then again, maybe not… if Ryan was working in the kitchen, he didn't need all of the lights in his store on, did he? What did you say? Stop it. Of course, Ryan was there. Why would he lie?

After several minutes of knocking and peering through windows, I was forced to the conclusion that Ryan was not at the bakery baking a cake. Why would he lie? Maybe he was baking a cake from his apartment? I think not. That would be against the health code thingies.

I shrugged and decided not to be angry. There had to be a reasonable explanation. I would just ask him tomorrow. No big deal, right? Right. Of course, I wasn't alarmed. Or angry.

I continued on my way down the street to Crabapple Yarns, where I was going to do my breaking and entering. Well, it wasn't really breaking and entering. I did have a key. It was just against the law to use it because the building was condemned. Details…details…

I know what you're wondering. You're wondering what I'm up to, aren't you? Well, maybe I'm just not going to tell you. It's my dastardly deed after, all, not yours. You, my friend, don't need to know everything.

Fifteen minutes later, I was back outside, locking the door to the poor, condemned building securely behind me. Mr. Morrie was standing by his door solemnly watching me as I walked by.

"Good evening, Mr. Morrie," I said in my most friendly voice. "How are you?"

He nodded his head at me but did not reply. I was just opening my mouth to chat some more when the door behind him opened and a tall form came out.

Well. Be still my beating heart. It was Nathaniel Goldmyer.

I blinked in surprise at him, and he stared at me for just a second too long before his face cracked and he smiled. But I had already seen the emptiness in his eyes.

I managed to croak out a very eloquent, "Hi." Perfect. Mr. Morrie turned around and went inside. What's even stranger than Mr. Morrie's behavior was that if any other person in the world had done the exact same thing, it would have been rude. But with Mr. Morrie and his eccentric ways… no… you're right. It was still rude.

"Good evening, Molly," Nathaniel said calmly, walking towards me like nothing weird was going on.

I narrowed my eyes at him, "What are you doing here?" It probably wasn't the nicest almost-greeting I had ever given, but Nathaniel's track record wasn't the greatest.

He raised his eyebrows mischievously, "What do you think I'm doing?" Unbelievable. He was actually smiling.

"Planning world domination," I retorted. "Or figuring out a way to steal Mr. Morrie's store or…"

He laughed and held up a hand, "Stop," he said, and then held up his other hand which contained a shiny hunk of metal. "Maybe I was just buying a new deadbolt for my door."

A likely story.

In the end, he walked me to my car. And it was a rather enjoyable walk, too. What? Don't judge. Even a rat can be sweet. Sometimes. Don't worry. I wouldn't forget that he was a rat.

He held the door open to Mr. Darcy and smiled down at me as I settled in behind the wheel. There was a look in his eyes, an emptiness behind the smile that had a strange echo in my own soul. Impulsively, I leaned forward, "Is everything ok, Nate?"

He blinked in surprise and paused for a moment, "You're a nice person, Molly," he said slowly, as if choosing his words carefully. "I appreciate your concern, however," he sighed, "everything is fine."

Of course it was.

He closed the door gently, but before he took a step back, he reached into his inside coat pocket and pulled out a card, offering it to me through my open window. I took it with a little bit of confusion. It was his business card.

The lost look was suddenly gone from his eyes, and he smiled his most charming. "In case you ever need me or my services," he said, "you call me."

And with that, he was gone.

A weird sort of feeling was twisting in my stomach, and it was somehow exciting and… disgusting. I rested my head on Mr. Darcy's rather old steering wheel that always smelled faintly of stale coffee and contemplated the difficulty of life. And why people lie. And why…

I was so deep into this philosophical contemplation that somehow I failed to notice the noise of several women running past the car, but there was no disguising the laugh that floated behind them. Helen has a very distinctive laugh. A less-than-kind person might just call it a snort. I stuck my head back up and peered through the gloom of dusk to see three familiar figures. I smiled to myself. It looked like the ladies were out for a little night on the town. Suddenly, the Helen-shaped shadow stopped and putting a hand up (possibly to her lips – this detail was supplied by my imagination, but probably correct), peered both ways. What? I leaned forward with more interest. The three of them slipped between the buildings, melting seamlessly into the growing darkness.

I suddenly realized that I was standing outside of Mr. Darcy on the sidewalk, already heading towards the spot where the ladies had disappeared. They were up to no good, I told myself, feet walking briskly, I should just turn right around and go back home. There was a nice comfy bed waiting for me with a really good mystery sitting on the table next to it. I should just mind my own beeswax and let them… huh… they were going in the back door of Happy Knits. This was bad. Really bad.

I'm not sure how long I stood outside the back door. What a chicken, I jeered at myself, just open the door and go in and see what they are up to. A sudden thought popped into my tiny little brain. Maybe they were supposed to be there.

Maybe they were Happy Knit customers now and there was a midnight sale on yarn… no… that didn't make sense… then they would use the front door. Maybe they were earning some extra money and cleaning stores at night? Maybe? You're right. They weren't doing anything legit in there.

But the question remained – what should I do?

"Ok," I said, "enough is enough. We're going in there and…" I still didn't know what, but I grabbed the handle with authority and (unfortunately) it turned easily in my hand. Bummer. I was rather sort of hoping that it would have been locked. Chicken.

They had not turned the lights on. Further proof of their malicious intent. I crept through the darkness of the back room and headed straight for the whispered giggles coming from the far end of the store. Thankfully, the owners and employees of Happy Knits were weird little minimalists so there weren't too many things to watch out for. At Crabapple Yarns, I would have been flat on my face within five steps.

I saw them now. They were backlit by the streetlights outside quite clearly… Helen, Rachel and Abby. Poor Abby. I'm sure they dragged her along. She really wasn't the type to… err… whatever they were doing. Even stranger was the fact that Abby was a customer of both stores. This was just plain weird.

A little scare was just what they needed. Breaking and entering. What was this world coming to? What did you say? I told you – that wasn't breaking and entering - I had a key.

"Alright," I said, loudly and commandingly, "just what is going on here?"

Helen and Rachel jumped. Abby fainted.

In the end, since we had no water to spritz her face with, Helen, very gently slapped Abby's cheeks until she woke up. She was not amused. I've never seen her so angry. "You could have killed us," she hissed at me. "What were you thinking scaring us like that?"

Pffft. It's not my fault that she wasn't cut out for the criminal line of work. "Excuse me?" I said. "You're the ones breaking into Happy Knits."

"We didn't break and enter," Rachel argued. "I have a key."

"Where did you get the key?" I demanded. Helen fidgeted and stared very hard at the ground.

I was on a roll now, "You stole a key? I don't even want to know how you did that. But, let's get back to the problem at hand… What were you thinking? Do you realize what's at stake if you get caught?"

Rachel glowered, "We weren't planning on getting caught. We were just here to let them go and then we were going to go, too."

Oh boy. That didn't sound good at all. "Let them go," I repeated slowly. "Let what go?"

As if on cue, something feathery whispered past my cheek. There may have been a small shriek and a (very minor and quick) jump back. There may also have been non-sympathetic, vindictive smirks on some faces, too. I sank to the ground on my rear end and looked up at the Three Musketeers. "Is that what I think it is?" I asked wearily.

Three heads nodded.

I pulled myself up to a more dignified position. "So you came all the way over here, in the dead of night, to release *moths* at Happy Knits?"

Helen tilted her head to one side, "Well, it doesn't sound as good coming from you as it did when we had our war meeting." She rubbed her hands together gleefully, "What we actually did was rally the troops and defend the honor and good name of our loyal and faithful knitting compatriot who was so cruelly…"

"I don't think Carolyn would be happy about this at all." They were so excited about their plan I almost hated to say it.

Helen's face fell, and Abby started pulling anxiously at her ponytail. Rachel was still not done. "When someone isn't capable of fighting for themselves, then others need to step forward and do what needs to be done."

I waved my hands around the store, "Basically, you're vandalizing Happy Knits," I argued. "I'm not sure how much damage a moth can do, but if they do eat the yarn, then you're responsible for ruining their inventory. Do you have any idea how much yarn costs? I'll tell you. A. Lot. Of. Money. What would Carolyn…" Actually, I wasn't even sure if they would know which type of moth was the yarn-chomping type, or how quickly moths ate wool, but that was a discussion for another day. A little guilt is sometimes good for the soul.

They looked like little kids who got kicked out of a birthday party.

Rachel was the first to stir. She sighed a deep and heavy sigh. "Fine," she said wearily, "maybe you're right."

Abby looked like someone waking up from a bad dream, "What have we done?" she whispered. "There must be thousands and thousands of dollars in here…"

"How many moths did you release?" I asked.

"Five," Helen squeaked.

Five? "That's it?" I know. I was really starting to sound like Natalie. I'm sorry. Maybe I was just spending too much time with her or something. She was really starting to rub off. Whether that was a good thing or a bad thing, remained to be seen.

"Well," Rachel said defensively, "we didn't have much time to prepare. And, really, five is plenty as long as *they* don't know it's only five."

All three of them forgot their shame momentarily and, looking at each other, chuckled evilly. I almost chuckled with them. Almost. It really was just a little bit clever.

I gave myself a mental shake. "If we collect all five moths and leave the place the way that we found it, we should be fine."

The arguing then began about the best way to collect the renegade moths. Rachel tried to google it on her smartphone, but couldn't get service in the building. In the end, we used the old cliché. "Like a moth to a flame". Rachel figured out how to turn one light on in the back of the store, after several failed attempts (one of which resulted in total store illumination for about 3 horrifying seconds) and the moths, quite simply, came to us. Strangely enough, we collected six.

"I think," Helen said primly, carefully adjusting the little paper bag of moths in her hand, "that we really did them a favor, didn't we?"

I stared at her, "How do you figure that?"

"Well, if we hadn't been here to collect our moths, they would have had a moth that could have, potentially, destroyed a lot of their inventory. I think that they will really thank us for that."

"Let's call them and find out," a deep, manly voice from behind us suggested.

Shrieking. Spinning. Clasping of hearts. And fainting (but that was just Abby).

Yes, my friends. It was the police. My first instinct was right. This was going to be bad. Really bad.

We were all marched swiftly outside. Helen, still carrying her little butterfly wanna-be's, talked quietly out of the side of her mouth, "Do I let them go or keep them?"

I shrugged. Would it be worse to have the proof of what we attempted– or not have the proof and then get booked for something even more dastardly than moth release? Get booked. Holy cow. I can't believe I was about to get booked for something. And for something that I didn't even agree with. Or help plan. That was the really insufferable part. Can you believe they had never even asked me to…? I mean, seriously, what's wrong with me? I can be devious. Not, of course, that I would. But it would have been nice to be asked.

The door swung shut behind us with an ominous thud. Just like the prison bars would after we were booked. I was going to throw up.

Holding up his flashlight, which was totally unnecessary, as we had plenty of light from the streetlamp, he paced in front of us. "Now, who," he said, in a rather menacing voice, "would like to tell me what's going on here tonight."

Whoosh. The flashlight illuminated Abby's wretched face. She looked incapable of speech.

Whoosh. Now it was on Rachel. She fidgeted nervously.

Whoosh. "Alright," Helen all but shouted, "we weren't supposed to be in there. It was just a harmless little joke." She let out a rather pathetic attempt at a chuckle and held up the bag of moths.

He reached out a meaty paw to grab the bag and opened it in a rather ill-advised fashion. All of the moths came out in their own victorious whoosh... making the intrepid officer jump back and drop the bag – and his flashlight.

I'm sorry. I know. It wasn't funny. But, sometimes, you know how it is... nerves can make you giggle at the exact wrong time. This was the exact wrong time. Also... have you ever noticed how nervous giggles are contagious?

"Alright," he yelled, scooping up his flashlight. "That's enough."

Totally did not help.

"I said that's enough," he repeated. "There is nothing funny about your situation – unless you think 3-5 years is hilarious."

Yeah. That totally helped. We suddenly found ourselves very sober and staring up at him with big eyes.

His little smirk was most unbecoming. "Yes," he said, "I kinda thought so." It was my turn to be under the flashlight spotlight, "And what do you have in your pocket?" he demanded.

Oh dear.

Oh dear.

"Nothing," I said. Well. That was stupid. Obviously, there was something in my pocket. But, before I could gather the words I needed to explain that the contents of my pocket had nothing whatsoever to do with this little incident, he had already reached forward and pulled it out. "Hey!" was my meager, but outraged reply. My heartbeat was roaring in my ears.

The other ladies stepped forward to protest, too, but one look from Officer... I checked his uniform... Douglas, had them all wisely retreating.

He was examining the small book with interest. "Excuse me, Officer Douglas," I said as sweetly as I could, "but that actually has nothing to do with this."

A calculating smile lit up his face as he flipped the cover open. No. No. No. He wouldn't dare.

He flipped a page and smirked some more. He flipped further, "I am so sick of knitters," he read. "They are all incredibly out of their minds. I'm not sure if there is another group of people out there who are so out of touch with reality and incredibly self-absorbed."

Have you ever, truly, wished that the ground would open up and eat you? Have you ever been so humiliated and ashamed that your only desire was to fall down and pretend you were dead? Yes, my horrified friends, you guessed correctly. It was my diary.

"They are never going to like me," he continued, obviously fascinated by what he was reading. "They only find me useful when they can't figure something out themselves. Or they don't want to. They are so…"

"That's enough," Helen said in a low voice.

"Stop it," Rachel said at the same time.

I couldn't look at them. Not as we were marching to the police station. Or, as we sat on the benches in the foyer of the police station. But that's ok. They were doing their best not to look at me either.

I believe Officer Douglas was in one of the back rooms arguing with a superior about how best to proceed with three, no, I guess I was there, four, four vandalizing little knitters when a thought hit me. Ok. It didn't really hit me. What happened was… I was cold, so I tucked my fingers into my pockets in the desperate attempt to believe that the cold I was feeling was physical when I felt something else in my pocket.

I didn't even think about it. I stood up and walked across the room to where the only other officer on duty was sitting with his feet up on a desk, extremely occupied with the contents of his smartphone. It looked like a dating website. Obviously not much happened in Springgate at night.

"Excuse me," I said, "but I believe I get a phone call."

I felt the other knitters perk up behind me. Officer Stuart looked to where Officer Douglas had exited the room, and with a small shrug, gestured me into the room behind him. Two minutes later, I was back out and sitting by – if not with – Rachel, Helen and Abby. They were curious, I could tell, but none of them bothered to ask.

Thankfully, Officer Douglas still had not re-entered the room when Nathaniel Goldmyer came striding in confidently. He winked at me and spoke to Officer Stuart before walking through the same door that Officer Douglas had left through.

That broke them out of their silence. "What's HE doing here?" Rachel demanded.

"Did you call him, Molly?" Helen asked breathlessly. She looked scandalized – and hopeful – at the same time.

I found I couldn't meet their gazes – or their questions - and kept my eyes firmly riveted to the fascinating flooring pattern of chipped laminate.

A few minutes later, Sherriff Roger Jones (the predecessor of the recently deposed Sherriff Finn, whom you may remember) came out with Nathaniel.

"Ladies," he said sternly, "we do not take kindly to breaking and entering or vandalism here in Springgate." We wilted under his glare like spinach in a pot of noodles. "However," and here, amazingly, a kind smile cracked his face, "I have some knowledge of all of you and I know that this is very out of character. I don't believe any of you are about to embark on a life of crime. So, I'm going to let you go," he held up a warning finger at the three delighted gasps, "but I will warn you – I will not be so lenient ever again." His gaze sought each of our faces. I believed him. "Now, go home before I change my mind."

Abby fled. Helen and Rachel gave Nate a rather grudging, "Thank you" before following suit.

The Sherriff and the other officers, apparently feeling that they had devoted enough time to us, went back to whatever they were doing before. Officer Douglas gave me a particularly malevolent stare as he exited, presumably to go back on his rounds. I pitied whoever he found next to pick on.

Nate sank down next to me on the wooden bench. I tried to manage a small smile, but before I could speak, he said, "When I said to call me if you ever needed me, I certainly wasn't expecting that to happen an hour later." His eyes were warm, without any hint of condemnation, for which I was ridiculously grateful.

I blushed. I hate it when I do that. "I wasn't expecting to have to ever call you," I said honestly. "But thanks."

He shrugged. "I was just debating whether or not to heat up my leftover Chinese or do the laundry when you called. This was …" and here there was a little lawyerly gleam of glee as he scanned the small police station, "a little more exciting." He looked down at me, "So, not that it matters or anything, but why were you in Happy Knits releasing moths?"

I fidgeted with the edge of my coat, "I wasn't releasing moths," I said irritably. "I have no idea why they were. Rachel said something about when someone can't fight for themselves… I don't know. It's all very confusing. We had just gotten them rounded back up when the officer… stopped us."

He laughed, and I glared half-heartedly at him. "Here's a quick tip," he said, bending down low so that he could whisper. "Next time, don't turn on the lights when you're doing something sneaky."

I couldn't help the small laugh, "You're actually not the first person to ever tell me that," I admitted.

His eyebrows rose. "Really? So this isn't your first criminal adventure? I'm impressed. You'll have to tell me about it sometime." We shared a small smile, and then he frowned, "So was it my imagination or were those other ladies… upset with you?" The frown deepened, "They didn't even wait for you to leave."

"OH!" I grabbed his sleeve. "That horrible officer still has my…"

"Diary?" he asked, pulling my poor, abused little friend from his inside coat pocket.

I snatched it from his hand and tucked it under the flap of my coat protectively. "Thank you." I looked at him suspiciously, "Did you read it?"

"Why?" He wiggled his eyebrows suggestively, "Am I in it?"

Men.

CHAPTER 5

G oing down to breakfast the next morning might have been one of the bravest things I have ever done. What I really wanted to do was hide in my room until everyone forgot what had happened. Or that I ever existed in the first place. But, that wasn't likely to happen, now was it?

Coming home yesterday, I had been met by Natalie at the door. Rachel had conveniently phoned prior to my arrival. She had inquired politely if I was alright. I had replied that I was fine and continued dragging myself up the stairs to my room. Not the most auspicious of beginnings.

Carolyn, Natalie and Jack were waiting for me in the kitchen. Three big spiders waiting for a little fly.

"Good morning," I said hesitantly.

Carolyn came sweeping around the table. "Oh my dear," she said, "I've heard about your horrible ordeal last night."

I wonder which of my ordeals she considered the most horrible – the vandalism or the public reading of my diary?

She hugged me hard, and I stepped away to sink down into the relative personal space of a kitchen chair, rubbing my already aching head.

"Rachel told me everything," Natalie said. "She said that you had no part in the 'The Great Moth Plot'" – other than talking them out of it. Is that true?" Her eyes were like razors.

I rolled my eyes, "Do I look like someone who would plan 'The Great Moth Plot?'" I demanded, little sparks of outrage waking me up.

Her face softened slightly, "I wouldn't put it past you," she said with a small smile, "however, I don't really see it."

Jack crossed his arms and leaned back against the counter, "What I would like to know is why you called that... that..." Natalie patted his arm nervously and hissed something that I couldn't hear. "Why you would call Nathaniel Goldmyer?" His face was creased with confusion, "Why not call Ryan? Or me? Or Carolyn? Or..."

I rolled my eyes, "Yes, because you all have such a great reputation in the Sherriff's office," I said. "You know they're still upset about everything that happened, and even if it's not your fault – they still..."

He waved an impatient hand, "Yeah, ok... but why not Ryan?"

"Ryan wasn't home," I all but shouted. "He said he was going to be baking a cake and he wasn't there. I don't know what he was doing. I didn't know what Rachel and Helen and Abby were doing. No one seems to want to tell me anything. So you can all stop looking at me like I'm a traitor."

To my complete horror, two little tears ran down my cheeks, and I wiped them away angrily.

Jack took a step forward and then hesitated, "Oh, don't cry, Molly," he said helplessly. "I didn't mean..."

"Yes, you did," I managed to get out. "And I know that Rachel told you what was written in my diary, too." Their faces were proof enough of that. "But diaries are meant to be private. It was taken out of context and..."

I turned and fled the room.

When I went back to my room, I realized something. My diary was missing. Someone had my diary. And they were probably reading it.

I haven't ever been what anyone would call the athletic type, so it surprised me that running felt so good. Never have I felt as much as even a little twitch of an inclination to run, but as I headed down the road through the haunted forest, I felt free. Every strike of my foot against the tar was in tandem with a beat of my heart, and it spurred me to go on faster – harder. The urge, no the need, the desperate need to get away... to be somewhere, anywhere, by myself... was uncontrollable. To be somewhere where no eye could see. No eye could judge. At some point, I must have left the road and started going cross-country, leaping like a newborn deer on shaky legs over roots and stumps and dodging trees. It was lack of oxygen and screaming lungs that finally stopped me. I fell to the ground, my fingers curling in the damp dirt and moss of the forest floor as I tried to regain my breath.

Failure stung hard in my eyes and stuck in my throat. I struggled to breathe and push back against the despair. I had ruined everything. The despair that had prompted me to seek this woody-solitude now choked me with its truth. Sobs came from so deep within me, that even as I cried, crouched on my knees and staring at the weeds under me, some part of me wondered, in a detached way, at their depth. I was paralyzed as every muscle in my body locked in an effort to hold them in. I had failed. I was a failure. Great gasping breaths blew through my mouth. I shut it tightly, refusing to let the emotion crumple me. I had failed.

With the last of the strength that was in me, I gave myself a hard shove and fell backward against a tree, its solid warmth strangely comforting. Rocking slightly back and forth, I put both arms over my head and tried to focus on... nothing.

Exactly how long I sat there, huddled against the tree and crying, I have no idea. Eventually, the tears stopped, and after that, my breathing finally evened out. Clarity and reality returned, as they usually do, with an unwelcome jolt of awareness.

I was an idiot.

How pathetic I would look to anyone else right now. I should really care about that, shouldn't I? But I couldn't. I was numb. Staring straight ahead, I found that I couldn't turn my focus anywhere but the tree ahead of me. I watched as a little black ant climbed up the rough bark faster than you would think possible, its little feet no thicker than a hair. How did something so small survive in this world? And, if something that fragile was capable of surviving and thriving, how was it possible that I couldn't... and here my thoughts forced me down the same path again. I had failed at my life. And somehow, I was not surprised. I thought I had friends. I thought I had a man who liked me... who I hoped maybe even loved me. And what did I really have? No home to speak of. Ryan was lying to me. The people I had counted as friends would never look at me the same way ever again. Never. They would all know. How long would it be until everyone knew? A tear trickled down my cheek and yet my gaze did not waver from the tree.

I should probably get up. I stared at the tree. I had people to apologize to. Another ant joined his friend. This one carried a large piece of something questionable. He struggled over an outcropping of bark. I had things to figure out. I had decisions to make. I had to figure out... The first ant joined in the struggle...

There was a large crashing sound on my right. Maybe it was a wolf. Did they have wolves in Springgate? I should probably care. The ants were almost out of sight now.

"Molly!" someone shouted frantically.

Something deep within me sighed sadly. It wasn't a wolf. Half of me wondered if a wolf would have been more bearable.

"She's over here," he yelled. Another voice answered and the crashing became louder.

Now was the time to suck it up and pull myself together. There was only a brief amount of time until this situation was irretrievable. I...couldn't. My peripheral vision saw two figures approaching me rapidly, dropping to their knees, one on each side.

A warm hand was on my face, "She's freezing," someone said, their voice angry. I flinched.

The other figure batted his hand away, "Stop it," he said. "You're scaring her."

I wasn't scared. I was tired. So tired.

Suddenly my vision of the tree was gone. I would probably never see those ants again. I mourned the loss even as my eyes adjusted to try to focus on what was now in front of me.

Red hair. A face puckered with concern. I should know this.

The mouth was opening and closing. Words flowed around me, but they were too much. I closed my eyes.

The warm hand was back on my face, and then another on the other side.

"Molly," a gentle voice said, "open your eyes."

I cracked them back open. "J-J-Ja..." I tried to say his name.

His eyes crinkled into a smile, "That's right," he said. "It's just me and Ryan. We were so worried. We're going to take you home now, alright?"

I tried to tell him that I didn't have a home, and probably didn't deserve one either, but no words came out and then darkness descended.

There was warmth and softness when I awoke. And blessed darkness. I was in bed. Thank heavens. How I got there, I have no idea. But I couldn't imagine a better place to be at the moment. Every muscle in my body throbbed, and I wasn't even moving. I tried an experimental leg wiggle. Yep. Just as I had thought. Nice and sore. Running was stupid.

My leg wiggle did more than confirm my doctor-ly diagnosis – it alerted someone that I was awake.

Natalie came cautiously into view, dropping a book onto the foot of the bed as she approached. She offered a small smile.

"Hi, Molly," she said softly, as if she knew I couldn't handle anything louder than a whisper.

I longed for my state of numbness to return.

"Hi," I croaked and realized my own throat was horribly parched. Like something had died in it three days ago.

She winced in sympathy and handed me a glass of water that magically appeared in her hand.

Ahhh. It was like liquid happiness. Too bad it only helped my throat and couldn't reach all the way down.

She perched cautiously on the edge of the bed, "I owe you an apology," she began.

I shook my head. Now was as good of a time as any to let her know that I would be moving on. Funny how just yesterday (was it yesterday?) I had been moaning about my small life and now, here, I was about to become homeless and jobless. And friendless. But maybe I had been friendless all along and was just now realizing it.

"Don't be silly," I said, clearing my throat to gain a few seconds of thought. "It's certainly not your fault that I went for a little run and got lost in the woods."

Her gaze was piercing. Anyone else would have probably gone along with my story to keep things friendly and non-confrontational. Not Natalie. She reached forward and squeezed my arm, "We shouldn't have ganged up on you like that. None of what happened was your fault. But you and I both know that you didn't 'go for a little run' yesterday." When I opened my mouth to protest, she just talked louder, "It's fine. I get it. You were angry and a little humiliated that someone read your diary. Who wouldn't be? And we weren't making it any easier for you. Gracious. But who cares what you wrote in there? Everyone gets frustrated from time to time, and from what I heard, you didn't mention names," here her eyes twinkled just a bit, "so really, it's not that big of a …"

"It's missing," I said suddenly. "When I came back to my room it was gone. Someone has my diary. Someone has…" My voice cracked even as it rose in volume… I swung the covers back to get up even as my body protested the movement. The need to escape was as real as the way my leg muscles shrieked their protest.

"Whoa. Whoa." Natalie grabbed my other arm, making it ridiculously easy for her to use her own weight to keep me from rising. "It's right here. I have it. I promise. No one stole your diary."

Relief hit me so hard I all but melted into the pillows behind me. Realizing that my escape attempt had been abandoned, she let go of my arms and ran over to the enormous dresser that was practically built into the wall. She pulled open the second drawer from the bottom and brought up the little leather-bound book triumphantly. I reached for it, handshaking.

She handed it to me, her expression contrite. "I'm so sorry. I came into your room in the morning, but you had already headed downstairs. I saw your little diary on the bed and thought you were probably not thinking clearly otherwise you would have put it into a hiding place. This house is so over-run by people sometimes, I didn't want to take the chance that anyone else would find it and…

"Thank you," I whispered. "Thank you. Thank you." I clutched it to my chest like a mother holds a child.

She smiled sadly and held up both hands, "I also promise you that I didn't even so much as open it."

I believed her.

Closing my eyes, I thanked God for saving me. No one had read it. I was still safe. Maybe I could still stay. Time would tell.

Even after a nice, hot bath, I was still a little bit stiff as I headed downstairs. My diary was now firmly tucked into a very convenient place under a floorboard. It was so handy to live in an old house with loose floorboards. I should have just made a little fire in the fireplace. It's a strange thing, isn't it, how we cling to things that aren't good for us. How inanimate objects can become just as real as flesh and blood? Maybe someday I will learn.

Ryan was sitting on the bottom step, his head held up with one hand. He looked forlorn and a bit ragged. His hair stood up in odd little tufts. The back of his shirt had dirt on it. I wondered if he had spent all night there, and felt a brief dart of pain. I had caused this. I was hurting people. Maybe...

His head shot up as my foot hit a particularly creaky step and he jumped to his feet. His expressive face lit up when he saw me, and my heart squeezed a little further. He was up the stairs before I even realized he was moving.

"Molly," he said, stopping just before he touched me, "are you alright?" His hands came out like he wanted to reach out, but they fell back reluctantly.

I smiled and dropped my eyes to stare at the floor, "I'm fine," I said softly. "I'm so sorry about all of the trouble I seem to have caused."

He snorted, and a soft touch on my hair drew my gaze upwards again. He was tucking a strand of hair behind my ear, "It's okay. I happen to like troublemakers," he said just as softly. "I'm so sorry I wasn't there and you had to go through the whole thing alone. It sounds brutal. My mom wasn't feeling well and I went home that night to be with her."

His gaze was earnest and bright. "Jack said you came to see me and that I wasn't there. I'm so sorry. I should have let you know. I just… she called… and I took off. I'm sorry."

I sighed and sank down onto the steps behind me, my legs too tired to stay up any longer. "You don't have to apologize," I said sadly. "I've been reading and writing about secrets and I think they've gotten to me. I'm seeing things that aren't there. When you weren't at the bakery… I thought… that…"

"You thought that I had lied about making a cake?" Ryan asked quietly. I nodded. "What did you think I was doing instead?"

I shrugged one shoulder, "I don't know. People tell lies all of the time." I took a deep, shaky breath, "Everyone has secrets. I'm so sorry that I thought…"

"Molly," Ryan said firmly, "look at me."

It took longer than it should have for my eyes to meet his. Instead of the (justified) frustration with me that he was probably feeling, his eyes were soft and kind, "No," he said, "I'm sorry."

I made a face at him, "For what? For not telling me every move you make? Sorry that I'm a crazy book-a-holic who sees plots everywhere around her? Sorry that I have a cynical disposition that looks for the worst in people? Sorry that…"

My last "Sorry" sentence never saw the light of day. It was swallowed in the most gentle kiss I have ever had. He broke away reluctantly. "No," he said, one hand on the side of my cheek, "I'm sorry that I haven't done that before. I'm sorry that I didn't tell you how I feel so that you have to wonder and…"

"Well, now, this is awkward," a voice from the bottom of the stairs said. Our expressions were identical mirrors of annoyance as we both looked to see Jack at the bottom of the stairs, wearing a triumphant expression of glee.

Ryan slid an arm behind me, and I happily snuggled in closer, even as my thoughts took off racing so much faster than my legs ever could. Did this mean he really loved me? A delicious ripple of happiness zinged from my heart all the way out to my toes. Followed quickly by the slippery coldness of fear. Was this a good idea?

Jack was now climbing the stairs, having the grace to look just a little bit embarrassed. "I'm sorry to interrupt," he said, as believably as possible, even though he was still grinning, "but I heard that Molly was awake and thought she could use some breakfast."

So it was true. I had slept through a whole day and a night. Wow.

He held a plate under my nose. Fluffy pieces of French toast, sprinkled with powdered sugar and slathered in syrup were calling me. I grabbed the plate and the fork from his hand and took three bites before I even realized I was eating.

Wiping my mouth with the back of my hand (he hadn't brought a napkin), I giggled rather self-consciously. "Thank you, Jack," I said. "This is so delicious. I didn't even realize I was starving."

Jack shrugged, "It was no big deal. I've been thinking about adding some brunch items to my menu." He paused to watch me eat with an expression somewhere between alarm and amusement. "I was going to ask how you liked my French toast, but I think you would be eating a deep-fried skunk with the same amount of enthusiasm right now…"

"Don't be silly," I argued. "Deep-fried skunk is horrible."

Ryan's phone went off in his pocket. He pulled it out and answered it with a smile. The smile slipped from his face as the other person began talking. I couldn't hear what was said, but it was definitely a female voice.

"Yeah," he said, in a surprisingly hard voice, "just hold on."

He stood, his smile somewhat strained as he looked and me and Jack, "Excuse me," he said. "I have to take this."

Because he couldn't talk to anyone here? Strange. And there it went again. My mind performing great feats of aerobic exercise as it jumped from one conclusion to another.

Jack leaned on my arm slightly, "Are you going to finish that?" he asked.

I looked up at him, surprised to find tears blurring my vision, "You know, Jack," I said, "I really hate secrets."

He leaned a little heavier against me as I reluctantly finished my French toast.

CHAPTER 6

"D o you know what I was thinking, my dear?" Carolyn asked.

Did I ever know what she was thinking? But, I merely shook my head and smiled. Carolyn had been very gracious about the moth event and the Reading of the Diary. Well, the partial reading of the diary. I thanked God every night that Officer Douglas had chosen that page to read. We'd be having a totally different kind of conversation if he had started at the beginning. Carolyn was optimistic that no one would be offended by my words… if the words got out… which, considering Abby's face… was bound to happen. I had offered to seek alternate employment, but she was insistent.

"Well," she said, her eyes happy, "I was setting up the class schedule and, do you know who I think would be perfect to teach the beginner's knitting class?"

I frowned over my knitting, "Don't you usually teach those?" I asked. "You're the perfect person for it." And she was, sweet and patient. Never making a nervous new knitter feel foolish for lack of knowledge. If you were going to learn how to knit, you couldn't do better than Carolyn.

She flushed a little, "Why, thank you," she said, "but I think it's time for some new faces to add a little spice to our classes."

I paused in my knitting to contemplate. "Rachel?"

She tilted her head, "Rachel is a very good teacher," she agreed. "But no. I was thinking of someone even better."

"Not…" I said cautiously, then cleared my throat. "You weren't thinking of Louise, were you?" I didn't want to hurt anyone's feelings, but…

She laughed, "No. Although," she said more soberly, "I think if you gave her a chance you'd see that she actually is very good with all levels of knitters."

"If I gave her a chance?" I muttered under my breath, completely missing Carolyn's last words. "Excuse me?" I could not have heard her correctly.

She made her eyes big and innocent as she finished inserting the latest patterns we had received into sheet protectors, straightening the pile with competent fingers as she worked. "You," she replied simply, grinning mischievously.

"Yeah," I said, "I think you'd have better luck with Louise." I rolled my eyes and re-attacked my knitting.

She sat down next to me, "No," she said, "I'm serious. You are my perfect candidate. And the knitters love you."

"Carolyn," I said patiently, "I can't teach other people how to knit. I just learned myself."

"I know," she replied. "That's one of the reasons you're the perfect candidate. You remember what it's like to be a new knitter – the emotions and the frustrations. You know exactly what to be on the lookout for and what should be explained more and what a new knitter needs to know and hear."

I patted the papery thin hand that was on the table, "You're very kind," I said, "but I think maybe you're just trying to…" I knew exactly what she was trying to do.

"I'm not trying to do anything," she protested. "And you're giving what happened way more emphasis than it needs."

I opened my mouth to protest just as Natalie came waltzing in. Abraham Lincoln stopped at the door and peered in. He still did not like coming into the ballroom. Why? Who knows? He had a few quirks. One of them being that you could not call him by anything other than his full and complete given name. Another one was… you were never to let him see himself in a mirror. Why? Who knows? No one, as yet, had been brave enough to find out if that were true. But, we digress.

"I think it's a perfect idea, too, Carolyn," Natalie agreed. She would. Rotten woman.

Let's just abbreviate this conversation. I argued. Eloquently. I was stubborn. I was steadfast. I was insistent.

Yes. In less than a month, I would be teaching "Beginning Knitting."

I normally loved fall. I loved the way the sun felt different as it fell across your shoulders. I loved the smell of fresh, crisp leaves and the explosion of colors. I loved the thought of warm, woolen sweaters and pink cheeks. I loved beautiful dreams of walking through the apple orchard, apples hanging from the trees like little red presents, sipping cool apple cider and eating hot, fresh, sugary donuts… even though the reality of having to crawl through the crowds, listen to wailing children and fighting tooth and nail for the last donut… left something to be desired. This fall promised to be no less than all of the other autumns of my somewhat long life. There was just one big, glaring, dark spot in the sky. An ominous raincloud that threatened to burst open and drown every apple tree from here to Oak Harbor. I was teaching a three-week knitting class.

I sat at the counter and stared at the class list that Carolyn had drawn up and had copies made of. Yes, she already had copies. It was either the quickest copy job in the history of mankind, or she had been very sure of herself when she printed them. I think you know which vote I would cast.

I would be teaching the class how to knit a hat. A hat. Good grief. Don't you think we should have started with something nice and easy like a scarf? I know. Me, too. But, no. Carolyn said that a scarf was too "basic" for a class. I argued that that was the point exactly. Now, in addition to learning how to cast on, they would also have to be taught how to knit in the round, how to use a circular needle, how to knit AND purl, do decreases and… and… I was clearly going to have to knit a hat before I did anything else. You know. Because if you're going to teach someone how to knit a hat, you should probably have, at some point, knitted a hat yourself. Geesh. You would think that Carolyn would have thought of all these things herself. Luckily, the pattern looked fairly easy. It was a cute little slouch hat with some ribbing at the bottom and just a few decreases on the top. How do I get myself into these situations?

I had chosen a rather beautiful shade of brown to complement my hair. Not, that I would probably ever get to wear it since it was a class sample, and really, the property of Crabapple Yarns. But, remember this, never knit with yarn you don't like. What's the point?

"It's here!" Natalie popped up by my elbow with a triumphant smile. "It actually came early! Can you believe it?"

I tore my eyes from the class description. "What's here?"

She waved a huge book in front of my face. "The book! The one I've been telling you about."

I grabbed the book from her and it fell to the counter with a rather loud thud. It was an older book, the leather already worn with time even though the spine showed very little wear. "This is a used book," I said in surprise.

She rolled her eyes, "You never listen to a thing I say," she said impatiently. "I told you that this was the only copy I could find. It must have had a limited print run."

I ran a hand over the front, tracing the faint outline of the title with one finger. I don't know if I've ever told you this, but I love old books. I love the way they smell and the way their pages crinkle with the history of every person who has ever turned them. I usually felt a glow of pleasant expectation just looking at one. What? You're right. It's not just old books. I love young ones, too. The enchanting lure of the world within a world. It never fails to call to me.

There was something... different... about this book though. There was something wrong with it. I flipped it over again. Perhaps it was because, even though it was clearly an old book, it looked like it had never been read before. Also, I had the uneasy feeling that we had met before. Which was, of course, entirely likely. I did use to work at the library, so there was a very good likelihood that I had checked this book in and out many times. Then again... wouldn't you think that "The Axe Murderer of Springiegate" would be a title to remember? Wouldn't anyone crack the cover of that one and read a page or two before putting it back on the shelf? Not, of course, that I was in the habit of reading during library hours. That's just silly. Where do you get these ideas?

"You can read it first," Natalie declared magnanimously, patting my arm.

"Thanks," I said slowly, turning the book one last time, "but you should read it first. You bought it, remember? Besides," I said with a sigh, "I'm going to be busy knitting a hat."

She grinned, "Well, you can't knit all of the time," she argued.

I flipped the book open almost reluctantly. "I wonder why someone would write a book called 'The Axe Murderer of Springiegate?'"

Natalie shrugged, her fingers absentmindedly petting my yarn, "Who knows why anyone writes anything," she said gloomily.

I couldn't help it. I chuckled, "Still with the writer's block, huh?"

Natalie rolled her eyes, "I don't know what you're talking about." She pulled the book across the counter towards her, "But I do know what you're talking about with this book. Maybe that's why I wanted to order it so bad. It's a fiction book, but…"

"But it sounds like a true story," I said excitedly. "I wonder if it is based on a true story, and that's… "

We both looked at each other with identical expressions of triumph and horror. "We need to do some research," Natalie whispered noisily, "and see if anyone here was murdered with an… "

Reality swept up and pulled me back down to earth where I belonged. "I seriously doubt that anyone here in Springgate is an axe murderer," I said, and then I paused to think, "but, I do have to tell you the first time that I saw Mr. Morrie… I wondered…"

I finally met her eye, and we both burst into giggles. "You're right," Natalie said reluctantly. "The entire idea is just absurd."

"Oh," a voice behind Natalie said, "I'd love to hear an absurd idea. It's been a rather boring day so far. I haven't even bailed anyone out of jail today."

She jumped, her blond hair spinning as she turned to see who had snuck up from behind. I tried to pretend I had seen them coming all along. "Hello, Nate," I said warmly. "Good afternoon, Mrs. Goldmyer," I tried to say just as warmly, but the words passed through my mouth with the same consistency as an extra thick slice of peanut butter toast.

Natalie's eyebrows were, by now, up to her hairline, but she tried to be gracious. It's a bit hard to be gracious to the person who once tried to put you out of business, but if it happens enough, it gets easier. "What can we do for you guys, today?" she asked smoothly. "Do you need any help selecting yarn?" This remark was accompanied with a pointed look at Nate, who actually turned a bit red. It was kind of adorable.

"I'm afraid I don't knit," he said, automatically taking a step back.

"That's alright," Natalie said, a wicked gleam coming into her eye. "We also offer classes for beginning knitters."

Oh, my word. If she were only on the same side of the counter as I was… she would get kicked right now.

"As a matter of fact," she continued, clearly warming towards her goal, "our very own MollyDear, will be teaching the class this time." She smiled, all of her teeth showing, "Would you like to sign up?"

Picture this… if someone came up to you and asked you to jump up on their shoulders and sing "The Star-Spangled Banner…" how would you look at them? Yep. That's what I thought. That was the same way Nate was currently looking at Natalie. I, however, was looking at Natalie like someone who would like to jump over the counter and clobber someone.

Mrs. Goldmyer looked up at her son, one side of her mouth actually quivering with the hint of a smile. I was mesmerized. Would she actually laugh? In public? Here in the store? A tidal river could not, at this point, have swept me away. "They say knitting is good for you," she said to Nate, the quiver still in evidence. "It lowers your blood pressure or something fascinating like that."

"That's right!" Natalie said happily. "It has all kinds of excellent health benefits, here… I think we have a paper on it…" she shoved the book out of the way so that she could reach behind the counter. Mrs. Goldmyer's smile disappeared as she leaned over to examine the title.

Her mouth now tipped down into a frown. "I would have thought that Carolyn would have better taste than to leave such literary garbage out on the main counter," she said with a haughty sniff. "If you insist upon reading during store hours, as I know some of you are prone to do," this with a significant glance at me, "I would encourage you to read something a little more worthy."

I quickly pulled the book out of eyesight, tucking it into the space under the counter. "Oh no, Mrs. Goldmyer," I said quickly, "we're not reading it for pleasure. We are using it as a research tool."

She stared at me coldly. "I see. And what sort of research do you expect to retrieve?"

I felt the need to stick up for, not only the book, but also for Natalie and tried to smile mysteriously. "You'll see," I said. "So far it looks very promising for what we need. It's already been very illuminating." Well. Not really. But by now it was a matter of pride.

Natalie caught my eye and smiled too, "Oh yes," she said, "it will be of monumental importance to the life of Springgate." I'm sure, if she won the writing contest it would be of monumental importance to her, but she was really pushing it now. Nate rolled his eyes and stepped away to examine a display of knitting magazines. It was amazing how interesting the knitted fall fashions could be when you were trying to ignore someone.

Finally, successful at reaching the paper that she had been trying to retrieve, she handed it over to Mrs. Goldmyer, as Nate had backed far enough away from the counter to not be within arm's reach anymore. "Well," she said, looking somewhat flustered by the unwavering, pale stare of Mrs. Goldmyer, "if Nate doesn't want to learn to knit, can we entice you?"

What the…??

"I'm sure Mrs. Goldmyer has better things to do with her time, Natalie," I interrupted. Let's just nip this in the bud right now. Can you imagine teaching a knitting class for the first time with Mrs. Goldmyer as one of your students? Can you? Can you? I can't.

Mrs. Goldmyer took the paper from Natalie. "Lowers stress, excellent for…" she scanned through the flyer slowly, while I shot daggers at Natalie. Natalie shrugged helplessly.

"Right," Natalie said. "It does all those things and more. I think that it would be very good for you to learn how to knit." She thumped the book for emphasis, "You'd be amazed."

"And you ladies are telling me to take this class for my own good?" she asked slowly.

"Oh yes," Natalie said enthusiastically, digging herself in even deeper. "I think it would be a great idea. Don't you, Molly?"

I choked down every single word that I really wanted to say. "Knitting is a good idea for everyone," I agreed reluctantly.

A lady came up behind Mrs. Goldmyer. She was tall with an angular face and an unusual expression that could easily go from pleasant to sour. "Did someone say knitting class?" she asked.

And, with that, I had my first two students. Mrs. Goldmyer and Rebecca Flannery. I was going to kill Natalie.

Rebecca Flannery had just moved to Springgate from sunny California. The concept of crisp falls and sweater weather had her completely enthralled and eager to learn how to knit. Yes, she thought that she would knit herself sweaters (notice the plural) for when "it got cold." What she failed to realize that it was about to "get cold" in a couple weeks… and it took more than a day or two to knit a sweater. Oh well. New knitters are usually super enthusiastic, and I, for one, didn't want to be responsible for poking holes in my student's happy balloons. At least not until class was over. We didn't want anything ugly happening in class.

I escorted her over to the wool area, where I attempted to explain to her the difference between different types of wool. It wasn't easy when every few seconds she interrupted me to get clarification. "Yes," I said patiently, for the third time, "wool does come from sheep, but no sheep are harmed in the process."

She peered worriedly at me over a skein of dove grey wool, "Are you quite certain?" she asked. "I mean, all of their fur is just taken off. That can't be good for them. Don't they get cold?" She examined the yarn again more carefully, "Also, isn't it just a little bit gross that you're basically knitting with… hair?"

Sigh. It was going to be a really long day.

After reassuring her about the humanity of sheep shearing and reciting the benefits (and the lengthy process of cleaning the wool – actually I didn't really know much about that – I just made it up, but she didn't seem to notice) of wool one more time, I decided to take a step back and give her some time to become one with the yarn herself and listen to which one spoke to her. I know. That is a really great line. I would have to remember that one when dealing with customers that I wanted to get away from in the future. If I chose my customers carefully, I could probably get, say, 10-15 uses out of that, more if I mixed it up occasionally.

"Oh," she said suddenly, dropping the yarn, and halting my progress back to the counter, "before you go, I was wondering if you could tell me who the person is that I was reading about this morning in the newspaper."

"Which newspaper was that?" I asked politely, slightly perturbed that my retreat plan was not working the way it was supposed to.

She was only half-listening (which I suspected was a well-honed art form with her)… "The article about the cranky knitter who works here and rants about the customers after they're gone, of course," she said, reaching down to rummage in the absurdly large purse slung over her shoulder. She pulled out what I presumed was this morning's copy of The Springgate Gazette (I recognized their logo even at this distance) and handed it to me. I hoped she could not see my hands shaking. I scanned it as quickly as I could. It was an article under the advice and opinion section. About two paragraphs long, relatively short in terms of articles, but still large enough to damage a reputation and ruin a life (my life). Thankfully… amazingly… it did not list names, nor did it mention the moth-releasing incident. It did, however, malign "a certain yarn store on a hill" quite badly, implying that the store was ridiculously over-priced, under-staffed and lacking in knowledge.

I was disappointed in myself all over again. "I'm sorry," I said, "but I wouldn't believe everything you read in the papers." I smiled my most dismissive smile, "Some people have a really big imagination."

She pursed her lips into a very unattractive pout, "Well, that's too bad," she said. "Although I'm not sure if I believe you or not. You could just be covering for someone."

Now that was an interesting idea. Perhaps I could introduce her to Louise and let her jump to her own conclusions. I'm sorry. That wasn't nice. But – still - a good idea nonetheless.

I approached Carolyn warily, but she had already seen the article. I tried apologizing once more, but she hugged me again instead. "I don't know why you keep trying to apologize, Molly," she said. "You certainly didn't write the article, did you?" And then she had the audacity to wink at me, "Besides, publicity is publicity even when it's bad." I gaped at her and she giggled, twirling the end of her scarf, "You'll see," she said, "we'll have a big increase in business for a few days." She rubbed her hands together in a perfect caricature of a cartoon villain cackling with glee, "The only thing that could make it better would be if one of us started yelling at customers and calling them names." I couldn't help it. I giggled with her, even though it was horrible. Carolyn was a beautiful soul, but I still felt guilty.

I slunk away to contemplate my forthcoming nightmare. Now that I had two people in my knitting class, it was time to actually learn how to knit a hat. The pattern used a small circular needle, which was a relief, because, as you may or may not know, there are two main ways to knit in the round… on a circular needle or on double pointed needles. When you use double pointed needles, you need to split all of your stitches between at least three needles and then knit with the fourth needle around. Sounds confusing, doesn't it? Well, it really isn't – not when you know what you're doing, but can you imagine trying to teach new knitters how to hang onto not two, but four needles, all at the same time? I can't. I tried, but my brain shut off and I ended up staring at the wall for 15 minutes before Natalie very obligingly came along and poked me in the side.

"Wake up, sleepyhead," she teased. "You could at least look like you're trying to work."

I groaned and laid my head on the polished wood counter, "I am trying to work. At least, I was, and then I started thinking about what it would be like to teach beginning knitters to knit this hat on double pointed needles."

She grinned, "I would totally sit in on the class so I could watch," she said. I gave her my best stare of death, "To make sure I was available to help, of course," she quickly amended. Wow. My scary looks must be improving. This called for chocolate. My stomach growled in agreement.

"Haven't had your lunch break yet?" Natalie asked, evil smile still firmly in place. "You could always go join Nathaniel and his mother in the café."

"They're eating in the café?" I asked incredulously. "Why?" I ducked out from behind the counter and scooted across the store to where I could peek between the bookcase dividers to see the patrons of the café. Natalie followed close behind. Sure enough, there was Nate and his lovely mother tucked into a little table for two, each devouring a huge sandwich.

She shrugged, "I don't know, but I overheard Nate say to Mr. Gibbs, who was sitting at the table next to him, that that's why they had come."

I blinked. "I'm not sure which is weirder – that they came here to have lunch or that YOU talked her into a knitting class." I glared at her again, "I will get you for that, you know that, right?"

She winced, "You are welcome to. I don't know what came over me. It just sort of… happened. She just looked at me with that horrible stare and the words came spilling out and it just happened."

"No. It didn't. Things like that don't just happen. You don't…."

Natalie took a step back, pulling me back with her. She put her arm around my shoulders as we returned to where we were supposed to be. The ballroom that temporarily housed the yarn store and the café was large, but not large enough to be able to gawk without being seen for any considerable length of time. The mirrors down all the walls did nothing to contribute towards secrecy either.

"Let's not think about that right now," she said in her most soothing voice, which immediately put me on guard. "I want you to come see who's here."

I didn't like the sound of that. At all. But I went with her. What else could I do?

I missed the charm and location of Carolyn's "real" store dreadfully, but no one could deny that the ballroom of Raspberry Hill wasn't an equally charming location. It had taken a lot of back-breaking work to drag the bookcases and tables and chairs and sofas and etc. and etc. into the ballroom, but it was so worth it. I don't think there's another yarn store in the whole world that has as much adorableness as Crabapple Yarns. Multiple seating areas were scattered amongst the yarn, like little oases in the desert. Some areas were larger, like the big round table, set slightly off-center in the middle of the store where we would have our classes, and some were smaller. There was even a knitting area for just one knitter. I knew Natalie loved that spot. I did, too. But, it was to the seating area towards the back of the ballroom where Natalie was dragging me.

Two little chintz loveseats sat cozily across from each other with a large footstool in between. A comfortably ragged leather chair, gleaming with polish, but proudly showing its battle scars sat on one end. And on these cute little loveseats sat Rachel and Helen.

I wilted onto the footstool. Retreating would have been my first choice, but Natalie had very rudely shoved me in this direction and then blocked the passageway.

They both offered me timid smiles.

Natalie sank comfortably into the leather chair, her dangling legs a barrier between me and escape.

"Hi, Molly," Helen said. "Ummm… how are you?"

I looked from face to face. The tension was like a thick blanket over my head. I took a breath and tried to do what I always do. Make it better. "Well," I said thoughtfully, "I'd probably be a lot worse if I was in jail today."

That broke the ice a little. Both Helen and Rachel twittered gratefully, although a bit nervously. "We're sorry for the way we acted. And then, after everything, we didn't know how to talk to you," Rachel admitted. "We were just so embarrassed about everything. We thought you'd be super angry with us, didn't we, Helen?"

Helen nodded, her lovely brown hair bobbing up and down in agreement. "We did. We behaved so badly. Can you ever forgive us?"

"I'm confused," I said slowly. "I thought you'd be angry with me." Identical expressions of astonishment lit up their faces, too quickly to be anything but genuine. "Because of what I wrote in my diary…?"

This time, Helen's laugh was thoroughly hearty, "Are you kidding me? You should read mine. Patrick would probably divorce me if he ever knew what I said about him in there – and I totally and completely love him." Her smile turned mischievous. "Most of the time."

Rachel nodded; her expression still serious. "Our Great Moth Plot seemed so perfect on the surface, but it was really such a bad idea. But, seriously, no one cares about what you wrote in your diary. Everyone is entitled to vent. And it was probably taken out of context, too."

"Then I don't suppose you've seen the newspaper today," I said slowly, feeling strangely irritated with their quick dismissal of the event.

Their heads bobbed in unison solemnly, "We did," Helen said. "It was kind of strange though, wasn't it?" She brightened up a little, "It never mentioned any names, so that's good right?"

"Well," I said slowly, "there's not too many yarn stores on a hill here in town."

Their guilty faces matched the queasy guilt still floating around in my stomach. It was time to change the subject. There was one thing still bugging me. "Why did you do it, anyway?" I asked. "I think one of you said something about when someone can't stand up for themselves…"

Helen perked up on the sofa, "Our intentions were totally honorable, Molly," she said, her eyes wide, and hand going over her heart. "We were avenging Carolyn's honor and trying to right a wrong by…" her voice began to rise in volume

Rachel snorted and swatted Helen's arm, "Would you stop?" she said, sounding mildly exasperated, "It was talking like that that got us into trouble in the first place. If you start with the avenging and honor baloney, we'll all get crazy and riled up again and go back to Happy Knits with six moths this time."

Helen flushed. "Baloney?" she repeated. "Carolyn's honor and good name is not baloney."

I laughed, "I think what Rachel is trying to say is that you are an excellent orator and your calls for action are so inspiring that they make people do crazy things… like breaking into Happy Knits with a bag of moths."

Helen turned even brighter red, "I do have a tendency to act before I think," she said, dropping her eyes.

I reached over from the footstool to squeeze her hand, "But we love you for it," I said. "I only hope that wasn't our last crazy knitting adventure."

Her eyes met mine in remembered memory for a moment and we both laughed.

But my question was still unanswered. "So, let's try to stay on task this time. Why did you…"

Rachel's eyes narrowed, "It was like this…" she said.

Well, dear reader, unfortunately, Rachel and Helen are not gifted with the ability to present a coherent narrative. I will attempt to reassemble it here for you, without all of the annoying pauses and interruptions and corrections that I was forced to endure. You can thank me later.

Rachel and Helen were shopping downtown together when they passed by Happy Knits. Abby, a somewhat friend, was in Happy Knits and saw them pass by. Abby met them outside and forced them to come in and look at a particular yarn that had just been placed on the shelf. Rachel and Helen reluctantly agreed (even though they felt it was being just a teensy disloyal to Carolyn). While they were in there, they saw the Fall Class List and Event Schedule and became so enraged that the three of them retreated to the diner to plan The Great Moth Plot. You see, once a month, Crabapple Yarns hosted "Sit and Knit" where, knitters were, of course, invited to come and sit and knit. And eat goodies. It was a very popular event here in Springgate amongst the knitters. Apparently, Happy Knits had decided to have, on the exact day of each month, "Knit Night." Their version of Knit Night, however, while it included sitting and knitting and snacks, took it a step further and offered a free speaker of the month as well. It was clearly aimed at taking away the knitters from Crabapple Yarns. The rest of the evening was history.

"That is despicable." I had to admit it… I was furious, too. I may have even felt the urge to gather a few moths myself. "How dare they try to keep putting Carolyn out of business? Who was here first? Why can't we all just…"

"Get along?" Rachel mocked. "Yeah. I don't think that's going to happen."

Me, neither. But… "What if we did something better than their stupid speaker this month?" I asked, an idea blooming. "What if… we had a Knitter's Halloween Party?"

Sometimes I really am a genius.

CHAPTER 7

I t was a great idea. A Knitter's Halloween Party was going to be a huge hit, everyone would want to come. Wouldn't you? Knitters were welcome to come in costume, there would be food and games, and a contest for best 'Knitted Mask.' Thankfully, Carolyn had also agreed. I had almost wondered if she wouldn't, to keep things more peaceable. The Halloween Party, would, after all, be declaring virtual war with Happy Knits.

I had also been a little excited to show her the book Natalie had ordered. Her eyebrows rose (like everyone's seemed to do) when she saw the title and she looked at me with some consternation. "Exactly what kind of book are you trying to write?" she asked with a little forced laugh.

"Do you mean you've never heard of this book?" I asked, grinning. "According to Natalie, it's a classic that is specifically designed to cure writer's block."

"No," Carolyn said, her smile finding its home again, "I've never heard of it, but I wish you good luck."

As I sat snuggled in my little reading chair later that evening, I tried to decide if I would knit a mask. I had suggested to Natalie that she knit a mask and wear a costume so that everyone would think she was Abraham Lincoln – the dog, not the man. That wouldn't be too hard of a mask to knit. Just some wild and crazy black yarn with the furry stuff mixed in and she'd be good to go. Now… what should I go as? Maybe Abraham Lincoln, the man? Now, that would be funny, wouldn't it?

I couldn't decide, so instead, I pulled out "The Ax Murderer of Springiegate" intending to read a few chapters. Hours later, the night burning away into the dawn, I closed the book. My life would never be the same again. Throwing the book on the ground, I went to sleep with burning eyes and a heavy heart. Carolyn had lied to me.

I was supposed to go wedding dress shopping with Natalie and Celia in the morning, so I pulled my groggy, grumpy self out of bed only a few hours after I had gotten in there. It was nobody's fault but my own, really. I mean, it's not like I *had* to read the entire book in one night. I just had to. Do you know what I mean?

I decided to wear something extra pretty for wedding dress shopping. We were headed a couple of towns over (as we had already exhausted – literally - the only little wedding dress shop in Springgate) where not one but three wedding shops were awaiting the pleasure of our arrival today. I stifled a groan. Natalie was just so… intense… about the details of the wedding. It's like she thought if the wedding were perfect, the marriage would be, too. Whoa. Deep. I gave the thought another trip through my head. A really, really deep thought. And probably spot-on. I'd have to share that with her. Later. Maybe much later. I had no desire to be smacked upside the head (figuratively speaking) by Natalie.

I put on my favorite black dress that ended in a little flounce with some black tights and black heels (well – little heels – you know how clumsy I can be). And then, upon looking at myself in the mirror, I realized that I was, perhaps, just a tad over-dressed, so I put on my faded denim jacket over the top. I smiled at my reflection. Adorable. "Thank you," I told the kind girl in the mirror, "you look very nice, too."

Abraham Lincoln was waiting at my door to escort me down to breakfast. He kept his distance, but padded alongside me all the way along the hall and down the steps. "You just want to eat my crust, don't you?" He paused to consider, tilting his head in what Natalie considered the most adorable way. "What if I want to have cereal, instead?" The ears went back with a growl. I couldn't help the small smile that crept along my face. Sometimes, he was really adorable. In a horrible way.

It was Friday today, which meant that Natalie was in the yarn store already helping Carolyn to put away the delivery that came last night. For some reason, deliveries seemed to be coming in on Thursdays. I don't know if Carolyn did that on purpose to keep the weekend sales even higher, or if it just happened that way, but it sure made for a busy Friday. I smiled to myself… that meant I wouldn't have to hurry through breakfast.

Rose was still eating her breakfast in the kitchen when I stopped by. "My, don't you look nice today," she said with a kind smile. She looked rather cute herself. Rose was fond of dressing in outrageous styles and today she was wearing a pumpkin orange fuzzy sweater over printed black pants. The pants had giant flowers (some sort of daisy, maybe) all over them. Character definitely ran in that family. I wish it ran in mine like that. An outrageous style in my family was wearing white the day after Labor Day – if it was still hot outside – and only the day after because the day after the day after was just out of the question.

"I still can't believe you don't want to go wedding dress shopping with us," I teased. "It's going to be a great day." I popped a piece of toast in the toaster and set the kettle on the stove to heat up again while getting a cup out. There's nothing better than a cup of tea in the morning. Don't even talk to me about coffee. Everyone tells me that it's an acquired taste. My question is… why would anyone want to acquire it? I think it all comes down to peer pressure. It's just what all the cool kids are drinking.

She set down her own teacup, "I'll wait until she makes up her mind," she said firmly. "I'm too old to be hopping around from store to store."

"Well," I said sincerely, "we'll miss you."

I finished fixing my breakfast and brought it over to where she lingered over the newspaper. Abraham Lincoln parked by my feet and gave a small little doggy cough. I ignored him. "Can I ask you something?"

"You just did," she said with a hint of the same humor that Natalie had.

I rolled my eyes, "No," I replied, "I'm serious. I don't quite know what to do about something, and I don't know who I should even talk to."

Rose sighed, "Sounds like you're pretty upset." Her wrinkled face puckered in sympathy. "What can I do?"

And just like that, I found that I did not want to burden Rose with my problems. She was very kind, but she had lived through too many problems of her own to make me want to add to them. I shook my head and dropped a piece of crust on the floor, "It's nothing," I said, shrugging.

"It's not nothing," Jack said, coming in through the swinging door, making me jump in surprise. "I think that dog has gained about 50 pounds since we all started living here." He walked over towards the oven where delicious smells were already coming out of, and I wondered what the café patrons would be treated to today.

"Don't be ridiculous," Rose said briskly. "He barely weighs 5 pounds. Poor baby. He needs feeding up."

Jack snorted. "That little monster steals food from everyone. I don't know why you give in to it. He has…"

"POT!" yelled Rose, coming to her feet, startling me yet again and causing the last piece of my toast to hit the floor. Abraham Lincoln very obligingly scooped it up. "The pot is calling the kettle black. I saw you feeding him yourself last night…"

I rolled my eyes, picked up my dishes and discretely left the room before I became involved in what sounded like another fantastic argument. It's a sad day when a person can't even eat a little breakfast in peace.

I headed back towards the ballroom, passing Abigail in the hallway. "Watch out," I warned her. "Trouble in the kitchen. The pros and cons of feeding Abraham Lincoln table scraps are now being discussed."

She winked at me, "Like any decision made by humans is going to affect Abraham Lincoln," she said. "Have fun shopping today."

She, too, preferred to wait until Natalie had, at least, narrowed it down to 2-3 dresses. The fact that most people choose their wedding dress months and months before time, simply didn't seem to bother Natalie. Not even when the seamstresses protested that there wouldn't be enough time for fittings and whatever else goes on with wedding dresses, Natalie waved her hand and blithely assumed that everything would turn out right. Maybe it would. I hoped it would. It was going to get awfully ugly if it didn't.

I paused before opening the door to the ballroom, hearing a different voice. Oh great. Louise was here. It really was time to hit the road.

I cracked open the door and slunk my way in, determined to find Natalie before I had to speak with anyone else. I didn't particularly feel up to talking with Carolyn right now either. I snuck down the row that had baby yarn in it and did a quick turn at the beautiful desk that stored the sock yarn. I loved that desk. It kept the sock yarn so nice and neat. Not at all like the way it was displayed at the other store. I could hear Natalie and Carolyn talking by the counter. I continued my sneaking in that direction. But where was Louise? I would have to watch out...

"Good morning, Molly," a voice said from behind me. "Practicing our stealth techniques, are we? Perhaps learning more ways to avoid customers? It is the next logical step after insulting them." I turned slowly, trying very hard to keep the grimace off of my face.

It was really too bad that we couldn't be friends. Louise was a fantastic knitter, and I know I could learn a lot from her. Today she was wearing a creation that I knew she had designed herself. It was done using a technique called "intarsia" where you knit with multiple colors at the same time. Sometimes intarsia sweaters were geometric designs or blocks of color, and sometimes they were scenes or drawings. She had designed a fall scene with tall trees that went up the front of the sweater with colorful fall leaves dancing their way to the ground. It was very pretty. "I'm sure I don't practice things like that, Louise," I said sternly, eyeing her up and down.

Her thin face cracked into a grotesque version of a smile. "Then how lucky that it just comes naturally to you."

Instead of the usual spark of outrage that normally came with her sly comments and hurtful digs, I felt nothing but unbearable weariness. "What have I ever done to you, Louise?" I asked. "Please just tell me."

She sneered at me, "You took a job here. A job you're unqualified for and that takes money away from Carolyn. And I can just guess where all that nonsense in the newspaper has come from, too. We did just fine without you, and I'll tell you the truth is that we don't...."

I turned around and left her talking to herself by the sock yarn. Sometimes that's all you can do with people. "Are you ready to go, Natalie?" I asked. Carolyn and Natalie were standing by the counter. Natalie was also dressed nicely, although a bit seasonally inappropriate in a floral sleeveless dress. "Better grab your sweater," I advised her, turning to leave and assuming she'd follow. I really wanted to hit the road.

"But, my dear," Carolyn said. "What's wrong, you seem so..." and here she faltered for words, her hands reaching up to fidget anxiously with her long string of pearls, "so unlike yourself. Is everything alright?"

I forced myself to meet her gaze. She looked pale and worried as she, in turn, studied me. "I'm fine," I said, pulling my lips back over my teeth into what I hoped looked like a smile. "I just didn't sleep well last night."

Natalie's gaze flew to mine, "We can wait to go shopping," she said. "It's no problem. Celia was called into work today, too, so it would be just you and me."

That sounded perfect. Plenty of time to talk. "Nope," I said, "I don't get all dressed up and then stay home. Come on. Let's go."

It wasn't until we were safely in Mr. Darcy and headed down the hill through the haunted forest that I felt like I could talk.

"I finished the book last night," I said.

"You did?" Natalie swerved a bit in her surprise. She is a very emotional driver. "All in one sitting? That was one big book." She looked over at me, "No wonder you couldn't sleep. You were busy reading."

"Yes," I confirmed, suddenly not knowing how to continue.

"Well?" Natalie demanded eagerly. "How was it?"

I studied the town passing by my window at an alarming rate, "You're going a little fast," I said. "Watch out for the..." and here there was a squeal of brakes and a turn of the wheel that had me grateful for Mr. Darcy's seatbelt system.

"It's fine," she said. "Next time he'll learn to look both ways before crossing the street."

"He was in a pedestrian crosswalk!" I protested.

She shrugged, "That doesn't give him the right of way."

"I think it does," I said, aghast. "That's why the sign said, 'Yield for pedestrians.'"

"Did it?" she asked curiously, craning her neck to look behind her. "Huh. Well. That puts a whole new spin on things. I'll google it when we get home to see if you're right."

"You also took the wrong street," I added. "This is not the way to the highway at all." I tried very hard not to sigh.

"Scenic route," she said cheerfully, even as she discretely looked around, trying to get her bearings. We were currently in the middle of a residential-type neighborhood. "Anyways," she said, "you were going to tell me how the book was so that I didn't have to spend my time reading it."

"And here I thought you let me read it first because you were nice."

She giggled, "I know you did."

"Sometimes I really don't know about you," I said, trying to sound sad. "I think that you're… STOP the car!"

Mr. Darcy came to a violent and somewhat screeching halt. It's a good thing he was used to it. "What?" she demanded, swinging her head wildly. "Who did I hit? Was it a pedestrian crossing again?"

"No," I said dreamily, opening the door, "it's the most perfect thing I've ever seen." And, my friends, it was. It was the house of my dreams. A little cottage (I do have a weakness for cottages), in golden yellow brick. The roof rose in two dramatic peaks, one over the front door and the other directly to the right over what I imagine would be the living room. Stone steps led up to the front door which was delightfully rounded at the top and painted a deep shade of red. On each side of the front door, two brick walls came out in curved angles, almost like the house was attempting to reach out and hug you. The window in the living room reached to the ground and soared almost to the top of the arch and was rounded at the top as well. A beautiful line of jewel-toned stones followed the line of the window all the way up, around the curved top and back down the other side. Quaint scalloped wood trim finished off the peaks beautifully, and the square windows to the left of the front door lent balance and charm. It also didn't hurt that the window panes were painted the exact shade as the front door. An eyebrow window winked out of the roofline over the square windows. But the best part of all? The "For Sale" sign right out front.

"That is so cute," I said to Natalie, who had also gotten out of the car and walked around the front of it to stare up at the house.

She wrinkled her nose, "And we stopped because…"

I turned back around and hurried her back to the car. "Let's get going," I said briskly, "or we'll be late for our first appointment."

She got back into Mr. Darcy and repeated her question, "And you screamed like a hyena and made me stop because…?"

I made my eyes big and round and innocent. "Because I love cottages?"

She looked at me suspiciously, "What are you up to?"

"Nothing at the moment," I replied. "Now about that book."

It took me almost the whole drive to summarize the book for her. It was, surprisingly enough, very well-written in an engaging, almost cozy manner. Filled with miscellaneous facts about crime and small towns, and, strangely enough, even a recipe for raspberry jam, the book was completely not what I had been expecting. Looking back, I'm not sure what made it so un-put-a-downable (yes, that's a librarian term), but it was. It was the tale of two sisters, whose close bond was severed tragically, first by a triangle love affair that went horribly wrong, and then, fatefully, by the blade of an ax. While the book never completely said that the older sister had killed her younger sister, it hinted very strongly. The biggest mystery was the issue of the shoe. There was a bloody shoeprint five feet away from the body of her sister. Not too surprising, really… with all of that blood. However, the strange thing was that the shoeprint matched the shoe that the murdered sister was wearing. Only one shoe had blood on the bottom. The other shoe was perfectly clean. How, after being… shall we say… so brutally attacked, had she managed to stand up, on just one foot and leave a shoeprint (and only one) five feet away? It was a mystery to this day.

"Wow," Natalie said, after a significant pause in which I assumed she was thinking. With Natalie, it was hard to tell. "What happened to the other sister?" We were pulling up to the first wedding dress store, somewhat charmingly entitled, "Happily Ever After"... if you liked that kind of thing.

"I don't know," I said. "The book didn't say. It just leaves you hanging with this weird, uneasy feeling that you've missed something important. It was totally unsettling."

Natalie pulled Mr. Darcy deftly into a parking place and turned off the ignition. "But something else is bothering you, isn't it?"

She was a good people-reader. I turned in my seat so that I could face her, "Yes," I said quietly, "something is bothering me. Last night, I showed the book to Carolyn and she said that she had never seen it before."

Natalie shrugged, shaking her head as she did, "So?"

I leaned forward, "Natalie," I said urgently, "it's the same book." Sometimes, when I get upset, I don't make much sense.

She tilted her head, "The same book as what?"

I tried again, "Remember? I told you the story. On the day that I was fired from the library, Carolyn returned a book that was 45 years overdue. This was the book." I grabbed Natalie's arm, "She had kept 'The Ax Murderer of Springiegate' checked out of the library for 45 years. She lied to me."

For once in her life, Natalie had nothing to say.

Some people just make me so sick. Some people like Natalie. She looked perfect in every single wedding dress that she tried on. It didn't hurt that she had a flawless figure with no extra... you know... lumps around the middle or anything. Obviously, she hadn't been eating too many cinnamon rolls, unlike me, whose jeans kept shrinking, just a bit, in the wash. And her beautiful blond hair shone like an angel's halo in the lights of the dressing room.

'I love that one," I said honestly, "but I've loved all of them on you."

She glared at me through the mirror's reflection. "There must be one that you liked better. You're really no help at all if you don't like one better than the other one."

I paused to reconsider, but everything was a blur of white and lace and yards and yards of fabric. "I'm sorry," I said a bit helplessly. "I can't remember." I really couldn't.

"Get my phone out," she said patiently, twirling again in front of the mirror. Oh brother. We had taken pictures, from 1200 different angles of her in every single dress. We were currently in store #2 and on our 4th dress. In store #1, we had tried on six. I doubted, given the time, that we would even make it to store #3. I don't know how many pictures that would be, but you can do the math. Which meant, if we didn't fall in love with one soon, we would have to come back. Perish the thought. Jack had given Natalie a smartphone as an engagement present. He had programmed himself into her "favorites" button five different times, with five different profiles. One was "Jack". I could live with that. The other ones were sickening things like… "Hubby to Be" or "The one who loves you the most." Yeah. You're right. I was just a bit jealous, too. I reluctantly flipped through her photos while she went to try on yet another dress that the amazingly patient storeowner brought in. I don't know how these ladies did it. It must be horribly difficult to, day after day, give love-struck women white dress after white dress and keep telling them how pretty they look…

"Ahem." Wow. She changed pretty quickly. I looked up. And dropped her phone. Thankfully, the floor was carpeted.

"That's the one," I breathed. "I've never seen a more beautiful dress."

I had been very amazed to see, right from the start, that Natalie preferred a more traditional wedding dress. Long train, lots of lace… these were the only gowns that she would try on. Given her usual love of, shall we say, a quite unique personal clothing style, it puzzled me for awhile. I would have thought we would be looking at a wedding dress that had a miniskirt or something that was, perhaps, pink, instead of white. But, I think that maybe, deep down, beat the heart of a little girl that still had a plan for how she wanted to spend her life- and that included a wedding with a white dress. I'm not sure that plan, until last year, included a haunted house, complete with yarn store and café, but all in all, I think for the first time, Natalie was feeling happy. Settled. Like she had found the exact place where she belonged. I wish…but anyways, back to the dress…

This dress was traditional – but it wasn't. It was white, but more of an antique white. It fell to the ground with a beautiful clean swoop of lace. It was, actually, made entirely of lace panels that ran up the dress vertically. Each line of lace different from the other, beautiful motifs of intricate circles, small inserts of floral lace, delicate lace ladders. It was gathered tightly at the waist with a beautiful wide, satin ribbon that tied sweetly at the back. Above the large ribbon, the lace rose in a lovely shawl collar to hug her shoulders and the most delicate, sheer lace possible closing the gap at the throat. The train dragged, just a bit, along the floor.

It was like Natalie had taken tradition and turned it into something of her own. Which, of course, was just like her.

"You are so beautiful," I said sincerely. "Jack is going to fall over."

She giggled self-consciously and turned to look at her reflection again. "It's the most perfect dress I've ever seen. I've got to have it."

"Wait!" I exclaimed, my conscience smiting me. "You weren't supposed to pick a dress today. Just narrow it down." The saleslady looked at me with a frown of slight disapproval and a seriously good stink eye. She probably thought I was going to ruin her sale. But even though I now had a deathly fear of the lady with all the pins attached to her wrist, I had to protest, "Now Celia and Rose won't be able to come to the store with you and see you in it… and that beautiful moment will be ruined…"

"They had their chance," Natalie said ruthlessly. "I'm not going to risk losing this dress." Her eyes met mine in the mirror again and she looked like a little kid who was being forced to give back her chocolate chip cookie, "Oh man," she wailed, "I can't take that away from them. What am I going to do?"

In the end, the intrepid saleslady, Ruth, saved the day again by suggesting that they all come together for a fitting next week. "After all, darling," she said, "you have a great figure, but we do need to make a few alterations so that it's perfect."

We both beamed at her. She was a genius. (And really good at her job).

CHAPTER 8

"You know," I said, "I completely and totally believe that is the most perfect wedding dress ever."

She giggled and squeezed my hand over the re-purposed and newly decoupaged table, "I know. I'm so excited about it! Did you see all of those different types of lace? I bet I can find lace that almost matches for decorating with." She sat back in her seat triumphantly, "And how many brides can say that they actually match with their entire wedding décor?" Natalie flipped her hair over her shoulder with a sniff, and a twinkle, "I bet hardly any."

I couldn't help the smile, she was so irresistible sometimes. "Hardly any," I said solemnly, trying not to chuckle as I scanned the menu once again. After all that trying on of dresses, Natalie had declared that she was starving and could not go three steps further without some type of food sustenance. Luckily, we were standing in front of a restaurant when she said it. Then again, that's probably why she said it. The odors wafting out the door as two customers left pulled us in. But, in my opinion, they had been rather deceitful odors. This, unfortunately, wasn't your typical restaurant… it was one of those new, super-healthy restaurants that only use food that has words in it like "organic", "locally sourced", "non-GMO" … which basically meant that their food was going to taste weird, am I right? Why couldn't I just have a nice, normal cheeseburger and fries? But, no. I was stuck looking at a menu, that had been printed on the back of a used grocery paper bag, where my choices included "broth bowls" and your choice of almost 1,000 different types of salad mixed with warm quinoa. Gag. I didn't even see anything with bacon on the menu. What's wrong with bacon? Bacon is healthy.

"Wow," Natalie said, scanning her menu hungrily, "this place is amazing. Can you believe that 98% of their food is all locally sourced? Even the meat."

"Great," I said glumly. "Now I can't eat anything that has meat in it."

She looked at me sideways, "What? Why?"

"Because if it's all locally sourced, there's a good chance that I've seen that cow before. I can't eat meat that I've seen before." I shuddered. "It's just too awful to even think about."

Natalie made a face, "Sometimes," she said slowly, "it's like you're from another planet. You do realize that all meat comes from…"

"Stop!" I protested, fingers firmly in ears. "I prefer to live in a pleasant – and permanent – land of denial where meat comes from the store…"

Natalie was watching in amusement mixed with worry for my mental state of mind, when suddenly her face turned pale, "Shhhh," she whispered, "stop talking." She lowered her face to the table and put a hand up to shield herself from being recognized, which, in my opinion, just makes people look at you more. But, that's beside the point.

I froze and dropped my voice, afraid to look to the right or the left. "Who is it?" I hissed. "What's wrong?"

She shifted slightly, moving her fingers so that she could peer between them. "Oh good," she said. "They can't see us." She dropped her hand and shifted even further to the left.

"Who can't see us?" I demanded. I know how curiosity killed the cat. He was literally too curious to see what type of horrible person was sitting in the restaurant behind him, fell into a pile of kale and was never heard from again.

I've never seen Natalie look so worried, "I don't know how to tell you this, Molly," she said, her eyes bright with anguish.

I slowly turned around to see for myself. At first, I didn't see what had Natalie so upset. I didn't even see anyone familiar. I scanned over to the corner table. Oh. Now I saw him. The red hair was always a big giveaway. He had his back mostly towards us. Ryan was here. I felt a brief glow of happiness before reality bit me in the… shall we say… rear. Natalie was not happy to see Ryan, which meant he was here with someone else. I jiggled my chair carefully around the table just a little so I could see who he was with. I think my mouth might have hung open. Natalie's hand came tentatively up my arm. "Now," she said nervously, "let's not jump to conclusions."

As we watched, the cute little blond reached up to kiss Ryan's cheek. I couldn't watch any more.

She hadn't turned the car on yet. It was horribly stuffy in Mr. Darcy, but the amount of effort it would have taken to reach over and unroll the window was too much to even think about. I felt… I don't know how I felt. It was such a shock – but it wasn't really that much of a surprise. Does that make sense?

Natalie grabbed the steering wheel with two hands and clenched them so tightly that her knuckles completely drained of their color.

"At least we didn't have to eat the quinoa," I said weakly. "See. There is a bright side to everything."

"I'm going back in there," she said decisively. "We shouldn't have snuck out like that."

I could just imagine her in there confronting Ryan. It brought a little spark back to life deep inside me. But it also brought out the little voice that I hated. My inner voice. *Why don't you go back in there? You were his girlfriend. Or whatever you were. You should be the one who fights. What does that say about you that you'd send your friend in instead of you? Are you just going to let someone walk all over you? Don't you have any self-respect? Maybe you don't deserve a relationship when you don't even have the gumption…"*

The sound of Natalie's door opening was like a gunshot. "No," I grabbed her arm to stop her from exiting the car, "please don't. I should be the one that goes in there, anyways."

She looked at me like I was crazy, "Are you kidding me? I'm your best friend, right?" I nodded weakly. "This is what best friends do." All I could do was look at her pleadingly.

"Alright," she said. "No confrontations today." I sighed with relief. She sighed, too, and laid her head back on the seat behind her. "Molly," she said slowly, "are you sure that Ryan doesn't have a sister?"

I was so glad that Natalie was my best friend. "No," I said. "He's an only child. But it was a sweet thought."

"Perhaps an overly affectionate cousin?" she suggested. I couldn't help the small giggle.

"Maybe."

Maybe. But probably not. It was just like every movie I'd ever seen where the (clearly deluded) female wonders why her boyfriend/husband/whatever was mysteriously answering phone calls and not saying who it was… would be gone for extended periods of time with no reasonable explanation. And the clearly deluded female just accepts everything as normal until the real truth comes out. How boring. I was living a total cliché. I was really going to have to try harder at this whole "life" thing.

Natalie hadn't wanted to leave me alone. Once we got home, she insisted that we go "straight to the kitchen" and cook something to eat. That alone told me she was really worried. Natalie hates to cook. I told her that I was going to go upstairs, take a bath and go to bed. She could possibly expect to see me sometime after the new year. She hugged me hard, then whispered to use the back stairs or I'd have to stop and chat with everyone. I thanked her and followed her advice, getting back to my room without having run into a single knitter or well-meaning old person.

But I had lied. I did not feel like taking a bath. Or going to bed. I felt jittery and sick. I curled up in the chair in front of my big picture window, pulling an old quilt over me, hoping that any comfort it might have gathered with its advancing years would be transferred to me. The thing that it comes down to is this… I just don't see Ryan as the two-timing type, do you? I mean, if this is a cliché and I'm living a horrible movie, then Ryan would have to be a cliché, too, right? I mean, naturally, I was entirely believable as the deluded female, but… Ryan? He should have slicked back hair, a pocket full of money and ooze charm out of every pore. And we all know that Ryan's hair was crazy and unruly, and he was rather shy. I wasn't sure about the money part. We had never had to sneak out on a bill or anything, so I assumed that he had enough to live on. Maybe he did have a sister-type person in his life. After all, it's not like he had kissed her. She had kissed him. *Or maybe you just didn't wait long enough to see him kiss her.* Then again, doesn't everyone always say so-and-so just isn't the type to do whatever they clearly just did? Maybe that was the true cliché.

I threw the blankets back decidedly. There was really only one way to know.

I snuck back down the servant's stairs that ended up by the kitchen and crept on tiptoes to the side door. I could have found Natalie and asked to take Mr. Darcy, but that would involve having to explain what I was going to do, which would involve discussion and input from Natalie. I really didn't want anyone's input. I just wanted to go talk to Ryan. This was going to involve a bit of a walk, but after I was done with Ryan, I could always call for a ride home. I left a sticky note on the side door and walked out onto the porch.

A familiar silhouette was already there.

I saw him first, as I was coming from the side of the house, and he was facing the front door expectantly, like he had already knocked. That was unfortunate. I made a slight scuffing noise with my shoe, and his face lit up when he saw me. I gestured for him to follow me, but it was too late. The front door was already cracking open.

"Ryan." It was Jack.

"Hey," Ryan said rather uncertainly, probably due to the look on Jack's face, which although I couldn't see, physically, at the moment, I could see in my mind's eye.

I ventured further down the porch so that I could see them both, the ancient wood smooth under my dragging feet. Why had I thought it was a good idea to see Ryan today? I should have waited until a bit of time had lulled me back into my beautiful false sense of reality.

Ryan's head swiveled back and forth between me and Jack, bewilderment clearly written all over his expressive face.

Jack looked surprised to see me out on the porch. Probably because he thought that I was hiding, I mean, resting, upstairs. I smiled tightly at Jack. "It's ok, Jack," I said. "I'm just going to talk to Ryan for a minute out here."

Jack stepped out the door and carefully shut it behind him. "I think I'll just stay," he said.

This must be what it was like to have an older brother. It was rather touching - and just a bit comical at the same time. I shook my head, even as Ryan said, "What is going on here?" He looked down at me with concern, "Has something happened? Are you ok?"

When he started reaching for me, Jack twitched forward, making Ryan pause. He looked between me and Jack, the picture of bewilderment. But was it an innocent bewilderment or the bewilderment of every cliché that ever lived? I wish I knew.

"Oh, for pity's sake," I said impatiently. "Please go inside, Jack. I want to talk to Ryan alone."

There was a great deal of reluctance and a lot said in his glower that he did not take off from Ryan, but he eventually went back inside. I could, however, see the curtained windows twitching, so I don't think he went far. A second window twitched. Great. Natalie had arrived.

Ryan's face was still lined with concern when he finally spoke, "What did I miss?" he asked quietly, tucking his hands in his front pockets. "Since when does Jack not want me in the house – or me to be alone with you?" I went and sat on the porch steps, and he joined me, hesitatingly, but wisely, sitting an arm's length away.

I put my elbows on my knees, resting my head on my hands. "Did you eat lunch today?" I asked. I know. It's not fair to try to trick someone, is it? But, how else can you know if you can trust someone? I turned to look directly into his face, watching for the tell-tale looks of dishonesty.

He stared for a full three seconds before what little color was left in his face drained away. And then one hand shot out to grab mine. "Please don't," he said desperately and I was surprised to see tears forming in the corners of his eyes.

I couldn't help it. I squeezed his hand in comfort. "Please don't?" I asked, trying hard to understand. "Please don't, what?"

"Break up with me about this," he said hoarsely, his hand squeezing mine a bit too tightly. "I can…"

I raised my eyebrows and pulled my hand away from his, "Explain?" I asked somewhat, I'm afraid, sarcastically. "A blond lady was kissing you in a restaurant and you think that there's a reasonable…"

"Her father and my father have been friends for years and years and years," Ryan said, speaking rapidly, almost as if he were trying to get all the words out before I could have time to get up and walk away. "We've known each other since we were babies. My mom hasn't been well lately, and her family has helped out a lot. She met me for lunch so that we could discuss… an issue… I swear…. That's all there is. I offered to do something to help her in return, and she was grateful so she kissed my cheek. Nothing else happened. Nothing is going to happen, because I don't see her that way at all."

I tucked my hands together under my arms, suddenly cold. He sounded so believable. I wanted to believe him. "This has been going on for some time, though, hasn't it?" I thought of the phone calls and the mysterious disappearances and a little bit of anger warmed me again.

He stood up, and for one, horrifying and shocking moment I thought he was leaving, but instead, he walked down a few stairs and then turned so that he could look directly at me. He put his hands on my shoulders, and, this time, I did not pull away. "My mom hasn't been well since before I met you," he said honestly. "I moved here to start my bakery, because it wouldn't have worked at home, but then my mom got sick and," his voice broke a little, "it's really hard to run a bakery by yourself and take care of your mom who lives in another town at the same time. It's no excuse, but sometimes I just get so tired and I don't think things all the way through. I never, ever wanted to hurt you. I just didn't want you to think that I couldn't…"

"That you couldn't take care of everything yourself?" I asked.

He nodded, his eyes never leaving mine, "You were like the sun coming out from behind the clouds," he said, a soft smile forming, and he tucked a strand of hair almost absently behind my ear, "but I didn't know how to tell you that. Jack finally made me see that I didn't have to be stuck in the same situation forever, and life could change. I could change. And I thought that, someday, the time would be right to explain everything. But…"

I sighed again, "Things got out of hand?" I supplied helpfully, reaching forward to pull him down to sit next to me again. It was getting cold on the step, and his warmth next to me would be most welcome. He obliged, but stared uncomfortably at the wooden steps below him. "It seems like the only thing I see right now are secrets," I said. "I'm starting to think that secrets need more than just knowledge and time." He looked up questioningly, "I think that they take root and grow in… I don't know what the exact word is, but maybe it's… pride." He looked away, cheeks heating up slightly, and I felt ashamed. "I'm sorry, Ryan," I said hastily. "That's not what I meant…"

He half-laughed and my heart fell when I saw tears in his eyes, "You see me being kissed by another girl in a restaurant and you end up apologizing?" He reached over to squeeze my hand, and this time I welcomed it, sliding closer. He kissed the top of my head, "I'm so sorry," he said seriously. "I never, ever wanted to hurt you."

I stared at him, frozen in the moment. Secrets hurt everyone. It's what I wanted to say, but couldn't. I knew he wasn't telling all of his. But neither was I. So why was I angry with him? What would he say if he ever found out…?

Ryan leaned forward to peer down into my face. He looked terrible. "It's always worse when you get quiet," he said miserably. "Do you think you'll ever be able to forgive me?"

Something inside of me cracked. I don't know how to explain it. It just did. Realization hit me so hard that I felt breathless. I was broken. More broken than he could ever be, and I didn't deserve to forgive him. Maybe… maybe this was all for the best? Maybe… I took a deep breath.

It didn't take long. And then, he was gone, fading away into the darkness of the night. I heard his car start up and saw lights swish their way through the trees as he turned his car and headed back to Springgate.

CHAPTER 9

The days passed with relative, and blessed, monotony. Yarn came in. We put it away. Customers bought it, and it went away again. Knitters dropped stitches, and I helped pick them up. My little class was filling up fast. Carolyn had assured me that I would not probably have more than 3-4 students. The class list was currently at 7, with 8 the max capacity. Terror gripped me with cold, wet hands every time I thought about it. My little hat, however, was almost done and turning out adorably. I could only hope that my students would feel as happy about theirs as I did mine. Panic grabbed me again, as it had been doing for a while now, in a brief, but choking hold. What if I couldn't do this? What if…?

"Are you alright, Molly?" Carolyn's kind voice broke through the panicked fog beautifully, and I forced myself to take a deep breath.

"Of course," I said as brightly as I could, "why wouldn't I be?"

She looked at me doubtfully. "I don't know. You haven't seemed like yourself for quite some time now. I wish I knew what was bothering you so that I could help."

I was tempted. I was so tempted to ask her about the book. It was eating away at me… the way she had lied about it. Why had she lied? And if she lied so convincingly about a simple, overdue book, had she lied about other things as well? I just didn't know. Like Ryan, she seemed so sincere, and her attitude towards me had never been anything but kind and loving, but, somehow, it seemed I was getting good at seeing secrets in everyone. And I saw some big ones hiding in the shadows of her faded blue eyes. Whether or not they were my business was another story. Wasn't a person allowed to have their secrets? Were they obligated to tell me every little detail about their life? I didn't think so, but, at the same time, I thought so. Do you know what I mean? Of course you don't. That would mean you are just as weird as I am.

"Molly?" my name came out of her mouth like a question, and I wondered how many times she had called it before I snapped out of yet another daydream.

I blinked at her, "I'm so sorry, Carolyn," I said honestly. "I lost my train of thought. What were you saying?"

She was wearing her long grey hair down today, which, on some people would look absolutely ridiculous, but looked charming on her, half of her hair pulled back into a braid behind her head. She tucked a stray strand of hair behind her ear before replying. "You know what?" she said. "I think you need a break." Her face erupted into wrinkles when she smiled like she did now, "It could be you have Fall Fever. Get out of the store for the rest of the day and go for a walk, kick up some leaves and eat an apple or something…"

I protested, but it was no use. Ten minutes later I found myself on the driveway with Mr. Darcy's keys firmly in hand and an admonition not to come back for three hours. I smiled to myself. I knew exactly where I wanted to go.

It really was the most perfect little house that I had ever seen. Totally and completely adorable. Perfect. I could see myself living quite happily here for the rest of my life. I allowed myself to take the bait and picture myself buying my own little piece of peace. A house. All to myself. Just mine. It almost soothed the constant pounding ache of regret that I felt with each breath.

I sank down to sit on the sidewalk and contemplate what life would be like as a proud house owner. Of course, it would take years before I could save enough on what I made at the yarn store to have even a decent sized down payment. *You could always…* my little voice began. No. I wouldn't do that. *But you know you could…* No. I'm not going to.

"You know," an amused voice said from somewhere overhead, "sitting in the middle of the sidewalk could get you run over."

I knew that voice. Trying to suppress a groan, I looked up at Nathaniel Goldmyer. "Maybe," I said with a small smile. "But it's got to be better odds than sitting in the street."

"True," he acknowledged, with a twinkle still firmly in place. "But it does make one wonder why Molly Stevenson would choose to come all the way down to Water Street just to sit on the sidewalk and stare at a weird looking house." He offered his hand to help me up, which I took. The moment was ruined now anyway.

"It's not weird," I protested hotly. "It's completely perfect."

His eyebrows rose, and he turned to re-survey the house again, "Well," he said, "why don't you buy it then?"

I shrugged and tried to discreetly brush the dirt off my rear end. He then surveyed me from head to toe, which had me blushing. Have I mentioned how much I hate it when I do that?

"Actually," he said, thoughtfully, "you may be the only person in town who could pull off having a house like this."

"What's that supposed to mean?" I looked down at myself self-consciously. I was wearing leather boots, jeans and a white sweater with a cheerful long red coat. My hair had obligingly curled this morning into what I considered adorable brown ringlets that fell halfway down my back.

"You look like little red riding hood," he said. "But I guess you would be coming from grandmother's house instead of going…"

"Speaking of going…I should be going," I said, not feeling up to his brand of teasing today.

"Have you been inside?" He asked, abruptly switching moods. "You really shouldn't make up your mind by just staring at the front."

I admitted I hadn't, and he pulled his cell phone out of his coat pocket. "Hey, Julie," he said, "I'm standing in front of the cottage monstrosity on Water Street with someone who might be interested. What's the code for the front door?" He waited for the reply, laughed and said something else I couldn't hear, and strode confidently for the front door.

"Wait!" I protested somewhat belatedly. "What are you doing?"

"You want to see inside, right?" he asked, lip curling again. "I know you do. It's going to kill you unless you can go in. I recognize the signs of love all over you."

I threw him a mean look, "Stop it," I said. "I can't afford…"

He shrugged and finished putting the code into the little realtor's box on the front door, "It doesn't cost anything to look," he said, holding up the key triumphantly. "Shall we?"

I was torn. I did not want to go in there with Nathaniel Goldmyer. But I so wanted to go in there. I nodded, "We shall." I grabbed the key from him. He wasn't going to have the fun of opening that cute red door. The first time only happens once you know. He certainly wouldn't be able to appreciate the experience like I would.

I put the key in the lock and gave the enchanted door a small push. It was one step into the house. One step that divided street from the interior. Standing on the outside of the door, I was but a hopeful dreamer, one step in and I was… home. Darn. This was what I had been afraid of. I was home. My heart leapt up in acknowledgment even as my mind soared to the top of the vaulted ceilings. I think the two even met somewhere up there and did a waltz of absolute contentment. I was home. This is where I was supposed to be. Just like the first time that I had stepped foot inside of Crabapple Yarns, something in my soul called to this place. Home. Shelter. Sanctuary. Peace.

Great.

Now what was I going to do?

I walked mesmerized through the small foyer and turned instinctively to the right which led directly into the large living room complete with cozy stone fireplace with an enormous mantle. The ceilings probably stopped somewhere around the Milky Way. Stepping into the living room, I turned to look behind me, pleased to see that the floor plan was fairly open. No walls stood between the living room and the dining room – separated naturally instead with three large pillars.

"Look farther up," Nate said, his eyes gleaming. I stepped further into the living room to see what he meant, my heartbeat speeding up as I saw… the loft. "Oh my goodness," I breathed reverently. "I have never seen anything so magical."

The loft wasn't large, the staircase to the loft hardly anything more than a ladder, but it was amazing. Amazing. I was so excited that I don't even remember the trip up – and normally heights don't agree with me. The entire back wall of the loft was one large bookcase, the shape matching the lines of the ceiling, so that some of the shelves of the bookcase were but little triangles. There was even a little darling half-ladder to help you reach the top shelves. The loft was just wide enough to fit a comfortable reading chair. Ancient iron railings prevented you from falling to your death from the loft. I tested them warily, but they seemed secure. Nate practically had to drag me back down to see the rest of the house, but, really, after that… there could have been a great gaping hole in the roof and I would have thought it was a-dor-a-ble. This is why you should never make a big purchase on impulse, my friends. Then again, sometimes you have to go with your heart, right? There were two bedrooms… the "master" bedroom was amazingly quite large, its big, bay windows overlooking the moderately sized backyard, which laid pale and forlorn in contrast to the cuteness of the house. I was already making plans that included a deck with a gazebo top over it and a garden that ran the entire length of the yard, when I realized there was something else in the backyard. I glued my face to the window, captivated. It couldn't be.

I stared.

It was.

A darling little stream was winding its way through my backyard. Oops. I mean the backyard of the house. The ground sloped gently down to greet the lovely little ribbon of water. The sweetness of it squeezed my heart so hard a tear ran down my face.

"Well," Nate said, following my gaze, "why else do you think they call it "Water Street?" Talk about a mood-spoiler. "Good grief," he snorted. "You had better never go house shopping by yourself. You have no concept of what you should really be looking at." And with that, he yanked me in to look at the kitchen. It was… well… let's just say that it was vintage. Quite vintage. Almost grossly vintage. I was wrinkling my nose at the cracked and peeling laminate when another thought occurred to me. If this is what the kitchen looked like…what about the… Striding past Nate, I walked further down to the hall to where I had glimpsed the bathroom. With a hesitant hand, I pushed the door open. And stared. I felt Nate come up behind me and heard him suck in a breath.

"That's…" he was uncharacteristically at a loss for words. "That's really…"

"Pink," I squeaked.

The sound he was now making was probably some type of suppressed laughter and I turned to glare at him before turning my attention once more to the intolerably pink bathroom. People. Let me tell you. I'm not joking when I say it was pink. The walls were pink… a really pale pink, which the previous owner (or maybe the original owner 200 years ago) thought contrasted nicely with the slightly darker pink of the sink, counter, bathtub (and entire shower surround)… and yes, even the… umm… toilet. Sorry. I know it's not polite to talk about toilets, but when you have a pink toilet, I think it's ok to mention it. The toilet paper holder was pink. The soap dish was pink. The shower curtain was pink stripes. Even the lamp fixtures were… well… you get the picture. The entire room was pink. I stepped further in to examine the cleanliness of the room… which was ok. It could definitely use a good cleaning, but I didn't see any horrible mold growing anywhere, although there was a somewhat questionable ring around the tub.

Nate cleared his throat and took a step away from the bathroom. "I can feel my manhood diminishing the longer I stand next to the door."

I rolled my eyes. "A true man can feel at home in any color."

"Ouch."

I continued the tour trying to keep a more critical eye open. The second bedroom was painted a cheerful yellow with gingham curtains hanging in the windows. All in all, with the exception of the kitchen and the bathroom, it was a lovely little house. With its very own little stream. I took a deep, fortifying breath and strolled back down the hallway to where Nate was leaning up against a wall in the dining room, typing away on his phone.

"I hope you're not telling the realtor that I'm an easy sell," I only half-joked, because… you and I both know that I probably was.

He frowned over his phone, "No," he said, "I'm telling her that she's asking a ridiculous price for a place with a shabby, outdated kitchen, the most ridiculous pink bathroom I've ever seen, and a roof that needs some work." Well. That was nice of him. Or was it? I don't know. I'm not good at these kinds of games.

Without meaning to, I cast anxious eyes up to the ceiling, "The roof needs work?" I asked in dismay. "Is it leaking?"

"Not right now," he said cheerfully, with his trademark wink. "It's not raining." His smile turned a little creepy, "Actually, I think the roof is just fine, but it never hurts to exaggerate a bit when negotiating things like this." He did a double-take when he saw my face and gave me a reassuring smile, "It's ok, Molly," he said, "this is how it works. Everyone does it."

I stared at him, "Sometimes," I said slowly, studying his handsome face, "you really worry me. What does your conscience have to say about living like that?"

He shrugged, "If it gets you a lower price, what does your conscience say?"

I sighed. "This is all crazy talk anyway," I said reluctantly. "I'm not going to buy it."

"She says she'll go down 15%," he said without looking up from his phone. "I think we can get more. You'll definitely need some money for the remodel. Just let me… what did you say?"

"I'm not going to buy this house," I said firmly, ignoring the shaft of pain at the thought.

"You're kidding, right?"

I shook my head, gathered up my heart, which felt like it had already melted and oozed into all of the cracks and crannies of the little cottage and prepared to leave the sweetest house I had ever seen. I would love to own this house. I truly would. But how could I do it, knowing what it would mean? What I would have to do to get it.

Nate looked up in surprise, even as I walked determinedly towards the front door. "But," he said, looking genuinely bewildered, but following me nonetheless, "you love this house."

I locked the door regretfully behind us and handed Nate the key. "Life isn't about getting what you want," I said sadly, walking back to Mr. Darcy.

"Then what is it about?" he asked from behind me.

"What were you doing here, anyway?" I interrupted. He blinked at the sudden conversation twist.

"What?"

"What were you doing here?" I asked again. "I was just sitting on the sidewalk for a few minutes to look at this house and then… boom… there you were. Again." I narrowed my eyes at him. "Are you stalking me?"

He laughed, and it was a hearty and appealing laugh, making me smile with it. "You're nuts," he said. "I live right over there," and here he pointed down the tree-lined street to a neat little white Cape Cod with black shutters. "Also, I hate to tell you this, but you were sitting on the sidewalk for over 20 minutes staring at the cottage. I think there may even have been some drooling -there was a suspicious puddle by your left knee. I came out to save you from the Neighborhood Watch. You had about 5 more minutes before you were cornered and detained indefinitely." He raised his eyebrows at my expression, "What? Don't you believe me? Mr. and Mrs. Malone are hardcore about loitering."

I couldn't help it. He was amusing in an annoying, yet charming, *I wish I could shove a pie in your face* kind of way. "I think you're probably exaggerating for your own purposes again," I said, softening my words with a smile and quickly stepping into Mr. Darcy. "But thank you so much for the impromptu home tour. I really did enjoy it. I hope you get a super nice neighbor someday."

The drive home was all too short. Not nearly enough time to collect my thoughts. Because I know what you're thinking. You're thinking the same thing I am. What *was* Nathaniel Goldmyer up to?

I had been gone longer than I had thought. It's amazing how long it takes to drive into town, tour a magical cottage and come back. Carolyn had already closed up Crabapple Yarns and was on her way out when she saw me floating in. Her face lit up with delight, and I couldn't help but smile back.

"I can tell by your face that you had a pleasant afternoon," she said happily, clasping her hands together in symbolic pleasure. "Do you feel better?"

I had to admit to her that I did. She wrapped (a totally unnecessary, but very pretty) striped scarf around her neck as she prepared to leave and had one hand on the door when she turned towards me suddenly. "Oh," she said, "I almost forgot. I left you a note. It's on the counter. I'd explain it to you now instead of making you read it, but I'm afraid I'm soooo late for dinner with Irene." She pulled a funny face, that made her nose look even longer than normal, "And you know how she gets."

"Let her wait," I said sassily, one hand on a hip. "It'll be good for her."

Carolyn hooted with laughter as she left, the ends of her scarf blowing merrily in the wind. Maybe the scarf was necessary after all. Funny that I hadn't noticed how much colder it was getting out there. I waved goodbye to her and gratefully shut the door, feeling enveloped by the warm house.

Back in the living room, it sounded like Celia, Jack and Rose were having an argument about who was picking the TV program of the night. I smirked to myself. Jack enjoyed those TV shows where there was a dead body in some horribly terrible state of decay and half of the show was dedicated to looking at the ruined corpse. This, funnily enough, was not anyone else's idea of appropriate entertainment, and when it was Jack's turn, Rose and Celia would spend half of the time holding a pillow in front of their face and howling forlornly every time an eyeball rolled out. It was, bizarrely, a lot of fun. Abigail, being made of sterner stuff, would have a running commentary with Jack as to the authenticity of the state of the body, medical condition, etc. Natalie? I don't think she even watched. She sat tucked under Jack's arm and stared at the TV with the look of someone who is totally and utterly content. I doubt she would have even realized if the TV was off.

I headed down the hallway to the ballroom to retrieve my note from Carolyn when a whoosh of fabric, motion, and light collided with me halfway there.

"Good," she said, in her best stage whisper, "you're home. Let's talk."

I took a deep breath. The drama continued. I was thankful that I knew the subject would not be Ryan. My one attempt to explain what had happened had ended up with both of us crying and she had promised to wait until I could talk about it. "What's the matter?" I asked. "Did Jack have the gall to suggest that the wedding colors be changed again?" We had just reached the door to the ballroom, and I turned the lights on before entering. It was already almost dark outside, and I was beginning to get an uneasy feeling that perhaps we should have curtains installed. It was impossible to see if anyone stood outside on the porch looking in, and those prickly feelings of being watched weren't pleasant. Not, of course, that anyone would stand outside of Crabapple Yarns and stare in to watch the exciting goings-on of the yarn store – or the café – but, who knows, maybe that was exciting to people out there. Kind of like watching a soap opera with the sound turned off.

Natalie whizzed in in front of me. "This isn't about the wedding, Molly," she said excitedly. "I think I know what's going on." Her cheeks were positively pink with excitement.

I was feeling a bit confused. Which event was she talking about? Had she guessed about the house..??

She grabbed my arm and pulled me behind the book display, obviously feeling the same way I did about the disturbing lack of curtains. "I know who the axe murderer is."

"Who the axe murderer is," I repeated dumbly. I don't think, in a million years, I would be capable of keeping up with Natalie.

Her grip tightened, "It all makes sense when you stop to think about it. One. Why wasn't the book in the library? Mrs. Goldmyer said it had been checked out, but I don't really see that happening, do you?" I had to admit that she was right about that. "Two. You were fired after the book was returned. Why?" She didn't give me time to answer that one. "Three. Carolyn kept the book for 45 years. Out of the library for 45 years. Why?"

She really did sound like she was on to something. My eyes were round as I stared at her, "Why?" I whispered obediently.

"Because," she said triumphantly, "Mrs. Goldmyer is an axe murderer."

I sank down to the floor. "What are you talking about?" I asked weakly.

She fluttered down next to me. On the end of the bookshelf was a little hook from which a few shawls normally hung. They were pretty, but also served a very useful purpose – people bought the pattern – and the yarn to go with it. Carolyn wasn't a first-year knitter – that's for sure. Samples sold patterns and samples sold yarn. Period. Almost. Samples also kept people warm when they started freaking out about axe murderers. She took one of the shawls and wrapped it around her shoulders. I don't know if she was shivering with apprehension - or with delight. She leaned forward, her blond hair gleaming like a halo in the light of the store. "It's the only reasonable explanation," she said, speaking softly, her eyes worried yet elated. "It comes down to this. Either Carolyn is the axe murderer – or Mrs. Goldmyer."

I shoved Natalie in the shoulder, "Carolyn is not an axe murderer," I hissed. I may be a little upset with her right now, but that didn't mean that I thought she was an axe murderer.

"I know," Natalie said, head bobbing enthusiastically. "That's why it has to be Mrs. G."

"What? Why?" I asked, totally bewildered and unable to follow Natalie's train of thought (actually that part was not that unusual).

Natalie gave the sigh of one who is long-suffering. "There's only one reason to keep a book for 45 years, Molly," she said seriously. "Why would Carolyn keep it that long unless it meant something?" I shook my head cluelessly. "Here's what I think. Carolyn kept the book out of the library because… I don't know… maybe it was like insurance or something because of what she knew."

"Oh. My. Word." I put my head into my hands, "Now you think that Carolyn is a blackmailer," I wailed. "I don't think I want to…"

"Shhhh," she said sharply, "Just listen to me. I don't know why Carolyn kept the book. But she did. And the very first thing that happened was that you saw it and Mrs. Goldmyer saw you trying to hide it. Maybe she thought you were going to read it and you'd find out about her...."

"I was trying to save Carolyn the overdue fees," I objected.

I was shushed again. "I know that, but she didn't," Natalie pointed out logically. "It must have looked pretty suspicious to her, too, when you went straight to work for Carolyn. She must have wondered if you two were in cahoots."

"I've never cahooted in my life," I said primly, folding my fingers.

She cracked a reluctant smile, "Liar. Anyways, she gets rid of you and then gets rid of the book. Don't you remember her face when we told her the title of the book we were looking for?"

I did. Rats. Natalie was actually starting to make sense.

"Just because the title of the book sort of sounds like Springgate, doesn't mean that anything actually happened in Springgate," I pointed out. "This could all be just a couple of crazy coincidences."

Natalie pursed her lips, "I don't think so," she said slowly. "I read that book pretty slowly, and I'm seeing some definite similarities. The street layout is the same."

"Most towns have a 'Main Street'," I pointed out helpfully. She, of course, totally ignored me.

"The character descriptions match perfectly."

"I'm not so sure about that," I objected.

"Well then," she retorted, "you didn't read the book very closely. I'll bet you're one of those readers who only reads the good stuff. You probably skipped all of the boring, descriptive parts, didn't you?" I felt my face heat slightly. "Didn't you?"

"Ok," I said impatiently. "So I skipped some of the parts where it was like blah, blah... this is what the house looked like... blah... sunset... blah."

She snorted, and flipped her hair over her shoulder absent-mindedly, "I knew it. Because, you know what? I recognized her right away. 'The cold smile that never reached her eyes.' '…hair pulled severely back.' 'The lack of compassion.'" She looked at me impatiently, "I can't believe you missed all that."

I groaned, "Give me a break, will you? I read it all in one night. Let me re-read it again and I'll tell you what I think."

She nodded and smacked my knee in agreement, "I'll put the book back in your room," she said. "Let's see if you end up thinking what I'm thinking."

A thought popped helpfully into my head. "But don't you think people would remember an axe murderer on the loose? Even an accused axe murderer 50 years ago wouldn't be calmly working as Head Librarian of Springgate, would she?"

She nodded thoughtfully. "That's a really good point. I haven't figured that out yet either. But I'm going to do some research and see what kind of deaths there have been around here in the last 60 years."

This was starting to get weird, and I squirmed uncomfortably. "I think you're wrong," I said. "Things like this don't happen…"

She raised her eyebrows, "And this is coming from someone who has actually seen a Knitting Fairy."

She was right. "Two of them," I corrected her. I shivered and pulled down the other shawl from the hook, wrapping it securely around me. "If you're right," I said, "then we have to be careful. Because she knows that we read the book."

Natalie nodded, her eyes wide and serious. "I know."

"Do you think," I said cautiously, "that we should maybe tell…Jack…or someone?" My heart squeezed painfully with the desire to add "or Ryan" to the end of that sentence.

Natalie shook her head, "Maybe when we have proof, but right now, if we told anyone, they would just laugh at us. And," she continued seriously, "if we're in danger because we've read the book, we can't put them in danger too, can we?"

Maybe she was right. And maybe we would really regret our decision of silence. Only time would tell.

The door to the ballroom creaked open, and we both squealed in fright, momentarily paralyzed with the shock of it. Jack's head appeared around the corner, "Everything ok?" he asked cautiously, eyeing our shawl-draped selves huddled on the floor.

"Of course," Natalie said with her most believable smile.

"Of course," I said with my most believable smile.

"I totally do not believe either one of you," Jack said. "But supper's ready, so get your little rears in gear. You have five minutes to get to the table." And with that, he was gone, taking with him the aroma of chili and cornbread. My stomach was already watering.

We both stood up and hung our shawls back on the hook. Hopefully, they would keep what they had seen and heard to themselves.

"Oh," I said, "I almost forgot. Carolyn said she left a note for me on the counter."

The note was helpfully under the large paperweight right on the counter by the cash register, next to the list of dreaded classes.

Dear Molly (it read), *There is something very important that I have to retrieve from the other store, but I need younger legs than mine. Would you be so kind as to meet me there tonight at 8:30, after I have supper with Irene? Please don't tell anyone else about this, as I don't want to get anyone else in trouble for being in the condemned store. I know I can trust you. Thank you, Carolyn*

I sighed and turned to look at Natalie, who was reading over my shoulder, "Can I borrow Mr. Darcy again?" I asked timidly. I was just a little bit afraid that I was wearing out my car privileges.

"Of course you can," she said without hesitation. "But I think I'd better go with you."

It took a bit of arguing, but in the end, she conceded that I was right and we should honor Carolyn's request to keep it to ourselves. It sounded like a good idea at the time. They always do, don't they?

CHAPTER 10

M r. Darcy puffed reluctantly into action, clearly preferring to remain at home than have to chug, once more, down the hill on another knitterly mission. I patted his dashboard affectionately, "Just a little trip," I said happily, "and then you can come right back home." I was seriously losing it.

The night was dark and wet. A fine, misty rain was falling, obscuring my vision of the road. I drove slowly and carefully, unwilling to hit an animal – or – perish the thought – get stuck out on this road after dark. Thanks to my careful driving, however, I was a few minutes late for my rendezvous with Carolyn. I felt a little spark of excitement. I wonder what she needed from the old store? How fun to be with her, once more, in the little store where I first learned to love the art of knitting. No matter what her reasons were for lying to me – or for hiring me – I would always be grateful to Carolyn for showing me how to knit with love. Anyone can teach you how to knit. But it takes a true knitter to show you how to knit love into every stitch. And yes, it makes all of the difference in the world.

It was all dark down Robert's Alley. The only lights were the streetlights, even Mr. Morrie's store was dark. I drove slowly down the street and then pulled around the building to the parking lot in the back. That's strange. Where was Carolyn's car? Putting Mr. Darcy temporarily into park, I switched on his dome light to check my watch. Yes, I was definitely late. Which made Carolyn… even later. Tiny little alarm bells started going off in my head. Perhaps the best idea would just be to go home? The idea was extremely tempting. But if Carolyn needed me, I couldn't just leave her.

I puttered Mr. Darcy back around to the front of the store and pulled into one of the parking spaces there to peer anxiously into the store. I made sure all of the doors were locked, left the engine running and settled in to wait. Have you ever waited in a dark car at night? Let me tell you... It. Is. Creepy. The normally soothing sounds of Mr. Darcy's engine were now grating on my nerves. Each rumble turning in time with the rumblings in my stomach. I wished, not for the first time, that I had a smartphone. Why didn't I have a smartphone? Here I was. Out in the middle of nowhere. All by myself. Ok. I know downtown Springgate isn't exactly the middle of nowhere, but when it's 9:00 p.m., on a cold, dark and windy night... oh great, I'm beginning to sound like the opening to Natalie's mystery story. Maybe she was right. Never underestimate a classic. It was sure scaring me.

Suddenly – a light popped on in the store. It looked like a flashlight. My heart jumped into my throat. What? I strained forward to see better, clutching the steering wheel tightly. Was there someone walking through the store? It was... my body deflated with relief like a popped balloon... it was Carolyn. I could see her distinctive hair even through the dim lighting. I breathed a silent prayer of thankfulness and put Mr. Darcy into park. Probably not the best place to park – right in front of the condemned store, but even though I was completely relieved to see Carolyn, I was in no mood to go back to the dark, scary parking lot. I'm not completely stupid. I also made sure to lock the car before going up to the front door. Carolyn must have unlocked it before turning on the light, which was kind of her. Maybe she had arrived just as I was going around to the back of the building. We had totally missed each other. How... funny? I pushed the door open, and the familiar and comforting sound of the entry bell soothed my still slightly rumpled spirits. "Carolyn?" I called, attempting to switch on the lights. Unfortunately, even though they made their familiar "click" sound, no reassuring beams of light emitted from the bulbs. Well. That did make sense. Why would there be power in a condemned building? Had I tried the lights on my top-secret diary retrieval run? I couldn't remember. Why hadn't I thought of that and brought my own flashlight?

It wasn't completely dark, thanks to the lights outside of the store, so I bravely shuffled forward, relying on my (hopefully) wonderful memory of how the store was laid out. Of course, I promptly knocked my knee painfully against a bookcase. Well – so much for the stellar memory.

"Carolyn?" I called out again, rubbing what was sure to be a bruise later. I caught a whiff of her favorite perfume and smiled. She must have gotten dressed up for dinner with Irene. She was so cute sometimes.

"Back here," her voice called. Since her flashlight beam was no longer in the store itself, it only made sense that she was in the back room. Strange. It, too, was dark. A tiny tendril of fear perked back up inside my stomach.

"Carolyn?" My voice was, pathetically, barely a whisper. I was starting to feel like this was not such a good idea. I peeked up into the stairwell that led to the upstairs apartment. My apartment.

A beam of light wafted down at me from up the stairs. "Up here," she called. "Watch your step on the stairs." Her voice sounded strange as it echoed down the stairwell.

I held up my hand to shield myself from the glare. I could just barely make out her form behind the light. "What is going on?" I asked, just a bit too loud, climbing up slowly, as she patiently held the light on the stairs for me.

I waited for her reassuring answer, but she was strangely silent. The wood under my hand suddenly felt slick, and it took me a few seconds to realize it was because my own hand was cold and damp with sweat. I paused, wondering at the feeling of dread pooling in the pit of my stomach. How silly was I being? This was just Crabapple Yarns. It was just Carolyn. What was wrong? I gripped the stairs to continue my climb, and in a burst of emotion, everything in me, down to my heartbeat, began chanting, "Run. Run. Run. Run." I swallowed. I think I knew then, but I just couldn't admit it. I could barely breathe and, as I peered up at the top of the stairs, I was paralyzed with fear. "God," I whispered under my breath, "what should I do?" I felt His answer… "Run."

I never got the chance to run. The flashlight went off silently and without warning. The sudden darkness left me blinded and dazed. Real horror grabbed me then, and I turned, panicked, my foot slipping on the lip of the step. I turned again to keep myself from falling, before remembering, hysterically, that going up the steps was not a smart alternative. Swinging my head the other way, I realized, with a horrified indrawn breath that I no longer knew which way was up – and which way was down. Wasting precious micro-seconds, I reached out for the reassuring solidity of the handrail. I'm not really sure what happened next, but there was a lot of noise, the feeling of being brutally shoved and then…finally… the disorienting sensation of falling down the steps that I could not see.

Falling is always such a strange feeling. Almost an out of body experience. It's like you know it's happening, but you just can't process that it's really happening to you - right now. This very minute. It's like your brain just takes a step back. Body and soul and feeling all reconnected, though, at the bottom of the stairs. I lay there, trembling and shaking with the most horrible pain that I have ever felt. I didn't even know where it was coming from, but I couldn't move. I could feel tears rolling down my face, and I lifted my head as far as I could before it fell with a thump back to the carpeted floor of its own accord.

Then - the worst sound I have ever heard came from up the stairs. A footstep. On the stairs. I tried to raise myself again, but a piercing pain through my left arm had me slumping back to the floor, gasping through the waves of agony. I didn't want to think about what I had felt poking out of my arm. Nausea churned oily in my stomach. Another footstep slid softly. "Oh God, help me," I prayed….she was coming down the stairs. I didn't think it was possible to feel any more afraid. I was wrong. I tried to move again, using my right arm to hold the left one, which I now knew was definitely broken, and shoving my feet frantically against the floor in an attempt to move even a little, but it was no good. There was something slippery on the floor, which I guessed to be blood, making any attempt to gain traction impossible. Another step. Breathing was becoming difficult. I fell limp again, trying to catch my breath for enough energy to try moving one more time. Another step. Even as I gathered my strength, I knew it was useless. There was no way I could move fast enough. Choking back a sob, I realized the truth. I was going to die.

There was an incredibly loud "bang" from the front of the store and, almost immediately after, the sound of panicked voices and running feet. I felt the feet coming towards me, the vibrations on the floor getting closer with each step. And for the second time tonight, relief hit me like a tidal wave, and this time, this time, I knew I was safe because… I knew that voice.

My rescuers had thought to bring flashlights, and for a few horrible seconds, I was illuminated by them just as I had been on the stairs. I squeezed my eyes closed and tried not to think about before… and to try to forget what I had seen, briefly of my poor arm. I'm pretty sure no one was meant to see what I just saw. Pain pierced through my side, as I tried to turn to avoid the light, spiking the nausea further. After that, I just focused on breathing.

"Molly!" I've never heard anyone say my name like that before. Ryan threw his flashlight down to the ground, where it rolled to stop somewhere by my leg. Jack was right behind him, and he propped his flashlight on end to illuminate the back room quite nicely. Ryan dropped to his knees beside me, his face ashen. "Sweetheart," he said hoarsely, his hands fluttering over me, "don't try to move." His hand was blessedly warm on the side of my face, "We're here. Everything is going to be fine." Huh. That's what they always say. He would have been more believable if he didn't look so scared.

Jack already had his phone out and was speaking on it. Then I remembered. She was still here. She was up there. Waiting for me. Maybe for Jack and Ryan, too. I reached out, feebly with my good hand towards Ryan and tried to tell him.

He shook his head worriedly, rubbing warmth into my hand, "I'm so sorry," he said. "I don't understand." Well, that was probably because my teeth were chattering so hard I couldn't even talk. The world went a little fuzzy after that. I vaguely registered the urgent voices, and even though I knew they were calling my name, there was no possible way for me to answer them.

Someone must have tried to move me, because the pain was so sharp and intense, I cried out with it. It was, actually, just what I needed, and I blinked hard and tried to refocus. Memory returned almost at once. Not-Carolyn. Had she come down the stairs? Where was Ryan? With strength I didn't know I had, I almost succeeded in sitting up. It was a ridiculously short trip. Ryan caught me before I fell back down to the floor and the heat and comfort coming from him made me cry harder. I hadn't even remembered I was crying. Ryan leaned me gently back against his chest, supporting my bad arm carefully, and holding my right hand as Jack took his coat off to drape over me, tucking the sides around me securely.

Ryan made soothing noises, the sounds rumbling through his chest comfortingly. Blackness at the corner of my eyes called me invitingly, but I pushed it back as hard as I could, shifting uncomfortably. Jack looked worried. "What, Molly?" he asked, kneeling next to me. "What are you trying to say?"

"U….u…uppppp…" I tried desperately to warn them. Jack's face suddenly sharpened.

"Upstairs?" he asked, leaning down to look in my face. "Is someone up there?" He exchanged a look with Ryan, whose face I so badly wanted to see.

Ryan's hold on me tightened, "It's ok, Molly," he said fiercely. "You're safe now." He tucked me in just a bit closer.

Jack stood up swiftly and turned towards the stairs. I let out a cry, which had him immediately turning back. Even though I couldn't talk, he knew what I wanted. "It's ok," he soothed. "We'll stay together." That was all I needed to know, and I welcomed the blackness as an escape from the bone-cold terror and pain.

CHAPTER 11

I t was still dark outside when I woke up, the window of the hospital room showed a large, glowing moon. Something hard and cumbersome covered the length of my arm, and my arm felt too tight in the confines. I could feel it throbbing gently. Thankfully, I was completely warm, although I did wonder if I had every blanket in the hospital on top of me. It was quite a stack. The thought of pushing them all back to climb out of bed was exhausting just to think about. I turned my head to the side and was surprised to find two eyes staring back at me. I jumped slightly.

"Sorry," Ryan said softly, "I didn't mean to scare you."

I blinked at him, recognizing the feel of some really effective drugs coursing through my system. "You're here," I said, rather stupidly. Later, I'll blame that on the drugs.

Ryan pulled his chair right up to the side of the bed and grabbed my hand which had somehow started reaching for him already. I'll blame that on the drugs, too. I loved the feeling of my hand encased in Ryan's two large ones. It was strange how safe and peaceful it made me feel. If only I hadn't broken up with him.

Ryan noticed my wince at once, "Are you in pain?" he asked worriedly. "Let me call the nurse."

"No." I squeezed his hands tighter, keeping him where he was, "I'm not... was just thinking about...about..." my voice cracked. Stupid drugs.

"About what happened?" he asked gently though his voice strained with emotion. "It makes me so sick to think of what you went through…"

"No," I stopped him again, studying his face like it was the first time I had seen it. The pucker in the forehead was new – but easily attributed to the events of this evening. The lines around his eyes were new, too. It looked like he had been spending a lot of time worrying lately. My heart clenched. I pulled my hand reluctantly out of Ryan's secure hold to touch the lines on his face. "I was wondering why you were here when I…and last night… you came… I thought…"

"Sweetheart," he said, "do you think just because you tell me that you don't want to see me anymore that I'm going to agree with you?"

My mouth might have fallen open just a little bit. "You should have been mad at me for the way I treated you," I argued. "I wasn't very fair." Memories zinged me hard. "Or kind."

He grabbed my hand again and held it up to his face so close that I could feel his eyelashes when he blinked. "You were upset," he said sadly. "And with good reason." He kissed my hand and laid it gently back on the bed before pushing his chair back and standing up. The sudden activity made me dizzy. He turned towards the door, and I panicked for just a second thinking he was leaving when he turned back and paced the other direction. He gave a frustrated sigh. "Jack is right."

Maybe there was such a thing as too much pain medication. This was making absolutely no sense. I felt like Alice down the rabbit hole. He looked down at me and groaned. "And now I'm making no sense and confusing you." Finally. Even though he made no sense he understood me perfectly. It was almost funny.

Running a hand through hair that was already standing up, he crossed the room again, pausing with his back towards me. "I don't know how to say this," he said. "Jack told me that…."

"Ryan," I said, "please don't feel like you have to say anything. You've done more for me than I deserve…"

He spun around, and I was surprised to see a flush of anger across his face, "Don't say that," he said in a low voice. "That's not true."

I couldn't meet his gaze, "It is true," I insisted. "I said I didn't want to see you anymore, remember? You should find someone who…"

He was suddenly crouching beside my bed, "I don't want someone else," he said slowly and clearly. "I only want you." And then he leaned over and kissed me so sweetly, I felt tears beginning to rise. He groaned, "Oh man, and now I've said the wrong thing."

I laughed a little, even as I wiped away a trickle, "No," I assured him, "you said exactly the right thing."

There was no talking for a few minutes after that, and when Ryan finally pulled away, I met his eyes, "I want to apologize," I began. He shook his head, his red hair whipping about with emphasis.

"Please don't," he said softly. "Can we just... I don't know... not forget everything that happened, but... just go forward?"

"It's not just you," I argued, despite the fact that my heart felt like it was melting. "There are things I haven't told you.."

"Shhh," he said softly. "Of course there are. That's how life is. I think maybe that's what it's about. Growing together and sharing life as you go." His eyes grew moist. "And I'd like to do that with you."

I stared at him, a smile starting to bloom, "I'd really like that, too."

The first real smile I had seen from him in a long time began making its way up his face, too. It made me warm. Really warm. But maybe that was all of the blankets. I kicked at them feebly with my feet, which still felt tired and leaden.

"Getting warm?" he asked. "Would you like me to take a few layers off?" When I nodded, he peeled off three blankets and plopped them into the chair next to the bed. His face took on the worried look again, "You were so cold," he said. "The doctors said you went into shock. They were really concerned."

Oh. That's right. Someone had tried to kill me tonight. I'm not quite sure how I forgot about that, but, somehow... I shivered. "May I please have one of those blankets back?" I asked Ryan timidly. The puckers around his eyes grew even more pronounced as he graciously re-tucked all the blankets again.

I grabbed his hand with my good one. "Someone tried to kill me tonight," I said, not quite able to stop the quiver in my voice. "I thought I was going to die." Images flashed through my mind like lightning strikes. The stairs. The person at the top. The flashlight. The fear.

He used his leg to reach back and hook the chair to draw it closer to the bed so that he could resume his position of careful watching. His eyes darkened, even as he pushed the hair back from my forehead gently, "But you didn't," he said, firmly. "And you won't. Not as long as I'm around." He sighed, "Later, when you feel up to, we'll talk about it. For now, I'm just content that you're safe and almost all in one piece. I'm sure the police will be here again in the morning. They have been hounding us for hours for some answers.

"Hours?" I said. "What time is it?"

He shrugged, "About 7:00, I think. Why?" My brain did somersaults trying to figure that one out. "What's the matter?"

"How is it possible that it's 7:00 now, when all of this happened just after 8:30?" I asked slowly, feeling like I was missing a huge piece of a weird, floating puzzle.

Ryan snorted, "Sweetheart," he said, "that was last night."

I stared at him in disbelief. "Are you telling me that I've been here for almost 24 hours?"

His eyes were kind, "You were in and out of consciousness. First, you were in shock and then you were in surgery and then recovery… the doctors said it could be awhile before you woke back up."

"I had surgery?" I gasped. How was it possible to have had surgery and not remember a thing?

Ryan winced, "Yeah," he said. "Your arm was broken pretty badly. The doctor will explain it all later, but you have some plates and pins in there now."

Nausea returned like a slippery serpent with the memory of my bone sticking out of my arm, and I swallowed hard.

"Hey," Ryan said, leaning forward to get my attention, "look at me." He waited for me to comply. "It's all over now. You're safe and your arm will heal just fine, so let's not think about what happened right now, ok? Why don't you get some sleep instead?" He released my hands to pull the blankets up higher around me.

"You mean I've been here for 24 hours?" I repeated. He nodded, still fluffing blankets. "Then," I said slowly, "you've been here this whole time, too?"

He nodded, "Of course I have." He glanced up to catch my incredulous expression, his own growing slightly angry. "Do you really think that I would leave you all alone after someone tried to…" his voice broke and he glanced away. "And just so you know," he said, "Jack and Natalie are both out there in the waiting room. Celia, Rose and Abigail left about an hour ago to go get food and some rest, dragging Carolyn home with them. They'll keep an eye on her until they come back tomorrow. We practically had to have her sedated to get her to leave, but she really looked like she needed some rest."

A strange feeling caught at my heart and held it ferociously, leaving a tear to trickle down my face. I think it was love. I thought I knew what love felt like, but I was wrong. This was different. It was better. And worse.

"Awwww," Ryan said soothingly, "don't cry." Which of course, made me cry harder.

"You should go home, too," I said, trying to pull myself under control, and wiping away the tears that wouldn't stop falling.

"Not a chance," he said firmly. "I'm staying here all night." He met my gaze with a small smile, "It's really for my own piece of mind. I don't think it's possible for you to get into trouble while I'm actually here, do you?"

I snorted a laugh, which was very unladylike. "Don't underestimate me," I said, making him growl a reply that I couldn't decipher. I frowned at the chair he was sitting on. Some hospitals that I have been in had nice comfy chairs for people who visited and spent the night. "You can't sleep there all night," I protested. "That is way too uncomfortable."

He smiled reassuringly, the corners of his eyes crinkling just a bit, "Stop worrying about me," he said, "and get your little self to sleep."

I considered the problem. On one hand, I was so grateful that I wouldn't have to worry about being alone. Because, yes, even though we weren't discussing it right now, I remembered the feeling of being pushed down the stairs. It wasn't even the fall that made me shiver, but the violence of the push. Whoever had been up on the landing had intended real harm. What if I had been further up the steps? Would I have even survived the fall?

"Why don't you sleep up here?" I asked finally, patting the bed next to me with my good hand.

He looked shocked. "I couldn't do that," he sputtered.

"What would people think?" I teased him, adoring that his face turned slightly red.

"No," he argued back, "I was thinking of your comfort. The doctor said not to let you jostle your arm and to keep you quiet and comfortable."

"I promise that I'll be quiet and comfortable if you just prop yourself up right next to me." I fiddled with the edge of the blanket and didn't meet his eyes. "Actually, I'd feel better if you were right next to me," I confessed. "I'd feel safer."

He sighed and rolled his eyes, but in less than five minutes, I was propped up against him and already feeling sleepy. Until I remembered a question that was still swirling.

I snuggled closer to him. "So, what was Jack right about?" I asked curiously.

He stirred, as if he had been teetering on the edge of sleeping, which made me feel just a little bit bad. "He said that I had communication issues and if I didn't want to lose you, I had to start finding a way to say what I felt." Ryan kissed the top of my head, "And right now, I'm going to communicate with you that you need rest, so no more talking until the morning."

"I doubt the nurses will let me sleep that long," I grumbled. "I probably won't be able to sleep at all."

Ryan tucked his arm tighter around my shoulder, and, fully intending to argue with him a little longer, I don't even remember falling asleep.

"What do you mean, there's no evidence of anyone else there?" an angry voice demanded. I stirred, and the voices abruptly stopped.

"Now look what you've done," Ryan said, anger coloring his tone. "You're waking her up."

There was a great sigh, and an unfamiliar voice spoke with a tone of practiced patience, "If you had done as I requested and spoken to me out in the hallway…"

"I told you I wasn't going to leave her…"

I opened my eyes to see Ryan facing down a police officer, his back to me. I noticed, with great relief, that it was not Officer Douglas. The officer noticed that I was awake and the change in his expression had Ryan immediately turning around.

I made my best attempt at a smile, although I knew that I looked terrible. Before either of them could say anything, a nurse came bustling in. She was comfortably middle-aged and had a kindly face. She sent them both skittering from the room with an efficiency that was impressive.

"Now," she said, "my dear, please don't take this the wrong way – but you could use some cleaning up."

I wholeheartedly agreed.

Almost 45 minutes later, she had me resting back in bed again, my arm propped up on a mountain of pillows. It was a beautiful feeling to feel fresh and clean again, and I could almost imagine that last night was only a horrible nightmare. My stomach grumbled loudly. She grinned, "I'll bring you some breakfast right away," she said. "The doctor said you could eat whatever you wanted as long as you weren't feeling nauseous?" The last sentence was part statement and part question. I assured her that I was not feeling nauseous at all, and that eggs and toast would be lovely.

As soon as she left, the officer and Ryan were back in the room, joined by Jack and Natalie, who both looked pale and worried. Natalie rushed to my side, grabbing my good hand. "Oh, Molly," she cried, "I'm so sorry."

I squeezed her hand back, "I'll be fine," I assured her. Whether or not this was true, I really didn't know, but Ryan had said something to that effect last night, so that was good enough for me.

Her face puckered in misery, "I should never have let you go alone last night," she said. "If only I had…"

I stopped her, "Knock it off," I said. "There's no way we could know. I certainly never doubted that the note was left by Carolyn, so why should you?"

"About that," the officer stepped in. "I do need you to answer a few questions about last night."

Jack wrapped an arm around Natalie, pulling her back so that the officer could step closer. Ryan took Natalie's place and held my hand firmly.

He was an older officer, with graying hair and a kind smile. "My name is Joe Shaw," he said. "Do you feel up to telling me what happened last night?" He shot an amused look at my entourage, "These people have all given me their versions, multiple times, but I'd like to hear from you."

I took a deep breath and, beginning with the note that Natalie and I found from Carolyn, and ending with the brutal shove that had sent me flying down the stairs. "I think," I said slowly, "that she really wanted me to come up to the top of the stairs so she could push me from there." I shuddered, and felt it ripple through Ryan, too, "I don't know what would have happened if I had fallen from there."

The officer's eyes were sympathetic, but they didn't quite meet mine as he looked down to jot a few notes on his notepad. Then I remembered what I had heard before I was almost quite awake. "You don't believe me?" I asked incredulously. "You think I'm making this up?"

Officer Shaw's eyes shot up to mine. "Did you feel any hesitation about meeting your boss in a condemned building?" he asked.

Natalie and I both snorted. "It's not condemned," I protested hotly. "It was condemned wrongly and we're in the process of having it un-condemned." Natalie opened her mouth to speak but a warning glance from Officer Shaw stopped her.

"I'm here to speak with Ms. Stevenson," he said. "If you have trouble remaining silent, I'm going to have to ask you to leave."

She glared at him, but didn't speak.

Had I thought his face was kind? It now looked stern and sober. I was feeling really confused. "So you think I made up the note and went to Crabapple Yarns so that I could throw myself down the steps?" I asked.

He rolled his eyes just a bit, "No," he said slowly, "we don't think that. We do think, however, that this was just a joke gone bad." He obviously had not felt the venom in that shove. His gaze sharpened on mine, "Were you not one of four women who was found," his lips quirked reflexively, "vandalizing a rival yarn store with moths?"

My gaze went from his to Ryan, Jack and Natalie, who all looked angrily back at the officer. So that's how this was going to be. No one had tried to kill me. It was merely a revenge prank gone askew. The matter would be superficially looked into, but nothing beyond that. Which, in the end, is exactly what happened.

CHAPTER 12

I t was one of those beautiful, rare fall days where the temperatures were happily summer-ish, yet the leaves shone brightly in their autumn hues. I was comfortably parked outside on the front porch in an enormous wicker chair with colorful cushions. Natalie sat next to me snuggled down into her own chair. It was Sunday, and our day off. The hospital had let me go home with strict orders to rest for a few days, and I had a follow-up appointment scheduled for next week. I had expected my arm to hurt more than it did, but other than an occasional throb, it was a blissfully numb dead weight over my lap. My biggest problem at the moment was my self-appointed babysitter. Natalie was currently rather unhappy.

"What was I supposed to do, Natalie?" I demanded. "I certainly couldn't tell the police our crazy theories about ax murderers." Well. I could have. I was even tempted to, but I don't think that would have escalated our case – except to make us all laughingstocks – well, more so than normal, I guess.

She shrugged helplessly, "I don't know," she said. "It just makes me so mad that someone lured you to the store, pushed you down the steps and it's just 'Oh, those crazy knitters.'" I heartily agreed with her, but before we could talk any more, Jack and Ryan came bounding up the steps, a newspaper flapping from Jack's hand. I met Natalie's eyes apprehensively. Both of their faces were grim.

"Now what?" Natalie demanded, yanking the paper from his grasp. Ryan settled on the arm of my chair, and I looked questioningly up at him.

"Another article not-quite about Crabapple Yarns," he said with a sigh. "This time, you're a vindictive, jealous store for scheduling an idiotic Halloween Party on the same night as another store has scheduled an intellectual, groundbreaking and innovative event." He frowned, "And there's also a really weird reference to one of the sales people accusing a former neighbor of criminal activity."

We had to wait until the guys went inside to fetch refreshments before we could talk about it. I snatched the newspaper from Natalie with my good arm to re-read it one more time. "Can this possibly be referring to the comment I made about when I first met Mr. Morrie?" I asked anxiously, peering over the paper at Natalie.

She chewed her bottom lip. "I can't remember who was around when you said that. I thought we were alone."

"I…I just meant that as a joke," I stammered. Here I was – singlehandedly taking down Crabapple Yarns. Quite an accomplishment, wasn't it?

She rolled her eyes, "I know that," she snapped. I dropped my eyes, which had somehow filled with tears, back to the paper. "Oh Molly," she said softly, "I'm not angry with you." She was suddenly sitting next to me on the chair, causing me to scoot over – it wasn't that big of a chair. "I'm so angry at whoever is messing with you that I could just…"

"Spit?" I suggested helpfully, smiling in spite of myself.

"Yeah," she agreed, "spit." So she did. Right over the railing.

We both giggled, "That was really gross," I said. I sobered. "We need to figure out what's really going on," I said softly, as I could hear the guys coming back. "This is getting seriously out of hand."

"I'm going to spend tomorrow googling," Natalie promised, "and see if there was ever an axe murderer of Springgate."

I know. You're dying to know (not literally of course – goodness – that phrase really isn't even funny anymore – my apologies) about what Natalie found out about The Axe Murderer of Springgate, aren't you? Well. I can't tell you.

No. Seriously. I can't tell you because there was nothing to find out. There were no horrible murderers in Springgate since 1842 when a man accidentally shot his friend while out hunting. It was either a grisly murder – or a horrible, heart-rending accident. But, either way, not likely to have any bearing on our current predicament. And certainly, in no way, were we able to connect that with Mrs. Goldmyer.

"Probably," I said to Natalie, "because there is no axe murderer. We've made all this up based on a theory we developed ourselves from reading a weird old book that was probably written by someone across the country and has nothing whatsoever to do with Springgate."

She shook her head sadly, "But it made so much sense," she said mournfully. "It really did."

Secretly, I agreed with her. But there was no evidence. Or, at least, no evidence that we had found yet. After all, do you really think someone lured me to Crabapple Yarns to push me down the steps as revenge for setting moths free in our rival yarn store? No. Me either. After all, I wasn't even the mastermind, or for that matter, a willing participant in The Great Moth Plot. Not, I suppose, that anyone would know that. The truth was - someone wanted me out of the way. But who? At this point, it could, literally, be anyone.

I said goodnight to Natalie and then went to say goodnight to the rest of the family all curled up in the living room watching an old Cary Grant movie. "I just love him," Rose was saying dreamily to Abigail. "He was just so…"

"He was," Abigail sighed back. I agreed with them both, said goodnight and retired to my room to, once again, examine "The Axe Murderer of Springiegate." I pulled it towards me and studied it again for clues. We had already established that it had been a self-published book with a very limited print run. Natalie had estimated it to be about 500 books, based on her "research". How she came up with that number, I have no idea, but she said it with a great deal of authority, so I didn't argue with her. There were no clues as to who the author was, though. "R. Waters" could be anyone. Actually, it could be a lot of someones. I won't even tell you how many people named "R. Waters" popped up on Google. If that was even his or her real name. Which it probably wasn't. We did discover that "R. Waters" never wrote another book. And that was a real shame, wasn't it?

With a first book like this, a second follow-up book on the "The Strangler of WhateverVille" would have been a great bestseller, don't you think? But I digress.

With a sigh, I opened the book back up and began re-reading it – promising myself not to skip any boring passages this time. An hour later, I flopped the book closed again. There was something tingling at the back of my mind, but it would not quite come to the surface where I could see it. Something about this book felt familiar. Like I had read it before… or…? I don't know.

There was a soft knock on my door. "Come in," I called, happy for any interruption in my frustrating thoughts.

Rose peeked her head in, "I thought I'd check on you before I headed to bed," she said cheerfully, "and see if you needed anything."

These people were so cute. Just because I was unable to use my left hand somehow made me completely helpless. "No thank you," I said, waving her in. "I was just reading a little and then I'll head to bed myself. It's a big day tomorrow."

She grinned, "I am curious to see how you're going to teach eight beginning knitters how to knit one-handed."

I groaned, "Don't remind me," I protested. "I'm already feeling nauseous about it. I've never considered myself the teacher type at all, and now everyone will be watching me extra close. Besides," I said, "Natalie said that she would help by doing all of the physical demonstrations and I can just talk everyone through it." I grimaced. "Doesn't that sound like fun?"

Rose smiled gently, coming fully into the room. Her little-striped socks shuffled their way through the dense carpet. "I have a feeling that you don't even know that you were born to be a teacher."

"I have no idea what gave you that idea."

She shook her head, "I've been watching you in the store. You always try to find something positive and affirming to everyone." As she was talking, she turned the book around to see the title, making a face as she read it.

"I'm not quite sure that qualifies me to be a teacher," I began.

She shook her head, "The most important thing a teacher does is inspire self-confidence," she said firmly. "When people feel good about themselves, they believe they can do anything and then… bang…" and here she slapped the book for emphasis, "learning is no problem at all." I stared at her in confusion. "What I'm saying," she said patiently, "is that teaching people how to do something isn't the only job of the teacher. You have to teach them to trust themselves. To believe in themselves, and then they won't be scared of trying… anything… and when that happens they stop becoming students and become teachers themselves (even though they don't realize it) and, because they love themselves, they show other people how to do the same thing…" she broke off, looking slightly embarrassed, her little pink cheeks flushing.

I put my good hand over hers, "I love you," I said sincerely. "I'm so glad that I got to know you. You're an amazing woman."

She placed her other hand over mine, "Likewise," she said warmly. "And I know that you'll be a great teacher." She frowned down at the book on the table between us, "Now, perhaps we should discuss your reading habits."

I giggled nervously, "I promise you that is not my typical reading material," I said. "This is an experiment of Natalie's, and it's totally backfired." Which was true. Because if this was supposed to get us over our writer's block, it wasn't helping. Well, perhaps it would help, if I wasn't so busy wondering about axe murderers and made some time to write.

She snorted, "Well, that explains a lot," she said. "That girl is just like me when I was her age."

"Then we know she'll turn out lovely, right?" I said, because Rose was starting to look a little pensive. It was time to change the subject. "Have you ever seen this book, Rose?" I asked.

She sat down on the little chintz chair across from me and pulled the book over to examine it more closely. "I feel like I have," she said slowly. "For some reason, the cover feels familiar." I raised my eyebrows. It was a perfectly plain leather cover, nothing unusual or worth remembering. She must have read my mind, "I know there's nothing significant about it," she said. "Maybe that's what feels familiar."

Well. She was absolutely no help at all.

There was a hard knock on the door that had both of us jumping, Rose clutching the book to her chest.

"Yes?" I called. My room was certainly a popular place these days. Jack cracked the door, just barely sticking his nose in.

"Do you feel up to a visitor, Molly?" he asked. "If not, I'll just tell him to come back tomorrow." His nose started a slow retreat with the door.

Him? Now this sounded interesting. It was obviously a "him" that Jack didn't want me to see. "Don't be silly, Jack," I said with a laugh. "Of course I'll see someone."

The door flew open and Nate pushed past Jack a little bit rudely. He was wearing jeans and a flannel shirt, which looked so incongruous that I had to blink before I recognized him. I had never seen him dress so informally. Even his normally polished hair was sticking up just a bit in the back, like he had run a hand through it before leaving the house. His eyes were big and concerned. "I just heard about what happened," he said, somewhat hoarsely. "Are you alright?" His eyes did not lose their concern as they looked me up and down. That was understandable. I had seen myself in the mirror, too.

I gave him my most comforting smile, which was just a little bit wobbly due to the bruises on my cheekbone. "Of course," I said. "I'm perfectly fine." He still did not look convinced, stopping a few feet away from where Rose and I sat. "The only problem is that this," and here I waved my casted arm in the air, "isn't going to get me out of teaching beginning knitting." He stared at me for a full five seconds before my feeble joke finally sank in.

"Oh," was the brilliant reply.

"How did you hear about what happened?" Jack demanded, a bit sharply. He, too, had come into the room with Nate.

Nate turned slowly, and his charming smile was magically back again, "I have my sources," he said with dignity. He turned to smile at both Rose and I conspiratorially while Jack sputtered. This time, though, he took pity on Jack, "I heard down at the police station where I was, shall we say, assisting someone with a legal predicament."

Jack did not reply verbally, but if looks could speak, it would have been a speech that even Shakespeare would have been proud of.

Nate looked back down at me, "Are you really alright?" he asked. "Shaw was quite concerned about the extent of your injuries."

I shook my head, "I was very fortunate... just some bruises and a broken arm."

"Four hours in surgery," Jack interrupted darkly, "lacerations and extensive bruising."

Nate looked pale, "What were you even doing at that store in the dark?" he asked. "What happened?"

Are you thinking what I'm thinking? Yeah. This was all a bit suspicious, wasn't it? On one hand, he did look really worried. On the other hand, he was Nathaniel Goldmyer.

I said I couldn't talk about it as it was an ongoing investigation, which had Jack relaxing and nodding his head in approval behind Nate. Nate did not linger long. "Just remember," he said, leaning forward towards me slightly, "my offer still stands." Jack moved slightly, and I looked up at him quizzically. He smiled broadly, well aware of Jack's attitude, "If you ever need anything, call me."

"Hopefully you won't have to bail me out of jail again," I said with a small smile, the incident almost tolerable to talk about now. He turned to say goodbye to Rose, who set the book down to shake his hand sweetly. I'm pretty sure it wasn't my imagination that he flinched slightly when he saw it. Interesting.

"She'll be fine," Jack said firmly, escorting Nate to the door. Nate resisted the arm at his back and turned one more time towards us.

"Oh," he said, "and, Molly - the other item that we discussed the other day?" I froze, worried that he would blab my secret, but I should have known better. "It's still available – at a 24% reduction." And smiling his best shark smile at Jack, he walked out.

"So what was Nate talking about?" Natalie demanded, tucking sock yarn into its little bins at a speed she normally did not have.

I proceeded to re-arrange the yarn behind her as she went, pretending ignorance. "I don't know, Natalie," I said, making my eyes big and innocent.

She snorted, and shoved the last ball into place. "Ok," she said, "have your little secret."

I winced, regretting her choice of words. "Natalie," I said, "it was just..."

She held up her hand, "It's ok, Molly," she said with a rueful smile. "I didn't mean to make you feel guilty. You don't have to tell me every little detail of your life." She paused. "Even if I do want to know it."

We both laughed. "There," she said with satisfaction. "All of the new yarn is put away. Now, we should have about 15 minutes before Carolyn comes back from her lunch break. Let's conspire."

We hunkered down behind the counter to keep a weather eye on the two customers that were in the store. Rebecca Flannery was over by the wool yarn, once again trying to decide what yarn to use for her class that began this evening. She had already purchased - and returned - three different yarns. The good news was that this would be her last purchase. She was going to have to keep whichever one she picked now, as class started in less than five hours. The other shopper was most definitely pregnant and trying to decide what to knit for her baby. In my opinion, she had better pick something with big needles and chunky yarn because that baby looked like he was going to pop out any day.

"So," Natalie said, returning my attention to our predicament, "what did you discover?"

I took a deep breath, meeting her eyes squarely. "Nothing." Her face fell in disappointment. "You?"

She shook her head, "Nothing here either. It was definitely printed 46 years ago. That's about all I could get out of Google. Man, I really expected better out of Google."

"Well," I said helpfully, "the book is even older than Google, so maybe that's the problem."

"That doesn't necessarily make sense," she argued. "The Crimean War was also before Google's time and there's plenty of information on that."

"Why were you looking up The Crimean…"

She smacked me on my good arm, "Stop it. That was just an example. Stay focused."

"Owww," I hissed at her. "There's a bruise there."

She looked guilty. "Sorry."

"So we know it was printed 46 years ago. Shortly after that, it was checked out of the library where it remained with Carolyn for 45 years. The second it comes back to the library, I'm fired and the book disappears again." I stared at Natalie, "There has to be some significance in that."

She nodded, "That's what I'm telling you," she said. "It's too coincidental to not mean something."

"I tried talking to Carolyn about the book again," I admitted, idly straightening the bags under the counter. "But she wouldn't say anything."

"Did you tell her that you knew that this was the book she returned?" Natalie asked excitedly.

I sighed again. "No. I just didn't know how. She still feels so guilty for what happened at the store…"

"I know," Natalie said glumly. "I don't blame you. I tried, too, and couldn't do it either."

"I feel like maybe she hired me for the same reason Mrs. Goldmyer may have fired me." At Natalie's bewildered look, I explained, "To keep me quiet about the book." I lowered my eyes to the countertop, tracing dents in the woodgrain with my finger.

"That's ridiculous," Natalie said firmly, and my heart lifted slightly. "I know Carolyn just loves you. She's not pretending."

I shrugged. "I hope not," swallowing past the lump in my throat.

"Well," Natalie said brightly, changing the subject neatly, "if we can't pump Carolyn for more information, there's just one thing left to do." She wiggled her eyebrows evilly. "We'll see what we can get out of Mrs. Goldmyer. Tonight."

CHAPTER 13

There was one big figurative fly in the ointment, though. Carolyn, in all of her kind-heartedness, had allowed Louise to also assist with the class. Louise, apparently, had made a very good case about my injury and Natalie's lack of experiencing in dealing with classes. Carolyn had been planning on working on some new patterns with Rachel during class time in case we should need her, but Louise, the little doll that she was, just insisted on helping. The joy. Now everyone would be on hand to witness my total and complete failure as a teacher. Because, if Louise was there, it was sure to be a spectacular failure. Louise would make sure of that.

"Good evening, ladies," I said as brightly as I could. "Welcome to beginning knitting." There were nervous smiles around the table. "If you think that knitting is just about wrapping some string around a couple of sticks – you're so wrong." Rebecca looked at me in confusion, and Louise scowled. *Get to the point* her expression said. I smiled sweetly at her. "With every loop that goes around your needles, a little bit of your love goes with it, every time. You can knit love into every stitch. And when you knit with other people, the loop going around your needles also goes all the way around the room. You're knitting yourself together with all the knitters around you – joining hearts and minds…" I went through the rest of my little prepared speech about the wonderful benefits of knitting quite nicely and was pleased to see warm smiles on almost everyone's faces already. I'm sure you can guess who wasn't smiling. "And now," I said, "I think it's important that we all get to know each other better, after all, if my theory is correct, we will also be knitting ourselves together, so my lovely assistant, Natalie," and here Natalie presented herself with a cute little curtsy that had (almost) everyone chuckling, "is going to pass out nametags. If you could please put yours on, we will get started in just a moment." There was a general fluttering and shuffling as everyone grabbed a nametag and a Sharpie from Natalie. I grabbed the little garbage can that I had, very wisely, prepared before time, and went around from person to person to collect the little paper from the back, and also, to greet them by name. "Rebecca," I said warmly, "so glad you could come. I see you settled on the chocolate brown. That will match your hair so nicely." She beamed at me, and I continued around until I reached Mrs. Goldmyer, skipping nimbly past the glowering Louise, whom I presented with a nice big smile. "Good evening, Mrs. Goldm-" I stopped halfway through her name, caught in a sudden coughing fit while she looked at me with an expression between disgust and concern.

"I do hope you're quite alright, Molly," she said. "Please refrain from coughing on my yarn." I valiantly choked back another cough, "Perhaps some water?" she said crossly.

I fled, heading for the counter and the bottle of water that I usually kept hidden behind there. Natalie was close on my heels and waited impatiently for me to finish drinking before demanding to know what had happened.

I grabbed her arm, "Did you see?" I demanded. "I would never have guessed. Never."

She shook me a little, and a little hysterical giggle floated its way out, "Molly," she said sternly, "get a hold of yourself. What did you see?"

I took a deep breath, "I guess I never thought about it. I mean, I know I should have. Everyone has one, right? I just expected it to say 'Mrs. Goldmyer'. I never thought," I was babbling and I knew it, but somehow, couldn't stop. "I mean. I just never thought. If I had thought I would have said it would be something sensible and stern, like…"

She peered into my face anxiously. "Do you mean all of this is because you saw Mrs. Goldmyer's first name?" she demanded.

"Charity," I said, choking back another cough. "Her name is Charity." I took another deep swig of water, internally battened my hatches and left a gaping Natalie behind me as I returned to the group gathered around the big table.

The next step was to explain the pattern and how it was knit, which I don't think made sense to anyone and no one would remember later. Oh well. It was all part of the fun, I guess. After that, with the assistance of Natalie, I showed everyone how to cast on. I had decided to use the knitted cast on method, as it is almost the same technique as the knitting stitch, which, in my opinion, makes it easy to transition from casting on to knitting. Natalie and Louise both then began working their way around the circle to make sure everyone was "getting" it, while I also walked around to give pep talks and compliment others on their technique or offer inspiring words of advice. At least that's what I hoped to do. At one point, Louise very rudely shoved me aside as I was discussing the knit stitch with a very nice young lady named, "Kari".

"Let me show you how to do it," Louise insisted, effectively elbowing me even further out of the way (she has a very bony elbow). "You don't want to start off doing it wrong. It's very important to have a good, firm foundation of the basics without any confusion."

Kari colored a bit, "I think she was explaining it just fine," she protested.

"Of course Louise is right," I said graciously, smiling kindly at Kari. "You want to learn it right the first time. I'm sure Louise would love to sit right here and help you until you get it." Hee hee. That should keep Louise busy for a while. I left them to it, moving to stand behind Mrs. Goldmyer… Charity… there was no way in this world that I could ever call her that. Ever.

"How is it going, Mrs. Goldmyer?" I asked, leaning over to see her progress.

"Fine," she said shortly, her fingers moving confidently over her yarn. I had to steady myself with my good hand on her chair. The second surprise from the night – and from the same person.

"Gracious," I said, "it looks like you've done this before." She was already well through the cast on, had joined her yarn into a perfect circle with no twists and was knitting and purling her way through the border just fine.

She paused to look up at me, her eyes glinting strangely in the light. "I never said I hadn't," she said shortly. "I have known the fundamentals of knitting for years. I have simply chosen not to employ them."

I didn't quite know how to reply. "Perhaps beginning knitting wasn't the best choice for you then," I said slowly.

Her frown deepened, "This is the class you and your friend strongly recommended to me," she said. "So this is what I took. Is there a problem?"

I smiled brightly, "Of course not." And then I moved quickly on to the next person, but not before catching Natalie's eye. She shook her head in bewilderment, and I shrugged with one shoulder. Just when you thought things couldn't get stranger… they did.

We were now halfway through the class. Everyone had cast on and learned how to knit and purl and were working their way, somewhat laboriously, through the ribbing at the bottom. There was complete silence around the table, the only sound that of sliding needles and the noise of uncertain knitters chanting and counting under their breath, "Knit One, Purl One."

Only Mrs. Goldmyer and Louise seemed immune from the tension of the beginning knitters. Louise, finally happy that everyone was doing fine, eventually settled in the chair next to Mrs. Goldmyer, pulling out her own knitting confidently. "How are you, Charity?" she asked.

Mrs. Goldmyer did not stop knitting, she just nodded at Louise, "Fine, Louise. How's your mother?"

Well. Who knew these two were buddies? Perhaps that explained a lot. A lot.

Louise's little twig face folded up into a grimace, "She's fine. Cranky as ever." Huh. Imagine that. A cranky woman in her family. Both women chortled briefly as if some shared joke passed between them. "And Faith? Is she still a nurse?"

Mrs. Goldmyer rolled her eyes, "Why my sister seems to love soothing fevered brows and contaminating herself with all of those germs is completely beyond my comprehension." Her fingers twirled through another set of ribbing stitches perfectly.

I lost track of their conversation for a few moments. My mind was whirling. Faith. Charity. What was missing? Why did that sound familiar? I stood, smiling at all of the ladies and announced a brief pause in knitting for a well-deserved snack break. There was a massive run on the brownies and chocolate chip cookies, and I found myself behind Mrs. Goldmyer in line for some of Carolyn's famous punch, somehow surprised that she would condescend to eat snacks. Charity, I still couldn't believe it - such a sweet name. I wondered what she was like as a child. I tried to imagine her with little braids and a toothless smile, playing dolls with her sister… Little Charity… and little Faith. A lightning bolt whacked me upside the head. Of course! Faith, hope and charity – you know – from the Bible. "And now these three things remain, faith, hope and love. But the greatest of these is love." (In the Bible – that's I Corinthians 13:13 – just in case you're wondering – or you don't believe me.). In some of the older versions, charity was used instead of the word love. There had to be three sisters then, right? I'd be willing to bet that Mrs. Goldmyer also had a sister named "Hope." Wow. I was really smart. I congratulated myself on my brilliant detective work and sat my punch glass carefully down at the knitting table again, as the ladies all returned, balancing plates of goodies with their knitting.

Finally. This could be a great way to break the ice and start building a communication bridge with Mrs. Goldmyer. Then, I could really start pumping her for information.

"And do you have a sister named Hope, too?" I asked, smiling my friendliest smile.

Mrs. Goldmyer froze. Louise froze. The moment was so uncomfortable that Natalie's head whipped around to see what was causing the frost to grow and stretch across the table. It only lasted a moment until Louise replied, "I don't know where you get these ridiculous ideas, Molly," she said, "but could we please stick to knitting?"

My cheeks grew warm, but I wasn't sure why. I had obviously stumbled across a subject Mrs. Goldmyer didn't want to talk about. Perhaps Hope was the… excuse the pun… black sheep of the family? It was Kari who came to my rescue, bless her little beginning knitter heart. "I'm the first person in my family to learn to knit," she admitted. "Except for my grandmother." She made a sad face, "She knitted so beautifully. I wished I had been smart enough to ask her to teach me."

Natalie was quick to embrace the subject change, "Is your grandmother no longer with us?" she inquired gently. "I'm so sorry."

Kari shook her head and looked down at the yarn on her needles, "I wish she could see me now," she said softly. "She would have been so happy."

"Oh, she can see you," someone said.

Holy cow. I think it was Mrs. Goldmyer.

"Do you think so?" Kari asked eagerly. "What a beautiful thought."

Mrs. Goldmyer was staring at her strangely, "I'm not sure if it's beautiful," she said, "to know that you're always being watched by dead people."

Kari's smile began slipping just a bit. "What makes you think that those who have already passed on watch over us?" The question came from Rebecca, who was looking faintly disturbed. I knew the feeling.

"It's in the Bible," Mrs. Goldmyer said simply. "If you don't believe it, that's up to you, but it's in there, and whether or not you believe it you're always being watched."

"I think it's true that God is with us every moment," I said, trying to recapture the situation, "however, I'm not so sure the Bible says...."

The look passed from Mrs. Goldmyer's face and she looked around the table at the faces currently staring at her. "My goodness," she said, and for the first time that I had ever seen she looked nervous, "I certainly didn't mean to make anyone uncomfortable," she said stiffly. "I would think that it would be a great comfort to know that your grandmother is watching over you," and here she actually tried to smile kindly at Kari. Kari, who did not have the past history that I did with Mrs. Goldmyer, unexpectedly smiled back.

"Of course," she said, quite happy to leave the awkwardness. "It is a beautiful thought." A little dimple popped out in her cheek, "I'm not sure I believe it though."

The rest of the ladies twittered nervously and resumed knitting.

I was helping Carolyn tidy up the store, picking up used cups and paper plates. "I think everything went perfectly tonight," Carolyn said happily. "I knew you'd be so great at this." I was not convinced. After all, it had taken me, Natalie and Louise just to get through the first class. I was almost glad that I had broken my arm. I seriously don't know how I would have handled that if I had been on my own.

The yarn store glowed cozily from the lights of a dozen or so lamps around the store, as I had just begun the process of turning them off. "I'm not so sure, Carolyn," I objected. "I feel really weird about the whole thing."

She frowned, pausing as her hand reached for the last scrap of yarn on the table. "Why would you say that?" she asked. "Everyone had cast on nicely and were well on their way to knitting the main body of the hat."

I sighed and sank down onto one of the chairs. "I don't know," I confessed. "Maybe it was just really strange to have Mrs. Goldmyer in the class."

Her mouth twisted in sympathy, and she took a chair next to me, patting my hand sympathetically. "You always handle yourself well – even when others don't."

If only that were true. I opened my mouth to make a flippant remark to end the conversation, but to my humiliation, two tears rolled down my face.

Carolyn looked surprised, wrapping me up in a sudden hug. She likes to do that. It usually made me super uncomfortable, however, tonight… I was thankful for it. I hugged her back, as well as I could one-armed. She pulled back, wiping away another tear. "What is it, my dear?" she asked. "What's troubling you?"

You would think that this would have been the perfect time to discuss the book or Ryan or something even remotely relevant, wouldn't you? I don't know what made me say, "Mrs. Goldmyer says that the people who die watch us from heaven," and I was appalled to hear my sentence end with a slight sob. I took a wobbly breath and pulled away from Carolyn, trying to regain my composure.

Her face puckered into a million wrinkles. "She did?" She was silent for a long moment, while I wiped my eyes. She raised troubled eyes to mine. "And this bothers you?" I tried shrugging, but something in her eyes made me nod my head.

"Why?" she asked softly, her eyes glowing in the soft light.

I shook my head, unable to speak. The silence lengthened between us, and I made a movement to get up. Maybe we could pretend that this never happened. She reached out unexpectedly and grabbed my hand in a surprisingly strong grip. "We haven't really known each other that long, have we, Molly?" I shook my head. It would be all too easy to tell her everything. I tried pulling away, but she held firm. "I'm sure that there are things in your past that you would rather forget." She smiled sadly, "Just like me. Just like everyone." Tears trickled down my face again, and she leaned forward, a new look in her eyes. "But just because something horrible happened doesn't mean it has to control your life forever."

"B-but," I protested.

"Do you believe in God?" Carolyn asked. I nodded firmly. "I know you do. It's evident to everyone that you have a relationship with Him. You grow the fruit of the Spirit so easily – love, joy, patience," she paused reflectively, "but I think you're missing out on peace." She looked me in the eye, "What was the whole point of Jesus coming to earth?" she asked.

I squirmed, but she held firm. I knew where she was going, and I didn't really want to hear it. She waited. I sighed, "Forgiveness of our sins so that we can be right with God."

She smiled, "So if you believe that God has forgiven your sins, how could anything in your past still haunt you?"

I blinked back tears, "But that's not what you said," I replied.

She looked confused. "What? When?"

"When we were talking about secrets. You said 'look for the person with the secrets to be someone who is starting over. But you can't really start over because the ghosts always follow you forever and ever and you can never lose them.'"

She released my hand in order to put it behind my back, pulling me closer. Somehow, my head found its way to her shoulder. "I don't think that's exactly how I said it," she said softly, I could feel her smile against my hair, "and I should have known better to say something like that to an over-thinker like you."

"Even if you didn't say it you would still have thought it," I mumbled. "That's the same thing."

"It is not," she argued, "and it's not what I meant." She pulled away so that she could look me in the eye. "When you run away from something, it will follow you." She wiped a tear away gently. "But, when you confront something and ask for forgiveness, it's over. God forgives you. You can have peace again. I promise."

"I can't have peace," I wailed. "Not..."

She looked suddenly fierce, "Yes. You can."

"You don't know what…"

Carolyn shook her white head, "It doesn't matter what you did, or what you think you did or what happened. If you ask for God's forgiveness, He will forgive you and you will find peace if you accept that forgiveness."

I grabbed her hand frantically. She didn't understand. "But how can I have peace when there are other people who…"

She sighed and pulled me into another hug, "Oh, Molly," she said in an anguished voice, "I'm so sorry. I never realized you were suffering so much." She clutched me tighter. "I'm so sorry. It is true. When we hurt other people, it lasts a long time. But you can't live with guilt every day of your life. God doesn't want that for you. That's what I'm trying to tell you. The only way to find healing is to pray, believe God and then let it go."

"But how?" I sobbed. "How can you just…"

"Listen," she said, "I've hurt people by what I've done in the past. And, I'll be honest. If I let it, if I let myself remember… it still hurts me." She took a long, shuddering breath, "But I don't let it. It's wrong to let it. If you've asked for forgiveness, then you are forgiven. It's a gift. I don't deserve it. You don't deserve it. That's what makes it a gift. A gift from God. But it's just like any gift," she pulled away and stared at me hard. "You have to accept it."

She held my gaze for a long time until I could get my composure under control. "I don't know how," I finally whispered.

Her eyes filled with tears, too, "It's only hard because it's so easy," she said softly. "Stop torturing yourself. Forcing yourself to stay feeling guilty doesn't help anyone. I don't know why it's so human of us to think that keeping yourself miserable can somehow atone for past mistakes." She shook her head sadly, "That path only makes you bitter and miserable." She pulled me in for one last hug before standing up abruptly, "Now, knock it off, young lady," she said with mock sternness. "Be the first person in the history of the world to listen to your elders and save yourself years of misery by learning from my mistakes."

She kissed me on the head, eyes still watery, adjusted her sweater and proceeded to empty the last trashcan. I watched her, unable to move. Was she right? Was it hard because it was so easy?

CHAPTER 14

N atalie had us packed into Mr. Darcy like well-dressed little sardines. Rose held the place of honor in the front seat and she presided over the event in her most queenly fashion, from directing the rest of us on an appropriate seating arrangement to advising Natalie on the best route to the wedding dress store. Natalie was, for once, being amazingly obedient – even slowing down for the pedestrians in the crosswalk. I may have remarked on this astounding behavior, which earned me a scorching look in the rearview mirror.

There really was not much room in the back seat. I sat perched in the middle, trying not to slide to the left or the right whenever the car curved around a corner and holding my casted arm firmly in my lap so as not to hit anyone with it as we went around another aforementioned corner on two wheels. Abigail sighed and cracked her window. She was sulking just a bit, as she had vied quite hard for the front seat honor. She was now insisting that car sickness was her fatal enemy and making suggestive noises. Abigail was a consummate actress who loved to play whatever role she was in to the hilt…I dearly hoped she would not resort to actually being sick in the back seat just to prove her point. She moaned a little and closed her eyes, placing one wrinkled hand against her brow heavily. Celia wiggled a little more to the left to get her rear even closer to her door. I promptly followed her, giving Abigail even more room, which left me practically sitting on poor Celia's lap. Celia groaned. Abigail cracked one eye open, and seeing our position, abruptly changed her mood and giggled. "You two look so silly," she said and pulled on my right arm with a surprisingly firm grip. "Get your little tush over here." She lowered her voice, "Rose wouldn't have nearly so much fun being extra special in the front seat if she didn't think I wanted to be there, too."

Celia snorted and rolled her eyes, "You two," she said, "are just like three-year-olds."

Abigail patted my knee, "So, honey," she began, "the police still haven't come up with anything?"

It was my turn to sigh, "No, they haven't. If someone was there, they got out through the upstairs apartment door after I fell. The police can't find any evidence…"

Abigail smacked herself in the forehead, causing both me and Celia to jump a little, "Now there's a surprise," she said. "You know what I ought to do is just get involved. I think with a little brainpower and digging we could get to the bottom of this in no time."

Gracious heavens. That was the last thing I needed -for Abigail to throw herself in whatever crosshairs I had. It's a good thing Natalie and I never shared our suspicions about the "Axe Murderer of Springiegate" with anyone. "Nonsense," I said firmly, "the police are doing everything they can. I have complete faith in them."

Celia flipped her long blond hair which was currently plaited into an elaborate braid over her shoulder, "I'm sure," she said with a sniff, "that you're right, Abigail. Why the police can't take anything serious just because knitters happen to be involved is beyond me." She paused thoughtfully, "Although, it does seem a little peculiar that so many strange things happen to knitters that don't seem to happen to normal people."

And that was the end of that. Quite a loud argument erupted over that last statement of whether or not being a knitter made you abnormal. I don't know what their problem is. I certainly didn't want to be normal. How boring.

We made it home just as darkness fell, everyone completely happy and completely stuffed. We had stopped at a delicious little steakhouse on the way home and had eaten way too much. Natalie had tentatively suggested the organic restaurant that we had tried to eat at before, but she was emphatically outvoted. Thank goodness. The trip had been a resounding success. The dress was heartily approved of, and, not only that, but the shop also sold "regular" dresses, so Rose and Abigail had each also purchased a dress for the occasion. As Maid of Honor (and the only attendant for Natalie), my dress was also selected in a lovely shade of steely blue. I believe that normally bridesmaids and such are usually disappointed in their dresses, but mine was just perfect... with an empire waist, long flowing skirt, lacey sleeves and an embroidered bodice, it was beautiful. I just hoped my cast was off in time for the wedding. It really didn't do much for the dress.

"How strange," Rose remarked, bringing my attention back to Raspberry Hill. The house was awash in light and activity.

"What is going on here?" Natalie spoke for all of us as she locked Mr. Darcy carefully before shutting the door. There must have been 20 cars, if not more, parked rather haphazardly all over what we used as a parking lot, "Who are all these people?"

The door to the house opened and Abraham Lincoln came flying out. As we approached the steps leading up to the front of the house, he moved to the top of the stairs. His ugly little fur stood completely out around his neck and head and he stared at us with a malevolence that we could all feel, his black eyes almost seeming to glow in the dim light. We were...rather reluctant to approach the stairs.

In the end, Rose was the bravest. She put one foot up on the first step, and Abraham Lincoln's lip curled back from his face, "Grrrr..." She put her foot back on solid ground.

"Oh no," I said. "We're locked out of the house."

Natalie looked worried. "I don't think we're going to make it past him," she said speaking in a low voice so that Abraham Lincoln could not hear. "Maybe we should go around to the back of the house and see if one of those doors are open."

Abraham Lincoln bristled even more, moving so that he stood at the very end of the top step, his eyes boring into Abigail's.

"Oh!" Abigail said. "I do believe someone has forgotten to feed poor Mr. Abraham Lincoln." She turned her full attention on the little furball, "Is that right, my little baby?" she crooned. "Did that mean ol' Jack forget to feed you?"

Abraham Lincoln blinked in what could only be relief. He plunked down, twisting his body so that he could give himself a good lick down as we now freely walked up the stairs.

"I can't believe it," Natalie said with disgust. "He was actually holding us hostage out of our own house. We need to get that dog trained with some manners."

Rose scooped up the suddenly pliant and winsome Abraham Lincoln who obligingly curled himself over her shoulder. "I'll just go get this little guy's supper ready," she said. "I think it was very clever of him to tell us what he needed." She patted his little rump as she walked away, and the expression on Abraham Lincoln's face as he rode triumphantly on the top of her shoulder could only be described as smug.

Natalie and Celia exchanged identical looks of amusement. "She's your grandmother," Celia said. "I don't know what to say."

Natalie's face darkened, "Yeah," she agreed, "and it probably runs in the family so you'll probably turn out just like her."

Celia gasped and pretended to pull a dagger from her heart, "My own daughter," she moaned dramatically, "thinking such horrible thoughts."

Jack came into the hall looking more than a bit frazzled. "Hey girls," he said, giving Natalie a quick kiss, "the Amelda Tartan Welcome Committee had to move their meeting here because it was against fire code to have that many people in the back room of the pub." He shrugged helplessly. "They called and asked if they could come… I didn't know what to do, so I said it would be fine, and I would make snacks… but there's like 50 of them in there and they're all arguing and fighting over what flavor of cake to offer Amelda Tartan, and I've got apple tarts in the oven that need to come out and…"

"Say no more," Natalie said. "You go rescue the apple tarts; I'll go settle the natives down. Celia, you go see if everything is set up for snacks and drinks, and Abigail…"

"Hey," Abigail protested, "don't give me a job. I already have one."

"Oh yeah?" Natalie said, eyeing her critically. "What's that?"

Abigail made her eyes big and innocent. "Security."

So, that's how it happened that while everyone else was running around making themselves useful, Abigail and I snuck into the back of the meeting to watch democracy in action.

"Aren't you supposed to have rules for when people talk and have the floor?" Abigail whispered, obviously enjoying the goat rodeo of a meeting. I shrugged helplessly. These were not the kinds of things I liked to see. Everyone should be working together to make this a great event, and not fighting. What a total waste of time. And somehow disappointing.

Carolyn was suddenly standing at my elbow and she gave me a tight smile. "I'm starting to think that this wasn't such a good idea," she said, looking more worried than I had seen her in a long time.

"Oh, but Carolyn," I protested, "it's such an honor to have her here. I just can't wait to meet her. She's practically a hero to me..."

Carolyn gave me a hard look, "You shouldn't put people up on pedestals, my dear," she said. "No one can live on one." She softened when she saw my face, "And how's your entry coming for the contest?" she asked kindly, more like the Carolyn I was used to seeing.

My cheeks heated just a bit, "I think I'm giving up on that," I said. "I don't think I was meant to be a writer. There's too much going on."

She frowned at me, "I think that's a mistake," she said. "You seemed to really enjoy writing. Don't give up on it just because it's getting a little hard. You know what they say..."

I didn't know. So, even though knowing the answer wasn't something I wanted to hear, I was forced to say, "What?"

"The road to success is paved with many tempting parking spaces."

The only way to answer that one was to stick out my tongue. Which I did.

"Alright," said the gentleman up front with the gavel (what he was going to bang it on, I had no idea). "Alright. That's enough". He brought the gavel down hard on the marble column next to him, which really made hardly any noise, but made my blood boil.

"Hey!" I yelled.

Strangely enough, my outraged cry caught the attention of the crowd. Oh. Oh dear. All eyes were on me. I heard Carolyn snicker. I cleared my throat. "Please respect the property," I said simply, trying my best to remember how to smile, "and don't use your gavel on the marble."

The man had the politeness to look embarrassed, and he lowered his gavel with a sigh, "I apologize," he said stiffly, "and now that I have your attention, let's try this again." A collective sigh could be heard through the whole crowd.

For some reason, the man stayed staring at me, "You look confused," he said. "Is there something about this that you don't understand?" He used the handle of the gavel to rub the back of his head, fluffing his white hair adorably.

"I'm sorry," I said, "I don't really belong in here, as I'm not on the committee." Something like a warning bell began clanging in my head, so I took a step discretely back towards the door.

His face lit up, "A fresh opinion!" he exclaimed. "Just what we need. Come right on up here, little lady."

A fresh opinion. Yeah, right. I was fresh meat. Listen to me, my friends…this is what happens when you go to meetings where you don't belong. There was no way out. In less than 10 seconds, I found myself up on the improvised platform at the front with the white-haired man who turned out to be the Mayor, Mr. Loring. He shook my hand heartily. Evidently, he thought I was his ticket out of here tonight. Boy, was he going to be wrong. "Now, Molly," he said, "our biggest problem here is we are trying to decide two things: What to serve and how to entertain our guests at the Amelda Tartan Celebration. What do you suggest?"

He looked at me expectantly.

The crowd looked at me expectantly.

How do I get myself into these situations?

I opened my mouth to speak and only a croak came out. I tried again. "Well," I said, "what have you discussed so far?" Ooohhh. That was a wise remark, right? Totally bought me some time.

The mayor rolled his eyes, "We haven't made it past what to serve," he admitted. "Some of us think a full dinner would be appropriate, considering the importance of the event, while others rather strongly maintain that such a cost would bankrupt us and be totally and completely uncalled for and think that cake and punch would be entirely appropriate and sufficient." Hmmm… I wonder which side he was on.

I nodded thoughtfully. The crowd tensed and shifted restlessly. This could get ugly fast. I scanned the room looking for inspiration, and to my surprise saw Ryan standing towards the middle. He smiled proudly at me. I couldn't help smile back, my heart suddenly inspired.

"Why don't you do dinner-like hors-d'oeuvres with bite-sized desserts instead of a cake? That way you can have the best of both worlds, and you won't have to worry about what flavor of cake to get, because you can do all sorts of flavors. Just in small bites." I smiled to myself, remembering the delivery of bite-sized desserts from Ryan's bakery that had officially started our relationship. I met his eyes again, and I knew he was thinking the same thing. I just loved the way his eyes crinkled.

The mayor was staring at me quizzically, the crowd surprisingly quiet. "I like the idea of hors-d'oeuvres," he said, "and I like the idea of bite-sized desserts, but I'm not quite sure that the deli/bakery can handle those at the supermarket…"

"I can do it," a loud voice said. I looked to see Ryan coming my way. "I would love to. I'll send you over a cost estimate tomorrow."

The mayor looked inordinately relieved. "Done," he said, reaching down and shaking Ryan's hand. The crowd erupted into applause. "Now, what about entertainment?"

"I'm not sure that's my specialty," I murmured, backing delicately away. I think I had done enough, don't you? The mayor, however, did not think so and gripped my good hand to keep me from leaving.

"Oh, come now," he said. "I was totally right that we needed fresh eyes on this. Just look at what we've accomplished so far. Now, for entertainment, we were thinking about a re-enactment of a few scenes."

"A re-enactment?" I said hesitantly, "Do you mean like a play? With sets and lights and costumes…"

He nodded heartily, and the crowd began a low murmur again, "Exactly," he said. "It's just what we need."

"But doesn't that kind of thing take a lot of planning and time?" I asked.

"That's right, you old beanpole," someone yelled from the crowd. "We don't have time for that!"

There was a swell of agreement. I risked a look at Ryan again, who shrugged his shoulders helplessly. He was going to be no help at all with this one, wasn't he? I wondered what it would look like when the crowd swamped the little platform and gobbled us up. Would there be bones left… or nothing at all?

"Who is going to write the plays?" a blond lady with extremely red lipstick yelled. "You can't just read them out of the book, you know, it has to be re-written."

She was a genius. "What a great idea," I said, causing the blond lady to glare at me.

Before I could hastily continue my thought, someone else said, "How about instead of a re-enactment, we have people read their favorite passages?" Wow. That was a really good idea. It was actually my idea, but it had come from… I swallowed my disbelief, Mrs. Goldmyer. How had I missed her before? She stood like a crane in the middle of a flock of seagulls, ramrod straight and serene in her own self-importance.

To my amazement, I agreed with her verbally, "That's a really good idea." A thought occurred to me, "And if they wanted to, they could dress up like their favorite character while they read it."

The mayor pulled a handkerchief from deep within his trouser pocket and mopped his face with it, "That's a fine idea, girls," he said. "You two can be in charge of that. It's very fitting. Very fitting. After all, what could be a finer way to show Amelda how much we love her than by reading our favorite passages. An excellent idea. So, if you two would figure out how that will work, that would be fine. You can have 35 minutes of the program for that. Please be sure it runs like clockwork. For those of you who would like to sign up to read a passage, please contact Mrs. Goldmyer at the library and they will be in contact with you with further instructions."

The mayor looked very pleased with himself, and I have a feeling that he now thought everything was his own idea. He shooed me off the stage and right into the vicinity of Mrs. Goldmyer, who did not look particularly thrilled with this turn of events. "Now," he said authoritatively, "we've taken care of the food and most of the entertainment. After the reading of the passages, we will have a brief presentation in which we will give Amelda Tartan the keys to the city and then we will have the winner announced in the Amelda Tartan contest, after which he/she will read a portion of their story. Copies of the winning story will be handed out to everyone for their full reading enjoyment in the final moments of the party, at which time, Amelda will reveal her latest book and sign copies for anyone who would like to purchase one." And, with that, the meeting was over.

"I'll expect you tomorrow at 1:00 p.m.," Mrs. Goldmyer said.

The only thing left for everyone else to do was eat Jack's apple tarts and go home. Let this be a lesson to you, my friends. Don't ever crash a committee meeting. Not unless you want more things to do.

CHAPTER 15

I met Mrs. Goldmyer at her requested appointed time right on the dot. Which, apparently, was the exact wrong thing to do. "Civilized people do not come flying in the door at the last possible moment, Ms. Stevenson," she said icily. "Civilized people are present and ready to begin at the appointed time."

She was just such a… such a … knitpicker. I giggled to myself. Yes, that was right. She was a born knitpicker. Never happy with anything. No one was ever good enough. A real knitpicker.

"Have you heard a thing I said?" she asked, with a greatly affected sigh, tapping her fingers against the beautiful counter with annoyance.

I had to admit that I hadn't. Because, if I had, she would have asked me to repeat it, word for word. And, since I had been busy thinking of her as a knitpicker, I couldn't possibly do that, now could I? If only I were braver and could tell her that I think she was just a big ol' knitpicker.

"I will collect the names of everyone who would like to read and which passage they would like to read. The deadline to do so will be next Friday at Noon. After that, you will take the list of names, make sure that no one is doing the same passage, check the passages for appropriateness, arrange them in some sort of coherent order and then make a schedule of performers, alert them to their performance time, perhaps have a small rehearsal the evening before and make sure we do not go over our allotted time."

Wow. The division of labor had been equally divided, hadn't it? I almost added, "And don't forget to give you all of the credit and none to me, right?" but I didn't. I wasn't brave enough.

I meekly agreed to her terms and left the library with the same sense of relief that I'm sure a mouse feels when they've seen a cat and escaped back through their hole in the wall. If I was lucky I wouldn't have to see her again until the next class.

I was that lucky. I didn't see her until class time. About halfway through the week, I thought about calling to see how many people had signed up, but the chicken in me decided against it. As a result, my week went rather smoothly. Right up until class time.

The knitters came bustling in – right on the dot. It was interesting how they never really came early. Not even Mrs. Goldmyer.

"Good evening, Kari," I said. "How did it go?"

Her cheeks were flushed becomingly from the brisk air outside, and she quickly removed her coat, sitting down at the table and proudly pulled her knitting out from her bag. She had done all of the required "homework" and was ready to keep going. I praised her work, making her eyes glow, and my heart glowed right with it. Maybe Carolyn was right. Being a teacher was rewarding. Sometimes. Mrs. Goldmyer came in and sat down at the table across from me. "And how did it go for you, Mrs. Goldmyer?" I asked.

With an irritated sigh, she pulled her finished hat out of her knitting bag and flopped it on the table. "You're done?" I squeaked. Uh-oh. This wasn't in the instruction booklet. What was I supposed to do with a student who finished her work by the 2nd class? And, we still had one more class after this. I reached across the table to pick it up and examine it, hoping for a fatal flaw that would justify me telling her to start over. I know. That's not nice. It was, of course, perfect.

"Wow," Kari said, her expression obviously impressed, "that's beautiful. You're an amazing knitter."

To my astonishment, Mrs. Goldmyer's cheeks colored, just a bit. "Thank you," she said stiffly.

Huh. Maybe that's all she needed. Love and encouragement. I smiled warmly, "Kari's right," I said. "This is just so beautiful. You've done an excellent job. It's perfect."

She snatched it back from me. "I'm going to give it to the school in case there is a child in need," she said, "unless you'd like to keep it to replace the class sample? I noticed there were a few points in your hat that could be improved upon."

Love and encouragement my foot. I opened my mouth to reply, but Natalie beat me to it, "That's a very kind offer, but we are completely satisfied with our class sample."

I forced myself to remember my manners. It wasn't easy. "What would you like to knit now?" I asked. "You still have two classes left." Knowing her, she probably wanted me to show her how to knit an intarsia sweater with embroidery thread.

She pulled a new skein of yarn out of her knitting bag. "I doubt there is anything I need to learn from you, Molly," she said. "I will content myself with repeating these same instructions and knitting for the less fortunate."

"I'm sure the less fortunate will feel the love you have knitted into every stitch," I said, hoping that I sounded sincere.

The other knitters had all filtered in. The only person we were missing was Louise, who had decided not to come tonight, claiming she had a headache and that she wouldn't be needed anyways now that everyone knew what they were doing. Which, of course, implied that without her last week, no one would know what they were doing.

"So," I said, "let's see how we did last week. Did everyone get their homework completed?"

To my surprise, only Kari and Jennie, a shy young lady with brown hair and large brown eyes, had finished their required knitting to go on to the next step. What was up with that? I mean, if you were going to take a class, wouldn't you finish your homework? The others were either still working on getting there, or, in Rebecca's case, going to have to start over.

Natalie got Kari and Jennie started on the next step, the others started doing what they should have had already done, and I settled in next to Rebecca to see what she had done wrong. I picked up her knitting, turning it over and over in my hands in wonderment. How could someone get their knitting so messed up?

I looked across the room to where Carolyn and Rachel sat with their heads together working on their new patterns. She gave me a smirk. Obviously, this was not something new to her. Oh well. I examined Rebecca's piece again, as she waited expectantly. There had to be something positive to say. My job was not only to teach but to encourage. The only problem was there was nothing encouraging about her knitting. Not only was their no ribbing to speak of, as she had not, it seemed, bothered to knit one, purl one, but rather, knitted and purled in merry abandonment, but there were also dropped stitches, some sticking their little heads out halfway down the knitting while others had run to the bottom never to be seen or heard from again. She had also managed to twist her circle, so that it was no longer a circle, but a twisted figure eight. How had she done this? Last week when she left she was doing so good.

I stopped my examining of her knitting to look her in the face, "I can tell," I said slowly, "that you are going to be a great knitter."

Her face dropped. I paused. That was a strange reaction. "How can you tell?" she asked warily.

"Because you're going to have so much practice," I said with a grin.

She grinned back. "Is that your way of telling someone they need to start over?"

"I'm afraid it is," I said, "but first, let's talk about what happened here." And we began, patiently, going over the fundamentals of knit and purl one more time. "Let's just practice doing knit one, purl one for a little bit on your knitting right now so that when you start over, you'll be able to do it perfectly."

She agreed with me that this was a wise idea, and I watched her carefully for a few moments. "Ahhh," I said, "I believe I see where you went wrong. When you go from a knit to a purl stitch, remember you have to move your yarn to the front of the needle."

"Oh," she said, embarrassed, "I keep forgetting that. Then I get these extra loops, which were making my hat too big so I just shoved them off."

That certainly explained the amount of dropped stitches. "That was very wise of you to realize that you had too many stitches," I said brightly, "and now you'll know why you had too many stitches so that won't happen again."

I caught Mrs. Goldmyer looking at me, and she hastily returned her eyes to her knitting. I'd probably hear about all the ways I could improve my teaching later. I could hardly wait.

"Hello, Mother," a low voice said. "I've come for your hat."

Mrs. Goldmyer looked up, her face, transforming in an instant from a knitpicking knitpicker to proud mother. I couldn't help but stare. She was so different when she smiled. "I have it right here," she said. She looked around the table, "I wanted to show it to you before I donated it," she said with a slight sniff, "otherwise you might not believe I had finished it." There was a titter of laughter from the ladies around the table. "And my son is headed to the school tonight and said he would drop it off."

Nathaniel was certainly dressed well for an appointment at the school. His navy blue overcoat fit like it had been tailored just for him, his hair curling nicely around the collar. In his hands, he held two cups of something that steamed and smelled delicious.

"Whew," a soft voice next to me said. "What a cutie." I rolled my eyes at Rebecca who was smiling as she leaned back down to study her knitting pattern.

A cup suddenly appeared in front of me. I looked up in wonderment to find Nate's eyes on me, "Hot chocolate," he said, "with whipped cream for you and straight up for my mother." His smile was his most dazzling, "I know you love hot chocolate, so it didn't seem right not to bring you some, too. After all, you're the teacher… now, Mother can be Teacher's Pet." His smile turned wicked.

"Thank you," I stammered, surprised. It did look delicious.

"It's so cold in here," Mrs. Goldmyer said, "that I asked Nathaniel to bring me something warm when he came."

My gaze flew indignantly to hers and then to Nate's who rolled his eyes and shrugged good-naturedly. He took the hat from his mother, teased Jennie about the color of her yarn and left in a cloud of expensive cologne. I wondered what type of meeting at the school could he be possibly going to… and then I decided I probably did not want to know.

Mrs. Goldmyer took a hearty sip of her hot chocolate, eyes closing in pleasure. I had a very strong urge to accidentally dump mine on her lap, having no desire to drink the delicious concoction of melting whipped cream and chocolate fragrantly steaming under my nose now. She was really a total and complete toad.

I turned to help Sarah, to my right, with her first decrease for a moment, so that I didn't have to look at her. This could have been such a nice little beginning knitting class. What if her attitude was rubbing off on everyone else? That happened, you know. Negativity is highly contagious. These new knitters may never knit again… all because… Rebecca pulled on my sleeve to show me her first round of perfect ribbed stitches, which I praised highly. "I think he likes you," she whispered, eyes glowing. "I could tell."

"Who?" I whispered innocently, heart thumping uncomfortably. "Nathaniel?" She nodded enthusiastically. "No," I said firmly, "I don't think so." I certainly hoped not.

"Whatever you say," she said gleefully. "But I saw the way he looked at you." She nodded at my cup, "Do you really love hot chocolate?" I bobbed my head. "Then I'd drink that if I were you, why let her nastiness win? After all," she lowered her voice even further, "she'd be lucky to have a daughter-in-law like you."

"Stop it," I hissed, "I don't like him. It's not like that at all." But I took a hesitant sip of my hot chocolate anyways, after all, Rebecca was right – why let the knitpicker ruin the happiness of my taste buds? She knew hot chocolate was my favorite, and that was probably her way of keeping me from enjoying it. It was just like her.

"Ahhh," I said blissfully. "And now, everyone, please go help yourself to a snack break as well." It would be rude to drink this in front of my class when they had nothing, wouldn't it? Everyone except Kari dove for the snack table. Jack and Ryan kept us well supplied with delicious treats, which they now knew.

"I hope they save me some," Kari said, concentration lining her face as she kept her eyes trained on her knitting. "I just want to get through the decrease row."

I assured her that there was plenty and kept her company while she counted and I sipped. Maybe I was wrong. Positivity could be just as catchy as negativity. Mrs. Goldmyer was certainly outvoted on that. Maybe these knitters would change her instead of her changing them. I watched as Carolyn and Mrs. Goldmyer accidentally crossed paths in front of the counter, neither acknowledging the other. Then again, maybe people can't really ever change.

Rebecca was the first to return. She wasn't exactly someone that you would think was built for speed, but somehow she had made it to the head of the line. I looked down with interest at her chocolate chip cookie, also one of my favorites, but my stomach rolled uncomfortably at the sight. Strange. Oh! Something hot and greasy was floating in my stomach. Sara set her plate of goodies down next to me, and the smell of warm cinnamon confirmed the nausea that was rising slowly but steadily. It twisted like an ugly beast through my torso and up my throat. Not trusting myself to say anything, I rose and made my way hastily towards the only place I wanted to be at the moment. The bathroom. I only made it as far as the hallway, throwing up everything I had ever eaten into the poor, helpless, umbrella stand.

"Oh my dear," a soft voice said, "just hold on."

The umbrella stand was wrenched away from me and replaced with a stronger feeling trashcan. I used that as well, too sick to even be embarrassed when I moaned in misery.

"Is she sick?" an appalled voice asked. Great. What was Mrs. Goldmyer doing out in the hallway?

"If you could just give us a moment, we would appreciate it." I had never loved the smooth voice of Celia more. "Rose, could you go find Jack, please." And to me, "You poor thing," she soothed. "Just hang on. You'll feel better soon."

But I did not feel better soon. The misery lasted for another hour, even after Jack carried me upstairs to my room, I was repeatedly sick until I could be sick no more, and then I could only lay helplessly on my bed shivering and huddled pathetically under the blankets until it either passed or I died. I didn't really care which happened.

"Do you think we should call a doctor?" It was the worried voice of Carolyn that brought me back to the land of the somewhat living. I cracked an experimental eye open. The sky outside my window was still dark, so it must still be the same night.

"Maybe," Celia whispered back. "I'll go call."

"I've already called." It was Rose, coming in and closing the door softly behind her. She crossed to my bed and placed a welcome, cool hand on my forehead. She noticed my eyes were open. "Hello," she said, eyes crinkling kindly, "welcome back."

I tried to say "Thank you," but it came out as "Uarbhlluuuuu…" and I stopped trying before I could embarrass myself any further. After tonight, I don't think it was even actually possible to embarrass myself further. Once you've thrown up in someone's umbrella stand, you've pretty much reached your limit, don't you think?

Carolyn and Celia crowded around the bed as well, Carolyn taking one of my cold hands in her warm one. She frowned. "Are you feeling any better?" she asked.

Still not trusting my voice, I did my best to nod, swallowing against the remaining nausea that the motion caused. Jack was suddenly standing next to Carolyn, and I blinked in surprise, wondering if I had dozed off or if he had magically appeared. He handed Carolyn a glass with something sparkly and rather clear– with a straw.

"Try a sip of this, my dear," she suggested, bringing the straw down to my level. And here I thought my humiliation couldn't get any worse. But, I did as she suggested and the ginger ale was immediately soothing to my unhappy stomach. I took a few more tentative sips. She set the glass on the small table next to my bed, within reaching distance, if I was up to reaching.

"Were you feeling ill at all earlier?" she asked. "You should have told me, and I would have taken over your class."

I cleared my throat gently, "I was fine," I said, my voice feeling gravelly and harsh, "until I wasn't."

Jack's face was dark, "I'm telling you," he said softly, "it was the hot chocolate." I opened my mouth to protest, but… he could be right. Everything happened right after drinking it. "And the proof is in the fact that his mother got rid of the evidence."

"What?" I gasped. Carolyn patted my hand while Celia gave Jack a scalding look.

"We can't prove a thing," she said in a conciliatory voice.

"We could if we still had the evidence," Jack said, "but by the time we thought of it, she had already cleaned it all up."

Rose cleared her throat delicately, "Well," she said, "Charity did also clean up everyone's snack plates and glasses, so that's hardly proof."

"Ha," Jack said.

"Ha," Carolyn said, and then looked ashamed of herself. "Excuse me," she said, "sometimes I let my feelings about Mrs. Goldmyer come out just a little bit strong. I'm sorry. The truth is, I don't believe either she or Nathaniel would poison your hot chocolate. I'm sure there's an entirely natural explanation for why you got sick."

"Ha," Jack said.

It was well into supper time of the next day before I felt truly well enough to attempt getting out of bed for anything other than the necessities of life. My stomach felt like it had been used as a piñata for particularly enthusiastic children, but it was no longer erupting or rejecting food, so I took that as a sign that the worst was officially over.

I drew myself a nice hot bath and, afterward, comfortably wrapped up in sweatshirt and jeans, I ventured downstairs. I could tell by the smells and the noises coming from the kitchen that they were just about to eat dinner. I wasn't quite up to that, so, I crept carefully and quietly down the hallway to the comfortable living room and curled up on the couch. My laptop was still sitting where I had left it the last time I had gotten the urge to write, and I opened the lid slowly, turning it on and typing in my password. I read and then re-read the opening to my Amelda Tartan story. Secrets. Maybe we had all had enough of them. I reached for the cordless phone that was next to me and, with fingers that shook just a little, dialed a familiar number. Tension coiled in my stomach as soon as I heard it ringing on the other line, but this time, the nausea was of my own making. I tightened my grip on the phone. It wasn't too late. I could just hang up. Just hang up and pretend that this never…

"Hello?"

I took a deep breath and tried to think what I should say. Maybe I should have planned this out better before I dialed.

"Hello?"

This was probably a big mistake.

"Hello? Is anyone there?"

Now was the time to hang up.

"Hi," I said softly, "it's Molly."

CHAPTER 16

"My goodness," Carolyn said, her fingers flying over her knitting, "you are certainly cheerful today."

I tidied the needle display absently, smiling happily at the sight of Carolyn perched on a stool next to me, knitting away on a chunky cowl meant as a present for Natalie. Of course, Natalie didn't know that. She thought Carolyn was making a store sample.

"I feel… lighter," I said, flipping a package of size 4 double points back to where they belonged. Why did people pick up needles and then put them back on the wrong hook?

"That would probably be the throwing up," Carolyn said mischievously, kicking her shoes off so she could tuck her feet around the rungs of the stool. She had on a denim skirt with a light purple sweater and purple and lilac-striped socks – hand knit socks, of course.

"Ugh," I groaned. "You promised you wouldn't talk about that."

She tilted her head, "No," she said, "I don't think I did." We giggled. She gave me a hard look. "I think I know what it is." That scared me into sobriety for a moment. Sometimes it was frightening the things that Carolyn knew. "I think you've finally realized that it's so easy and not hard anymore."

Any lingering customers would have no idea what she was talking about, so I put my needles down and hugged her, "Yes," I whispered in her ear, "I did." She squeezed me back. "I'm not saying it's all fixed or even better, but I feel like maybe I don't have to let it be the biggest thing in my life anymore."

"Good for you," she said. "Just keep giving it to God, and He'll do the healing."

She was right. God was doing the healing. I could feel it already. Last night, lying in bed and thinking things through, I had been swamped again by a familiar wave of guilt, although, this time… this time… it had felt like I was standing behind a tall rock and when the wave washed over my head, I was only a little damp – not completely soaked. Does that make sense?

I sighed and stepped back from Carolyn and the needle display, glancing around the spacious ballroom, at the yarn store and the adorable café that was half full of patrons even in the morning and my heart felt like it was literally going to crack from the beauty of it. "Sometimes," I said to Carolyn, "I feel like this is all so perfect."

She smiled, and slid off the stool, tapping me on the nose with her long, bony finger, "Sometimes," she said, "it is." She sauntered off to greet Mrs. Royston whose yarn delivery had come in yesterday. Mrs. Royston was going to start an Icelandic Fair Isle sweater with her special order yarn. This could be the beginning of a very close relationship with Mrs. Royston. As of today, she had only knit one scarf and one felted purse – and the felted purse had turned out the size of a wallet, so I'm not sure how well that boded for the sweater. Oh well. Everyone has to have a dream, right?

I crossed the yarn store, noting that all the customers were happily engaged in a yarn hunt or by the big bookcase of knitting books and settled in behind the counter. I examined the sign-up sheet for the Halloween party. Already over 100 people coming, and not just knitters, either. Ladies had invited their husbands and friends who obviously felt that a Halloween party at the somewhat haunted Raspberry Hill was something not to be missed. I almost felt bad for them. I'm not sure how exciting it was going to be. Maybe we should arrange some sort of entertainment. I knew Natalie was just dying to dress up in a sheet and float around the room. I'm sure Abigail could give us plenty of pointers on how to haunt the place…

I know what you're thinking. How can she just sit there so calmly and talk about a stupid Halloween party when, over the course of the last two weeks, someone had shoved her down a flight of stairs and (probably) poisoned her somehow? Well. Sorry. What do you want me to do? What would you do? Run around screaming, "Help! Help!" Yeah. I didn't think so. I bet you'd be sitting here trying to think of something else too.

After all, each incident taken separately could be logically explained away, couldn't it? We didn't have any proof that Mrs. Goldmyer was an axe murderer, now did we? Why would anyone want to get rid of me just because of a book that I had read? For that matter, Natalie had read it too, so why wasn't someone out to get her? See. There's absolutely nothing to worry about.

Maybe if we keep telling ourselves that, we'll both believe it.

At lunchtime, Louise came in with the air of a queen visiting her loyal subjects. It was just too bad that the only people in the store were Carolyn and I. Carolyn had made a mistake in her cowl (I know. That surprised me, too. It doesn't happen often.) and was busy dropping stitches off her needle and picking them up again as the correct stitch. She was amazing. However, she barely grunted a "Hello" to Louise, which did not go over well. And, as for me, by the time she made it to the counter, I had my purse in hand and passed her in a blur, waving over my shoulder, "Have a good day!" to the both of them. I was in no mood for snide remarks about puking during a class. Or on any other subject, for that matter.

Natalie was waiting for me by the front door, her own purse and keys to Mr. Darcy well in hand. "Come on," she hissed. "Hurry up before someone sees us." That was both the blessing and the curse of living with so many people. You were never alone.

We snuck out the door like well-practiced ninjas, and were safely ensconced in Mr. Darcy before we dared say anything else. She put the keys in the ignition and headed down the driveway towards town.

"Where is it?" I asked. She gestured towards her purse, which could also function for someone less persnickety as a small suitcase, and I bravely reached in to find what I was looking for. It wasn't hard. A newspaper takes up quite a bit of room.

Not all yarn stores are created equal, my knitting friends, please remember that. ("That's right," I said with a snort, "ours is way better." Natalie nodded emphatically.) *One of the greatest virtues of a knitting store is its ability to replicate knitters. One store in our town does this well. The other... well... we don't want to speak unkindly of anyone, but let's just say that when beginners teach beginners, it shows. Teaching others how to knit is a time-honored tradition that, until recent years, has generally been done by passing one's skills down to the next generation. Thank goodness that time is over. Now, knitters have the option of getting sound knitting advice and basic fundamentals from people who have studied the art and science of knitting and know what they are doing. Does it not make sense that when embarking upon..."*

The paper was rudely snatched from my hands and thrown in the backseat. "Natalie," I yelled, "I was reading that!"

"I know," she said calmly. "You've read it five times already. You're just going to get yourself all worked up again."

"Impossible," I said, huffing and settling back down in my seat. "I'm already worked up. How rude. Who does this person think she is?" For, in my mind, it could be nothing but a female. "I'm telling you that it's Happy Knits. Someone at Happy Knits is writing for the paper now and trying to..."

Natalie nodded her blond head up and down obligingly, "I know," she said, trying to sound soothing. "I know and that's why we're going to find out today who B. Haven is."

"B. Haven," I repeated, "Do you think that's a pretend name? It sort of sounds like 'Behaving', doesn't it? Is that supposed to be funny?"

"We will find out," Natalie said grimly, pressing her foot down a little harder on the gas pedal as a middle-aged man in a suit coat leapt heroically out of her way. "Ooops," she said. "Was that a pedestrian crosswalk again? Shoot. I have got to start watching out for them better."

I looked over my shoulder, "Nope," I reassured her, "he was just jaywalking."

"Oh good," she said sounding relieved, "then a little scare might help him remember to cross at the crosswalk."

I rolled my eyes and said nothing, craning my neck when we got to Water Street to see if I could see my cute little house from here. I couldn't. I didn't want to see it anyways. What if someone had already bought it? I didn't want to know. I made myself a mental vow that I would never drive down that street again. That way, when someone did buy my cute little cottage, I would never know and I could live happily in my little daydream that it was mine. All mine.

Turning off at Main Street onto Hapers Boulevard, Natalie roared past City Hall and pulled up with a screeching of brakes to the Springgate Gazette. She reached behind her seat to grab the newspaper and we summoned all of our righteous indignation to storm up to the front door of the Springgate Gazette. Natalie tugged on the door. Locked. I tugged on the door. Locked.

"Huh," Natalie said. "Maybe they saw us coming."

"Maybe we should have read the sign," I said, pointing at the prominent sign in the middle of the glass door that read *Please use the side door.* I peered through the glass and could see a secretary sitting at a desk facing our door, trying to look like she wasn't laughing at us. She was not doing a very good job of it. I pointed this out to Natalie who scowled.

"There's probably nothing wrong with the door," she grumped. "Probably only that girl in there wants some entertainment."

I agreed with her, and we marched back down the sidewalk to find the side door, which we entered a bit more meekly than we had anticipated. It's just disheartening to look silly when you're trying to look tough… do you know what I mean?

The inside of the paper building was rather boring. I was expecting a little more…something. A little more excitement. A little more hustle and bustle. People running around, grumpy men yelling things like "I need that copy on my desk – STAT!" But yet, it was oddly calm, just a small, ordinary office building with a corridor and closed doors – and a bored secretary reading a novel at her desk.

We explained that we had come to see B. Haven. We were very polite and nice, if I do say so myself. Which, for Natalie especially, quite an impressive feat. The secretary, Amy, listened with wide-eyed interest and then tried to look regretful when she informed us that B. Haven did not accept visitors.

"Is B. Haven even a real person?" Natalie demanded, momentarily forgetting our *You catch more flies with honey* philosophy. "Or just a pen name. I bet she doesn't even have an office here. It's probably someone that writes one article a week."

"Oh, yes she does," Amy shot back. "She writes most of the newspaper, as a matter of fact, but only signs her name on the opinion columns." And then her face turned beet red. Obviously, this was more information than she was supposed to give out.

"Great," I said, smiling my most winning smile. "She must be an amazing writer. We would, seriously, just love the chance to meet her. Couldn't you break the rules, just this once? Please?"

In case you're wondering. No. No, she couldn't. Not even just this once.

We regrouped at Mr. Darcy, Natalie chewing intently on her fingernail. "There's got to be a way in," she muttered. "They do it all the time in the movies."

I had visions of us sneaking in on mail carts… or what's it called when you jump off the roof and kinda walk down the side of a building… I'm sure Natalie could do that. Alas, I had a cast on one arm. What a shame. I would just wait on the roof.

She slumped back in her seat and surveyed Springgate, or what we could see of it from the parking lot.

"Maybe we could pretend to be the cleaning crew," I said, brightly. "I'll dress up in a white uniform, and you can hide in the mop bucket."

Natalie suddenly straightened and snapped her fingers. "I've got it," she said triumphantly.

Oh no. This could not be good.

Mr. Darcy roared to life and we peeled out of our parking spot on two wheels, going backward. By the time I had caught my breath, we were across the street at the cutest flower shop in town, "Petals." Isn't that a darling name for a flower shop? I know. I think so, too. A few people had sent me flowers when I was in the hospital, and the arrangement that had come from this establishment was twelves times nicer than the other store that was called "Main Street Florist." In my humble opinion, you should always look for the stores that have cute names… that means their owner has a lot of imagination and… but I digress. We were at Petals and Natalie was wearing a frightening look of triumph on her face.

"So, you want to buy some flowers?" I asked, trying to follow Natalie's logic. It worked. That, in itself, was just a tiny bit scary. A light bulb went off. "Perfect!" I shrieked. "Natalie, you're a genius."

"I know," she said humbly.

The store was just as cute on the inside as I had hoped it would be. It was a dizzying array of eclectic flower vases, flower pots and assorted items that, even though they had nothing to do with flowers, were just adorable in their uniqueness. One whole wall of the shop was a flower market where you could pick out which flowers you would like to go in your own customized bouquet. A cooler next to the cash register kept arrangements that had already been made nice and cool. I passed by a display of stuffed animals, and a little bear wearing a chef's hat caught my attention. I squealed, "Natalie, look. I should get this for Ryan. Don't you think it's adorable?"

Ryan had been out of town the last few days to see his mother again, and I missed him already. Natalie rolled her eyes, "I'm not sure he's going to love a stuffed bear as much as you seem to think he is."

I picked up the little bear, even more delighted to see the little rolling pin tied to his little hand… I mean… paw. "Oh look at the darling little rolling pin," I cooed, "and look at his eyes. He has the sweetest eyes…"

Natalie gave me an exasperated look, "Buy the bear," she hissed, "but try to remember why we are here."

The lady behind the counter watched us with amusement. I set the bear gently down on the counter, arranging his moveable legs so that he could sit and not fall over.

"I see you've taken quite a shine to our Mr. Cook," she said, smiling welcomingly. "I'm almost sorry to sell him. I think he's adorable."

"I do, too," I said eager to discuss the cuteness of Mr. Cook with someone who was a bit more agreeable, but Natalie's elbow in my ribs stopped me effectively. "He's just adorable," I ended lamely, cheerfully forking over way more money than anyone should ever spend on a six-inch bear.

The saleslady tucked a strand of brown hair behind her ear and, winking at me in understanding, addressed Natalie, "You seem to be a woman on a mission," she said with a smile. "What can I do for you today?"

Natalie looked behind her into the cooler, "I really like the look of that arrangement there," she said, pointing to an enormous bouquet, wildly chaotic and extravagant in both flower choice and color.

"Oh," the saleslady said, "I'm so glad you like it! I put it together myself this morning, and then I thought… who is going to want this? It's so big."

"I want it," Natalie said enthusiastically. "Definitely. It's perfect."

The lady turned to get the price from the arrangement and I pulled at Natalie's sleeve, hissing, "Natalie, that's going to cost a fortune. Can you afford that?"

Natalie wiggled her eyebrows and produced a credit card from her wallet, grinning evilly. "I can't," she admitted, "but Celia can. She gave me this card to buy my wedding dress, but forgot to ask for it back. I'm sure she would be happy to contribute…"

I was appalled. Speechless. The lady returned with a price that had both of us gulping, Natalie handed over her mother's credit card and we left Petals.

The flowers would be delivered within the hour, the kind saleslady assured us. We did not have to worry about that.

Natalie parked Mr. Darcy across the street from the Springgate Gazette where we had a great view of the side door and the employee parking lot.

"But, Natalie," I argued, seeing a large flaw in our plan, "what if she doesn't take the flowers home with her?"

Natalie chuckled – a dark and sinister chuckle… "Why do you think I wanted the biggest arrangement they had?" she asked. "Of course she'll take it home. There won't be any room for flowers so large in that dinky little office building."

"Maybe," I said, not entirely convinced. "Who do you think B. Haven is?"

To pass the time, we took turns speculating on the identity of B. Haven until the little Petals van pulled up into the paper. "Hee hee," Natalie said, rubbing her hands together in anticipation. "The fun begins."

Minutes passed. The Petals van left. More minutes passed.

"This is boring," I complained. "If we had been smart, we would have had those flowers delivered closer to closing time. Now we have to sit here and wait…
"

"Pssshaw," Natalie said. "People like B. Haven don't stay until closing time."

"I bet they do," I argued. "They have a little thing called a 'work ethic'."

"Pssshaw," Natalie said again. "She's obviously high-up in the ranks otherwise that bored secretary would have told us more. Nope. She was scared of saying too much, which means B. Haven has authority. People with authority don't have to stick around until closing time."

I rolled my eyes. Natalie and I had very different ideas about the way that the world works. Just because someone has an important job doesn't mean…

"Ha!" Natalie said triumphantly, pointing excitedly at the side door. "Look! Here she comes."

It was true! She was coming out. You could see the outline of the enormous bouquet even from our parking spot. Natalie gripped the steering wheel tighter and leaned forward with me to stare intently out the front window. It was… it was… we groaned and fell back to our seats with a flop. It was a man. And, even worse than that, it was a man that I had never seen before. So much for our theory about the vengeful writer out to get Crabapple Yarns. He opened the passenger side door and deposited the flowers on the front seat of a sporty red utility vehicle. If I was a better car person, I would tell you what kind it was. But I'm not. You'll have to content yourself with knowing that it was a large SUV that was red. I hope that's enough. He bent the tops of the flowers ruthlessly to get them to fit. I sighed. What a waste of money. He obviously didn't even like the flowers. Then, he slammed the door and went back inside, shivering in his shirt sleeves.

Natalie was remarkably quiet.

I couldn't help myself. "You're going to be in so much trouble," I said in a sing-song voice. She rolled her head along the back of the seat, raising an eyebrow in question. I couldn't help my expression, "Just wait until Celia finds out that you spent a million dollars on a flower arrangement trying to catch the writer and it doesn't even work…."

She wrinkled her nose and rose to the bait, "You just shut up," she said. "It's not like you had a better idea."

"It's not like you waited until I had a better idea," I argued with her, just because it was fun. "As a matter of fact, I had several ideas perking away." None of them good, of course, but they had been perking.

"'Oh, Natalie,'" she said mockingly, "'you're just such a genius'. Isn't that what you said? Because I seem to remember those were your exact words."

"Now you're seriously losing it," I said, rolling my eyes, "if you think I'm calling you a genius."

We were having such a nice argument that we almost totally missed the most interesting thing that had happened in a long time. Rebecca Flannery came out the side door and got in the driver's side of the red SUV. Three seconds later, it roared to life and she drove away.

"Well," said Natalie in complete shock. "Well."

"Natalie," I said humbly, "you're a genius." Her expression was priceless. "Maybe we should follow her?"

Mr. Darcy obligingly took up the pursuit of the red SUV. Given her head start and the way that she had been driving (aggressive drivers always make me a little nuts), I wasn't too sure that we would be able to find her again, but she had stopped for gas.

"There she is," I hissed, grabbing Natalie's arm in excitement. "She's getting some gas." Natalie pulled into the gas station.

"This isn't good," she said in a stressed voice. "I didn't really want her to see us."

Rule #1 when you were tailing someone was to remain unseen, wasn't it? I saw the way out. "Go through the car wash!" I said excitedly. "If you hurry she won't see…"

Natalie had quick reflexes. She whipped Mr. Darcy into the car wash with an expert ease while I kept an eye on Rebecca. "I don't think she saw us," I whispered to Natalie, as Natalie handed the car wash attendant some money.

We were soon ensconced in the soothing blue light of the car wash tunnel.

"Great," Natalie said sarcastically, as a spray of water completely drenched Mr. Darcy's elderly body. "Now we're stuck in here and we'll never know which way she goes." Natalie grabbed a handful of tissues from the console and rapidly stuck them up by a gap in her window. "He has a bit of a leak from time to time," she said, by way of explanation.

The spray ended and the brushes descended upon us. "Oh no!" I squealed. "They've remodeled."

"When did this happen?" Natalie gasped. Our nice, dark carwash escape had turned into a spectacle for the whole world to see. The car wash had replaced all of its sides with glass. We were going to be parallel with Rebecca at any moment. "Oh no!" Natalie wailed. "She's totally going to see us."

"Maybe not," I said desperately, "I mean, I probably wouldn't think of looking into the car wash if I was pumping gas. Would you?"

Natalie glanced at Rebecca's profile nervously. "I don't know. I'm not a crazy writer who has it out for an adorable yarn store either, am I? Who knows what she will do."

"Should we duck?"

We looked at each other for a moment and then both ducked at the same time, cracking our foreheads together painfully. "Wow," I hissed, clutching my head. "Your skull must be made of steel."

She glared at me, "No," she said coldly. "Passengers should duck forwards so that the driver can go sideways. Everyone knows that."

"Who knows that?" I demanded. "Is there a rulebook for how to duck when you're in a car?"

We are horrible spies. We had completely forgotten about Rebecca. In my annoyance with Natalie, I glanced out the window so I could think of something clever to say and I saw Rebecca's puzzled face watching us from outside the window. "Natalie!" I gasped. She spun to see, as Mr. Darcy shuffled slowly down the track. I'm sure our faces were the very picture of guilt.

Mr. Darcy popped out of the end of the car wash bright and shiny (well, as bright and shiny as he was ever going to get), just as Rebecca was pulling away from the gas pump. She rolled her window down, "Hi girls," she yelled cheerfully, waving out her window as she drove away.

And that was the end of our great chase scene. We were too mortified to even try to continue. "I'm not even sure why we were following her," Natalie said dolefully. "She was probably just going home."

I sighed. All of that espionage and spending of Celia's money had given us quite the appetite, so we decided to duck into the diner for a bit of overdue lunch. I loved this diner. It wasn't much to look at, but it was amazingly comfortable and offered just the kind of food that you liked to eat. Natalie promptly ordered an enormous cheeseburger with French fries, while my stomach voted for my favorite Chicken Noodle soup with a fresh roll. They bought them fresh every morning from Ryan's bakery. So, it was just like having him here. Even though, technically, Jack had made them this morning because Ryan wasn't here, but you know what I mean.

"I just can't believe it," I said, once the food had been delivered and Natalie was chomping away at her French fries. "I mean. I can believe it. But I just can't believe it. What is going on?"

Natalie, her mouth full of food, of course, could make no reply, but made her eyes big and wide and shrugged cluelessly.

"So she's a spy?" I wondered out loud.

Natalie swallowed hard, the choice between not talking and eating being a very difficult one. "I don't know," she said.

"Well, that's certainly helpful," I said sarcastically.

She picked up another French fry and carefully chewed the top off as I slurped a noodle. "So, Rebecca Flannery is B. Haven. The secretary seemed to imply that it was her real name, didn't she? So, which name is right? IS she really Rebecca Flannery or B. Haven?"

My lightbulb went off again. Or maybe it went on again. Whatever. You know what I mean. "Maybe it's both," I said slowly. Natalie looked at me askance. "Maybe "B" is short for Becca or Becky or something. Rebecca can be shortened to a few different things, can't it? And maybe Haven is her maiden name."

Natalie looked impressed, "Molly, dear," she said sweetly, "I think you're a genius, too."

We smiled companionably at each other. It was nice to be in the company of a fellow genius – especially one that appreciated you. I studied my soup with a renewed appetite, feeling the warm glow of companionship and success. The glow lasted about five seconds.

"Why, that little…" I sputtered.

Natalie giggled, flipping her hair over her shoulder so that the ends didn't drip into her ketchup. "I was wondering how long it would take before you realized what this meant."

"She's been playing us all along," I said, feeling, somehow, deeply disappointed in humanity in general. "She took our beginner's knitting class to spy on us and write horrible things about us in the paper."

Natalie, unlike me, didn't look as surprised. "That takes guts," she admitted. "She had to know that her anonymity wouldn't last forever."

I sighed, breaking off pieces of my roll and letting them drown mercilessly in the chicken broth. "But why?"

"Why?" Natalie sighed, too. "That's the best question. I mean, those articles are hardly big news. They were little paragraphs on the back page. Most of our customers haven't even read them. So, why waste the time?"

"I don't know," I said. "Maybe she's Susan Holmes' daughter or something and is doing her mom a favor?"

At the sight of Natalie's wrinkled brow, I explained, "Susan is the owner of Happy Knits."

She shrugged, still eating her French fries absentmindedly, "Maybe. I don't know. You're the genius. You tell me."

I rolled my eyes, "I thought you were the genius and I was the sidekick?" It was quite clever of her, really, to use her maiden name, if that is, indeed, what she had done. It's funny how after you've been married for a while, people even forget that you used to be someone else. HOLY COW. "Holy cow," I said out loud, for the benefit of Natalie's hearing. "Holy cow."

She looked up at me with concern, "What? You've figured it out already?"

I tightened my grip on my spoon so hard that I was sure it was leaving indentations in my hand. "No," I said. "Holy cow."

Natalie did her best to look patient, "You're going to have to stop saying, 'Holy Cow' and start using your real words or I'm going to dunk you in your own soup."

My mind made feeble attempts at grasping for the right words, as I was pretty sure Natalie was capable of doing just that. "We need to find out what Mrs. Goldmyer's maiden name was."

Natalie's eyes went large. "Holy cow," she said. Then, she looked down at her plate, "Hey," she exclaimed, "who ate all my French fries?"

"How could I be so silly?" she wailed, carefully hanging her coat up on its little hook. "Why would I do research on Mrs. Goldmyer and expect to find any horrible skeletons in her closet with a name she probably didn't have until after her skeletons jumped in the closet? This is really embarrassing."

I pulled my coat carefully over the stupid cast. Casts were the worst. They stuck out like sore thumbs, wouldn't go through half of my clothes, and you don't even want to know what it was like trying to wash my hair or take a shower. "I'm not any better," I admitted, chagrined. "I never, ever, ever thought of looking under a different name. It's like… she's Mrs. Goldmyer, always has been and always will. I think that's why I was so surprised to find out her first name. She's always been so…."

"Impersonal?" Natalie agreed. "Like she's not real. Just like you can't imagine her putting her feet up on the end of the sofa and eating popcorn – you just can't imagine her ever being anything than she is right now."

"Ahhhh," Abigail said, floating in on a cloud of perfume that made me sneeze and Natalie fan the air with her hand, "the ignorance of youth."

"Excuse me?" Natalie demanded. "I don't think Molly and I quite fit into the…"

Abigail kissed Natalie's cheek sweetly, causing Natalie to stop her sentence and gape. "No, sweet child," she said warmly, "you simply haven't lived long enough to realize that these old wrinkled cheeks (and here she patted her two heavily rouged cheeks delicately with her hands) have ever been anything other than wrinkled. You see the elderly as elderly. You forget that once we were young and lively and in love." She gave a great sigh and twirled on her toes back down the hallway from the same direction she had come, arms flung out theatrically.

We stared after her. "Is she trying out for another play?" I finally asked.

Natalie looked at me and then looked doubtfully down the hall where Abigail had just danced down, "I have no idea," she said wearily. "It could be that was a call for help. Maybe she just needs more attention."

"Maybe," I said, "she needs to move to Hollywood and make a zillion dollars."

This made Natalie grin. "Definitely," she said. "I can totally see it." She waved her hand out the vestibule, "But she does need to buy some new perfume first." I had to agree with her on that. It smelled faintly like rose-scented bug spray. "There was a good point in there, though," Natalie conceded grudgingly. "We do forget that older people were once young."

We stepped across the hallway into the fancy sitting room. "I'm going to sit here and try to think about what Mrs. Goldmyer might have been like as a child," I said, plunking down on the chintz loveseat.

"Me, too," Natalie said, sitting next to me. We both gave it a decent interval. "What have you got?" Natalie asked. "What do you think she was like?"

"I think," I said slowly, "I think she had less gray hair."

"And I was thinking that she was probably a great deal shorter as a child."

"This isn't working."

"I know."

"Which one of our old ladies shall we choose for brain picking?" I asked.

"Hey," a voice protested, "I heard that. And for the record, I choose to think of myself as 'well-seasoned' and not 'old'."

My face flushed bright red, "I'm so sorry, Rose," I stammered. "I certainly didn't mean any disrespect."

She cackled happily and finished coming into the room, absently dusting a small figurine on the coffee table before she sat down. "If only you could see your face," she hooted. "I've seen tomatoes with less color."

"Now, Grandma Rose," Natalie chided, even though I could hear the smile in her voice too, "you know that it's not nice to tease Molly."

Rose wrinkled her nose at Natalie, "I was trying to tease you, too," she said, growing serious, "but you just don't know how to feel embarrassed."

Natalie rolled her eyes. "Come on in, Rose," she said warmly. "We want to pick your brain about something."

It took a little bit of sweet-talking from Natalie, and a quick cookie run (which means that I ran to the kitchen and raided the sweets for the café), but in the end, we got our man. Well, woman. Well… maiden name. Ross. Mrs. Goldmyer used to be Charity Ross. And we were going to track that little knitpicker down.

CHAPTER 17

I could hardly wait for supper to be over so that Natalie and I could steal away and Google. Jack, unfortunately, was in no hurry and kept going back for seconds… and then thirds… and then hinted at a dessert that was still coming. I could have pulled my hair out. Well. Not really. That would be horribly uncomfortable. I forced myself to relax and look around the table at these lovely people who were rapidly becoming more than friends. They were becoming family.

Abigail was, indeed, trying out for a play. I wasn't paying attention, so I can't tell you what the name was, but the Senior and Youth Community Center was going to do a big performance in early December, and Abigail was positive she was going to get the leading role, which was, of course, a doting grandmother who gets into terrible scrapes and has to be rescued several times by her chauffeur and reluctant grandson. It sounded entertaining. Abigail was certainly a character actor. It's like she simply stopped being Abigail and started being "Evangeline". Evangeline was sweet, but flighty. She had the part down cold. I don't know how many times she "accidentally" misplaced her fork and had to be handed a new one. I actually saw her stick one down the front of her rather generous sweater. Rose saw it, too. She winked at me and rolled her eyes. She was going to try out for a part, too. She was going to be a maid. She, however, had no urge to practice and refused to play her part by going to get Abigail yet another fork. "But, darling," Abigail said, "you're the maid. That's your job."

Celia chose her moment well and pulled everyone's attention away from Abigail, much to Abigail's dismay when she announced that Friday was going to be her last day at the diner. "I'm so excited," she said, glowing with happiness. "I passed my Realtor's test and McMurphy & Sons Realty offered me a job."

"I didn't even know you were studying for…"

Celia made a face, "I'm so sorry, darling," she said to Natalie. "I didn't mean to keep it a secret. I was just so scared that I wasn't going to be able to do it, so I didn't tell you." She pinched her lip between her teeth for a moment, "I didn't mean to… that is… I'm sorry…"

Natalie, to my relief, laughed and stood up to give Celia a hug. Celia looked immensely relieved, as did Jack who looked to be bracing himself for a war between mother and daughter again. "I'm so proud of you!" Natalie exclaimed. "I think you'll be an awesome realtor."

Jack scraped up the last of his beef stew from his bowl and shoved his chair back. "Well," he said, "if this doesn't call for a slice of my Triple Death by Chocolate Cake, I don't know what would."

How I was going to fit a slice of Jack's Triple Death by Chocolate Cake in my stomach after all of that stew and biscuits and salad… I had no idea… but as he pulled it from the refrigerator, my mouth began to water, and I decided that just because something was hard didn't mean it wasn't worth doing. It also probably meant my jeans would be too tight tomorrow, but who cared about that right now?

"Did you two see the article in the paper?" Rose asked innocently, as we cleared the table to make room for the cake plates.

"Why?" Natalie asked in a high voice. "What do you mean?"

"She means," Celia said grimly, "that once again without naming names, that B. Haven is implying that Crabapple Yarns is a second-rate yarn store."

"She also implied that I'm a terrible teacher," I said, looking at the floor.

"That's weird," Natalie said slowly. "All of this time I've been thinking that she was attacking Crabapple Knits with her words, when, really, she has been attacking… you."

A horrid chill crept up my spine.

"I'm sure you're wrong," Jack protested.

Natalie sank back down to her chair. "Let's see. What did she say about us in the articles? She mentioned that someone, implying Molly, of course, was mean and grumpy and rude to customers. Then she implied that we spread rumors about our former neighbor. And then she suggested that we had a bad teacher. It all points to Molly."

Four pairs of eyes stared at me in wonder and concern.

"But why?" I protested feebly. "I don't even know her."

"Are you sure you don't?" Natalie demanded. "Are you really, really sure?"

I thought hard about it. I considered her face, trying, in my mind to make it younger, changing the hair color… but … no. I could think of nothing. "She doesn't even feel familiar," I said. "Nothing about her makes me think of anyone I know. Or have ever known. I mean, it's possible that we've met in the past, but I sure don't remember."

"Bummer," Natalie said. "I was hoping it was someone from your past that had it out for you. That would have made things so much easier."

My stomach lurched into my throat and I dropped my eyes to the ground so she wouldn't see any telltale emotion. "Ha," I said, somewhat hoarsely. "You're funny."

"Hey," she said, contritely, "I was just kidding. You know that, right? Who would want to hurt you? You're not capable of hurting anyone."

I stood up quickly, "I think what we need to do is forget about this for the night and have some cake." I looked up to Jack for support, who promptly flashed me a grin and pulled out his cake-cutting knife. "The first piece is for you," he promised.

I'm sure the cake was delicious, but I don't actually remember eating it. I remember smiling and talking about the play (I still can't remember the name), helping do the dishes and then going into the living room with Rose and Abigail to talk them through, one more time, how to play a DVD on the television. They were so amazed at how easy it was, but then, they always were. And tomorrow, when they wanted to watch another movie, they would be amazed again. I smiled warmly at them and surprised myself by giving Abigail a one-armed hug before trying to leave the room.

"I hope you know that we are here for you, Molly," Rose said, coming to stand next to me as well. She patted me on the shoulder somewhat awkwardly. "I'm not sure Natalie is right about you being the focus of those articles, but if you are, there's a reason, and we're going to help you figure it out."

"That's right," Abigail agreed, hugging me back firmly. "You're family now."

I was surprised to find tears in my eyes as I left the room. I was touched. And scared. I certainly didn't want to involve them in anything that could get them hurt. I snuck into the ballroom and crept to the agreed meeting spot with Natalie, the small sofa in the middle of the bookcases, sinking gratefully down into the worn cushions. What should I do? I decided to pray and closed my eyes.

I never even heard her come in. "Are you sleeping?" she asked hesitantly.

"Amen," I said, opening my eyes. "Nope. I was praying for guidance." I had never really talked about God with Natalie, and I wondered what she would say.

"Good idea," she said briskly. "That's the only way we're going to get to the bottom of this." Pushing me out of her way, she sat down next to me, and shoulder to shoulder, we opened her little laptop, waiting for it to warm up.

We googled.

And then we sat in frozen silence.

Hope Ross had, indeed, been Mrs. Goldmyer's sister. She had died when she was quite young. The police have ruled it as a suicide, but, according to several articles, there were some very strong suspicions that it was not suicide, but murder. The only suspect had been… I'm sure you guessed it… Charity Ross.

It was a rather sleepless night. Despite my nice, cozy bedroom, I could not settle down. Shadows flickered at the window. Rustling outside my window had me scurrying for the lights more than once. It was one thing to plot with Natalie that Mrs. Goldmyer might secretly be the Axe Murderer of Springiegate. But I had never really believed it. Had you? I mean, given Mrs. Goldmyer's rather nasty personality, it had, I admit, been just a teensy bit of fun to imagine her as a villain. But, no, I had never really believed it. Even with everything that was going on, I still couldn't believe it. But now… this! Mrs. Goldmyer had once been accused of murdering her own sister. Why? It was just so awful. Ok. You're probably dying of curiosity, aren't you? Here are the facts:

Hope Ross was found dead by her sister, Charity, on a cold, gray Saturday afternoon. The rest of the family was out doing errands, and Charity, having a headache, had gone home early. (I'm so sorry – if you're squeamish cover your eyes for a minute)… She had found her sister lying in a pool of her own blood, her wrists cut. The problem: No knife or razor blade had been found. The other problem: One shoeprint in Hope's blood, about five feet away from the body. Just one. And the shoe used to make it? Hope's shoe, still on her foot. One bloody footprint. Which, of course, was improbable and impossible, and left a big question mark in everybody's head. There had also not been a suicide note. Suspicion naturally fell on Charity, but since no evidence was found, the police declared Hope's death a suicide. One paragraph stuck out in my mind, its words emblazoned forever in my brain. "I'll never forget Charity's face," the coroner said, "when I gave my verdict as a suicide. I have never, and hope to never, see again the cold calculation that I saw there."

I picked up "The Axe Murderer of Springiegate" yet again, flipping idly through its pages. So it was true. Natalie had been correct. The Axe Murderer of Springiegate was, in fact, about Springgate. And, it was, in fact, about Mrs. Goldmyer. Someone had written this book about Mrs. Goldmyer. The clue of the bloody footprint was too big to be coincidental. I shivered again. Mrs. Goldmyer. All of the time I had worked with her, she had been harboring this secret. She was a true secret keeper. Had she murdered her own sister? Or… another thought occurred to me… did she know who did and was afraid to tell? The idea also had merit. Even though the idea of living with such a thing made me nauseous. If that was true, did she see her sister's killer at the grocery store? Did they stop, occasionally, into the library to check out a book and re-kindle fear? Or did she live every day with the guilt and remorse of what she had done?

The articles online had given no hint of a motive. There was no obvious source of tension in the family, although, one article quoted an anonymous "friend" of the family as stating "the family had recently weathered some troubled times," but, annoyingly, had left out any juicy details. The girls were apparently all straight-A students and members of many committees both at school and at church. Perfect little role models. Everyone said what a sweet girl Hope had been. She had graduated high school a year early and had spent the last year at a prestigious Women's College studying to become a teacher.

My fingers traced the lettering on the front of the book. There was no doubt in my mind that this was the book Carolyn had returned. Hers had been dustier and more worn, but it was the same book. She had kept it out of the library for 45 years. But why?

I thumped the book back down and tried to remember the day that Carolyn had returned it to the library. The day that had changed my life. Literally. She had been wearing an enormous hat with little fruit hanging off of it, a flowing purple dress, a shawl and she had carried the book into the library in an enormous basket. I remember thinking that she had looked like Mother Goose.

I shivered. The room was chilly at night and so I crawled gratefully between the covers again, pulling the heavy comforter up over my shoulders. While it was true that Carolyn had a bit of, shall we say, an eccentric style I had never seen the dress or the hat ever again. A sudden thought had me sitting straight up in bed. She had dressed outlandishly- even for her, because she had wanted to attract attention. She had wanted Mrs. Goldmyer to see her and to see that the book was returned. In all reality, I almost spoiled her plans by hiding the book. How strange. How very strange.

"You know," Natalie said thoughtfully, stuffing little treats into pumpkin-shaped bags haphazardly, "the library has all the copies of the newspapers on that film stuff."

"No," I said firmly, "we are not going to the library." I took her full bag and gave her another one, carefully twisting the top of the full one into a neat spiral so that I could tie a green piece of yarn around the top. Adorable. My super great idea in one-upping Happy Knits was going to cost us a small fortune. Now, in addition to the delicious goodies, we already had planned, Carolyn was preparing door prizes, goodie bags, games, a live spinning demonstration and... I think I heard something about... square dancing?? I was determined to help as much as humanly possible, as this little "Knit Night" was turning into its own Halloween monster with a speed that was truly frightening.

The door prizes were already packaged up into tantalizingly decorated bags proudly on display all along the counter. Why Carolyn was trying to tempt even more people to come, I had no idea. I was pretty sure we had enough people coming. Over 150 at the last look. And that was only people that bothered to RSVP. The party was tomorrow, and the phone would be ringing off the hook tomorrow afternoon with people saying, "I'm so sorry I forgot to call earlier… can I still come?" And we would graciously take their name and say, "It's no trouble at all. Of course, you can still come." Sigh. I just hoped we would have enough goodies to go around. It got real ugly when someone didn't get a goodie bag.

Tonight was my last class, and I was a bit nervous. Would Mrs. Goldmyer come back? Would Rebecca? What should I do? Should I let Rebecca know that I knew that she was also B. Haven? Should I just pretend everything was the same way it was last week? Should I…

"How many ribbons are you going to tie around that poor pumpkin?" Natalie asked with some amusement.

I looked down, slightly appalled to see no less than five around the poor pumpkin's little stem. I grimaced, "I just wanted him to look extra special," I lied, trying to sound perky.

She reached across the table to squeeze my hand, "I'm worried about the class tonight, too," she admitted. "I just don't know what to do about Rebecca – or the knitpicker."

The nickname made me smile slightly. It was just so perfect. "Well," I said slowly, "for one thing, we won't eat or drink anything."

Natalie shook her head solemnly, "You got that right," she said.

Feeling eyes upon us, I looked across the store to the café, where Jack stood looking at us with a troubled expression. I smiled and waved to him, but he stalked off towards the kitchen without a change of expression. "Sometimes I think we're wrong not to tell Jack about what's going on," I said softly, watching Natalie's face carefully. "You would be mad if it was the other way around, wouldn't you? He's worried and doesn't even know why. I hate seeing him like this."

Her face puckered, "Me, too."

"Tell him."

"But he's going to think we're crazy."

"Tell him."

"Tell me what?" We both jumped, and the contents of Natalie's bag went flying through the air, scattering chocolate and assorted goodies over the floor. Jack did not look amused.

"Oh look," I said, "there's a customer who needs help." And I fled. To keep up appearances, I went in search of a customer who looked like she needed help. There was actually only one customer in the store, but after I spoke with her, she realized that she did, indeed, need help. That worked out well. I do not like lying.

Natalie and Jack walked slowly out of the store, Natalie's fair head bobbing with emphasis as she talked, one hand gestured theatrically, in what I can only imagine was some sort of axe murderer motion. Jack's face was impressively blank. I did not expect it to stay that way for long.

I waited for them to leave completely before I went back to our table and picked up everything that had fallen on the floor. I sighed. There were still about 50 bags to fill. A quick glance at my watch confirmed what I already knew – that I didn't have a lot of time left before Rachel, Helen and an assortment of knitters arrived to "decorate". I wasn't really feeling up to that, truth be told. It was hard to laugh and have fun, with these big questions and secrets gnawing at my insides.

I looked up as I heard the door open again, surprised that Natalie would be returning so quickly. But it was Carolyn breezing in. When I get old and gray, I hope I resemble her. Her energy and enthusiasm for life were contagious.

"Good morning, my dear," she said happily, setting a small stack of papers down on the table. "I thought I'd come in early and lend a hand."

"Weren't you supposed to be getting some rest?" I asked sternly, even though a small smile was already forming. I felt more energized already. "Your lovely niece told us that the doctor had said…"

"Oh, psshaw," she waved a dismissive hand. "Irene is such a worrywart and never wants anyone to have fun. I'm perfectly fine."

I studied her hard for a minute, even as she began filling bags with a speed that Natalie had not quite seemed to manage. She certainly looked fine. She had braided her long grey hair into French braids this morning and wore a striped blue turtleneck under her cabled sweater. In truth, she had never looked better. I was so relieved. With all of the drama that had been happening, she had begun to look… old. And that worried me.

"So," I teased, "what have you been up to?"

She looked down her crooked nose at me, "Your tone implies that you think I've been up to something bad," she said, her eyes twinkling from behind her glasses, "but you should know, by now, that I wouldn't even know how to start."

"Oh, right," I said with an eye roll. "Whatever was I thinking?" I glanced down at the papers she held in her hand. "And what's this?"

She giggled self-consciously and pulled the papers closer, turning them over so that I couldn't read them. Rats. The pages had been full of writing… laid out like a …

"Are you writing a play?" I asked in amazement, kindled with a bit of wondering disbelief.

Interesting. One hardly ever saw Carolyn blush. "Well," she stammered slightly, "I thought maybe I'd do something fun for the Knitter's Halloween Party."

I stared at her. "You are truly the most amazing person I've ever met," I said in all sincerity. "Is there anything you can't do?"

For one moment, the twinkle in her blue eyes dimmed, and I felt that maybe I had said the wrong thing, but then she smiled again, "You are such a blessing to me, Molly," she said. "You'll never know what a gift you've been." Her eyes were kind and gentle, and I felt… loved.

Rats again. I couldn't ask her about the book now, could I?

CHAPTER 18

C rabapple Yarns looked like Halloween had come in and thrown up on it. We were completely decked out in orange and black crepe paper. Helen had even hung a disco ball, complete with an annoying, I mean, fun, strobe light in the center of what would be the "dance floor". Little ghosts, goblins and witches peeked out from various corners and angles. We had carved pumpkins until we were literally sick of seeing another pumpkin seed. Jack, however, had gathered up all of the pumpkin seeds and promised us that we would love them roasted and salted. I'm still not sure if he was kidding or not. Rose had even shown us how to hook up some wire and fly a ghost across the room. Jack's contribution had been an elaborate timer and contraption that made this process automatic. Every 15 minutes, Casper, as we had already affectionately named him, would make his journey across the enormous ballroom. He had also offered to stuff Casper full of confetti, so that on one trip across, magical confetti would fall like snow over everyone. Carolyn had actually turned pale. Can you imagine the process of cleaning up confetti tomorrow? Me, neither. But, she thanked him politely for his offer and declined. I'm sure the mischievous glint in his eyes as he walked away was just a trick of the light.

"Do we have enough tea lights?" Helen asked, tucking a strand of hair behind her ear expertly. "I can stop at the store on my way home and get some more."

Oh dear. Was it that time already? I checked my watch. It was. Class would begin in an hour. Rachel tidied the last rolls of unused crepe paper, while Carolyn rummaged under the counter.

"Oh yes," Carolyn said, pulling out a big box, "I've got a ton here. We should be fine." She looked around the room gratefully, "Thank you so much for coming and doing all of this work. I've never seen Crabapple Yarns look quite so....

spooktacular… before." The knitters all giggled and looked like they would rather be doing nothing else. Carolyn had that effect on people.

I still had two black cats that needed hanging. One had two green jewels for eyes and appeared to be hissing, and the other had dangling feet that moved in the breeze. I literally had no idea where to put them. Even the café was full of decorations. I was debating the merits of stuffing them under the counter – or a convenient bookshelf, when Jack appeared by my elbow. He didn't look too happy. Guilt squirmed inside me like a child caught red-handed.

"Jack," I began, but he shook his head.

"I need to speak with you," he said and then turned and walked towards the back door. I guess he expected me to follow. I did.

He was waiting just outside the door and pulled me into the little room where, I believe, you are supposed to grow plants in. It was cold and dark. I shivered, but not just from the cold. I didn't blame him for being angry. I would be, too, if I was him.

He shut the door, but did not turn on the overhead light. There was still enough daylight coming in that we could see clearly. Even though maybe I would have preferred a bit more darkness. There was a terrible sinking feeling in my stomach. I had once likened Jack to having a big brother. The idea had appealed to me. Now I may have lost that forever. And it was my own fault. Again.

He crossed his arms and leaned back against the door.

I cleared my throat, "So," I said nervously, "I'm guessing that Natalie told you… everything?"

He shrugged, "I don't know. Did she?"

I dropped my gaze briefly to the floor, "Did she tell you about the book and Mrs. Goldmyer and her sister's maybe suicide and about how it's the same book Carolyn returned 45 years overdue and how we think that Mrs. Goldmyer is the character in the book and…"

He snorted, "Ok. Stop. Yes, I guess she told me everything." His gaze was hard, "But what I'm wondering is… why didn't you?" He ran an aggravated hand through his spiky hair, every freckle across his nose standing out in the greying light, "Why would you two keep this a secret and not let me know…"

I put a hand on his arm, it felt like stone. "I'm so sorry," I whispered brokenly. "I can imagine how you must feel. At first, we didn't really believe it was true, and then, it seemed more like a coincidence and then we didn't want you to get hurt."

"Didn't want me to get hurt?" He replied softly. Scarily. I studied the floor again. It was tile, maybe slate. Probably great for plants because if you spilled water the water would just... "Didn't want ME to get hurt," he repeated, drawing my attention reluctantly back to him, his eyes bright. "Did you ever think that I wouldn't want you to get hurt?" I could feel my eyes getting bigger, my heart jumping with emotion. "That I would rather die than have anything happen to Natalie," he paused, "or to you?"

I shook my head, unable to speak. And then, suddenly, amazingly, I was enveloped in warmth. It happened so fast that it took me a few seconds before it even registered what was happening. Jack was hugging me. It took me two more seconds before I hugged him back. We stood that way for several moments, and then his arms tightened before he pulled back to look me in the face. "I consider you a sister now," he said, his eyes gentle. "I don't even know if you have any brothers or sisters, and I feel bad that I never asked, but from now on you're my sister. And I love you." Two hot tears ran down my cheeks, but I didn't let go of his arms to brush them away. "And I'm here for you. I promise." He wiped a tear off gently, and I was surprised to see them gathering in his own eyes, "But I can't help you if you don't let me know what's going on."

"I love you, too," I whispered. "Thank you for being the best big brother in the world. I'm so sorry and I promise not to keep things from you again..." and I found I couldn't go on. He pulled me in tight again, and now that I didn't have to look at him, the words came out freely. "I thought maybe you were going to ask me to leave," I confessed to his plaid shirt.

"Never," he said.

I believed him. The bonds of family slipped around us, and the tightness of their loop was comforting.

Today was the day. The day knitters all over had been waiting for. It was… "The Knitter's Halloween Party." The phone was, as predicted, ringing off the hook with knitters getting their last minute RSVPs in. Natalie had already taken Mr. Darcy into town to purchase 50 more goodie bags and contents. Sigh. I could hardly wait to tie more green yarn around the little pumpkin stems.

What was that? Oh- sorry – I totally forgot to tell you about the class last night, didn't I? Well. There's a good reason for that – there was nothing to tell. Mrs. Goldmyer had called to inform us that she had, in fact, not learned anything from the class other than how to clean up afterward and as she had absolutely no desire to eat ill-baked cookies and watch knitters struggle with the basics that should have already been mastered, she saw no reason for coming. Rebecca had called in to say that she was not feeling well and would, regretfully, be unable to join us. That left me with a nice little class of amiable knitters. A few of them even finished their hats. The others were still happily knitting along, and I had promised them that even though the class was over, I was still available to assist them. It was, all in all, a really great evening. Which just goes to show you that worrying is never a good idea. It serves absolutely no useful purpose. And, like the Bible says, "Cast your cares upon Him, for He cares for you." Doesn't it make more sense to turn it all over to God rather than trying to figure it out on your own? I think so too. I had a long talk with Him last night about that, and I have to say it made all the difference.

Helen and Rachel had shown up early this morning, their faces glowing with knitterly sneakiness and had conferred with Carolyn in the front parlor for almost two hours. I had a feeling we were in for a great performance tonight. Carolyn, however, when asked about it, merely winked and would say nothing.

You would have thought that with the party happening this evening, that we would have been slow in the yarn store, wouldn't you? The truth was completely the opposite. Carolyn even called Louise to come in and help. That was a real treat. She immediately stationed herself behind the counter and insisted upon ringing up every purchase herself. I, in turn, resisted the impulse to hide and spent every spare moment trying to think of nice things to say to her. It was really hard at first. I literally could not think of anything to say. Nothing. Not one nice thing to say to her. Isn't that sad? So I prayed. "God, You love Louise too. Please help me to reach her with Your love and be kind. You are always good to me, even when I don't deserve it. Please give me more of Your great love so that I can be the same way to Louise." Right after that, the first perfect thing to say popped into my head and I marched right up to the counter to say it. She was so astounded that she picked up her knitting and totally ignored me. I was not deterred, however, and also not surprised, an hour later, as I was bringing a nice gentleman named "Steve" up to the counter to have his purchases rung up, when another perfect thought popped into my head, "And here's Louise," I said warmly. "I know you're going to be knitting an intarsia sweater, so if you have any questions, you should ask her. She is an amazing knitter. You should see some of the intarsia sweaters that she has designed herself. They're breathtaking." I didn't even have to choke the words out. I meant every word.

She gaped at me, and I left her and Steve discussing the pros and cons of using bobbins to manage your yarn, feeling grateful to God for the blessing of love. Because I knew it was His love, not mine, that was making it not only easy, but fun to find ways to be kind to Louise.

Carolyn squeezed my arm as she walked by, "What are you smiling about?" she asked.

I answered honestly, "I was just thinking about how beautiful it is to have God's love."

Her eyebrows rose, "It is, indeed," she agreed.

"Ahem," Louise approached from behind us. "I have a phone message for Molly." She held it out in one thin hand, almost as if she were afraid of our hands touching.

"Why, thank you, Louise," I said, smiling, "how kind of you to bring it over to me." I took the note from her.

"Well," she said, withdrawing slightly and looking between Carolyn and me, "it had a time frame listed and as I'm never sure where you disappear to sometimes, I thought I'd better find you." She sniffed and left.

I tried really, really hard not to roll my eyes, and glanced uneasily at Carolyn to see how she felt about what just happened. She smiled happily at me, "I think Louise is really warming up to you," she said.

I shook my head. I was clearly going to have to pray again. I was out of nice things to say. Mrs. Royston walked in just then and wondered if she could have "just a minute" of Carolyn's time to discuss her Icelandic sweater. I suppressed a grin as they walked to the big class table, where I knew that Mrs. Royston would pull out every skein of yarn, her pattern, her sweater that she, so far, knitted an inch of, and ask Carolyn to explain the process one more time.

The note was from Mrs. Goldmyer. It was Friday. I was to report to the library at Noon to get my list of readers from her for the Amelda Tartan Reception. Huh. I'm not sure how, but I had almost totally forgotten about Amelda and her new book. That was, in itself, strange. And was I ever going to finish the story that I had started? It had to be turned in by next Friday. Was it even feasible anymore? I sighed, feeling like a traitor. My favorite author in the whole world and I had forgotten.

The bigger problem was this… I had to go to the library. I looked over at Natalie who was embroiled in deep conversation with a young girl in braids about the pros and cons of circular needles. I couldn't take her with me. That wouldn't be fair to Carolyn.

The café was closed today due to the party this evening. Jack couldn't cope with that and all of the things he was making for tonight. Would it be fair to ask him to leave for a few minutes? Probably not. But after letting Carolyn know I was taking my lunch hour, I went in search of my… brother.

I found him in the kitchen, pulling two big trays out of the oven. They were his famous chocolate chip cookies. Yummm… I eyed them even as I tried to get his attention.

He flipped the oven doors closed with an expert foot kick that I'm sure would have had Natalie protesting and grinned at me. "Are you hungry?" he asked. "I made some sandwiches."

I pulled at my sweater somewhat nervously, "No," I said, "I can see you're really busy, but…"

He pulled the oven mitts off, setting them down on the spotless counter. How he did that I have no idea. If I was in the kitchen for more than 3 minutes there were puffs of flour everywhere, melting butter dripping off the counter and more pans in the sink than you could count.

"What's the matter?" he asked seriously.

"I have to go to the library," I said. "Is it ok if…" I lost my nerve to ask him, "if I borrow Mr. Darcy?"

"I'll go with you," he said quickly, already looking around for his wallet.

"No," I said just as quickly, "don't be silly. Nothing is going to happen. It's broad daylight and I just have to pop in to pick up a list."

"I'll go with you," he repeated, pulling Mr. Darcy's keys off the hook. He took a look at my face and smiled reassuringly. "It would keep me happy," he said, "and maybe we could stop at the store and buy some more butter."

I seriously doubted that he needed more butter, but I was grateful for his presence.

Abraham Lincoln trotted forlornly after us down the hallway to the back door. Jack had to push him back by his little nose in order to get the door closed. Even then, we could hear him howling with a broken heart about being left behind.

"I swear," Jack said. "I told Rose it wasn't a good idea to bring him with when she went to town the other day… but nooooo… she said it would be good for him to get out and "broaden his horizons." Now he wants his horizons broadened every time someone leaves. It's getting out of hand."

I climbed into Mr. Darcy reluctantly, the odd howls twisting my heartstrings, "It's a very effective howl," I said sadly.

"Don't fall for it," Jack said with a grin. "I think Abigail is training him. If you went back up to the door, you'd probably find him gone already."

At least that made me feel a bit better. "So," I said, buckling my seat belt and watching the woods fly by as we headed into town, "are you ready for tonight?"

He rolled his eyes, "Do I really have to do this?" he asked.

"If you don't play your part, the whole thing falls apart," I said, trying to swallow a smile and frown at him.

"You say that like it's a bad thing," he said, with a reluctant grin.

He parked Mr. Darcy expertly and waited patiently for me to untangle my cast from the seatbelt – for some reason, I seem to do that a lot, before we entered the library. His presence was solid and comforting next to me, and I felt none of my usual anxiousness about seeing Mrs. Goldmyer – even if she was a murderer, nothing would happen to us today. I was sure of it.

"Good afternoon, Mrs. Goldmyer," I called to her, spotting her at the circulation desk across the room.

She looked frostily at me from over her glasses. "Please refrain from bellowing, Ms. Stevenson," she said. "This is a library."

I looked up at Jack and he pretended to shiver. Then, he looped his arm through mine as we crossed the foyer. I think that's what saved us both. One second we were walking, and the next our feet were flying out from underneath us. Jack's quick thinking and strength were amazing. The floor was flying up towards me when I felt a sharp tug backward and landed on a much softer surface.

"Ouch," Jack said. I opened one eye experimentally and was greeted by plaid. Jack's favorite shirts were always plaid.

"Are you ok?" I asked worriedly, hurrying to straighten up. He sat up with me, a careful arm still around my back and peered down at me.

"Are you ok?" he asked.

Mrs. Goldmyer came hurriedly across the foyer, "No, stop!" Jack barked. She froze , one foot slipping on a wet patch of ground in front of her, her arms helicoptering comically before she regained her balance.

"It's slippery right there," Jack growled, pushing me off of him and rising slowly to his feet. He helped me to my feet, and we cautiously shuffled away from the slippery patch on the floor. Our pants were soaked with the stuff. Jack bent down to touch it with two fingers, glaring daggers at Mrs. Goldmyer who appeared, for once, incapable of speech.

I fingered a wet patch by my knee in much the same way, marveling at the sheer slipperiness of it. "Oil," Jack said, answering my unspoken question. "Possibly cooking oil." He bit his lip, "I should have seen the shine of it on the floor."

"But why would there be oil on the floor?" For the first time in my life, Mrs. Goldmyer looked like any other confused human being. She also looked a little scared. Interesting.

Jack crossed his arms and did his best to look intimidating, which, actually was very effective. "Why don't you tell me," he said.

She blinked in confusion to me and then Jack and back to me again. And then, just like a television screen going dead, the expression faded out and Mrs. Goldmyer was back. "I have no idea what you're talking about," she said. "I certainly hope you're not implying that I spilled cooking oil on my own floor. What a mess. And it's not even Herbert's day to work." She sounded disgusted. Like we hadn't almost just had our brains knocked out of our heads. Herbert was, of course, the maintenance man at the Library. He worked part-time and was expected to work full-time. You know how that is.

"You knew Molly was coming, didn't you?" Jack asked evenly. "I'm guessing you don't have a lot of customers today and it would have been very easy to know when to spill a little oil on the floor. I'm not sure it would have done any permanent damage, but who knows, especially with her arm already in a cast. It could have gotten her out of the way for a nice, long time." I took a step closer to Jack. He was right. It was broad daylight and I had thought nothing would happen. I looked up at him, and he put an arm around me.

"Nonsense," Mrs. Goldmyer said briskly. "Where do you get these preposterous ideas?" But she looked nervous and her eyes flicked back to the library stacks almost involuntarily.

Jack saw it, too. "Come on, Molly," he said, "if you feel up to it, I suddenly have the desire to check out a book." My legs were still a bit rubbery, and if my heart pumped any harder, I would probably have a stroke, but I followed him willingly, for some reason hanging on to the sleeve of his coat. He carefully skirted the puddle on the floor and walked with purpose towards the library stacks. The library was arranged so that the shelves formed squares within squares, with the children's section in the middle. The theory behind this was that the parents could keep an eye on their children while they browsed for their own books. In reality, this never worked, but it was a good theory. It also created a bit of a dilemma when searching the library. The shelves were full and built close together. It would be all too easy to hide around a corner.

"What are we looking for?" I whispered, well aware that Mrs. Goldmyer had not moved from her spot in the foyer, and was watching us with anxious eyes.

He huffed a small laugh, "You know" he said, "I'm not really sure, but I got the feeling that she didn't want us to come in here, so…"

So. That was a good enough reason for me. Especially since I had had the same feeling. The first person we found was a man, possibly in his mid-50's hunkered down on the floor with about 10 books scattered around him. He looked startled to see us and did not look like the floor-oiling type. "Uh…" he said, "I'll put them back. I'm trying to remember which ones I've already read."

I nodded in understanding. "It's so much easier to make a list," I suggested helpfully, "then when you read one…"

"Come on," Jack hissed, trying not to laugh, "I can't believe you're trying to give advice while we're hunting down someone nefarious."

That stung. "It's always the right time to be helpful," I replied.

A mother sat with her little daughter on the floor reading "Frog and Toad" in the Children's Section. Jack obviously considered them harmless and we passed them without speaking. We peeked around the corner into the card catalog room where the computer was and I gasped. Rebecca Flannery sat there, serenely clicking the mouse.

I wasn't sure if Jack knew who she was, so I grabbed his sleeve harder. He leaned down so I could whisper, "That's her." I know. Not really helpful. Have I mentioned that in times of stress I can be a little less than coherent? He shook his head in silent confusion. "That's the newspaper lady," I whispered. "The one who came to our knitting class and wrote those articles."

Realization came to his face. "I wonder…" he whispered.

"Oh, dear," a voice behind us said, "this looks just like a scene out of a movie. Two slightly shady characters whispering in the corner of a library." Nate tutted, shaking his head sadly, "They can't possibly be up to any good." He looked us carefully up and down, "Especially since they both seem to be a bit… damp."

Jack took a lunging step forward, stopped only by my outstretched arm. "Yeah," he said darkly, "you would know all about being up to no good, wouldn't you?"

Nate looked genuinely baffled. I pulled Jack's arm back further. "I don't think it's him," I hissed.

"Him?" Nate asked, foolishly taking a step forward. "Are you sure that's proper English? I can never remember." He grinned, "It might be more proper to say, 'I don't think it is he.'" Jack's muscles tensed under my hand. Nate paused, as if, for the first time, fully taking in the look on our faces. "What's going on?" he asked seriously.

Mrs. Goldmyer appeared on the scene looking calm and unruffled. "They slipped in the foyer," she said smoothly, "and seem to think that someone is out to get them."

"Slipped?" Nate asked sharply, his head swiveling towards his mother. "How?"

"How long have you been here?" Jack asked instead.

"He's been here for hours," his mother said smoothly. Nate's expression did not change, except for a brief tightening around his mouth that told me Mrs. Goldmyer was lying.

"Really," Jack said flatly. Jack and Nate stared at each other until I began to squirm with the uncomfortableness of it. This was getting nowhere. I fidgeted. "Then, maybe," Jack said, "you wouldn't mind if I called the police and let them know about the oil on the floor." He was already reaching into his pocket.

"Oh dear," Mrs. Goldmyer said emotionlessly. "I'm terribly sorry, but that mess has already been taken care of." Nate's gaze flew from Jack to his mother again.

"That was fast," Jack said, and I could feel the anger growing again. "Almost like you had it planned that way."

"Nonsense," Mrs. Goldmyer repeated for the second time this afternoon. "I couldn't very well leave it there to let someone else fall on, now could I? Herbert leaves all of his cleaning supplies in a small cabinet up by the foyer. It was a very small spill, after all. I'm surprised you were even able to slip on it. You really should be more careful."

Jack's face was flushed with suppressed anger, "I'm still going to go to the police station," he said slowly, "and tell them I slipped here. There's plenty of evidence right on my pants. Maybe I'll even contact the insurance company."

"Ah," Nate said. "That would be covered under the city's insurance policy. I would be happy to give you their number."

"I think," Jack said between clenched teeth, "that it would be in your best interests for a continued happy and long life if you went about your business and left us alone. Stay away from Molly. And stay away from our house. I can't be responsible for what will happen if I see you two anywhere within twenty feet of her."

Nate gave a nervous laugh, "Why would you say something like that?" He looked at me carefully before studying Jack. "Why would we want to hurt Molly?"

"The hot chocolate you gave her was poisoned," Jack growled, "there was an oil spill waiting for her when she walks into the library," he looked Mrs. Goldmyer up and down, "and I'm pretty sure your mother would make for an appropriate substitute for Carolyn in a darkened store."

Mrs. Goldmyer gasped, looked outraged. Nate went pale. "Poisoned?" he asked weakly. "How is that possible?"

Nate and Mrs. Goldmyer both took a step back as Jack and I ventured forward to leave. "Stay away," Jack repeated. "I mean it."

"Good afternoon, guys," a cheerful voice behind us said. "It must have been the day to go to the library."

Mrs. Goldmyer eyed Rebecca with distaste… and something else… I glared at her, wishing, not for the first time, that I was a more confrontational person – and that I could think of things to say when I wanted to say them. As it turned out, the only thing I could do was clutch Jack's coat tighter. Nate frowned, noticing this, and took a step forward, stopping when he saw Jack's expression. I hope that expression never gets sent my way. I would just curl up and die, I think.

"And you," Jack said carefully, "can either print a retraction of the lies you've said about Molly and Crabapple Yarns or stay away."

I finally found my voice, "Yeah," I said. "We know who you are."

Rebecca's mouth opened and closed in a most unbecoming fashion. We left her that way.

It was only once we were back outside in the bracing autumn cold that I let go of the breath I had been holding. I found myself, for the second time in two days, hugging Jack. "Thank you," I said fervently, "for coming with me and saving me from falling and sticking up for me and being…" Rats. I was crying.

"Shhhhh," he said, patting my back awkwardly. "Don't cry. I'm glad I was here." He squeezed me tighter. "Thank you," he said, "for coming into the kitchen and asking me to help you."

My stupid conscience forced me to remind him, "But I didn't," I said miserably. "I wanted to. I was going to. But I chickened out."

He leaned back and I was happy to see that the anger was gone – at least for now, and he smiled gently. "That's what your words said, but that's not what your face said," he replied, finally letting me go and contemplating his pants and then mine. "We can't get back into Mr. Darcy like this," he said regretfully. "Natalie would kill me."

I loved that he was afraid of Natalie, too.

In the end, we left the car at the library, securely locked, and decided to walk down to Mr. Morrie's store and purchase some plastic to drape over the seats. Removing our pants would have also served the purpose, but I don't really see that happening, do you?

"She'll probably have Mr. Darcy towed," I said glumly, kicking an innocent pebble out of the way with more force than was strictly necessary.

"If she does," Jack said grimly, "she'll be sorry. We're parked there legally."

I wasn't so sure about that. Nate, was, after all, a lawyer. And Jack had probably just ticked him off good. But we'd worry about that problem when we came to it.

Mr. Morrie was in his store re-arranging his hammers. "Hi Mr. Morrie," I said cheerfully. He barely looked at me but smiled almost warmly at Jack.

"Hey Jack," he said.

Jack frowned and looked between the two of us. "Do you have a problem with Molly?" he asked bluntly. I gasped. I wasn't used to such forthwritedness (if that's a word – which it probably isn't).

Mr. Morrie pulled at his beard thoughtfully, not even seeming to be offended by the rudeness of the question. "Well," he said slowly, "I read something in the paper about her thinking I was up to criminal activities." His pale stare was horrifying, and I was struck with guilt for having even made a joke with Natalie. I opened my mouth to reply, but Jack beat me to it. "You also probably read that she's mean to customers and rude and can't teach a knitting class. Do you think that's true?"

Mr. Morrie looked at him for several long moments before transferring his stare to me, "No," he said, "I don't believe so. I apologize little lady. I shouldn't let things get to me."

I smiled warmly at him, "I'm honestly sorry for any confusion and trouble, Mr. Morrie," I said honestly. "I would never, ever want to hurt you."

And that was that. Do you know what I think? Big brothers can come in very handy. My happiness with my new brother lasted all the way until we were tucked back into Mr. Darcy with our protective sheeting in place for the short drive home.

"Ummmm… Molly…." Jack said, "I think I need to talk about something."

I sighed and leaned my head against the cool window. "Again?" I asked, but softened my words with a half-smile.

He looked a little worried. "I think it's time you told Ryan what's going on."

I nodded, "I agree with you. But he's still out of town and I don't want to…"

"Bother him?" Jack finished somewhat sarcastically. "Do you know how mad he was to find out what's been going on? You've been calling him and never said a thing about…"

"Wait a minute," I cut in. "He's mad? How do you know he's mad?" A bright spot of color appeared on Jack's right cheek, and a terrible suspicion began to bloom with it. "Jack," I said slowly and clearly, "are you telling me that you called Ryan and told him?"

He nodded, never taking his eyes off the road.

"Everything?"

He nodded again.

"Oh boy."

He nodded. "Yep," he said, "he's pretty upset."

I'm sure that was the understatement of the century. I was about to tell Jack what I thought of people who meddled in other peoples' affairs when a thought occurred to me. "Oh no!" I exclaimed, turning to look back in the direction of town.

My tone caused Jack to wince and swerve. "What?" he demanded, hitting the brakes.

"I forgot to get the list from Mrs. Goldmyer," I said meekly. "Now I'm going to have to go back."

Jack gripped the steering wheel tightly before accelerating slowly back up the hill. "Mrs. Goldmyer can do the work herself," he said. And then he said words that I can't really repeat or reprint here.

CHAPTER 19

I tied the white apron securely around my waist and double-checked that my braids were sufficiently straight before pulling the red cape over the whole ensemble. I picked up the basket full of knitting that I had gotten ready the night before and stood in front of my floor length mirror to contemplate the ensemble. I was probably a little old to be Red Riding Hood, but then again, Natalie was a bit young to be a grandmother, too. Jack, however, was perfect for his role as The Big Bad Wolf. Natalie's original thought was to go as Wizard of Oz, as we had our very own built-in Toto. Abraham Lincoln, however, had very serious doubts about his role, and Jack, still nursing his somewhat bitten finger, reluctantly agreed to be the wolf instead of the tin man. I peeked my head out into the hallway, careful to not let the door creak to see if I could hear any activity happening out in the hallway, and sure enough, I could hear Jack and Natalie arguing quite loudly. I smirked to myself. The idea of the Big Bad Wolf was one thing. Actually putting on a fuzzy costume and mask – now that was another. I had politely refused knitting a mask – even though, strangely it was my own idea. Natalie had knit one to look like glasses for herself and a fuzzy thing for Jack. There were actual bets happening downstairs between the old ladies and Celia as to whether he would actually wear it.

Carolyn had, naturally, embraced the idea of dressing up and was coming as "The Knitting Fairy" which I thought was a horrible idea, but she apparently loved. Rachel was, also, slightly appalled and I think briefly mortified once again over her role in that situation, but Carolyn's natural enthusiasm had turned The Knitting Fairy from something to be ashamed about to an exciting event. Rachel was coming as a dropped stitch. I'm not sure what that was going to look like, but it would probably be interesting. Helen and Patrick were coming as Raggedy

Ann and Andy, which would be a natural fit for them, and I'm sure their costumes would be fabulous.

Rose and Abigail were also attending, but would be dressed as their respective roles in the play. "Two for one," Rose crowed. "This makes buying our own costumes so much more worth it." Yes, it was a small theater, and just opening, so the actors were kindly asked to purchase their own costumes. I'm sure, after a few performances, they would be able to have a budget. Someday.

Jack was worried that one of our "enemies" was going to sneak in – in costume - and had set up a camera at the front door with a funky strobe light. He reasoned that the light of the strobe light would hide the flash of the camera. He would be monitoring the camera closely while the guests arrived. I was instructed not to eat or drink – or be alone with anyone – or to talk to strangers… basically, I really should have just stayed upstairs.

I had spent the afternoon rushing around trying to help get the last minute details of the party ready – and trying to call Ryan. But there was no answer. He was probably ignoring my calls. That was bad. Stupid, sweet, stupid Jack.

I straightened the bow at the end of my braid and decided that it was time to stop procrastinating and go down to the party that had been my idea in the first place. The guests were due to arrive in less than half an hour. There were probably some people already parked outside, but Jack had insisted that we leave the doors closed and locked until 10 minutes before the party to help with "crowd" control. How that helped to control the crowd, I wasn't sure – it seemed like it was making the crowd even bigger.

There was a scratching near the bottom of my door. "Come in, Abraham Lincoln," I called and the door creaked open. Someday I would love to know how he did that. He strolled into the room and paused at the foot of my bed, tilting his head.

"If I were you," I said, "I'd stay upstairs tonight. There's going to be a lot of people out there and you're just a little dog."

"Arf," he said, coming closer and scratching at my foot. I set my basket down on the floor and, feeling brave, reached out a tentative arm to pat his head. I held my breath in anticipation. I was way beyond the normal 2.25 feet boundary. I was… almost there. Oh my goodness. I was there. I patted his tiny head, marveling at the silkiness of his hair.

"Wow," I said. "Thank you, Abraham Lincoln. It's a great privilege." His reply was to throw himself down on the ground and offer his stomach to my hand. Well. I never. Seriously. I never thought. I was almost a little choked up. Without warning, he shot to his feet and jumped on top of my basket. "Oh," I said, trying to remain calm. "Ok. You are certainly a changeable little dog, aren't you? I've got to go now, ok?" I reached for the basket handle, and little teeth emerged, along with a warning growl. Oh great. Well, that friendship certainly didn't last long. I slunk an arm up the side of my pillow and pulled a book down (What? You don't have books on your bed?) and used it to try to poke the basket and get him to jump off. He held on with the alacrity of a world-class surfer. Then, he plumped his little rear down on the cover. A strange, totally bizarre thought occurred to me. "You don't want to get in the basket, do you?" I asked. Listen to me. I was talking to a dog like it could understand me.

The tail wagged. Oh brother. Abraham Lincoln wanted to go to the party. I reached out a cautious hand and flipped the lid open, while he scooted back to allow me room. I reluctantly pulled out the knitting that I was going to sneak into the party and spread a pillowcase down in the bottom. "Alright," I said, "get in you little troublemaker."

He hopped in and I shut the basket over his head. If Natalie found out, she was going to freak. Toto was going to go see the wonderful wizard after all. Jack would be furious.

This was the strangest party I had ever been to. People were dancing on the dance floor, doing wonderful and strange things as the square dance teacher instructed them on which way to jig and which way to jog. He was a bit of a strange man, though, because I have never seen a square dance where the people are told to flap like a chicken, have you? But, everyone seemed to enjoy it. The entire counter and surrounding area were taken up by an assortment of delicious autumn-themed treats and delights. In one corner, people were dunking for apples, a process which was exciting, and slightly disgusting. After all, there was a lot of spit going into that water, and no one was changing the water in between turns. I politely refused to participate. A little growl from my basket reminded me that I was still carrying half of a sugar cookie in the shape of a pumpkin (don't worry – it was a pre-approved cookie). I broke it in half and slipped a piece into my basket where it was met with a delighted purr of contentment. Yes, I said purr.

At the center of the store, Old Mrs. Harrison was enchanting everyone with her spinning technique. I didn't even know that she had a spinning wheel, and apparently, she had two. One she used to demonstrate and one that people could take turns practicing on. She was wearing a golden wig that hit the floor and a long pink dress. I'm pretty sure she was supposed to be the beautiful daughter of the Miller who could spin straw into gold. Her (well-behaved) dog, Harold sat next to her wearing a little goblin hat, and was, apparently, Rumpelstiltskin. So cute. I tried to get closer, as the concept of spinning has always fascinated me. How in the world did that fluffy stuff turn into yarn? Did it go all the way around the wheel? I couldn't tell from here. Somehow Abraham Lincoln must know that Harold was here because a warning growl stopped me from getting too close. It looked highly entertaining though, and Abby appeared to be having a lot of fun with her mini-lesson. The crowd around her hooted every time the fluff got away from her and was sucked into the wheel. If only I didn't have this monster in my basket. Carolyn was brilliant, though. She really was. I would be willing to bet that Crabapple Yarns would soon be carrying spinning supplies. Take that Happy Knits.

A few more games were scattered around, and it was fun to watch people try to pin the tail on the werewolf and get their fortune told by "Madame Yarnbeebe" who was, in fact… Louise. Shocking, right? But she seemed to be having a great time, and the line to her little chair was always long. Did I get my fortune told? Alas, no. I know exactly what she would see for me. Death. Certain Death.

At the "guess how many beads in the jar" table, I stood behind two women who were trying to mathematically deduce how many beads there could be in the jar by figuring out how many beads there were in a cubed inch. I was getting ready to ask them to move along (in a nice way, of course), when their conversation stopped me in my tracks.

"These cookies are divine," the lady with the rabbit ears said, polishing off the last of the cookie she held in her hand, "and did you try the pumpkin cheesecake?"

The other lady, obviously dressed as a skein of yarn, at least that's what I hope she was, nodded enthusiastically, "No one bakes like Ryan," she said. "I swear he has a secret ingredient that makes everything taste so scandalously delicious."

"Speaking of scandalously delicious," the rabbit said, standing closer to the skein, "I heard that Ryan has two girlfriends now."

"Stop," the skein said. "He's dating Molly."

"Nope," the rabbit's ears shook violently, "I saw him the other day with her. She's a cute little thing – blond and adorable. He had his arm around her and she was whispering in his ear. They crossed the street right in front of me."

I decided to let them cheat as much as they wanted and wandered off to feel sick and tell myself that, of course, it wasn't true. Rabbits lie all the time. Don't they?

Jack had finally ventured out of his "security booth" content that everyone who wanted to come in had already done so and had let me know that he had seen no one "suspicious." However, I was not so sure. The noise and the movement of the crowd and the stuffiness surged around me in stifling waves, and I couldn't think of anything nicer than this party being over. The thing is, when people were in costume, they didn't look like people anymore. The person in the gorilla suit… for example… could be anyone. He or she could be Nate. Heck. It could be Mrs. Goldmyer. And the guy wearing a Zorro cape and mask coming towards me looked almost exactly like Ryan. Jack's confidence in his security system was a tad overrated in my opinion. I stepped aside to allow Zorro to get past to the food tables, and my heart jumped into my throat when he stopped in front of me and grabbed my good arm. I squeaked a bit before I got a hold of myself.

With his other hand, he lifted his mask. I pulled away from him and punched him in the shoulder. "You scared me," I hissed.

Jack was right. Ryan was not happy. "And what do you think I felt when I heard you had been poisoned?" he said lowly. "And almost got yourself killed at the library?"

Jack the Rat. Apparently, Ryan was still taking HIS phone calls. I was surprised to feel anger flowing through me. I should have been feeling guilty, right? "Well," I said slowly, "I suppose that you'd have to answer your phone if you wanted to talk to me."

His brow lowered, "Don't give me that," he said. "You already knew something was going on when you went to the store by yourself. In the dark. It's a miracle you weren't killed. And I was right there. You could have told me."

"Well," I said again, "we were broken up at the time."

"That was your choice," he argued. "Not mine."

"And I suppose it was my choice that you were kissing someone else in that restaurant?" I shot back.

Jack came up behind Ryan and whispered something I could not hear. "I'll be right back," Ryan muttered, leaving with Jack.

I fed Abraham Lincoln the rest of the cookie and decided that I would not be here when he came back. I wasn't needed right now anyways. Carolyn's little Halloween production would begin at 8:00 p.m. I would just hide... I mean... seek alternate amusement until then. Besides, Abraham Lincoln would be thirsty after all of that cookie. I would go and get him a drink. That wouldn't be cowardly at all, would it? Actually, I would call it humane.

I snuck out of the ballroom all too easily and, making sure the door shut securely behind me, headed down the back hallway towards the kitchen to grab a bowl of water. I put the basket on the counter while I filled the little dish. For a little dog, he sure did get heavy. I decided that the kitchen was too... busy of a location and headed towards the second floor in search of some privacy when I remembered that Jack had set up his security cameras on the stairs. That would never do. I wanted to be alone. I altered my course and headed towards the basement stairs. No. Not stairs. Not in the dark. The sitting rooms and conservatory were all out. Jack planned to patrol them regularly. Darn him and his security. Wasn't there anywhere a girl could go to collect her thoughts? And then it hit me.

I ended up in the pantry. The little door closed behind me, and I sank down gratefully to the floor, the shelving units oddly comfortable against my back. I let out a sigh of relief. Finally. Safe and out of all those prying eyes. Abraham Lincoln appeared to be in no great hurry to come out of his basket, so I set the water dish down on one side, and he slurped happily and then snuggled into the pillowcase. He was clearly worn out from all of his socializing.

The problem was… Ryan. I loved him. I loved him. The realization of that was almost as scary as the figure at the top of the stairs had been, and it took my breath away. That was the problem. I was afraid, and Ryan's attitude at the party had only confirmed that fear. Here in the privacy of the pantry I would take my thoughts out and arrange them in order to see if they were only crazy thoughts or if what I was thinking was true. In books and in movies, love is usually portrayed as either beautiful and uplifting – a goal – a dream – to aspire to – or something terrible and tortuous that rips your heart right out of your body. I was more inclined to agree with the last version at the moment. Because if you loved someone, that didn't mean they loved you back, did it? I mean, even though they say they do, you can't really know, can you? And here was my real fear… Ryan was an honorable person. A protective soul. What if he…

The door cracked open, and my heart jumped into my throat. I should have prepared a feasible explanation for sitting in the pantry in case this situation occurred. I should have brought a really big and sharp knife with me. I should have told someone where I was going. Why must I always be so unprepared? It was a hard life lesson.

"Molly?" A voice whispered and the door opened fully.

Ryan was a tall guy. It took me a long time from my position on the floor to look all the way up to his face. "Yes?" I asked calmly, as though sitting on the pantry floor in the middle of a party was the most reasonable thing to do.

"Are you ok?" he was still whispering.

"Fine, thank you," I replied. He came into the pantry, and to my surprise, shut the door behind him. The little light from the nightlight on the shelf gave a weak but adequate glow to the little room. Ryan sank to the ground, his back to the door.

"Are you sure?" he asked, his face kind and so unlike the angry Ryan I had seen in the ballroom.

"No," I sighed. "I'm not. But I'm sure I will be."

He scooched closer so that our knees were touching and reached out a hesitant hand towards mine. "Your hands are freezing," he exclaimed. "How long have you been sitting in here?"

"Just a few minutes," I protested, instinctively clenching my hands into fists, but he was quicker and wrapped both his hands around mine. I pretended like I wasn't grateful for the warmth.

"It's been almost 45 minutes since I saw you in the ballroom," he said. "When I couldn't find you again, I was starting to get worried."

I groaned and let my head fall back against the shelf behind me. "I just can't seem to get it right," I said with an inappropriate amount of self-pity. "It seems like no matter what I do it's not the right thing and I'm just so tired…"

"Hey," Ryan said gently, "stop it. I'm sorry, Molly. Don't talk like that. I shouldn't have been so angry with you. I know you had your reasons. And I also know that if you had told me that you thought Mrs. Goldmyer was an axe murderer based on a totally unrelated book that Natalie found on the internet, I would have thought you were… err… being… overly-imaginative." His honesty seemed to come so naturally.

I looked him in the eyes. "Thank you," I said. "That's kind of you to say. But I should have…"

"The truth is," he interrupted, "I should have done a lot of things different, too."

I looked away sadly.

He squeezed my hands one last time before sliding around into what little space there was next to me and putting his arm around me. I put my head on his shoulder. "I have a feeling, though, that the whole death and destruction thing is not really what's bothering you."

I made a very fake sounding chuckle, "If I have problems that are bigger than death and destruction, that would be bad, wouldn't it?"

"Tell me," he said quietly, "please. What's wrong?"

To my amazement, I did. "I'm afraid," I said simply.

The smooth rhythm of his breathing didn't change. "Of what?"

"Two things, actually."

His chest rumbled a bit. "Only two?" he teased lightly. "I have at least three on my list." Then he sobered. "Tell me."

"I'm afraid that you're going to realize that you'd be happier with someone else and leave," I felt his quick indrawn breath and hurried to continue, "and I'm afraid that you're going to realize that you'd be happier with someone else and not leave."

For an agonizingly long minute, he did not reply. "I'm confused," he finally said. "For one, how in the world could I possibly be happy with anyone other than you?" I couldn't stop the small sob that escaped my throat, and his arm pulled me closer. I felt him kiss the top of my head. "And two, I don't know what you mean by 'not leave'."

"I mean," I said, with a voice that was horribly scratchy with tears, "that you're an honorable person and you might think that you have to stay because you feel like you're too far in to get out but you don't want to be, you want to be out, but you'll pretend to be in so that I don't know you want to be out."

He moved fast, and suddenly I was done talking and busy kissing Ryan. "You are such an over-thinker," he said affectionately, kissing my forehead and brushing the tears away. "I love you. Get that through your thick head. And I'm never going to leave. And I'm always going to be honest about what I feel." He bent down to look me in the eye, "I promise," he said solemnly. "Could you tell that I was angry tonight?" I nodded reluctantly. He looked pleased. "See," he said, "I didn't try to hide what I was feeling, did I?"

It was a remarkably cheering thought. "I'm so glad that you were angry with me," I whispered, kissing him on the cheek. "Thank you."

He let go of me and pulled something out of his pocket. "I can see that I obviously can't leave you alone for too long," he said with mock seriousness, "you totally forget everything that I say. So do you know what I'm going to do about it?"

I looked at the pen in his hand and shook my head. "I can't even begin to guess. Write a book?"

"I'm going to give you a reminder that you can look at. Every time you begin to get scared and think crazy things I want you to look at this and remember. Can you do that?" He brandished the pen in front of my face.

Isn't it funny how you can feel so happy and free sitting with the person you love on the floor of a pantry in the middle of a Knitter's Halloween Party? I obligingly held up my cast for him, but he shook his head. "Nope," he said, tapping my nose with the end of the pen, "that cast is temporary. This is forever." And he picked up my left hand, drawing a perfect heart on the inside of my ring finger. I think we were both crying by then and I flung myself at him.

"I should have known you two would be in the pantry," a disgusted voice said from the doorway. "I should have started my total and complete search of the house here instead of everywhere else."

I looked up at Jack who towered over us in the doorway. "What big eyes you have," I said.

The door slammed back shut.

I hope he couldn't hear our laughing through the door.

The party obviously did not realize we had been gone. It looked much the same as it had before we left. Ryan and I watched the square dancers dip and twirl in silence. When the dance ended, everyone applauded and the announcer shouted for more people to come out on the floor for the next "mixer" dance. You can probably tell I'm not that much of a dancer, and I have no idea what that was, but when Ryan turned to me and asked if I wanted to try it, I agreed. A wiggle from the basket over my arm had me second-guessing my decision, but then I saw Rose standing by the fringe and asked her to hold my basket. She looked at me in confusion until Abraham Lincoln poked his nose out and licked her hand. She rolled her eyes. "The little stinker," she said. "He just never ceases to surprise me."

I took Ryan's hand happily out to the dance floor, even though my heart was pounding with dread. I had absolutely no sense of rhythm and sometimes couldn't remember which was the right hand and which was the left. I shifted to avoid the gorilla who was going to dance with a ballerina. Huh. I guess that meant the gorilla was a man in there. Well…. Then again… The music started with a screeching fiddle sound and distracted me from that particular train of thought.

Soon, I was laughing and doing figure eights around Ryan, dosey-doeing, and clapping. I even managed to clap at the same time everyone else was clapping – most of the time. And then, I discovered what it meant to be a mixer dance, as I noticed in disappointment that all the men dancers shifted partners one to the right. Sigh. I was dancing with the gorilla. Deciding to be brave – and really praying that it wasn't Mrs. Goldmyer in there – I took the gorilla's hand for the first dosey-do.

"Molly," the gorilla hissed, "I have to talk to you."

I gasped and stumbled, only the strong hand of the gorilla saving me from face planting on the floor. I quickly caught myself and made a face at Ryan so that he would not be worried before glaring at the gorilla. "Do you know what will happen if Jack catches you in here?" I demanded hotly.

"I know," Nate whispered urgently, "but this is urgent. There's something you don't know. I need to speak with you outside."

Oh yeah. And I was born yesterday. I gave him my best stare, "Do you really think that's going to happen?" I asked.

And then, it was time to change partners again, and I was dancing with the friendly mayor. Between the steps, he asked me how the readings were progressing. I answered as honestly as I could that everything seemed to be on schedule. I mean, can you imagine Mrs. Goldmyer not having something on schedule? Me, either.

Three more exhausting partners later, the dance ended. I could have sat down on the floor and wept tears of gratitude. That was the longest square dance of my life. Now if only I could avoid the gorilla and go find Ryan, everything would be fine. If the gorilla had the sense of… well, a gorilla… he would get out of here before I had the good sense to tell Ryan and Jack about our uninvited guest. Ryan and I had ended up on opposite sides of the dance floor. I wound my way over to where I could see his black hat sticking up over the sea of heads, scooping my basket from Rose who waited on the sidelines. Not, that she couldn't handle watching her dog for a while, but you never know, she might enjoy a good square dance herself. One was certainly enough for me tonight.

Ryan was talking to two women and a man who were all not in costume. How strange. Then again, maybe they were dressed up as someone famous that didn't require a costume. I popped up by Ryan's elbow and smiled up into his face when he looked down at me. "I don't think I like the mixer dances," I said, smiling at him and then turning to smile at the others in the little group. "You just never know who…" I trailed off, stopping in shock when I recognized the second woman. It was the blond from the restaurant. "Oh," I said brilliantly.

Jack and Natalie were suddenly circling around the little crowd as well, their worried eyes taking in the scene faster than I had. I knew Natalie also recognized the restaurant kissing girl.

The blond smiled brightly, her red lipstick in stark contrast to her pale skin, "Ryan," she said delightedly, "are these your friends from Springgate - the ones you always talk about?" Her golden curls bobbed excitedly in our direction. "And you must be the little Molly," she said. "The one who works at the yarn store and loves his cinnamon rolls." Even Natalie was speechless. I looked up at Ryan, but all the color was gone from his face. "Excuse me," she said, "Ryan can be so shy sometimes, can't he? I'm Jessica, his fiancé, this is his mother, Ruth, and this is my father, Stanley Ruebens."

"Fiancé?" Natalie repeated in disbelief. Jack pulled his furry mask off and stared at Ryan in bewilderment – probably the same expression that was on my face, too.

I studied them closer – Stanley was a tall, thin man who looked like he had been born a businessman and wearing a suit. He was respectably graying at the temples and probably never took his tie off. Ruth was not what I had expected at all. She was plump and… vibrating with the excitement of being at the party with Ryan and his fiancé. I could see that from here. She was the healthiest looking sick person I had ever seen. And Jessica… Jessica… was the perfect picture of a young woman in love. Her face was flushed and happy, adoration for Ryan shone in her eyes as she gazed up at him. Stanley looked on with paternal pride.

I felt sicker than I had when I had been poisoned by the hot chocolate. "Is this true, Ryan?" I whispered, turning to look up at him and studying his miserable face. "Are you two engaged?"

Something in his face switched off. And something else switched on. In an instant, the Ryan I knew and loved was gone and a different Ryan took his place. Just like that. It was a weak smile, but a smile nonetheless that he bestowed upon Jessica, "Of course," he said smoothly, "we've just been waiting for the right time to tell everyone."

"And now, ladies and gentlemen," a booming voice over the loudspeaker sang out, "please come over to the stage area for our very own presentation of "A Knitter's Halloween". Carolyn sounded so happy. I envied her being so blissfully unaware of what was happening at her own party. I found myself swept away and sandwiched between Natalie and Jack as we numbly watched Rachel and Helen act out the part of two knitters at Halloween. It was a tale, narrated by Carolyn, that had everyone shouting with laughter, some had tears running down their faces by the end. It was warm, funny and, at the same time, tender. It poked gentle fun at knitters but still showed the amazing love, friendship and resilience that all knitters have for each other and the world. It was beautiful. It also reminded me of something. The style and rhythm of it tickled something at the edge of my consciousness and I picked at it even as I watched Helen hunkered down on the stage, spinning around and around to ward off the scary monster in the fog (sorry – I'll have to tell you the whole story sometime when I'm more in the mood).

The show ended with a round of applause that went on for what felt like forever. And my brain, more than happy to have something else to think about other than Ryan and his fiancé, obediently chased down all the rabbit trails until I realized what it is that was bothering me about Carolyn's play. Huh. Strange, wasn't it? There are points in your life when you think –this is the worst. Nothing could be worse than this. And then… it gets worse. Betrayal stings hard. And it stings long.

I pulled myself away from Natalie and Jack, spotting the gorilla easily in the crowd a few rows back. "Good," he said with relief. "Can you talk now?"

"No," I said. "I can't. I was just wondering something."

"What's that?" he asked.

"Do you know if my house is still for sale?"

I think I shocked the gorilla. He stared down at me for five long seconds before answering slowly. "I believe it is," he said. "Are you ready to buy it now?"

"I am," I said. "I plan to start the process tomorrow, if possible."

"I'll help you," he said, quickly slipping into his familiar lawyer mode. "How much do you have for a down payment."

I gestured for him to lean down and whispered a figure in his ear. "Whoa," he said.

Jack and Natalie came up behind me, looking pale and sick themselves. "If you want to leave, Molly," Natalie said her face sympathetic, "we totally understand. We'll make sure no one gets upstairs."

"Nonsense," I said briskly, "I've got a job to do here and I plan to finish it." Even though the thought of going upstairs and crawling into bed sounded like the best idea in the world right now. "This is going to be a big mess to clean up and I've already got plans for tomorrow."

"Like what?" Jack asked, brow puckering in concern.

"Molly…" it was Ryan, approaching us, "please can I speak with you?" He must have managed to have his fiancé removed from his arm somehow. A small but amazing feat. I had watched them throughout the play and she seemed like a permanent fixture.

"I don't think so, Ryan," I said politely. "The guests will be leaving soon and I have work to do."

"I think you should leave, Ryan," Jack said firmly, anger simmering under his voice. "You've caused enough damage tonight."

"Not yet," Ryan said, reaching for my arm. I stepped back, even as Jack and the gorilla stepped forward. "Hey," Jack said, seeing the gorilla for the first time, "I don't remember seeing you come in. Who are you?"

"A guest at the party, obviously," Nate said, not even bothering to disguise his voice. Jack's face turned bright red, as did Ryan's and they both turned angrily towards Nate, who, I'm sure under his gorilla mask was smiling in delight. Men. They can be such boys.

"Why you…" it probably wasn't a very original thing to say. I'm sure, however, that whatever Jack was going to say next would be much more effective, but Abraham Lincoln had other plans. Jack pushed me back just a little, causing my basket to rattle, Abraham Lincoln did not enjoy such violent treatment. He erupted from the basket, barking and snarling. I knew he was in there. Natalie knew he was in there. Jack did not. Nor did Ryan. Or Nate. Jack and Ryan's faces wore identical expressions of horror and surprise as the small furry object exploded out of the confines of the basket. Unfortunately, Nate's expression was hidden by the mask, but he took a very manly step backward, hands flying up in the air to ward off whatever demon had been unleashed. Abraham Lincoln landed on the floor on all fours, his fur completely raised all over his body. The partygoers around him all leaped back in surprise and fear as he began circling them, spitting and hissing like a cat. Jack's arm had gone out in an involuntary gesture when the missile had launched, and Ryan had, for some reason, grabbed on to it. I couldn't help it. I giggled at their fearful expressions even as realization was slowly dawning on their faces. Natalie giggled, too. Hysterical giggles can be contagious. Soon everyone within ten feet of Abraham Lincoln was laughing and watching him spit and circle. This did not please Abraham Lincoln, who doubled his volume and widened his circle, nipping at ankles as he went. It was only when

I realized that my giggles were rapidly turning from laughing to crying that I fled the ballroom, Abraham Lincoln barking at my heels.

We ran all the way upstairs, and Abraham Lincoln jumped head first under the covers. I carefully locked my door and followed suit, not even bothering to take off my costume, pulling the covers over my head. Abraham Lincoln promptly curled his little body into the shape of mine and began snoring, clearly exhausted. I focused on the warmth and comfort of his presence and ignored everything else – the soft knocks on the door, the gentle turning of the door handle, all the voices… and stared, dry-eyed, at the pattern on the sheets. It wasn't until I turned over in bed and saw the heart on my finger that I cried.

CHAPTER 20

I f there was any sense of fairness in the world, then today would have been gray and cold and rainy. Big, fat clouds should have obscured the sun and any chance at a happy day for anyone. But, of course, that did not happen. By the time I crawled out of bed on Saturday, the sun was already halfway up the sky on its merry little route of spreading sunshine and good cheer, and I snarled at it even as I marveled at the view out of my window. Every tree in the forest looked like it had been hand painted by a master painter. The sun falling on the autumn tree caused each one to glow with an inner beauty that can never really be explained or photographed. It was like each tree was alive and shouting. I read once that Autumn was God's way of showing us how beautiful letting go could be. I pulled the braids out of my hair, blissfully numb and contemplated the possible truth in that. I didn't know if letting go was going to be beautiful or not, but I was going to do it. I was letting go. Of everything. Well. Not everything. I wasn't going to quit my job, but today I was going to start the process of having my own life. I was going to buy my own house and find a way to fill my life with beautiful things that did not depend on anyone else. I was going to trust God and God alone to get me through this. I had spent too long clinging to one thing or another for my own happiness – first my position at the library, then my job at Crabapple Yarns. I had let that get way out of control to the point where I didn't know where the job ended and my own life began. I should never have moved into this house. I should never have let Carolyn… I rested my head on the window in front of me. There were depths to Carolyn that I had no idea of. She had hinted, of course, that she earned money more than one way when Happy Knits had opened and we were in trouble because of The Knitting Fairy. I had, foolishly, allowed myself to think that she was doing something illegal.

A bird perched on the tree branch outside my window, and I opened the window just far enough so that I could hear her sing more clearly. So beautiful. Such a tiny, fragile thing out in the big world alone and still able to sing. I was determined to be like that bird. I would not wallow. I would move on. And hold my head up high. I was not going to be needy.

I closed the window and walked back over to the bed, looking for Abraham Lincoln amongst the covers but he was already gone. It was strange how he could go from room to room, but that's ok. He could have his little secrets. Everyone else in the world, apparently, had theirs.

I took a deep breath and went in to take a much-needed shower. To my dismay, though, the heart would not wash off. "Darn you, Ryan," I muttered scrubbing until my skin turned red. "Who carries a permanent ink pen?" Oh well. No wallowing.

Half an hour later, I was dressed for anything, my hair perfectly combed, make-up well in place and attitude confidently appropriate. I only hesitated briefly in front of the door, one hand on the doorknob, just long enough to offer a quick prayer to God to help me get through this day in the right way.

No one was downstairs in the kitchen. I did hear a lot of commotion coming from the ballroom, so I headed that way. My stomach flatly refused all offers of breakfast, even though an assortment of rolls and coffee cake were laid out on the counter. Even tea, at this point, felt like it would be pushing the limits.

I took a fortifying breath and strode down the hallway, greeted only by Abraham Lincoln who sat in the doorway to the living room, licking his paw like he hadn't a care in the world. I reached down to pat his little head, but he growled when I was within two feet. An exasperated laugh escaped me, "Really?" I asked him. "After all that last night, you're going to go back to that?"

He stood up, rubbing his body through my legs and sauntered down the hallway. "Crazy mutt," I muttered, careful not to let him hear me. I walked slowly towards the ballroom doors, appreciating again the beauty of this house. I would... I realized with a pang... I would miss it. Change is hard. Because to change you have to give up something you like for something else. And even if the something else is something you really, really want, the giving up is... terrible.

Like a death. Which, I suppose, it was. The death of what had been and never would be again.

The door to the ballroom was open and filled with a bunch of busy bees. Well, figurative busy bees. Some people were dismantling the stage, while others swept and picked up trash, while others were busy trying to move things back to where they were.

"No," Carolyn said patiently to two ladies who were huffing and puffing trying to pull a bookcase, "that's not where it was. It was over here just a bit more and tilted slightly left." I smiled sadly thinking that it would never be back where it was exactly. Then again, what would?

Her face lit up when she saw me. "Good morning, Molly," she said warmly. "How are you this morning?" She came towards me with an outstretched arm, which I ducked neatly and pretended not to see her hurt expression.

"I'm fine, Carolyn," I said and when her expression remained doubtful. "Truly I am. This will all work out." She patted my arm.

"Of course it will, my dear," she said.

Most of the work was already done, for which I felt more than a little guilt. While I had slept in bed, these poor people had been working hard. So, I pitched in with more gusto than I usually had and, in a couple of hours, it was… almost… like the party had never happened. Carolyn had, thankfully, the wisdom to have closed the store after the party for the rest of the weekend, so she thanked everyone heartily for their help, gave them all a free skein of sock yarn and their choice of a cute new sock pattern and sent everyone home. Natalie and Jack kept sending me worried looks, which I met with a perky smile each time. And, when Natalie sidled up to me to ask me if I was ok, I was quick to assure her that I was.

"Lunchtime," Jack announced, happy that the last knitter had already vanished and looking forward, I'm sure to the rest of the day off. He had worked harder than probably anyone, and I hoped he would take a well-deserved break.

"Jack," Carolyn gasped, "please tell me that you didn't actually cook something. I specifically told you that you weren't to…"

He laughed and held up a hand, "No worries," he said. "I know my own limits. I ordered pizza."

Carolyn, Rose, Celia and Abigail all sighed with relief and headed out to wash their hands and get ready for lunch.

"Thanks," I said to Jack and Natalie, "but I have something else to do this afternoon. I'll see you later this evening."

"Wait," Jack said, catching my arm. "Are you leaving? One of us will go with you." Natalie's blond head bobbed in agreement as she exchanged a significant look with Jack.

"Nope," I said, "please don't worry. I promise not to go to the library or the paper or anywhere remotely dangerous." That was, actually, not entirely true, as I would be spending the afternoon partially in Nathaniel Goldmyer's company, but despite what Jack and Natalie believed, I refused to accept that he meant me any harm. Yep. Sometimes I am really not that smart.

Despite efforts on both of their parts to dissuade me, I was on my way in less than 20 minutes. The only concession I had made was to take Mr. Darcy with me. I didn't really want to – as part of the Molly Stevenson Liberation Plan really didn't include borrowing someone else's car, but that's ok – we have to be flexible, right? And, besides, if I took Mr. Darcy maybe it would keep those two from having the means to follow me. True, they could always use someone else's car, but I was going to hope that they would behave and stay home and take a nap or something.

I drove carefully down the hill and through town, turning right on Water Street and pulling up the driveway to… my new house. Well. It would be. Excitement bubbled happily in my stomach, right along with the nauseasness of spending that much money. It was a do or die moment. Fish or cut bait. Move along or get out of the way.

A knock on my window stopped me mid-pep talk, and I saw Nate grinning at me. "You're going to get a reputation from the neighbors before you even move in if you keep doing weird things like talking to yourself in the car," he said, opening the door for me.

I rolled my eyes and smiled sassily, "They ain't seen nothing yet." His laugh was a welcome sound.

A sleek black car pulled up behind the battered Mr. Darcy. It oozed money and power. A very well-coifed and smartly dressed woman emerged, rings sparkling in gold and silver on each finger. She carried a leather clipboard and an expensive looking pen with her. "Good afternoon," she said, surprisingly warmly, "you must be Molly." She smiled up at Nate, "I told Nate that only a very special person would buy this house. I'm so glad we found one."

Me, too.

Four hours later, numb and shaking from what I had just done, I took Mr. Darcy home. Jack and Natalie were sitting in the front parlor with Celia, trying to look like they were playing a board game and weren't waiting for me to come home. They had gathered the little chintz loveseat and a few chairs around the little coffee table.

"Hi," I said, setting my purse down inside of the door.

"Hi," they all said, casually looking up from the game. "Did you have a good afternoon?" Natalie asked, just as casually, rolling the dice.

Oh brother. We might as well get this over with. It was, after all, Part 2 of the Molly Liberation Plan. "You know," I said, leaning over to inspect the board, "this would be a lot more believable if you actually had moved some of the pieces around."

Jack flushed. "We were just getting started."

"Oh," I said, "of course." I took a deep breath and sat down on the remaining chair around the coffee table. "Then it's ok if I interrupt?"

Their heads all bobbed up to look at me expectantly. "We could make the time," Celia said with a grin. "After all, we were just pretending to play so that it didn't look so obvious when you came home."

Natalie and Jack groaned, flopping back on the couch. "Mom!" Natalie wailed. "You weren't supposed to say that."

Celia rose and gave me a one-armed hug, sitting on the arm of my chair, almost like she knew I needed some moral support. "Let's not insult Molly's intelligence," she said. "Now what do you have to tell us?"

All three pairs of eyes were on me. I'm never good at this. Give me a pen and paper – and I'm fine. Have everyone look at me and wait for words of wisdom to come... "I bought a house today," I blurted out.

Jack and Natalie's faces fell. "I knew it," Celia said grimly. "I had a feeling that is who Sarah was meeting at the old Turner place."

That's right. I had forgotten that Celia was a realtor now. She glanced down at me, "I'm supposed to study what the other realtors are doing and who they're meeting with. I saw a M.S. on her schedule and I just... somehow... knew it."

Natalie came off the couch and went to her knees in front of me, "Why, Molly?" she asked, her face puckered with concern. "You don't have to move out of here. We love having you live here. Please don't go."

Jack leaned forward, resting his elbows on his knees, "I hope you didn't do this because of what happened last night," he said slowly. "It's never a good idea to make hasty decisions..."

"Please," I said laughing, "I didn't just decide last night. I promise. Don't you remember, Natalie, I saw that house on our way to go dress shopping and I literally fell in love with it."

Her mouth fell open. "You mean you bought that crazy-looking little dwarf cottage?"

I nodded happily, the first real smile of the day making its way across my face. "I did." I laughed, surprised that I could even as it happened, "I bought that adorable crazy-looking little dwarf cottage." I reached forward to grab her hands, "It's all mine, and I'm nervous and slightly sick and excited.... And I love it."

Her face split into a wide grin, too, and she pulled me forward into a hug, "I'm so happy for you, Molly," she said. "Not that I wanted you to leave, not at all. But I can tell that this is something you really want and..." here her eyes started watering, "I'm so happy for you," she sniffed.

Celia's hug tightened, "Me, too," she said softly. "It is an adorable little house. Just perfect for you. Did you see the stream in the backyard?"

I looked up at her, still grinning happily, "I did. Its perfect sweetness made me cry a little the first time I saw it. I'm going to put a gazebo back there and a huge garden and..." Celia and Natalie squealed with delight.

"And I don't think so," Jack said, looking between us like we had lost our minds. "Have you bird brains forgotten that Molly isn't safe right now? This is the worst possible time to move out on your own."

Natalie's face fell. "He's right," she said solemnly. "You can't leave right now."

I really liked the word that the knitpicker always seemed to use. "Nonsense," I said briskly, determined to take charge of my own destiny once more. "Everything that has happened has happened while I was living here," I reminded them. "I don't think it really matters where I live. Besides, who knows what this is even all about? Maybe it's over now. I mean, maybe it never began... maybe we just read too much..."

Jack stood up. "Maybe you just imagined the note that brought you to Crabapple Yarns and almost killed you?" he asked. "Maybe you just happened to get sick on the spur of the moment after drinking that hot chocolate? Maybe someone accidentally spilled cooking oil on the floor right before you were coming in?" He looked down his nose at me. "You really think that?"

I took an internal deep breath. "Maybe," I said. "But nothing serious has happened, has it?"

"I think I'd call this serious, Molly," Natalie said tapping my cast. "And the other things, too."

"But," I said as gently as I could, "they all happened while I was living here, so..."

Jack started pacing the room, "Oh yeah?" he challenged. "If you hadn't been living here then who would have come after you that night? Do you think you would have lived that night if Natalie hadn't known you were going and let us know?" He glared at both of us, obviously still a bit upset about being left in the dark.

I looked down at my hands. He was right. But I wasn't going to let that stop me. "How long?" I asked.

"How long what?" Jack sounded confused.

"How much longer should I live here because it's safer? How will we know when it's all over and when it's safe?"

He ran a hand through his hair and glowered at me, "Long enough."

I stood up and walked over to him, "Jack," I said, "there's always going to be a reason not to leave. A reason why it would be safer, smarter, more economical, more…" I flung an arm out for emphasis, "more something. And you're right. It probably would be safer to be here." I put a tentative hand on his forearm, "You guys have become like family to me. I love you. But I also… I can't describe it… but I need someplace that's my own. I need to create my own space – my own life that doesn't depend on other people. We never intended for this to be a forever arrangement – as soon as the store is un-condemned, I would have moved back there anyway."

He sighed and rolled his eyes at Natalie, "She has definitely been hanging around you for too long. She used to be so nice and quiet and un-argumentative." He pulled me forward for a hug, even as I opened my mouth to object. "Ok," he said, stepping back again. "Ok. I get it. This is something you need to do. If that's true, then there's something you need to do for us."

"What?"

"Let me install the best security system in the whole world."

Tears blurred my vision as Natalie and Celia and Jack and I all hugged together in the middle of the room, "Deal," I said happily. "And you guys have to promise to come over for dinner at least once a week."

"Just try keeping us away," Natalie said from somewhere by my right shoulder.

"Wow," Jack said, unable to keep his face neutral. "Just wow." He peeked back inside the door one more time, "That is the pinkest room I've ever seen in my life."

It was, actually, kinda growing on me. "I know," I said cheerfully. "Isn't it cute?"

"It's like Pepto Bismol exploded in there," he continued. "So if you think the cure for stomach problems is cute then…"

"Well," Natalie said, her eyes twinkling with mischief, "that is where you go when you have stomach…"

"Ewwwww!" we all exclaimed. Natalie laughed and went back to where she was cleaning the kitchen. She looked super cute today in denim overalls with a red scarf tied over her braids. Celia came back from the living room carrying a half-eaten stuffed animal.

"Look what I found," she exclaimed. "I bet it was someone's favorite little bear at one time. He's so cute. It almost looks like he's holding a little bear in his hand, I mean paw…"

Natalie snatched the dirty, ugly old toy from her mother's hand and dumped it quickly in the trash bag. I was grateful. It looked a lot like the bear I had bought Ryan and never got to give him, and she knew it. It's funny how reminders of Ryan were everywhere. I found that instead of ducking them, it hurt less if, when they came, I acknowledged them and then stuffed them way back down. Someday I'd probably run out of stuffing room, but until then, it was a system that seemed to be working just fine.

Rachel and Helen and Patrick, Helen's husband, were also somewhere around, helping me clean the house before I moved in. Things had moved along very quickly after the initial offer to purchase. There was one little tricky patch when Natalie had asked me, rather innocently, if I needed help with the purchase, but I had to confess that I already had legal counsel. Of course, this resulted in the next question of… "Who?"… and I had to confess that it was Nate. Jack had all but banged his head against the wall. "Are you kidding me?" he had demanded. "You actually went to him… him who might be responsible for…" I had felt like a worm, and Celia had very bravely stepped in to ask if she could see the paperwork, which I eagerly handed over. Jack stood there, breathing like a dragon and waiting for Celia to declare that I had been hoodwinked, swindled and scammed…

"Interesting," she said slowly.

"I knew it," Jack said lowly. "Just wait until I get my hands on…"

She rolled her eyes, "Calm down, honey," she said. "Molly has, in fact, received a very good deal. This is significantly under the asking price and includes a... car?"

That's right. I totally forgot to tell you, didn't I? The purchase of the house was a two-for-one deal of the best kind. Not only did I get a house – a home – but a car, too. Now, granted, it was a slightly rusted, very old-fashioned station wagon with vintage wood-looking trim down its elongated body, but it seemed to work and after Mr. Morrie had changed the oil and checked all the other... thingies... he declared it good to go. I certainly could fit 20 of my closest friends in the back, which would make a lot less trips when I moved later this week.

Patrick was so sweet. He fixed the garbage disposal and confirmed that the plumbing was in perfect order. Not, of course, that the building inspector hadn't already said so, but it's always nice to hear it from a familiar face, right? Nothing worse than always wondering if your toilet is *really* going to flush, am I right?

Patrick and Jack were now currently working on installing the security system that involved windows, doors, and who knows what else. I was a little scared of it, truth be told. I certainly wouldn't want to wake the entire neighborhood up at night just because I opened a window. But, Jack promised that it would be easy to use, and he was so anxious about having it on, that I agreed to whatever he said. It's a good thing Nate had saved me money on the sale of the house – the alarm system was going to cost its own small fortune. The roof would just have to wait until... it rained. Ha ha.

There was just one thing I had not told Jack, or any of my other sweet and willing helpers about. I saw no reason for them to know that Nate lived right down the street, do you?

There was only one person missing from the work crew – Carolyn. Since the night of the party, our relationship had been a little... strained. I know it was my fault. I tried, but I just couldn't seem to act the same since I had realized the Big Thing at the party. It changed everything. While Jack had, so amazingly, closed his café for a few days to help me get the house ready (even though I had begged him not to), he had. Which is the reason why both Jack, Celia and Natalie were here today. Once Sarah had realized that Celia was my... whatever she was... she had insisted that Celia take a few days off. So, what I once believed would take a month to accomplish, was going to be done in less than a week. Isn't that exciting? Carolyn, however, had let me have the week off, but kept the store open and was running it with Louise for help. Rose and Abigail were also on stand-by in case things got too busy. Rose was a good knitter herself, and she was quite content to park herself in the middle of the store and let the customers come to her.

I dumped my bucket of dirty floor-cleaning water down the sink, pleased to see the quick drain action and sighed happily. Tomorrow. Tomorrow I would move in.

There was but one flaw in my moving-in plan. My few humble, but paid for, furniture-type belongings were stuck at Crabapple Yarns. They were, too, condemned.

I'm embarrassed to say that this happy little thought actually did not occur to me until we were all sprawled around the living room eating take out and trying to re-gather energy for round #2. I let out a little cry of dismay.

Natalie giggled. I turned to her, "What?"

Her smile was wide, "I told Jack that you hadn't thought of It yet, and I was right."

"Nuts," I said. "So much for moving in tomorrow."

"Don't be silly," Natalie said. "Jack, Celia, Rose, Abigail, Abraham Lincoln and I have a few things we'd like to give you as a house-warming present."

"No," I breathed, setting down my cheeseburger in protest, "I couldn't accept."

"You can and will," Celia said with determination, "or you'll get no more help from us."

And that, my friends, is how I started life in my cute little dwarf cottage with the perfect furniture and accessories. There was a small dining room table, a couch, three comfy chairs – two for the living room and the extra-comfy one for the loft, the bed from my room, complete with sheets and comforter and pillows, towels, lamps, assorted dishes and pots and pans, and even a few knick-knacks that Natalie knew that I loved. And that first night, after everyone had left, and I had securely locked the door, bolted the door and carefully put my little code in the security system, I dropped to my knees and thanked God. I was home.

CHAPTER 21

My new car was quite happy to go back and forth every day to Raspberry Hill. I had gotten used to driving the long car surprisingly fast, and there was only one minor episode at the grocery store where I may have forgotten how long my tail was and backed into a light pole. The store manager was very kind, however, and as no damage was done to the pole, and my car didn't really care if it had one more scratch, I had gone on my way wiser and more careful about using reverse.

Despite Jack's dire warnings and predictions, life had settled down quite nicely. I had not seen or heard from Ryan since the party. I never saw Rebecca. Nate had stopped by only one time to make sure all was well, and I saw nothing and heard nothing from Mrs. Goldmyer. I felt a bit bad about that, as the "Amelda Tartan Welcome Party" was tomorrow, and I had done nothing to help her with our part of it. Not bad enough to venture to the library, however. I had even managed to behave relatively normal around Carolyn. I had not, however, managed to finish my manuscript for the contest. At this point, it seemed a farce anyway. Natalie, on the other hand, had finished hers in plenty of time and was anxiously biting her fingernails over it.

"The hardest part about writing," she had wailed one sunny day in the middle of the store, "is that there's just so many decisions. So many different ways things can turn out. And it's driving me crazy, because if I pick one, then the other ones will never get their turn, and that just doesn't seem right." Her eyes had held a crazy gleam. "And so, I write something and then delete it, then I write another thing and then delete it… and I never get anything done. I just… I just…"

"I believe that's common in the world of writing, my dear," Carolyn had commented, patting Natalie on the arm. "Just go with your instincts. You'll be fine."

I have a feeling that's what Natalie ended up doing. I also have a feeling that her story still began with, "It was a dark and stormy night." Speaking of which, I peeked out the floor-length windows on the doors, I think we were due for a dark and stormy night as well. Storm clouds were pulling together in the sky as if drawn together by a magnetic force. They whipped wildly across the sun, dizzying in their ability to block out the sun in one second and let it shine brightly the next. Natalie joined me at the window. "Why don't you spend the night here?" she suggested cheerfully, trying to pretend it was an innocent suggestion.

"No thanks," I said carefully, "I'll be fine. I've got a pot roast in the crockpot." I grinned at her, "Who knew being domestic could be such fun?" It was important, wasn't it, that when one began a quest to be brave and independent, that one stuck to it.

She rolled her eyes, "I'm sure the thrill will wear off."

I hoped not.

As I rolled through town, though, great big fat blobs of rain were already hitting my windshield, and I wondered if perhaps it would have been wiser to take a little vacation from being brave. I sighed. Oh well. This is what I had wanted, wasn't it? Freedom and independence. Even if it meant being on your own on a dark and stormy night.

I pulled into my driveway, happy to see the cheerful red door and the glow of the lamp I had left on in the living room. No. I would be fine. It didn't matter what the weather was like outside, the weather was always the same inside. A cheering thought. I pushed the button on the little rickety garage door and watched in delight as it creaked its way up. There was something so magical about coming home to your own garage, wasn't there? And, the benefits of a garage meant that you didn't have to scrape any frost off of your windshield, either. Double win.

I was greeted by the delectable smell of roast beef and potatoes as I walked through the door. My stomach growled in appreciation and anticipation. I decided that I would get myself a big plateful, and figure out how to climb the loft holding a plate and eat in my comfy chair up there. After, of course, I went and put on some sweatpants and a sweatshirt. You can't really be totally comfy in tights and a skirt, now can you?

The soaring ceiling of the living room was the perfect backdrop for the lightning currently flashing across the sky. I sat warm and snug, wrapped in a blanket and stretched out on the couch after supper, watching nature's fascinating light show as I tried to decide what I would do this evening. I could do any one of the many little house projects that still needed to happen. Or, I yawned, I could simply sit here and read a book. Climbing into the loft with dinner hadn't really worked out, so I was still due for some comfy chair time. That was important, right? Reading was also very important. I could, on the other hand, get some knitting done. I'm embarrassed to tell you that I still had to finish the bunny blanket. Carolyn's sample was done and hanging up next to the yarn and selling both patterns and yarn right off the shelf. Unless I got my sample done soon, it was both a waste of materials and time. Sigh. I guess part of being a homeowner is sitting down and mentally deciding which thing you should do is giving you the biggest guilt trip and then doing that. What do you think? Yeah, there is always the idea of ignoring it, too. Laziness, however, was going to have to be something to guard against. I yawned again. Maybe tomorrow. It was, after all, completely dark outside. Way too late to start anything now. If only I had a television – or a laptop - I could just snuggle in and…

Reality, as it often does, smacked me upside the head. This time, in the form of a tiny little raindrop. Right on my face.

"Oh no!" I wailed. "No. Please, not the roof." I waited. Nothing. I waited some more. Still nothing. I let out a sigh of relief. Plop. Darn. The inspector had said re-shingling the roof could wait a couple of years. Now, I had a leak already. I turned on all my lights and prowled the living room, dining room and kitchen for signs of other leakage. Then, I ran to my bedroom and spare bedroom and did the same. What a relief. The rain only seemed to be coming in that one spot. Perfect. Maybe it would be an easy fix, then. Perhaps something simple like a loose shingle. Maybe even a shingle knocked loose by the inspector's own foot.

Who knows? There was obviously a lot to learn about owning a house. It's a good thing I had purchased the buyer's insurance. I hope that this was covered. I jumped at the loud crash of thunder and waited for the corresponding flash of lightning. The storm must be right overhead now. It was sure to blow over soon, right? In the meantime, I would move the couch over just a bit, get a pail from the bathroom and set it under the leak.

It was a heavy couch, the frame being made of solid wood. It had caused just a little bit of swearing to pop out from both Jack and Patrick when they moved it in. But it was the couch I had wanted. I loved its wood frame and bright stripy cushions. They contrasted perfectly with the flowered armchair on the right and the deep, deep blue chair on the left. Probably not everyone's idea of perfect, but it was mine. I regretted, now, the heaviness of it, and realized I should have picked the cheap sofa from one of the upstairs sitting rooms. They, at least, would be easier to move and vacuum under. If, that is, I ever felt like vacuuming under my sofa. Which, of course, I would. I mean... who wouldn't? Ahem.

After some serious shoving, I managed to back the couch far enough away from the drip where it wouldn't be bothered, and then I shoved both armchairs back and the coffee table. Now, all I needed was the pail. The pink pail that was in the pink bathroom, currently doubling as the under-the-sink garbage can. I grinned to myself. I had been unable to resist its pinkness when I saw it at the supermarket. Natalie had protested quite loudly, but I had bought it anyway. Who knows – perhaps that is how the original owners had started as well – one pink thing leads to another...

There was another loud crash of thunder, and the sound of something falling from the vicinity of the back bedroom. The lights flickered and then dimmed. "Oh noooooo...." I whispered. My first thunderstorm in my own house, by myself, was one thing... my first thunderstorm in the dark... how was I going to...

"Nonsense," I told myself, trying to sound stern and cold like someone else I know. "Don't be ridiculous and do not be hysterical. The loss of power does not equal loss of your brain."

Dang. I could be pretty mean when I wanted to be. I decided that the drip was the most important thing right now, and so the candles would have to wait. I know. A flashlight would have been a good idea, too. It's just too bad I was so busy buying a pink bucket that I never thought of one. I would have to burn the candles that Rose and Abigail insisted I have to go with the candlesticks they had given me. It was a shame, though, they looked pretty old.

I walked towards the bathroom, one hand against the hallway door to find my way… and found it easy enough to get around. The brilliant flashes of lightning every 3 seconds were more than sufficient to light the way. I stepped into the bathroom, my hand automatically flipping the light switch. "Stupid," I muttered. "That was really stupid."

I opened the cupboard and pulled the pail out, placing it on the counter so that I could pull out the inner plastic bag. Lightning flashed outside brighter and harder than before. I glanced uneasily at my reflection in the mirror – and froze. That couldn't be….

I waited, frozen in horror for the next flash of lightning. *Please God. Please God. Please God,* chanting through my head. The lightning came as it had been doing with shocking regularity and strength. Its power zinged through the open window, illuminating the room for a horrifying half of a second. I literally did not know what to do. Horror gripped me with icy fingers.

There was someone behind the shower curtain.

In my bathtub.

I quickly put my head down so I wasn't looking in the mirror and tried to look as calm as I could. Two steps. Two steps away from me there was someone in my tub. Two steps. They could be out of there in one second. Did they have a gun? A knife?

My hands were shaking as I finished taking the bag out of the garbage can. I laid it casually on the sink and forced myself to walk out of the room slowly and calmly, sweat falling from my forehead into my eyes. I shut the bathroom door with what I hoped was a normal door shut and backed away down the hall. I knew what was going to happen. The doorknob would begin turning and then… *Oh God. Oh please God.* Oh. My. Goodness. The doorknob was turning. I stopped thinking then. It never occurred to me to grab a weapon and wait- or grab the phone and call the police. My only thought was – out. I needed to get out. I flew out the door – noticing in the back of my mind that that action should have sent the alarm screaming but it remained oddly silent– and ran across the road and down the street to the solid little white cape cod with black shutters.

I pounded on the door, soaked to the skin and shaking with fear and adrenaline. Maybe he wasn't home. Maybe he worked late. I pounded again, crying and calling his name. A horrible thought occurred to me... what if he wasn't here... because he was.... at my house... and I gasped in continued fear. This was taking too long, I looked anxiously over my shoulder... had I been followed... The light on Nate's front porch suddenly turned on, and I blinked in the steady glow of the light. But... the power... I realized with a growing dread that the power to my house only had been cut off. I looked closer and saw the house next door from me also had a light glowing from within, as did the house two houses down. Why hadn't I thought to look? Why hadn't I run there instead of here?

The door creaked open. "Molly?" It was Nate's shocked voice that pulled me from my contemplation of the houses on the street. He reached out an arm into the rain and pulled me in. I stood on the rug in front of his door and contemplated him carefully. His hair and clothing were completely dry. It would have been impossible, right, to have gotten back to his house and be completely dry already, right? I sighed, face crumpling. Right. I think it was safe here.

"Nate," I cried, pulling his arm, "there's someone in my house. They turned off the electricity and... the roof was leaking so I went to get the pail out of the bathroom and..."

"What?" he exclaimed, trying to pull me further into the house. "Come in and calm down."

"No!" I insisted, wiping the rain and tears away from my face. "Please. You have to call the police. There was..." I gulped, "there was someonebehindtheshowercurtainandithinktheywantedtokillme."

"What?" He asked. "What are you saying?" He grabbed me by the front of my arms. "Take a deep breath, calm down and say it slow."

I did as he suggested and was remarkably pleased to find that he was right. I did feel calmer. That fact could also have something to do with the fact that I was now dry and standing in a well-lit room with a person that was probably not trying to kill me.

"I'm trying to tell you," I said, "that the power went out. I went into the bathroom, and the lightning flashed. And…" I was still having a hard time saying it.

"Go on," he encouraged, his face worried.

"There was someone behind the shower curtain," I whispered. "I could see their silhouette."

He turned pale. "Are you sure?"

I nodded, sinking wearily to the floor, feeling like one of those ridiculous parade blimps that suddenly lose their helium. He grabbed his phone and dialed rapidly. I lost track of what he was saying, but was grateful when he threw a kitchen towel my way. I used it to dry what I could. I was starting to shiver. By the time my hair and face were fairly dry, he was off the phone and leaning down.

"Are you ok?" he asked.

I nodded shakily. "I was so scared," I whispered, feeling unable to speak any louder. "I thought I was going to die."

His face twisted in sympathy. "You poor thing," he said. "How about we get you a little drier and warmer? And then we'll wait for the police to come."

"That would be nice," I agreed.

He led me carefully down the hallway to his bathroom. I balked at going in the door. "Sorry," he said quickly, "let me check first." He left me clinging to the doorframe, while he turned on the light. I could see him in the mirror. He checked the bathtub, even, and this made me smile just a bit, even the little cabinet under the sink. He double-checked the lock on the window. "It's safe," he said. "I promise."

I looked back at the little wet trail I had left through his immaculate house. "Sorry," I offered.

He shrugged, zipping around me and going into another room and coming out quickly with an over-sized sweatshirt and sweatpants. "These are probably going to be way too big, but they're dry."

I took them gratefully, and he waited for me to step into the bathroom. "Do you want me to close the door?" he asked.

I might be scared, but I was obviously not scared enough to throw modesty out the window. I wondered, idly, what that would take. "Yes, please."

"Ok," he said, "take your time. I'll be in the kitchen."

I closed the door quietly and leaned back against it for a full five seconds. *Thank you, God* I prayed. I straightened away from the door and surveyed the neat and trim little black and white bathroom before looking at myself in the mirror. I looked like a drowned rat. Worse than a drowned rat. A scared drowned rat. I was sure that those circles under my eyes hadn't been there before, and I wouldn't be surprised to see that all of my hair was gray by tomorrow. I went to take off my soaking sweatshirt and realized that Nate had forgotten to give me a towel. The little kitchen towel I had used before was now completely useless.

I opened the bathroom door and squished my way back down the hallway, pausing in the shadow of the opening. Nate was on the phone. I hadn't heard it ring. My feet refused to move forward, which left me feeling slightly guilty for eavesdropping, but not really.

"I can never get anything right, can I?" he asked with an angry sigh. He paused to let the other person speak. "No. You always said that your parents were so hard and emotionless and that you wished they had known how to be kind. Now you're being the same way." My heart squeezed painfully. This was wrong. I should stop listening. "No," he said again, "that's not how it's going to work. You need to come clean about this whole business or it's going to get ugly." He continued speaking, and although I couldn't hear the exact words, I could hear the tone and timbre of the voice. I covered my mouth to hide my gasp. He was talking to his mother. He must have stepped away into the living room, because his voice became muffled. I shrugged, still shivering in my wet clothes. I would contemplate their family relationships later, after I was warm and dry. The towel closet had to be somewhere close to the bathroom, I'm sure he wouldn't mind me borrowing one. He had said to make myself at home, hadn't he? I wasn't sure. But it was the polite thing to say, so I would just assume that he said it before I died of the cold.

All of the doors down the hallway were closed – their handles identical. I could hear my teeth chattering as I considered them. I doubted it was the door down the hall where he had appeared out of with the clothes – that was probably his room. I tried the door across the hall. That seemed logical. I wiggled the door handle. Rats. It appeared to be stuck. I tried again, tightening my grip and twisting hard to turn the handle. It gave way relatively easily, and then I realized with a sinking feeling that it wasn't a linen closet at all – it was a small room – a room with lots of bookshelves. I looked down at the doorknob again and realized, as my stomach sank even lower, that the handle hadn't been stuck – it had been locked. Whoa. I had broken the lock. Not good. Not good at all. Try explaining this one, Molly, I chided myself. Then, as is bound to happen, curiosity got the better of me. Why would someone lock a room with bookshelves? I peered at them in the dim light – how strange they almost looked like… I decided to risk exposure – both from the cold and from Nate – by delaying my towel search and turning on the light.

Holy. Cow.

Holy. Cow.

This was not good.

Not only was the room absolutely stuffed with books – they crowded the bookshelves and were stacked in piles on the floor – it was filled with only one book. Sorry. I mean, they were all copies of one book. Yes, my friends, you guessed it. The room was filled with copies of "The Axe Murderer of Springiegate."

I quickly flipped the light off and stepped back into the hallway, pulling the door shut as best I could and hoping that the handle didn't look broken from the outside.

I took a step back and turned to re-enter the bathroom for a quick thinking session. This was big. What was I going to do? What did it mean? But then, naturally, Nate popped his head down the hallway. "Hey!" he said in surprise. "Why aren't you dry yet?"

My teeth were chattering even louder now that there were fear and cold in the equation. "T-T-Towel," I tried to stammer out.

He rolled his eyes, "How could I be so thoughtless? Of course, you'd need a towel. Here – let me get you one." He passed me in the hallway and went to the door just beyond the bathroom, reaching into the closet for a towel. He paused, mid-grab, the door blocking my view of the linens, and I saw his eyes slide to the ground by my feet.

I looked down quickly and saw what he saw. My wet footprints clearly going through the doorway. To the locked room. My eyes flashed back up to his – my panicked gaze colliding with his – and then I was running again.

"No," he yelled, "wait!" I could hear him running down the hall after me, and was surprised that his long legs had not yet caught up to mine, when I heard a skid and a thud. He must have slipped on the wet floor.

I ran straight to the front door, pausing only long enough to unlock the handle and then flew back outside in the dark and stormy night. I would never, ever mock Natalie for starting a story with those words. They were the scariest words I had ever heard. I ran down Water Street towards Main Street, praying as I huffed past my own house that whoever was in there would not see me. Thankfully the rain was still falling like a million stinging pellets of iciness, and I ran, slipping a bit as I turned onto Main Street. I knew where I was going. The only safe place I could think of. Even if he was engaged to someone else.

CHAPTER 22

For the second time that night I was banging on the outside of someone's door. Yes, you're right. I could have gone any number of places. I could have gone to the police station, for example. I could have gone to Raspberry Hill, for another example. That, my friends, though, was way too far for me to run. If you seriously think I can go that far you have seriously over-estimated my athletic ability. I was already huffing and puffing, the exercise doing just a little to warm me up. I could have also easily gone to Helen & Patrick's, or Rachel's or… Old Mrs. Harrison's. I didn't want them, though. I wanted Ryan.

"Ryan," I called, banging on his door as hard as I could, "please." Maybe he wasn't home. Maybe he was with Jessica. Maybe… I couldn't help the sob that escaped me and I leaned my forehead against the front of his door, knowing that I would not have the energy – or the courage- to venture out into the storm again. I would just slide right down here and hope that I wouldn't freeze to death by morning.

The door opened, and a sleepy-looking Ryan had to grab me to keep me from falling face-first into his apartment. "Molly!" he exclaimed. "What's wrong, sweetheart? What happened?" His long fingers were cupping my face and studying me with a scared expression.

And just like that, I knew what I had known since I had started running blindly to Ryan's apartment. He was mine.

My face puckered, and I shivered hard. "Come in," he said, pulling me in with him. "Come in. Here let's get you dried off and warm first. Ok? Don't try to talk yet. Let's just get you warm." And with that, he had already pulled a blanket off from the back of his couch and wrapped me in it, still pulling me down the hallway. He opened a door to what turned out to be the bathroom and I sank down onto the side of the tub, shivering violently. He plugged the tub up and started the hot water going. I focused on trying to keep my teeth from chattering out of my head, and he disappeared. Only to come back with fluffy towels, fresh clothes and a long, fleece robe.

"Ok," he said, "I'm going to leave you. Get out of those wet clothes and into the tub. Then, when you're a little warmer, get dressed and I'll make you some hot tea." He grabbed my elbow, forcing me to look up at him. "How does that sound?" he asked anxiously.

"G-g-g-great," I managed. "Did you l-l-lock the d-d-dr?"

His face got paler, the freckles standing out, "I did, Molly," he said seriously. "I promise. No one's getting in. I'm going to close the door and then wait right outside it. Ok? See – there's not even a window in here – you're perfectly safe."

I nodded feebly and he left. I could hear him slide down the door on the other side, as I'm sure I was meant to. "Take your time," he said. Just like Nate had earlier. But this time, the words warmed me from the inside.

I was out of my wet clothes and into the tub in no time. At first, the water still felt cold even though I could see steam rising from the tub. I waited, shivering in misery until warmth began returning. Ryan, bless his heart, began whistling softly outside the door, letting me know he was still there. I loved him even more for that.

When I no longer felt like I was going to die, I reluctantly pulled the plug, dried off and got dressed in Ryan's sweatpants and sweatshirt. They were yards too long, so I rolled up the cuffs and, finding a safety pin in the top drawer, pinned them securely on. The sweatshirt sleeves were also far too long, so they got rolled up as well. By the time I had the robe on with the sleeves rolled up, I felt a bit like the abominable snowman, but at least I was warm.

I opened the door, cautiously, and steam escaped and blew out down the hallway. Ryan quickly stood. "Hey," he said uncertainly. His lips curled when he saw my outfit.

I looked down self-consciously. "I must look pretty funny," I admitted.

"You look beautiful," Ryan said seriously and pulled me into a hard hug. "Now come to the kitchen and tell me what's going on. I'm about to burst with questions."

I told him, over two cups of tea and chicken salad sandwiches, what had happened this evening.

He put his warm hand over my still-cold one, "I'm so sorry" he said hoarsely. "That was terrible." His hand twitched to the phone, as it had done the first time I had sat in his store dripping wet and scared, "We should call the police."

"No," I said quickly. I couldn't bear the thought of talking to anyone else right now. I just wanted to talk to... Ryan. "Please don't. Nate already did." I puckered my head, thinking, "At least I think he did. It's all so muddled."

"Come on," Ryan said, standing and pulling me up with him, "let's go sit in the living room. I'll turn the fireplace on."

"That sounds heavenly," I agreed, curling into my own corner of the sofa immediately while Ryan fiddled with the dials of the gas fireplace. Now, normally I prefer a good old-fashioned wood blaze, but today, even the somewhat chemistry room scent of the gas was something trivial compared to the heat that it soon puffed out.

He draped a blanket over my lap. "Better?" he asked.

I nodded. "Much better. Thank you." I examined my cast, which had water spots all over it. "I think my cast got a little wet, but oh well."

He sat down next to me. "I owe you an explanation," he started.

"No," I said. "Can I go first?"

He sank back into his corner. "Go first?" he asked, puzzled. "What explanation would you possibly need to..."

"Please?" I asked.

He nodded and waited for me to start. I took a deep breath and prepared to tell him the thing I had promised never to tell anyone else. "When I broke up with you," I began, "I didn't break up with you because that girl kissed you." I refused to use her name.

Ryan started, "Molly," he said, "please don't..."

"No," I said, holding up my hand, "let me finish. I broke up with you because I thought I didn't deserve you and you'd figure that out someday and it would be easier just to get it over with."

Ryan closed his eyes briefly, as though in pain. "Molly, please…"

"My best friend in the whole world died because of me," I said suddenly, eager to just get it out of the way. He stared at me, wide-eyed. "Her name was Gretchen, and she was shy, but funny and so much fun. She would still be alive if it wasn't for me. You could say that I killed her."

I dropped my gaze and studied the pattern of the blanket over me. "I find that hard to believe," Ryan said gently. "Tell me what happened."

"Well," I said, not raising my eyes, "we had been friends since 2nd grade. She transferred in the middle of the year from another school and the teacher asked me if I could make sure she was included in the fun at recess. So I did, and somehow, we became best friends. We were inseparable until… until high school."

"What happened then?"

I sighed, "She became… different. Her parents told me she was suffering from depression. She would become irritable and moody. She didn't want to hang out with anyone else but me. Ever. Sometimes she would be different and we'd go to the movies together or go to the mall, but those were the rare times. So many times she would call me and say that she just couldn't go on. She wanted to end it all and felt that she would be better off dead. And so I would drop whatever I was doing and go over to her house and spend the night and try to be bright and cheerful and make life sound interesting. I told her parents, I promise you I did, but things never got better. The cycle would just keep repeating. And repeating. Sometimes," I raised agonized eyes to his, "sometimes, I thought she was doing it just to get attention because she'd call and I'd go over there and she'd be ok. It would make me mad."

"And then…" Ryan encouraged gently, reaching over to take my hand.

"And then… it was the Junior Prom. I had a date." I let out a shuddering sigh. "She didn't. She called that night. Said she was depressed and wanted to die. I told her to stick to the plan. We were still going to sit together at the same table.

A few other girls didn't have dates either, and they were sitting together with us. I told her it would be fine. She said she didn't want to. I got angry with her. I wanted to go to the prom. I had a pretty new dress and I was…" I broke off to catch a sob before it came out, "I was tired of cheering her up. I yelled at her. And she hung up the phone. I went to prom, but she never came." I pulled my hands away to cover my face. "Her parents found her in the morning."

Ryan was suddenly off the sofa and kneeling in front of me, pulling my hands down. "Stop it," he said sternly. "It wasn't your fault. You can't make someone better if they don't want to be – or even if they can't be. It wasn't your responsibility – and it certainly wasn't your fault."

I cried harder. "Yes, it was," I argued. "She was my best friend. I was the only one who…"

"No," he said firmly. "Didn't anyone tell you that that's not how mental illness works? If she couldn't control it- what makes you think you can?" He pulled me forward, picking me up and then sitting back down with me on his lap, "Shhhhh," he said, "it's going to be alright."

I cried into his shoulder, so embarrassed that I couldn't seem to stop. "It's never going to be alright," I said. "Never. Because she'll always be dead."

"Just because you don't see the reason doesn't mean there isn't one," he said quietly, into my hair. "You need to believe that. And you need to stop feeling guilty."

I took a deep, shuddering breath, and tried to compose myself. "I know that," I said honestly. "I thought I was doing better. I called her parents the other day."

He stiffened. "Please tell me they don't blame you."

I shook my head. "They don't. They never did. They were…" I had to pause to maintain some dignity, "grateful for our friendship."

He let out a sigh. "Of course they were. You have a beautiful heart. Anyone can see that. I'm sure it would kill them to know that you're still beating yourself up about this."

"I felt like a murderer," I said softly, into his shoulder. "I felt like a big fat hypocrite for being alive and healthy and for not listening…"

"Shhhhhh," he said again, waiting for me to calm down, "I'm going to say it again. You're not responsible for anyone's actions but your own. You did your best. You can't live your life just to keep someone else out of trouble. Not even her parents could do that. She had a disease. And it overcame her. Blame the disease if you want, but don't blame yourself."

"They gave me her college fund," I said, wiping my eyes. "I swore I would never use it. But I did."

His eyes crinkled. "You used it to buy your house, didn't you?"

I looked up at him in surprise. "How did you know that?"

"What?" he asked, a slight flush creeping up his neck. "Just because I tell you I'm engaged to another woman, you think I'd stop caring about you?"

"Yeah," I said straightening up a little, and blowing my nose in the tissue Ryan offered. "What was up with that, anyway. You had me fooled, you know. Right up until…" I trailed off.

"I'm sorry," he said, meeting my eyes honestly. "If I could have thought of any other way, I would have. I promise I would have. When did you realize…"

"On the way running over here tonight," I admitted with a small smile. "I realized that this was the only safe place in the whole world and the only place I wanted to be was with you – and – I just knew. I knew you had lied." I punched him in the shoulder, just as I had done that night at the party. "But why did you lie?"

He sighed and leaned back against the cushions, pulling me closer. "My mom is sick," he said, looking at the ceiling, "but not physically sick like I let everyone believe."

Ahhh. It all made sense now.

"She has a mental disorder?" I asked softly. "And you were…"

He looked ashamed. "I was embarrassed by her," he confessed. "Her behavior is sometimes atrocious – especially when she is off of her medication. She lives in a home where they monitor her medication and offer counseling and assistance around the clock. I tried to have her live with me - I really did – but it was impossible. She was just too…"

"Sick," I supplied. "I know you, Ryan," I said softly. "I know you would do everything you could for someone you love."

I was rewarded with a brief smile, "I would," he confirmed, and then he sighed. "I would even pretend to be engaged."

"Now that was probably not your best idea," I admitted, snuggling closer so that he knew I wasn't mad.

"My mom," he said with a sigh, "during one of her episodes, did some shoplifting and vandalism. She claims she doesn't remember doing any of it, but she…" he sighed again, "she lies a lot. That's one of the problems. And, despite the fact that she has medical proof that she is mentally incompetent, they were threatening to press charges which would mean that she would either go to jail or a state hospital. I didn't want either of those to happen. Jessica's father is an amazing lawyer. He was persuaded by Jessica to represent my mom, and, miraculously, they let her go with a firm warning and an admonition to stick to her treatment program. I think this might have scared her into actually doing that this time. She seems so much better now than she ever has. The problem is… Jessica wanted something for his help. She wanted…"

I sat up and stared at him, "She wanted you?"

He rolled his eyes, "You don't have to sound so surprised," he said somewhat indignantly. "After all, I am considered by many to be quite a catch."

"I meant," I said, unable to stop a small smile, "that she can't have you. Because you're already mine."

He pushed the hair back from my forehead affectionately. "I tried to tell her that. But her dad was pressuring her that it was time to get married. She thought maybe a long, fake engagement would buy her some time. If I didn't agree, she'd promised that she would tell her dad to change his mind about representing my mom, and possibly, to get the judgment reversed due to new evidence."

"New evidence?" I asked, puzzled.

"She kept some of the things my mom stole as proof."

I was indignant, "As blackmail!"

He smiled, "It's nice to see some color back in your face," he said. "Yes, as blackmail."

"So you're still engaged then?" I asked, making a face.

"Nope," he said, sounding smug. "I got it all straightened out last night. I was working up my nerve to come see you tomorrow, feeling pretty certain you'd throw me out on my ear. But I'm not engaged to Jessica any longer."

"How did you do it?" I asked in wonder.

"First," he said with his familiar mischievous smile, "I told her that I loved you. That didn't work. Then I had the brilliant idea to reverse blackmail." He laughed at my puzzled expression. "She had kept the jewelry my mother had stolen. She was, in fact, in possession of stolen items. I told her I would tell the police that she had them and had assisted my mom in her endeavors. Just like that... I wasn't engaged anymore."

"You're brilliant!" I exclaimed. "That's almost better than most books I've read."

"Almost better?" he teased, leaning down to kiss me lightly.

I took a deep breath. "I thought telling someone my worst secret in the world would feel like it happened all over again and I would want to burrow into the closest hole in the ground."

He pulled me closer, "What does it feel like instead?"

I looked up at him, "It feels like maybe I can really let it go."

The phone rang. Neither of us moved. It kept ringing.

"Don't you have an answering machine?" I asked sleepily, feeling warm and content and exhausted.

"I don't," he said. "What's the point?"

"So you don't have to get up and answer the phone when you're totally and completely comfortable," I suggested.

He kissed my nose and, when it became obvious that it was not going to stop ringing, I reluctantly moved so that he could get up and answer it.

"Hello?" he said. There was frantic talking. "Whoa," he said. "Slow down Natalie. It's ok. She's here." More frantic talking. "No, she's fine. I promise.... Hello? Hello?"

Uh-oh. How did Natalie know what had happened tonight? "So, I'm guessing she's on her way over here," Ryan said grimacing, putting the phone back down. "I'll make some coffee."

In less than 10 minutes, both Jack and Natalie were sitting in the chairs in Ryan's living room, not sipping their coffee and looking livid. "I'm sorry," I said lamely. "I didn't know the police would call you."

Jack looked like he was going to say something, thought better of it and stared at the floor. "Molly Dear," Natalie bit out, "when one is accosted in one's home, flees to another home and then runs for her life from that home as well, don't you think one's family should be made aware of the situation?"

"I do," I said emphatically. "I really do. I'm so sorry. I was just so cold. And then Ryan and I started talking and time just seemed to get away from us. If I had been thinking clearly, I would have called. I promise." I stood up, ready to grovel at their feet. I hated it when I caused anyone suffering.

"I think after all that Molly has been through tonight," Ryan said a bit severely, "that you could cut her a little slack." He looked embarrassed, "You can yell at me if you want to yell at someone. I should have thought of calling you. I only thought…"

Jack looked up, "You only thought about making sure she was ok first," he said with a small smile, "and that's exactly what I wanted to hear."

"You mean," I said, looking back and forth from Jack to Natalie, "you're not mad at me?"

Natalie jumped to her feet and hugged me hard, "Of course not. We were never mad. Scared out of our wits, yes. We heard that someone had attempted to kill you and you were missing. How would you feel?"

I hugged her back just as hard, "I would be scared and mad as hornets."

"Besides," Natalie added mischievously, "who could be mad at someone who looks like a little kid dressed up in play clothes?"

"I'll have you know," I said, feeling suddenly happy and waving my long sleeves in front of her face, "that this is what people refer to as stylishly over-sized."

Jack laughed, "You look like a midget," he said. "An adorable midget."

Natalie's phone rang, and she pulled it out of her back pocket. "Yes?" she answered. "I see. Tonight? Yes, I suppose that's possible. We'll be there in half an hour."

We all looked at her expectantly. "That was the police," she clarified. "They're holding Nathaniel Goldmyer and want you to come down and say if you want to press charges."

I shrugged helplessly. "Press charges for what?"

Jack and Ryan both looked at each other meaningfully, "I'm sure we could think of something," Jack said with an evil smile.

I rolled my eyes. "Guys," I said "it's not illegal to own hundreds of copies of the same book. And he never tried anything either. For all I know, he was going to explain it when I freaked out and hoofed it over here."

"I think…" Ryan began.

"Oh never mind," Natalie said impatiently, "and don't think we've forgotten all about that 'I'm engaged to this blond chick business either.'" She glared at him only half-seriously. She turned her attention to me. "I brought you some clothes if you want to change," she offered, picking up a bag from behind the sofa. "I figured if you made it here somehow you might be a tad damp." She grinned at me, "Of course, if you prefer the stylishly over-sized look, that's ok, too."

I took her bag of clothes gratefully. "Thank you," I said sincerely, "I can never repay you guys for all of your kindness…"

"Oh, go get dressed," she said, pushing me down the hall. "We'll save the sloppy sentiments for later."

She had brought me a pair of her own jeans and a nice, long comfy sweater. I was grateful for the sweater, especially since her jeans were a tad bit, shall we say, ill-fitting on me. Ok. Let's just be honest. I could not get the stinkers to zip up. That's just the way it was. We were built differently. I made good use of the safety pin as a temporary jean extender and guarantor of the jeans remaining where they should be, pulled the sweater down as far as it would go and tried to comb my hair so no one would mistake me for a scarecrow off of its stick and said a quick prayer. I had a feeling that this was still going to be a long night.

It continued to rain cats and dogs as we entered the police station. Nate sat on the same bench that I and the pesky knitters had sat on during our brief almost incarceration. He didn't look especially happy to see me.

"Hi," I said lamely.

He settled back on the bench and refused to meet my eyes.

Officer Douglas came out with a smirk. "I see the roles are reversed this time," he said, chuckling. "I can't wait to see the next combination of miscreants that you guys will think of."

"I'm sure there won't be a next time, Officer Douglas," Natalie said frostily.

The Sherriff popped his head out of the door, "Howdy, folks," he said. "I'll be right with you."

I went and sat on the bench by Nate. "I'm so sorry about dragging you into this," I said softly so that the others wouldn't hear. "I'm also so sorry for running away tonight. I know it was stupid and I shouldn't have behaved…"

"It's fine," he said shortly. "Whatever."

I snorted, "Whatever? I never thought I would hear Nathaniel Goldmyer using language like 'Whatever'. What are you? Three?"

He scooched even farther away from me on the bench. "I never thought Molly Stevenson would actually run away from me because she thought I was capable of…"

I turned to him, "I was scared because I saw all of those books," I confessed. "I didn't mean to break into that room. I thought it was the linen closet and the door was stuck. It was a total accident. I think you know that I know the truth about those books." I shrugged. "Sorry that I wasn't thinking clearly." I added somewhat sarcastically. "There was only some crazy person in my bathtub like 15 minutes earlier and I was still a little… upset… and not thinking clearly." I repeated somewhat lamely. I'm just not good at verbal communication during stressful times. I looked around the room, "So why would anyone think that I would want to press charges for anything you did tonight anyway?"

He sighed and slouched even further down the bench. "Oh," he said, "you haven't even heard the best part yet."

Sherriff Jones chose that moment to come out. I was struck, once again by his kind face. He smiled down at me. "Alright there, Ms. Stevenson?" he asked. "No harm done tonight?"

I shook my head, "No sir," I said. "I'm fine. I would like to know, though, if you were able to find the person that was in my house?"

He pursed his lips together and eyed both me and Nate before reaching over to pull an object in a plastic bag off of the nearest desk. "We did find this in your bathroom," he said softly. "Have you ever seen it before?"

He handed me the bag. My fingers shook a little as I saw what it was. A knife. A large kitchen butcher knife. I swallowed. "No. I don't think so." I tried to look braver than I actually felt at the moment. I could feel the tension flowing off of my three friends listening to every word that was said. They were practically vibrating with anxiety. I studied the knife closer, "But it shouldn't be too hard to trace with that distinctive pattern on the handle. It looks expensive."

Nate rose to his feet, "I'll save us all some trouble here," he said tiredly. "It's my knife. It came from my house."

I gaped up at him. "Someone stole a knife from your house and brought it to mine?"

His mouth fell open and he sat back down hard on the bench. Strange noises came from his throat. "What's wrong?" I asked in alarm. His shoulders were shaking.

The Sherriff shook his head sadly, as if I were an exceptionally slow student. "What we brought you down here for, Ms. Stevenson, is to see if you would like to press charges against this man for breaking and entering your house."

Nate raised his head to look straight at me. I stared at him in confusion, "When did you do that?"

"Oh for Pete's sake, Molly," Natalie said in exasperation. "The Sherriff thinks that Nate was your intruder in the bathtub. He is implying that Nate broke into your house and contemplated killing you with a knife. His fingerprints are all over the knife. His and no one else's."

"Oh," I said, turning back to the Sherriff, "why didn't you just say so?"

He frowned at me, the first time I had ever seen him frown, "I thought I just did."

"I don't," I said firmly.

He frowned again, scratching the back of his head in confusion as some men are prone to do. "You don't think I did?" he asked.

"No," I said as patiently as I could. Good grief. We were having some major communication problems here, weren't we? I was going to have to spell this out nice and slow before we all ended up behind bars. "No," I repeated, "I don't want to press any charges. Nate certainly wasn't in my bathtub tonight."

Jack cleared his throat, "Now, you don't really know that do you, Molly?"

I glared at him, "Of course I do," I protested hotly. "His hair was dry."

That must have been the last straw. The shaking of Nate's shoulders, apparently, hadn't been stress or emotion. He had been trying not to laugh. As if almost being accused of attempted murder was anything to laugh about. He was now laughing openly. The Sherriff shook his head sadly again, "Poor kid," he said. "Cracked under the pressure."

"Only you, Molly," Nate choked out, wiping tears out of his eyes. "Only you would be so crazy as to believe that it wasn't me in your bathtub tonight. 'His hair was dry.'" He snorted, then wiped a hand over his face, suddenly sober and tired looking. He stood up slowly, like someone thirty years his senior would do, and looked to the Sherriff. "Am I free to go?"

The Sherriff shrugged, "Your hair was dry, so you must be fine." He clapped Nate on the shoulder so hard Nate actually swayed, "I never really thought it was you," he confided, "but you have to follow the evidence."

"Oh, I know that," Nate said smiling. "No harm done." He turned to me, "Thanks, Molly. No hard feelings, I hope?"

I shook my head and tried to smile back. "Of course not. I'm sorry about…"

He waved his hand negligently. "It's always fun to see you at the police station," he said, "although I almost regret giving you my card." He winked at me and sauntered past Ryan, Natalie and Jack like he owned the place. He was almost to the door before he paused and turned around. "Oh, and Ryan," he said.

Ryan tried to glare at him, but it was a pretty weak glare. "What?" he asked.

"Keep an eye on Molly," he said. "I'd hate to be accused of her murder or anything."

Ryan stared at him, "You can count on that," he said grimly.

Sigh. Goodbye freedom and independence. It was fun while it lasted.

CHAPTER 23

Our evening, or should I say, morning, concluded with the four of us returning to Raspberry Hill to spend the night. It was a given that I wasn't returning home anytime soon, and so, like a wayward child, I was brought back into the welcoming fold. And, after all that excitement, Natalie and Jack had insisted that Ryan take a spare room as well. Everyone would sleep better, Jack had insisted, if we were all under one roof. And, what do you know? He was right. You'd think after almost being butchered to death (if the police were right and the person in the bathtub was, indeed, carrying Nate's knife) and running for my life at least twice last night, that sleep would be a long time in coming. The truth was – I was out like a light even before my head hit the pillow. At least that's what Natalie said. She also insisted that I snored the whole night, but you can't always believe everything she says. We had set a little bed up in her room just for the night, just like we had after I had seen the head in my bathroom closet. The Molly Stevenson Liberation Plan would just have to wait until no one was trying to murder me.

When I awoke, the sun was shining high through the window. I had obviously missed the crack of dawn several hours ago – if not more. I raised my weary head to peer over at Natalie's. Great. She was already up and probably working her tail off while I lazed about. I snuggled back down to think about that – just for a minute.

The next time I awoke the sun was definitely more in the afternoon-type sky as opposed to the morning sky. I sat straight up in bed. Oh no! I had way overslept and probably overstayed my welcome. Carolyn was going to fire me. I should have been working. And then, after work, I was supposed to help with the Amelda Tartan Welcome Celebration and serve hors-d'oeuvres and greet the people attending. A brief twinge of guilt snapped me even further awake. I sure hope Mrs. Goldmyer had finished taking care of the readers. It would be just like her to let it flop and then stand back and coolly say, "Well, Ms. Stevenson, obviously you did not follow through on your portion." The town would all boo and hiss. My name would be mud. I would be shunned at all future gatherings...never asked to do anything again... hey – I brightened... maybe there was a small bright side to this.

I groaned and flipped back the covers. That scenario, unfortunately, was very likely to happen. And, in all reality, maybe even what I deserved. After all, I had not done my part. I dressed quickly, performing my morning ablutions (or afternoon – whatever) and hurried downstairs, ready to work. Right after I ate something. I was starving.

I came up to Rose, also going down the stairs and matched my gait to her slower one. She eyed me worriedly. "How are you this morning, Molly?" she asked.

I nodded happily at her, "Just fine, Rose. And you?" I wasn't sure if Jack and Natalie had told everyone about what had happened last night, so I decided to play it cool. Well, at least as cool as I knew how to play things.

She smiled, looking relieved, "Great. I'm so glad to hear that. Natalie said you were spending the night, so I was a little worried that something was wrong." She turned to head back in the direction she had come from, "I'm just going to go let Abigail and Abraham Lincoln know that you're ok, too," she said, over her shoulder. "They were a teensy bit worried."

In a strange way, it was good to be back. Liberation is all well and good. But there's something really nice about having people care about you, too. Now, I just had to figure out how to have them both. What? Who says you can't have your cake and eat it, too?

I headed straight for the kitchen, expecting to find Jack. But he wasn't there, and the countertops were empty and sparkling. But, then again, they usually were even if he was here. Disappointed, I looked in the refrigerator and found a lonely piece of chocolate cake. Ah. The breakfast of champions. In order to make my breakfast completely nutritionally sound, I washed it all down with a glass of orange juice. Fortified and feeling a little perkier, I took a deep breath and decided to bite the bullet and visit the yarn store and see if Carolyn was upset with me for missing work.

I pushed the door open cautiously and peeked my head in, looking both ways carefully. Alright. I'll be honest. I was looking for Louise. I just wasn't up to seeing her today. But, I only saw Carolyn sitting on the customer's side of the counter on the three-legged stool, swinging her feet like a little kid. My heart filled at the sight, and all of the things I had been thinking about Carolyn flew out of my heart and out the window – hopefully never to be seen or heard from again. It didn't matter that she had kept it such a big secret. She wasn't obligated to tell me that…

"Oh, my dear!" Carolyn exclaimed, hopping off of her stool. "You're awake. How are you feeling?" She crossed the room quickly and I ran to give her a hug. I squeezed her gently, even as she enveloped me with her frail but surprisingly strong arms. "Jack and Natalie told me everything," she said into my shoulder. I pulled away from her a little so that I could see her face. She frowned a little, "At least I hope they did."

I laughed a little, "I'm sure they did," I assured her. "Where did they go?"

She stepped back and waved her hand, "They went to help Ryan finish the goodies for tonight."

I made a face, "While I slept in."

"Honey," she said, "it's a miracle you got out of bed at all today. I don't think I would have. You must have been terrified."

Without even realizing it, we had walked over to the large oak table, and I sank gratefully down into one of the solid chairs. "I was," I said seriously. "I don't think I've ever felt so totally and completely struck with fear as I was when I looked up and saw the shape of a person behind the shower curtain." I shivered remembering it. "It was…"

"Thank God that it's all over," she said soothingly, patting my hand. I smiled, pretending to agree with her, but I knew it wasn't over. Not yet anyway. "I'm sure they'll catch whoever it was soon."

Ah-ha. So Jack and Natalie hadn't quite told her everything. I nodded in agreement again, feeling bad for leaving her out of the loop. But, unless I was wrong, she had her own problems to deal with today.

I looked around the empty store. "No customers?"

She shook her gray head, a few wisps popping out of her bun, "It's been very slow," she said. "I think everyone is excited about the party downtown tonight."

Before I could answer, Abigail came bursting through the doors. "Have you read the paper today?" she breathed. "It's unbelievable."

I snatched it from her hands and scanned the article quickly. She was right. It was unbelievable. And, for once, the article wasn't about me. It was about Mrs. Goldmyer. And how she had murdered her younger sister. I gasped. It was full of "facts" that I had never heard of. Like, how, at the funeral, Mrs. Goldmyer had cackled evilly as her beloved sister had been lowered into the grave. It hinted of a scandalous secret in Hope's past and how that secret had caused a murderous jealousy to grow in Mrs. Goldmyer, inciting her to murder.

"Scandalous secret," Carolyn murmured over my shoulder. "How did anyone find out about that?"

I spun around. "Carolyn," I cried, "what are you talking about? Did Hope have a scandalous secret?"

She tried to take it back, but I needed to know. "Please, Carolyn," I said, trying to stay calm, "but I think this is somehow all related to what's happening to me, and I really need to know."

She looked old and frail and sat down again slowly. Abigail put her hand on Carolyn's shoulder. "I think it's time to let the old ghosts rest," she said softly. "Tell us what happened."

Carolyn put a wrinkled hand to her forehead, "I didn't find it out right away," she said, "and I never told anyone." She looked up at Abigail, "I promise I never told anyone."

Abigail patted her shoulder again, "Of course you didn't," she said soothingly. "I believe you." Abigail looked over at me. "I knew there was more to the story of Charity and Hope, but I was never close to either of them – Hope was younger than me, and Charity was, well…"

"Hope had a baby," Carolyn said swiftly. "That was her secret. She had had a baby. That's why she graduated a year early and went to "college", but she had never really gone to college. I found that out when I was researching… err… something. But I never told anyone."

"What became of the child?" I wondered.

She shrugged helplessly, "Adopted, I'm sure," she said. "Hopefully to a lovely family and never had to find out that…"

"Her mother was murdered…" I finished for her. She met my eyes bleakly across the table.

Mrs. Royston came in just then, a welcome diversion. I hugged Carolyn and told her that I had a few things to do for tonight and asked if she could live without me. She sent me off graciously, and Abigail confirmed that she would stay behind for moral support and knitting guidance. I'm pretty sure that neither of them suspected a thing.

I walked as normally as possible out of the yarn store, but as soon as the door was shut, I raced down the hallway. I had to find Nate. Because… because… what if the child had grown up and searched for its mother? What if the child had found out that his or her mother had been murdered? And, last but most importantly, what if that child was out for revenge?

With a timing so perfect that it could be nothing but a blessing from God, Helen came puttering up the hill to the yarn store just as I was shutting the front door behind me and contemplating the long walk down to town… and then through town… and then who knows where in my search of Nate.

"Hi, Helen," I said cheerfully, bending down to see her through her car window. "What do you say to another knitting adventure?"

Her face lit up.

We sped back to town remarkably fast, and she braked quickly in front of Nate's law office. I ran in to inquire if he was at work. I wasn't expecting him to be, so I wasn't really too disappointed to find out that he had taken the day off.

"Ok, Helen," I said, climbing back into her car, "the adventure is over. Can you take me to my new house?" I held my breath, hoping she had not, somehow, heard of what had happened last night.

She looked disappointed, "That's it?" she said, wrinkling her nose. "That was the big adventure?" she grinned. "We didn't even get arrested or catch a knitting fairy."

Whew. She was happily clueless and drove me obediently to my new house. I hopped out, thanking her profusely for the ride and waved as she drove away. She might have thought it was odd that I didn't go in, but there was no way I was going in there by myself today. I was entirely certain that the intruder was gone, but I certainly wasn't brave enough to really find out. As soon as her car was out of eyesight, I headed for my real destination – Nate's house, tucking Helen's phone securely in my back pocket as I ran. These were still Natalie's jeans, so there was no doubt in my mind that the phone would stay securely in the pocket. I would have to use a pry bar to get it back out. Yes, I'm not proud that I stole her phone but I was sure that she would understand. I'm sure she would. And it would have been very, very foolish of me to attempt this mission without back up. I shuddered to think about what Jack and Ryan would say if they knew where I was.

I knocked on the front door. No answer. I snuck around to the side of the garage and peered in through the little window. His car was in there. I grinned to myself. He couldn't hide forever. I went back to the front door and pounded some more. When I started singing show tunes at the top of my voice, the door reluctantly cracked open.

"Go away before the neighbors call the cops," he hissed through the crack.

"Gracious," I said, "I sure hope they don't send Officer Douglas."

The door opened all the way, and Nate gestured in resignation for me to come in. "I hope they do," he said, grinning almost wolfishly.

I rolled my eyes, "Men."

He leaned against the counter and folded his arms. "So what do you want?" he demanded, all niceness gone.

"I need to talk to you about…" I took a fortifying deep breath and met his glare with one of my own, "your mom and Hope."

"Get out," he said flatly.

I backed up against the door. "I can't," I said. "Because I think Hope's child is trying to kill me and frame one of you for it."

That shut him up.

For about 10 seconds.

"Get out," he repeated. "I don't have time for games, and I have no idea what you're talking about"

"Really?" I asked coolly. "You don't?" I stalked down the hallway and he followed me. I pointed at the room where I had broken into last night. "This room is full of books about your mom," I said.

"You've read too many books," he sneered, "and jump to conclusions faster than anyone else I've ever…"

"Give me a break, Nate," I all but shouted. "I know. Ok. I know it's your mom that the book is about. I don't know why. I don't know if it's true or not. But I know it's about her, so please, give me some credit and stop pretending."

He closed his eyes briefly. "Fine." He looked painfully thin and tired. I wished I didn't need to do what I knew had to be done.

"How long have you known the rumors about your mom?" I asked softly.

"I think I was six when I heard the first whisper," he said, finally, "and then I found the book hiding in my mom's closet when I was ten."

"When did you start collecting the books?"

He shrugged. "I was still in high school," he said. "At first, I rented a small storage locker, and then when I got my own place, I moved them here. I felt like they would be safer here." He twisted his mouth in a parody of a smile, "I never invite anyone over," he explained. "Ever."

"Does your mom know that you have them?"

He shook his head, "I don't think so. It was a really limited print run. Only 250 were ever printed." He saw the question in my eyes before I even asked. "I have 218. I used to look online almost every night and make sure no more were up for sale. I've been slacking off lately, which is probably how your friend got a book. When I hit 250, I'm going to burn all of them. Then, maybe, this nightmare will be over."

"But why do you need the books?" I asked.

"Because," he hissed, "you figured it out, so could other people. Anybody that reads the book is going to think my mother is a murderer." He glared at me. "She's not."

Ok. One thing at a time. "Did you know that Hope had a child?" I asked him.

He jumped slightly, "I thought you were lying when you said that earlier."

I put a hand on his arm. "I'm not lying," I whispered. "Hope had a child. What if, somehow, Hope's child tried to track down his or her birth mom, and in the process, somehow, horribly, came across this book?"

Nate looked up at me with dawning comprehension. "I have to go find my mom," he said, jumping up and scrambling around in his kitchen drawer for his keys.

"But… wait…." But he did not wait. He was gone.

There was just one thing to do now. Nate still didn't realize what we were up against. I needed to follow him, but this time, I wasn't going to be stupid and go by myself. This time, I was doing the right thing and asking for help. I wiggled Helen's phone out of my back pocket.

CHAPTER 24

O k. Asking for help was definitely doing the right thing. Getting yelled at for doing so was something I hadn't quite expected.

"Ryan," I said as reasonably as I could, "I did call you. I called you as soon as…"

His red hair was standing almost straight up on end. "As soon as you realized you needed a ride," he said with an eye roll.

"Not true," I argued back, "I have a car right inside the garage that I could use anytime."

He smiled knowingly, "But then you'd have to go inside the house to get your keys."

Darn. He had me there. He pulled me in for a quick hug suddenly, "Thanks for calling me," he said seriously. "Sorry I over-reacted just a little."

"Just a little?" I teased.

"Well, we were just sitting in the police station literally a few hours ago trying to decide whether or not to press charges against him for your attempted murder."

"Now you're just being dramatic," I said. "You know as well as I do that he was not going to murder me."

"Ok," Ryan said reluctantly, "get in. We'll go hunt down Nathaniel Goldmyer and his nefarious mother if you want to." I opened the door to his car happily. "But," he said, pausing before he put the key in the ignition, "if things get crazy I want you to promise me…"

"I promise," I said. "We play it safe today. And stick together."

He leaned over to kiss me. "Agreed."

We roared down the street. Gracious, he was driving almost as poorly as Natalie. "So you know where Mrs. Goldmyer lives?" I asked curiously. I had expected to have to google it or something. It was kind of handy having Helen's phone, actually. I would have to think about getting one. I wasn't quite sure what to do with the text that popped up from her husband, though. I had no way of getting a message to Helen right now which meant that he was going to be a little upset when she forgot to pick up cereal at the store on her way home.

The tips of his ears turned a bright red as he turned off of Main Street onto a pleasant little neighborhood street. "I may have, in my youth, you understand, I may have looked up her address once."

I couldn't help it. I giggled. "You went and teepeed her house, didn't you? What did you do? Get a late fine at the library?"

He half-laughed and glared at me, "Nope. Got kicked out for talking too loud and the old lady wouldn't let me back in to finish my report. I got a "D". My dad wasn't exactly happy about that."

"So you teepeed her house," I confirmed. "That's terrible." I tried to look disapproving.

"Well," he said, turning down another street where the houses stood a bit bigger and were a little further apart, "not exactly."

"Really? You had a change of heart? An attack of conscience?"

"Nope. I…"

"Chickened out?" I supplied helpfully.

"Not exactly," he said. "The truth is I did put toilet paper in her yard, but I didn't exactly… err… spread it around. I was so terrified of getting caught, I just threw the rolls at her bushes and took off running."

I laughed. "And she probably used that toilet paper, too," I hooted. "Waste not, want not."

He pulled into a driveway and, suddenly, reality was not so funny anymore."

"We're here," he whispered.

It was a beautiful brick colonial. Very well maintained with a symmetrical formal garden in the front and hedges, perfectly trimmed along both sides of the driveway. I was impressed.

We got out of the car slowly, looking for signs of activity. "There's Nate's car," I said unnecessarily to Ryan, who could clearly see the car for himself.

The garage door was open, and by unspoken mutual decision, we did not go to the front door like any other person would, but went to the back door. Ryan tested the handle. It was unlocked.

We entered cautiously. "Nate?" I called. "Mrs. Goldmyer?" The doorway entered directly into the kitchen. Ryan gaped.

"Wow," he breathed, "this is even more beautiful than the kitchen at Raspberry Hill." He started towards the stove, "Hey, I saw this stove in a magazine last month." He ran a hand along the dials, "Did you know that it can…"

"Would you focus?" I hissed.

"Sorry," he said with a small, apologetic grin. But his gaze lingered on the stove even as we left the kitchen and entered the formal dining room.

"Whoa," I said. "Maybe we should call the police."

"I wouldn't," Nate's voice had us both jumping. He strode rapidly into the room. "That idiot Douglas is probably on duty and will arrest you for breaking and entering."

I shook my head, "We didn't break anything."

Nate snorted, "Just entered." He eyed me, "You just might have a great life of crime in front of you after all. Keep my card," he said. "I could use the business."

"What's going on here?" Ryan asked, gesturing to the assortment of paraphernalia strewn all over the table and toppling over to the floor.

Nate shrugged. "Perhaps my mother was going for a brief stroll down memory lane," he theorized. "These are all of our old photo albums, and some are albums I've never seen before. It looks like she opened all of her old boxes that were in the attic."

"Is she home?" I already knew the answer, but needed to hear it. Nate's lips pulled together in a tight line and he shook his head. I gestured at the table. "Any idea of what she was looking for?" He shook his head again. "Mind if we take a peek?"

He sighed, "Might as well." He approached the table and began sifting through the mess of papers and photos. "Maybe we'll get a clue as to where she went."

"I don't suppose she's just working?" Ryan suggested helpfully. "Did you try the library?"

Nate's dark glance was more than enough answer. Ryan pulled a face at me and began his own sifting through the junk.

"Old land records," Nate muttered. "Old birth certificates." He cut me off before I could even suggest it, "No, I don't see *that* birth certificate. Old photos." He looked at the mess in bewilderment. "This is just so unlike my mother. If she had wanted to go through old records and pictures, I would have expected her to do it in some sort of orderly fashion."

"Unless," I said grimly, "she was in a hurry or upset about something."

"Maybe," he conceded. We continued our search. I looked, briefly at each photo that I passed, not knowing what I was looking for but hoping that I would know it when I did. The minutes turned into half an hour… and then an hour. Eventually, we started sorting all in one direction so that we didn't have to re-see what we had already seen and carelessly started dumping everything we had already checked over the side of the table where the papers and photos fluttered to the ground like leaves falling from a tree. Ha ha. I thought to myself. It was a family tree. Oh boy. Perhaps we needed to take a smallish break. We were clearly getting nowhere…wait a minute…

I had glanced, casually at the photo that Ryan was studying, in my quest not to giggle at my own stupid joke. Now, I grabbed his arm. It was a woman, dressed in 1920's style clothing, her hair bobbed fashionably and frowning darkly at the camera. It was the expression on her angular face that stopped me. It was familiar. Really familiar.

"What?" Ryan asked, peering more closely at the figure. "Do we know her?"

Nate came around to study the picture, too. He pulled it quickly out of Ryan's grasp and flipped it over. "Rachel Ross, Summer, 1925," he read. He looked at both of us, "So?"

"So, she's a relation to your mom, then, right?"

Nate's expression seemed to doubt my mental capacity. "Yes," he said slowly, as if speaking to a child, "and also, strangely to me."

Ryan covered his small laugh with a cough. I elbowed him and pulled the picture out of Nate's fingers. I was an idiot. I should have known. I mean, seriously. Duh.

"So," I said patiently, "if Hope had a child then it's just possible that she is also related to Rachel Ross, correct?"

Nate rolled his eyes, "I believe that is how it works."

I tried again… these guys were pretty slow, "Which means that it's also super possible that if Hope had a child that she might bear some family resemblance to other family members." I waved the picture in their faces. "Congratulations," I said. "You have a new aunt." I sighed at their still puzzled expressions. "Hope had a girl," I explained. "Her name is Rebecca Flannery – or possibly B. Haven. Look at that face, she's the spitting image of Rachel Ross. She's the one that's been writing all of those nasty pieces in the paper about me."

Nate grinned briefly, "I thought they were a little funny," he confessed. At Ryan's twitch, he amended, "I mean, come on, anyone who has ever met you for more than a minute wouldn't believe a word of it."

I pulled the dining room chair out from under the table and whisked it free of photos before sinking down onto it. "Don't you remember?" I asked. "She was standing right behind you when Natalie somehow talked Mrs. Goldmyer into taking the beginning knitting class. She signed up, too."

"That was her?" Nate asked in disbelief. "I wonder if she followed us in?"

I nodded. "Probably. She probably needed to dig up more information, do more research about your mother before she made her 'move', whatever that was going to be."

Nate's gaze turned dark, "And then she saw the book."

I smacked myself in the head, "That's right," I whispered. "The book was right there. Mrs. Goldmyer saw it." I looked up at Nate, eager for him to believe me, "I promise you that we didn't figure out that it was about your mom until much, much later," I said earnestly. "We had no idea. Natalie had seen the title on her search through the library catalog and, for whatever reason, it had caught her eye. She was trying to help us overcome writer's block. That's all. I swear."

A muscle twitched in Nate's jaw. "Really?" he asked. "My mom felt like you were pressuring her to take your class or you would reveal all that you knew."

I gasped, hand going to my throat. "That makes complete sense. She thought she was being blackmailed."

Ryan sank to his knees, a warm arm going around my shoulders. "No one thinks you're a blackmailer, Molly," he said firmly.

"That's right," Nate said with a sigh. "I can see how it looked that way."

My mind was spinning, "So, it was Rebecca who poisoned my hot chocolate," I said, turning to look at Ryan. "She had plenty of opportunity. She encouraged me to drink it before it got cold." I looked over at Nate, "You made it all too easy for her."

"I think," Nate said, his own logical mind spinning fast, "that when she saw you had the book, she panicked."

"She meaning Rebecca?" Ryan clarified.

"Right," Nate confirmed. "She wanted to come to town and get her revenge quietly. If you started broadcasting that my mother was a murderer it would ruin her plans."

"And then, then she must have changed her mind," Ryan broke in excitedly. "She saw that Mrs. Goldmyer and Molly didn't have a, shall we say, warm relationship, and she realized that maybe the perfect revenge wouldn't be killing Mrs. Goldmyer, but, perhaps, framing one of you for Molly's murder. She would," Ryan took a deep breath, "get rid of Molly and then helpfully supply facts and evidence that Molly was killed because she was investigating Hope's death, which would lead to one of you two as the key suspects."

I squeezed Ryan's hand hard. It made painful sense. "What could be worse," I whispered, "than for a mother to sit through her son's trial for murder and watch him waste away in prison?"

Nate sank to a chair as well, looking pale. We stared blindly at the table, numb and shaking. Well, at least I was. It wasn't every day that you realized someone heartlessly wanted you dead.

Ryan recovered first, "But that doesn't solve this problem," he said. "Where is your mother?"

Nate jumped up, "I don't know," he said, pacing. "I've called every place she usually goes and she's not there."

I felt sick. "Do you think Rebecca has figured out that we have it figured out?" My hands felt clammy. "Because then she'd have to give up her elaborate plan and just…"

"Finish it," Nate said hoarsely. "But… how… where would she go?"

"The Axe Murderer of Springiegate," I said suddenly, meeting Nate's horrified gaze with my own. I gulped. "Do you…" I paused to swallow. "Oh my word. I can't even say it. Does your mother have an… an…"

"Oh, Lord!" Nate exclaimed and ran to the garage, followed closely by Ryan. They were back within seconds. "It's gone." He looked like he was going to be sick at any minute. "The axe is gone."

And then it occurred to me. "I wonder…" I said out loud, pushing back from the table and standing up. Nate grabbed my arm. "You've thought of something?" he demanded, shaking my arm slightly. "What?"

"Hey!" Ryan protested, "Back off."

"No," I said, one hand on Ryan. "It's ok. I think I know where they went. Let's go."

We ran out the door, hopping into Ryan's car, Nate in the backseat. My theory made perfect sense. They both agreed. The only thing we could do now was pray. Pray that we weren't too late.

Ryan flagrantly disobeyed every single speed limit sign and even a stop sign or two on our way to the big old church on the outskirts of town. The graveyard parking lot was empty, except for one slightly battered looking black sedan and a Red SUV. "That's my mom's car," Nate said hoarsely, clutching the seat in front of him.

"And that's Rebecca's car," I said grimly. Ryan parked quickly and we all jumped out.

"Come on," Nate yelled, "Hope's grave is down the hill." Ryan and Nate took off running. I started to go after them, but something changed my mind.

Something wasn't right. The graveyard was immaculately well-tended, a few leaves had fallen since the last yard clean up, but the grass around each one was clipped short and evenly and respectfully cleaned off. A place like this probably had a... I looked around... there! A directory. A tall double-posted signboard stood securely in the ground with a map of the graves. It only took me a minute to find what I was looking for, and I took off running in the totally opposite direction. Would I ever learn?

She was there. Kneeling by a grave and sobbing. I almost didn't recognize her. Her normally perfect hair was free and uncontained, blowing wildly in the wind.

"I tried," she sobbed. "Every day I tried, but it was never good enough, was it?" She pounded the gravestone with her bare fists, and I winced at the sound. She would have bruises in the morning. "You picked on her constantly," she sobbed. "She didn't know what else to do. She thought she had nothing left to live for. You made her that way. She would have been ok. She just needed..." Mrs. Goldmyer's voice trailed off in broken sobs.

I stepped forward and knelt on the ground next to her. "Love," I said softly. "She needed love."

Mrs. Goldmyer looked at me with lost eyes. I've never seen such a hopeless look on anyone's face before. Tears ran unchecked. "Love," she nodded. "And they made her feel... wicked."

I reached for her cold hand, "It was just a baby," I whispered. "Just a baby. She gave it up for adoption, didn't she?"

Mrs. Goldmyer nodded miserably, "She wanted to keep it. She asked me to help her. But..." her face puckered with an age-old misery that I could feel myself, "I didn't. I didn't know how to stand up to them. They..."

"They were overbearing and tyrannical," I finished for her again, "and they made you feel less than a person if you ever did anything wrong."

She nodded, turning back to the gravestone. "They hated imperfection."

I spoke softly, hoping I wouldn't make matters worse, "That's why you made Hope's suicide look like a murder."

She spun to look at me, shaking her head vigorously, "No," she hissed, "don't say that. Don't ever say that."

"Why?" I asked gently. "Because they can hear you from heaven?" I remembered our conversation during that first knitting class, Mrs. Goldmyer's twisted reasoning making even more sense now. I sighed, feeling unutterably sad for this poor woman next to me. I slid an experimental hand up her shoulder and squeezed. "It's ok," I said. "It's ok for them to know what a good daughter you were. How you tried to protect Hope, even in death. If they can hear us, then it's ok. It's ok for them to know that they were wrong about Hope. You didn't want them to have one more thing to blame Hope for, did you?"

She hunched even further over, great sobs shaking her body. I braved sliding closer, pulling her closer so that I was almost completely hugging her. "I bet you even wore the same shoe size as she did, didn't you?" She nodded miserably. "So when you accidentally stepped in her blood, you just switched shoes with her." She nodded again, the storm of tears passing a little and took a hiccuping breath. "You took the razor blade away from her and replaced it with the kitchen knife. If there was a note, you took that too." I leaned a little harder against her "You incriminated yourself so that you could save Hope." I wiped the tears out of my own eyes, "You gave her love," I whispered. "You gave that to her."

"I didn't," she whispered brokenly. "I made everything worse. I always make everything worse.."

"Nonsense," I said briskly, hoping she would recognize her own determination with that one word. "You gave her love. She knew that you loved her. She just…" I started crying… "she just couldn't see past her own pain and see the beauty of tomorrow. She just couldn't see… Hope… like you could."

And then she said the thing that almost finished breaking my heart, "I'm just like them."

"No you're not," I said quickly. She pulled away from me, wiping her eyes. I was losing the moment. In a minute, she would have composed herself and risen to her feet and maybe even pretended like nothing had ever happened. "If you were like them, then Nate wouldn't be who he is."

She turned to me then. "What?"

"Look at Nate," I said. "He's great. He's successful. He absolutely loves you. He's warm and caring and kind." I conveniently left out the part where he was also ruthless and conniving. "When I was scared the other night, I ran to his house and stood in his kitchen dripping wet. And I knew I was safe." Well, for a few minutes anyway. She didn't need to know the whole story right now. "He's a beautiful person. That happened because of you. Because of your love."

She wiped her eyes and looked at me with an expression that I had never seen on her face before. She smiled. It was somewhat watery, and not very practiced, but it was a smile. I reached over to squeeze her hand. "Ok?"

To my surprise, she covered my hand with her other one, "Ok," she whispered.

We almost didn't see her coming. I saw the movement out of the corner of my eye and jumped, pushing Mrs. Goldmyer behind me. She caught herself on the gravestone, turning to see what had happened, just as I turned to see Rebecca. She held an axe up on her shoulder, ready to swing, and a wild look in her eye.

"You were supposed to meet me at Hope's grave," she snarled, taking a threatening step forward.

"I didn't even know who you were," Mrs. Goldmyer said. "You just said I had better come to the graveyard if I didn't want something terrible to happen to my son."

Rebecca's somewhat pretty face was twisted and turned into something terrible, "You killed my mother," she said lowly. "And today, I'm going to kill you." I shivered, believing her. She looked at me, grinning madly, "And you. You've been very stubborn about dying so far. But that ends today."

I was thinking fast. My legs and knees were sore and aching from crouching so long on the cold ground. Mrs. Goldmyer must be the same way. Would we be able to lurch to our feet and avoid the axe that was so clearly headed our way? It would be impossible for one lady to kill two ladies, wouldn't it? I began to feel desperate. What would we do? How would we get away? We needed a...

"Oh my word!" Mrs. Goldmyer gasped, looking at something in the distance behind Rebecca.

We needed a diversion. Rebecca spun, almost involuntarily to see what was behind her, and we sprang to our feet. Well, actually, we lurched and wobbled, especially poor Mrs. Goldmyer who was not a spring chicken and not used to athletic exercise. I grabbed her arm with my good hand and pulled her with me. Run. It was a familiar reaction now when confronted with Rebecca. Run. Run for your life. But this time, I was running for Mrs. Goldmyer's life, too. And what about…

Rebecca realized, precious seconds too late that she had been tricked and spun back towards us with a cry of rage. She ran forward, bringing the axe down, but missing us by a hair and hitting the gravestone so hard I thought I heard it crack. I also heard her hiss of pain and she fell to her knees. Good. Maybe that would slow her down.

"Run," I puffed neatly avoiding a gravestone. "We have to run."

"Hide," she puffed back.

Maybe she was right. She wasn't going to be able to run far. We only had to wait until Ryan and Nate figured out where we were in this ridiculously big graveyard. Maybe they would have the good sense to call the… HOLY COW. Helen's phone was still in my back pocket.

We ducked and bobbed behind gravestones until I saw the mausoleum. She saw it, too. It was as good of a place as any. We ran up to it, it was unlocked. "No," I gasped, "don't go in. Let's just do this." Wasting precious seconds, I dragged a heavy stone urn, complete with a beautifully carved angel behind the door, wedging myself out and pulling the door closed behind me so that it would appear that the door was wedged from the inside.

"Now, let's hide behind those two gravestones," I said, gesturing at two obscenely large and old tributes to someone's great-great grandparents.

We each took one, sliding into place and hopefully out of view, panting heavily. I looked over to make sure she was securely tucked behind hers, and to my surprise, her expression was one of respect. I felt a warm little glow and grinned cheekily at her. She hadn't seen anything yet. I pulled out my phone. Rats. I couldn't call the police. For one thing, Officer Stupid Douglas probably wouldn't take me seriously. For another thing, talking at all was out of the question. Absolute silence and a stone monument were all that stood between us and an axe murderer. I frowned and peeked over at Mrs. Goldmyer, embarrassed to have the means of saving us, but unable to use it. She made a motion with her fingers. What was she doing? Oh my goodness. She was a genius. Texting. Now, why didn't I think of that?

It was Helen's phone, and I looked through her phone list quickly. Oh, Helen, I thought, why can't you be a little more organized? She didn't have a single last name – and sometimes not a first name either. There was only one thing to do. Text Patrick. So I did. And, as I was hitting send, I heard a chilling sound. My head swiveled over to Mrs. Goldmyer, she heard it, too. A twig breaking under someone's foot. She was coming.

Just like I thought she would, she approached the mausoleum slowly. "I know you're in there," she called, her voice almost unrecognizable. "One little door will not stop me." I heard the sound of an axe hitting wood and splintering and was very grateful not to be in that little mausoleum.

The axe crunched again on the hardwood. "Come out, come out…" she sang mockingly, "wherever…" the rest of her sentence was cut off by a scream and a shout from a familiar voice. I wilted with relief against my tombstone.

"I got her feet," Nate said, grunting like he had been kicked, and then Ryan's voice, "What have you done to…"

"You'll never know," she cackled.

I struggled to my feet, comforted to see Rebecca safely pinned to the ground, writhing under both Nate and Ryan's grasp. Their faces were white with anxiety. "It's ok," I called. "We're here. We're fine."

The beautiful sound of a siren in the distance sounded like a lullaby.

"So," the Sherriff said, leaning back against the cemetery sign, "let me get this straight."

"Perhaps we could discuss this another time, Sherriff Jones," Mrs. Goldmyer said coolly. "I have a prior engagement that I simply must get to."

He cocked his head interestedly, "Oh really?" he asked. "You really have something more important to do than give an explanation to me for why this lady tried to kill you?"

Oh! I looked at Mrs. Goldmyer in astonishment. "She's right," I said. "We're in charge of the entertainment portion of the Amelda Tartan Welcome Committee."

The Sherriff rolled his eyes just as another car came screaming into the parking lot. "Helen," someone yelled out the window. "Where's Helen?"

"Who the heck is Helen?" the Sherriff asked, scratching his head as I was beginning to realize he did whenever he got frustrated.

"My wife," Patrick shouted. "She's out there in the cemetery with an axe murderer…" he paused, taking in Rebecca's disheveled appearance, handcuffs and axe laying on the ground."

"Oops," I said. "Did I forget to put in the text that I was sending it instead of Helen?"

Ryan tried to cover his smile by turning his head quickly to survey the rest of the cemetery.

After that, I think the Sherriff was completely happy to see the tail end of Mrs. Goldmyer and myself for a little while. Nate and Ryan promised to stay and explain everything. Not, of course, that they could. They didn't know everything. But maybe they knew enough to keep the Sherriff happy so that everything wouldn't need to be told and recorded. Patrick, still a little cranky and shaky was almost happy to give us a ride to the amphitheater downtown. He was, after all, I supposed to be working crowd control for the event. The entire way he muttered under his breath about crazy knitters and axe murderers and people who had the nerve to steal someone's phone.

But, he came around the car and held Mrs. Goldmyer's door open for her as she exited his vehicle. On the way over to the park, she had had the presence of mind to tidy herself, even scraping her hair back into its familiar bun. I felt better about that. I wasn't quite sure how to handle a Mrs. Goldmyer without her bun.

I handed Helen's phone sheepishly back to Patrick and tried to explain. "Stop it," he said sternly. "I'm glad you stole her phone so that you could text me. It all worked out." And then, surprisingly, he hugged me and strode off, whistling to do crowd control.

And now, the only thing left to do was, "Mrs. Goldmyer," I began... but she was already gone. Huh. I guess... I guess it was over.

I slipped and slithered my way through the crowd looking for a familiar silhouette – that was not anywhere to be seen. I neatly avoided the refreshments section, though, unwilling to spend the time necessary to bring Jack and Natalie up to speed, because once they saw my disheveledness, they would know that something had happened.

Huh. She wasn't here. But she had to be here. I walked further out into the park, scanning for any sign of... there... there she was. Under my tree. I should have known. We were back to where we had started.

"Hey," I said softly, making her jump. She had not seen me coming. She was perched on the tree roots in much the same fashion as I had been the day she had found me here after I had been fired for "Conduct Unbecoming a Librarian."

"Oh, Molly," she said her smile fading as she looked me up and down, "is everything ok?"

I nodded, smiling warmly, "Everything is better than it has been in a long time," I assured her, "and I think it's all going to be ok."

She smiled back, but it was a smile that was missing her familiar sparkle. I sank down next to her and tipped my head back to stare up at the tangle of branches overhead. This was an amazing tree. It was so old. It had been here – and been old – when Carolyn had been a baby. The stories it could tell.

"Aren't you coming into the party?" I asked.

She sighed and shook her head, "I don't think so," she said sadly. "I'll just stay out here."

I took a deep breath and prayed that I was taking the right path. "But won't everyone be disappointed when Amelda Tartan doesn't show up?"

This time she did jump. She looked at me, her periwinkle eyes huge behind her glasses, "What makes you say that?" she asked in a high voice.

I smiled gently, "It's ok, Carolyn," I said. "I know."

She did not stop staring. "You know?"

I brushed a strand of hair out of my face, "I know that you're Amelda Tartan." I took another deep breath, "I also know you're the author who wrote 'The Axe Murderer of SpringieGate."

Her face crumpled. "How did you figure it out?"

I shrugged, "Well," I said loftily, "I am a former librarian, you know, I'm highly trained to spot literary similarities."

"I don't see how that led you to me," she argued. "What on earth…"

I reached forward to squeeze her hands, which were wringing anxiously. "It was your knitter's Halloween story."

She rolled her eyes and flopped back against the tree. "A stupid idea," she said. "I should have known better, but I've always wanted to write about knitters and I just couldn't resist."

"Your style is unmistakable," I said. "I almost… almost… put it together after reading the Axe Murderer… there was just something so familiar and almost comforting about reading that book… but I couldn't put my finger on it." I looked at her with mock sternness, "Now, the picture on the back of all of your books is a bit of a lie, isn't it?"

"Not at all," she said, a spark of mischievousness returning to her eyes. "If one is writing under a pen name then that pen name can be its own person, right?"

"I don't think we have time to debate that," I said. "People are waiting for you to come."

"No," she said with a sigh, "they're waiting for Amelda Tartan."

"You are Amelda Tartan," I reminded her, "and you've kept so many people enchanted and delighted with your stories for years and years. It's time people knew who you were."

"I thought so, too," she said. "I was beginning to feel like a fraud, and I wanted to tell people. My publishers thought up the book tour idea." She looked at me self-consciously, "I've never done a book tour before, but I knew I would have to start it here and 'fess up' first." She picked at her sweater idly, "But now, I'm too chicken."

I stood up, "Carolyn Crabapple," I said sternly, "you've never backed down from anything in your life. You're the bravest, kindest, most giving person that I know. Now, get your little self off the ground and march over there to that stage."

"What if people are mad at me for deceiving them for so long?" she whispered. "I couldn't bear it if…"

"Nonsense," I said, my new favorite phrase, "and you certainly won't feel better for ducking out on your responsibilities. Just look at all of that food. And the entertainment. And," I twinkled at her, "the mayor's speech. You know how much he's looking forward to that."

"Oh, alright," she said, standing with a creak and a sigh, "but I do think you're being just a bit bossy."

We stared at each other for a long minute before her face cracked and split into the familiar smile I was used to seeing. I smiled back and reached out for a hug, completely forgetting that I had personal space issues.

We walked quickly back to the stage area, maneuvering carefully around the crowd until we got to the steps.

"Who's that on the stage now?" Carolyn asked curiously.

We could, in fact, hear a loud voice reciting what seemed to be a poem, "Not one of all the purple host who took the flag today can tell the definition so clear of victory" the lady shouted, and from her profile, I could see her throw up an arm for emphasis. She dropped her voice theatrically into the microphone, "As he defeated – dying" and here she gave a pathetic cough, "on whose forbidden ear the distant strains of triumph burst agonized and clear!"

The crowd roared in approval.

"What on earth is Celia doing up there?" I wondered out loud.

"I believe it is Emily Dickinson, Ms. Stevenson," Mrs. Goldmyer said from up the stairs. "You should probably know that."

I frowned. "But they were supposed to be reading Amelda Tartan… not… Emily Dickinson…."

Mrs. Goldmyer hurried down the stairs. "No," she said, her usual stoic expression firmly in place. "I thought we should wait to commence the Amelda

Tartan entertainment selections until she had arrived and was ready." She turned to look Carolyn up and down. "Are you ready now?"

We both gaped at her. "W-what…" I gasped.

Mrs. Goldmyer turned a knowing look on me, "I've known for years," she stated simply.

"You have?" Carolyn looked flabbergasted. "How?"

"Well," Mrs. Goldmyer said, and we watched in amazement as a small smile started to form, "after I stole your boyfriend and you wrote that stupid book to punish me, I could recognize your writing from the first paragraph of 'The Home Wrecker.'"

Carolyn grabbed her arm. "I'm sorry," she whispered. "I'm so sorry. I tried to return the book so that you'd know I didn't want to hurt you anymore…"

"But I ruined the whole plan," I said, feeling ashamed, "and made it look sinister."

Mrs. Goldmyer shrugged. "What's past is past," she said simply. "Let's let it remain there." She looked Carolyn up and down again. "So," she repeated, "are you ready?"

Carolyn's eyes were welling with tears but she nodded bravely. "Let's do this," she said.

I watched the two of them walk up to the stage door and go through. I should have hurried around to the front so that I could hear clearly what was said. As it was, I could do nothing but stare at the steps while I heard Mrs. Goldmyer making some sort of announcement. There was a stunned silence from the crowd that lasted a full six seconds, and then… then… the most beautiful thing happened… the crowd erupted into an explosion of clapping and cheering and hooting… the applause seemed to last forever.

And, somehow, I wasn't surprised when I felt Ryan's arms come around me. It felt like the most natural thing in the world. "I love you," he whispered in my ear.

I turned so that I could face him, "I love you too," I whispered back.

He pulled me with him to sit on the stairs even as I heard the mayor beginning his speech. I sat next to him, our arms entwined. "Sometimes," Ryan said into my hair, "I just get so scared that I'm going to lose you."

"That will never happen," I said firmly. "Look." I showed him my finger where my heart still would not rub off. "I couldn't even get rid of you when I wanted to. Your heart stayed there." On a gamble, I reached up to his shirt pocket. He looked at me like I was crazy, but it was there. I pulled the pen out and took his hand, carefully drawing an identical heart on his own finger. "Now you're stuck with me too."

There were tears in his eyes when he looked at me, "I think I can live with that," he said finally.

So, I guess you could say, after everything was considered, that Mrs. Goldmyer was not cut out to be a secret keeper. It would have been better for her if she had been able to share what she had felt and seen. But that's okay. It's all out now, and I truly believe it worked out for the best. Well, maybe not for Rebecca, but I hear that she is doing much better with professional counseling and maybe won't have to spend too much time in jail. After she heard the whole story, she was horrified by what she had tried to do. It almost made me feel sorry for her. Almost.

I guess it's just true that most people aren't meant to be secret keepers. Most people need to tell in order to stay healthy and whole. Not everyone knows how to keep the secrets in. They're not equipped to stuff them down, zip them up and go against every grain of instinct that encourages them to tell. It's just not who they are. They are not like me. It was true that I couldn't keep my own secret. I could, however, keep someone else's. It would die with me. Because... some things should never be told.

PSSSSSTT...

Hey, friend... did you find the secret code somewhere in this book that gets you a free knitting pattern? Better check it out! Hint: It's not on this page!

And... would you like to read the story that Carolyn wrote for The Knitter's Halloween Party? Just join my mailing list (and stay updated on all the latest news) and I'll send you a free copy. Go to: www.liveknitlove.com and click on the "Mailing List" link.

JAIME MARSMAN

Writer. Knitter. Daydreamer.
It's amazing, isn't it? Twenty-six humble letters in the alphabet.
By themselves... not very impressive. And yet, those tiny things
are put together in endless combinations and change the world.
Every day... every day... they change your world. That's a lot of
power. The same is true with knitting. One single (really, really
long) strand of yarn could be anything... a sweater, a scarf... a
turtleneck for a flag pole... and it's this endless combination of
words and fiber that inspire Jaime both as a writer and as a
knitwear designer for Live.Knit.Love. Her biggest wish for you
is that you, too, would use your powers for good, realize the joy of
creating, and follow your own dream and become who you are
supposed to be... YOU.
And no one else.

Made in the USA
Monee, IL
06 July 2023

38606438R00164